James Fenimore Cooper

VULCAN'S PEAK - A Tale of the Pacific
(Adventure Novel)

e-artnow 2018

Reading suggestions (available from e-artnow as Print & eBook)

Bram Stoker
THE MYSTERY OF THE SEA

Walter Scott
Ivanhoe

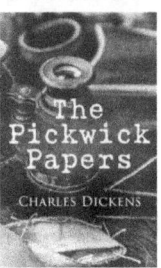

Charles Dickens
The Pickwick Papers

James Fenimore Cooper
THE ADVENTURES OF MILES WALLINGFORD: Afloat and Ashore & Miles Wallingford (Sea Adventure Classics)

Jack London
THE SEA ADVENTURES - Boxed Set: 20+ Maritime Novels & Tales of Seas and Sailors

Daniel Defoe
The Complete Adventures of Robinson Crusoe – 3 Books in One Volume (Illustrated)

James Fenimore Cooper
WYNADOTTÉ (Historical Novel)

James Fenimore Cooper
TALES OF THE SEA – Premium Collection: 12 Maritime Adventure Novels in One Volume (Illustrated)

Rudyard Kipling
Captain Courageous (Illustrated)

Jack London
TALES OF SEAS & SAILORS – Jack London Edition

James Fenimore Cooper

VULCAN'S PEAK
A Tale of the Pacific (Adventure Novel)

The Crater

e-artnow, 2018
Contact: info@e-artnow.org

ISBN 978-80-268-9222-9

Contents

Preface	11
Chapter I	13
Chapter II	20
Chapter III	27
Chapter IV	34
Chapter V	41
Chapter VI	49
Chapter VII	57
Chapter VIII	65
Chapter IX	73
Chapter X	81
Chapter XI	89
Chapter XII	97
Chapter XIII	105
Chapter XIV	113
Chapter XV	121
Chapter XVI	130
Chapter XVII	138
Chapter XVIII	146
Chapter XIX	154
Chapter XX.	162
Chapter XXI	170
Chapter XXII	177
Chapter XXIII	184
Chapter XXIV	191
Chapter XXV	199
Chapter XXVI	209
Chapter XXVII	217
Chapter XXVIII	224
Chapter XXIX	231
Chapter XXX	239
Footnotes	247

"Thus arise
Races of living things, glorious in strength
And perish, as the quickening breath of God
Fills them, or is withdrawn."

—Bryant

Preface

The reader of this book will very naturally be disposed to ask the question, why the geographies, histories, and other works of a similar character, have never made any mention of the regions and events that compose its subject. The answer is obvious enough, and ought to satisfy every mind, however "inquiring." The fact is, that the authors of the different works to which there is any allusion, most probably never heard there were any such places as the Reef, Rancocus Island, Vulcan's Peak, the Crater, and the other islands of which so much is said in our pages. In other words, they knew nothing about them.

We shall very freely admit that, under ordinary circumstances, it would be *prima facie* evidence against the existence of any spot on the face of this earth, that the geographies took no notice of it. It will be remembered, however, that the time was, and that only three centuries and a half since, when the geographies did not contain a syllable about the whole of the American continent; that it is not a century since they began to describe New Zealand, New Holland, Tahiti, Oahu, and a vast number of other places, that are now constantly alluded to, even in the daily journals. Very little is said in the largest geographies, of Japan, for instance; and it may be questioned if they might not just as well be altogether silent on the subject, as for any accurate information they do convey. In a word, much as is now known of the globe, a great deal still remains to be told, and we do not see why the "inquiring mind" should not seek for information in our pages, as well as in some that are ushered in to public notice by a flourish of literary trumpets, that are blown by presidents, vice-presidents and secretaries of various learned bodies.

One thing we shall ever maintain, and that in the face of all who may be disposed to underrate the value of our labours, which is this: —there is not a word in these volumes which we now lay before the reader, *as grave matter of fact*, that is not entitled to the most implicit credit. We scorn deception. Lest, however, some cavillers may be found, we will present a few of those reasons which occur to our mind, on the spur of the moment, as tending to show that everything related here *might* be just as true as Cook's voyages themselves. In the first place, this earth is large, and has sufficient surface to contain, not only all the islands mentioned in our pages, but a great many more. Something is established when the possibility of any hypothetical point is placed beyond dispute. Then, not one half as much was known of the islands of the Pacific, at the close of the last, and at the commencement of the present century, as is known to-day. In such a dearth of precise information, it may very well have happened that many things occurred touching which we have not said even one word. Again, it should never be forgotten that generations were born, lived their time, died, and have been forgotten, among those remote groups, about which no civilized man ever has, or ever will hear anything. If such be admitted to be the facts, why may not *all* that is here related have happened, and equally escape the knowledge of the rest of the civilized world? During the wars of the French revolution, trifling events attracted but little of the general attention, and we are not to think of interests of this nature, in that day, as one would think of them now.

Whatever may be thought of the authenticity of its incidents, we hope this book will be found not to be totally without a moral. Truth is not absolutely necessary to the illustration of a principle, the imaginary sometimes doing that office quite as effectually as the actual.

The reader may next wish to know why the wonderful events related in these volumes have so long been hidden from the world. In answer to this we would ask if anyone can tell how many thousands of years the waters have tumbled down the cliffs at Niagara, or why it was that civilized men heard of the existence of this wonderful cataract so lately as only three centuries since. The fact is, there must be a beginning to everything; and now there is a beginning to the world's knowing the history of Vulcan's Peak, and the Crater. Lest the reader, however, should feel disposed to reproach the past age with having been negligent in its collection of historical and geological incidents, we would again remind him of the magnitude of the events that so naturally occupied its attention. It is scarcely possible, for instance, for one who did not live forty years ago to have any notion how completely the world was engaged in wondering at Napoleon and his marvellous career, which last contained even more extraordinary features than anything related here; though certainly of a very different character. All wondering, for near a quarter of a century, was monopolized by the French Revolution and its consequences.

There are a few explanations, however, which are of a very humble nature compared with the principal events of our history, but which may as well be given here. The Woolston family still exists in Pennsylvania, and that, by the way, is something towards corroborating the truth of our narrative. Its most distinguished member is recently dead, and his journal has been the authority for most of the truths here related. He died at a good old age, having seen his three-score years and ten, leaving behind him, in addition to a very ample estate, not only a good character, which means neither more nor less than what "the neighbours," amid their ignorance, envy, love of detraction, jealousy and other similar qualities, might think proper to say of him, but the odour of a well-spent life, in which he struggled hard to live more in favour with God, than in favour with man. It was remarked in him, for the last forty years of his life, or after his return to Bucks, that he regarded all popular demonstrations with distaste, and, as some of his enemies pretended, with contempt. Nevertheless, he strictly acquitted himself of all his public duties, and never neglected to vote. It is believed that his hopes for the future, meaning in a social and earthly sense, were not very vivid, and he was often heard to repeat that warning text of Scripture which tells us, "Let him that thinketh he standeth, take heed lest he fall."

The faithful, and once lovely partner of this principal personage of our history is also dead. It would seem that it was not intended they should be long asunder. But their time was come, and they might almost be said to have departed in company. The same is true of Friends Robert and Martha, who have also filled their time, and gone hence, it is to be hoped to a better world. Some few of the younger persons of our drama still exist, but it has been remarked of them, that they avoid conversing of the events of their younger days. Youth is the season of hope, and hope disappointed has little to induce us to dwell on its deceptive pictures.

If those who now live in this republic, can see any grounds for a timely warning in the events here recorded, it may happen that the mercy of a divine Creator may still preserve that which he has hitherto cherished and protected.

It remains only to say that we have endeavoured to imitate the simplicity of Captain Woolston's journal, in writing this book, and should any homeliness of style be discovered, we trust it will be imputed to that circumstance.

Chapter I

> "'Twas a commodity lay fretting by you;
> 'Twill bring you gain, or perish on the seas."
>
> —Taming of the Shrew

There is nothing in which American Liberty, not always as much restrained as it might be, has manifested a more decided tendency to run riot, than in the use of names. As for Christian names, the Heathen Mythology, the Bible, Ancient History, and all the classics, have long since been exhausted, and the organ of invention has been at work with an exuberance of imagination that is really wonderful for such a matter-of-fact people. Whence all the strange sounds have been derived which have thus been pressed into the service of this human nomenclature, it would puzzle the most ingenious philologist to say. The days of the Kates, and Dollys, and Pattys, and Bettys, have passed away, and in their stead we hear of Lowinys, and Orchistrys, Philenys, Alminys, Cytherys, Sarahlettys, Amindys, Marindys, &c. &c. &c. All these last appellations terminate properly with an a, but this unfortunate vowel, when a final letter, being popularly pronounced like y, we have adapted our spelling to the sound, which produces a complete bathos to all these flights in taste.

The hero of this narrative was born fully sixty years since, and happily before the rage for modern appellations, though he just escaped being named after another system which we cannot say we altogether admire; that of using a family, for a christian name. This business of names is a sort of science in itself and we do believe that it is less understood and less attended to in this country than in almost all others. When a Spaniard writes his name as Juan de Castro y[1] Muños, we know that his father belonged to the family of Castro and his mother to that of Muños. The French, and Italian, and Russian woman, &c., writes on her card Madame this or that, *born* so and so; all which tells the whole history of her individuality Many French women, in signing their names, prefix those of their own family to those of their husbands, a sensible and simple usage that we are glad to see is beginning to obtain among ourselves. The records on tomb-stones, too, might be made much more clear and useful than they now are, by stating distinctly who the party was, on both sides of the house, or by father and mother; and each married woman ought to be commemorated in some such fashion as this: "Here lies Jane Smith, wife of John Jones," &c., or, "Jane, daughter of Thomas Smith and wife of John Jones." We believe that, in some countries, a woman's name is not properly considered to be changed by marriage, but she becomes a Mrs. only in connection with the name of her husband. Thus Jane Smith becomes Mrs. *John* Jones, but not Mrs. Jane Jones. It is on this idea we suppose that our ancestors the English-every Englishman, as a matter of course, being every American's ancestor-thus it is, we suppose, therefore, that our ancestors, who pay so much more attention to such matters than we do ourselves, in their table of courtesy, call the wife of Lord John Russell, Lady *John*, and not Lady-whatever her Christian name may happen to be. We suppose, moreover, it is on this principle that Mrs. General This, Mrs. Dr. That, and Mrs. Senator T'other, are as inaccurate as they are notoriously vulgar.

Mark Woolston came from a part of this great republic where the names are still as simple, unpretending, and as good Saxon English, as in the county of Kent itself. He was born in the little town of Bristol, Bucks county, Pennsylvania. This is a portion of the country that, Heaven be praised! still retains some of the good old-fashioned directness and simplicity. Bucks is full of Jacks, and Bens, and Dicks, and we question if there is such a creature, of native growth, in all that region, as an Ithusy, or a Seneky, or a Dianthy, or an Antonizetty, or a Deidamy.[2] The Woolstons, in particular, were a plain family, and very unpretending in their external appearance, but of solid and highly respectable habits around the domestic hearth. Knowing perfectly how to spell, they never dreamed anyone would suspect them of ignorance. They called themselves as their forefathers were called, that is to say, Wooster, or just as Worcester is pronounced; though a Yankee schoolmaster tried for a whole summer to persuade our hero, when a child, that he ought to be styled Wool-ston. This had no effect on Mark, who went on talking of his uncles and aunts, "Josy Wooster," and "Tommy Wooster," and "Peggy Wooster," precisely as if a New England academy did not exist on earth; or as if Webster had not actually put Johnson under his feet!

The father of Mark Woolston (or Wooster) was a physician, and, for the country and age, was a well-educated and skilful man. Mark was born in 1777, just seventy years since, and only ten days before the surrender of Burgoyne. A good deal of attention was paid to his instruction, and fortunately for himself, his servitude under the eastern pedagogue was of very short duration, and Mark continued to speak the English language as his fathers had spoken it before him. The difference on the score of language, between Pennsylvania and New Jersey and Maryland, always keeping in the counties that were not settled by Germans or Irish, and the New England states, and *through* them, New York, is really so obvious as to deserve a passing word. In the states first named, taverns, for instance, are still called the Dun Cow, the Indian Queen, or the Anchor: whereas such a thing would be hard to find, at this day, among the six millions of people who dwell in the latter. We question if there be such a thing as a coffee-house in all Philadelphia, though we admit it with grief, the respectable town of Brotherly Love has, in some respects, become infected with the spirit of innovation. Thus it is that good old "State House *Yard*" has been changed into "Independence Square." This certainly is not as bad as the *tour de force* of the aldermen of Manhattan when they altered "Bear Market" into "*Washington Market!*" for it is not a prostitution of the name of a great man, in the first place, and there is a direct historical allusion in the new name that everybody can understand. Still, it is to be regretted; and we hope this will be the last thing of the sort that will ever occur, though we confers our confidence in Philadelphian stability and consistency is a good deal lessened, since we have learned, by means of a late law-suit, that there are fifty or sixty aldermen in the place; a number of those worthies that is quite sufficient to upset the proprieties, in Athens itself!

Dr. Woolston had a competitor in another physician, who lived within a mile of him, and whose name was Yardley. Dr. Yardley was a very respectable person, had about the same degree of talents and knowledge as his neighbour and rival, but was much the richest man of the two. Dr. Yardley, however, had but one child, a daughter, whereas Dr. Woolston, with much less of means, had sons and daughters. Mark was the oldest of the family, and it was probably owing to this circumstance that he was so well educated, since the expense was not yet to be shared with that of keeping his brothers and sisters at schools of the same character.

In 1777 an American college was little better than a high school. It could not be called, in strictness, a grammar school, inasmuch as all the sciences were glanced at, if not studied; but, as respects the classics, more than a grammar school it was not, nor that of a very high order. It was a consequence of the light nature of the studies, that mere boys graduated in those institutions. Such was the case with Mark Woolston, who would have taken his degree as a Bachelor of Arts, at Nassau Hall, Princeton, had not an event occurred, in his sixteenth year, which produced an entire change in his plan of life, and nipped his academical honours in the bud.

Although it is unusual for square-rigged vessels of any size to ascend the Delaware higher than Philadelphia, the river is, in truth, navigable for such craft almost to Trenton Bridge. In the year 1793, when Mark Woolston was just sixteen, a full-rigged ship actually came up, and lay at the end of the wharf in Burlington, the little town nearly opposite to Bristol, where she attracted a great deal of the attention of all the youths of the vicinity. Mark was at home, in a vacation, and he passed half his time in and about that ship, crossing the river in a skiff of which he was the owner, in order to do so. From that hour young Mark affected the sea, and all the tears of his mother and eldest sister, the latter a pretty girl only two years his junior, and the more sober advice of his father, could not induce him to change his mind. A six weeks' vacation was passed in the discussion of this subject, when the Doctor yielded to his son's importunities, probably foreseeing he should have his hands full to educate his other children, and not unwilling to put this child, as early as possible, in the way of supporting himself.

The commerce of America, in 1793, was already flourishing, and Philadelphia was then much the most important place in the country. Its East India trade, in particular, was very large and growing, and Dr. Woolston knew that fortunes were rapidly made by many engaged in it. After, turning the thing well over in his mind, he determined to consult Mark's inclinations, and to make a sailor of him. He had a cousin married to the sister of an East India, or rather of a Canton ship-master, and to this person the father applied for advice and assistance. Captain Crutchely very willingly consented to receive Mark in his own vessel, the Rancocus, and promised "to make a man and an officer of him."

The very day Mark first saw the ocean he was sixteen years old. He had got his height, five feet eleven, and was strong for his years, and active. In fact, it would not have been easy to find a lad every way so well adapted to his new calling, as young Mark Woolston. The three years of his college life, if they had not made him a Newton, or a Bacon, had done him no harm, filling his mind with the germs of ideas that were destined afterwards to become extremely useful to him. The young man was already, indeed, a sort of factotum, being clever and handy at so many things and in so many different ways, as early to attract the attention of the officers. Long before the vessel reached the capes, he was at home in her, from her truck to her keelson, and Captain Crutchely remarked to his chief mate, the day they got to sea, that "young Mark Woolston was likely to turn up a trump."

As for Mark himself, he did not lose sight of the land, for the first time in his life, altogether without regrets. He had a good deal of feeling in connection with his parents, and his brothers and sisters; but, as it is our aim to conceal nothing which ought to be revealed, we must add there was still another who filled his thoughts more than all the rest united. This person was Bridget Yardley, the only child of his father's most formidable professional competitor.

The two physicians were obliged to keep up a sickly intercourse, not intending a pun. They were too often called in to consult together, to maintain an open war. While the heads of their respective families occasionally met, therefore, at the bed-side of their patients, the families themselves had no direct communications. It is true, that Mrs. Woolston and Mrs. Yardley were occasionally to be seen seated at the same tea-table, taking their hyson in company, for the recent trade with China had expelled the bohea from most of the better parlours of the country; nevertheless, these good ladies could not get to be cordial with each other. They themselves had a difference on religious points, that was almost as bitter as the differences of opinions between their husbands on the subject of alternatives. In that distant day, homoeopathy, and allopathy, and hydropathy, and all the opathies, were nearly unknown; but men could wrangle and abuse each other on medical points, just as well and as bitterly then, as they do now. Religion, too, quite as often failed to bear its proper fruits, in 1793, as it proves barren in these, our own times. On this subject of religion, we have one word to say, and that is, simply, that it never was a meet matter for self-gratulation and boasting. Here we have the Americo-Anglican church, just as it has finished a blast of trumpets, through the medium of numberless periodicals and a thousand letters from its confiding if not confident clergy, in honour of its quiet, and harmony, and superior polity, suspended on the very brink of the precipice of separation, if not of schism, and all because it has pleased certain ultra-sublimated divines in the other hemisphere, to write a parcel of tracts that nobody understands, themselves included. How many even of the ministers of the altar fall, at the very moment they are beginning to fancy themselves saints, and are ready to thank God they are "not like the publicans!"

Both. Mrs. Woolston and Mrs. Yardley were what is called 'pious;' that is, each said her prayers, each went to her particular church, and very *particular* churches they were; each fancied she had a sufficiency of saving faith, but neither was charitable enough to think, in a very friendly temper, of the other. This difference of religious opinion, added to the rival reputations of their husbands, made these ladies anything but good neighbours, and, as has been intimated, years had passed since either had entered the door of the other.

Very different was the feeling of the children. Anne Woolston, the oldest sister of Mark, and Bridget Yardley, were nearly of an age, and they were not only school-mates, but fast friends.

To give their mothers their due, they did not lessen this intimacy by hints, or intimations of any sort, but let the girls obey their own tastes, as if satisfied it was quite sufficient for "professors of religion" to hate in their own persons, without entailing the feeling on posterity. Anne and Bridget consequently became warm friends, the two sweet, pretty young things both believing, in the simplicity of their hearts, that the very circumstance which in truth caused the alienation, not to say the hostility of the elder members of their respective families, viz. professional identity, was an additional reason why *they* should love each other so much the more. The girls were about two and three years the juniors of Mark, but well grown for their time of life, and frank and affectionate as innocence and warm hearts could make them. Each was more than pretty, though it was in styles so very different, as scarcely to produce any of that other sort of rivalry, which is so apt to occur even in the gentler sex. Anne had bloom, and features, and fine teeth, and, a charm that is so very common in America, a good mouth; but Bridget had all these added to expression. Nothing could be more soft, gentle and feminine, than Bridget Yardley's countenance, in its ordinary state of rest; or more spirited, laughing, buoyant or pitying than it became, as the different passions or feelings were excited in her young bosom. As Mark was often sent to see his sister home, in her frequent visits to the madam's house, where the two girls held most of their intercourse, he was naturally enough admitted into their association. The connection commenced by Mark's agreeing to be Bridget's brother, as well as Anne's. This was generous, at least; for Bridget was an only child, and it was no more than right to repair the wrongs of fortune in this particular. The charming young thing declared that she would "rather have Mark Woolston for her brother than any other boy in Bristol; and that it was delightful to have the same person for a brother as Anne!" Notwithstanding this flight in the romantic, Bridget Yardley was as natural as it was possible for a female in a reasonably civilized condition of society to be. There was a vast deal of excellent, feminine self-devotion in her temperament, but not a particle of the exaggerated, in either sentiment or fueling. True as steel in all her impulses and opinions, in adopting Mark for a brother she merely yielded to a strong natural sympathy, without understanding its tendency or its origin. She would talk by the hour, with Anne, touching *their* brother, and what they must make him do, and where he must go with them, and in what they could oblige him most. The real sister was less active than her friend, in mind and body, and she listened to all these schemes and notions with a quiet submission that was not entirely free from wonder.

The result of all this intercourse was to awaken a feeling between Mark and Bridget, that was far more profound than might have been thought in breasts so young, and which coloured their future lives. Mark first became conscious of the strength of this feeling when he lost sight of the Capes, and fancied the dear little. Bucks county girl he had left behind him, talking with his sister of his own absence and risks. But Mark had too much of the true spirit of a sailor in him, to pine, or neglect his duty; and, long ere the ship had doubled the Cape of Good Hope, he had become an active and handy lad aloft. When the ship reached the China seas, he actually took his trick at the helm.

As was usual in that day, the voyage of the Rancocus lasted about a twelvemonth. If John Chinaman were only one-half as active as Jonathan Restless, it might be disposed of in about one-fourth less time; but teas are not transported along the canals of the Celestial Empire with anything like the rapidity with which wheat was sent to market over the rough roads of the Great Republic, in the age of which we are writing.

When Mark Woolston re-appeared in Bristol, after the arrival of the Rancocus below had been known there about twenty-four hours, he was the envy of all the lads in the place, and the admiration of most of the girls. There he was, a tall, straight, active, well-made, well-grown and decidedly handsome lad of seventeen, who had doubled the Cape of Good Hope, seen foreign parts, and had a real India handkerchief hanging out of each pocket of a blue round-about of superfine cloth, besides one around his half-open well-formed throat, that was carelessly tied in a true sailor knot! The questions he had to answer, and *did* answer, about whales, Chinese feet, and "mountain waves!" Although Bristol lies on a navigable river, up and down which frigates had actually been seen to pass in the revolution, it was but little that its people knew of the ocean. Most of the worthy inhabitants of the place actually fancied that the waves of the sea were as high as mountains, though their notions of the last were not very precise, there being no elevations in that part of the country fit even for a windmill.

But Mark cared little for these interrogatories. He was happy; happy enough, at being the object of so much attention; happier still in the bosom of a family of which he had always been the favourite and was now the pride; and happiest of all when he half ravished a kiss from the blushing cheek of Bridget Yardley. Twelve months had done a great deal for each of the young couple. If they had not quite made a man of Mark, they had made him manly, and his *soi-disant* sister wondered that any one could be so much improved by a sea-faring life. As for Bridget, herself, she was just bursting into young womanhood, resembling the bud as its leaves of green are opening to permit those of the deepest rose-coloured tint to be seen, before they expand into the full-blown flower. Mark was more than delighted, he was fascinated; and young as they were, the month he passed at home sufficed to enable him to tell his passion, and to obtain a half-ready, half-timid acceptance of the offer of his hand. All this time, the parents of these very youthful lovers were as profoundly ignorant of what was going on, as their children were unobservant of the height to which professional competition had carried hostilities between their respective parents. Doctors Woolston and Yardley no longer met even in consultations; or, if they did meet in the house of some patient whose patronage was of too much value to be slighted, it was only to dispute, and sometimes absolutely to quarrel.

At the end of one short month, however, Mark was once more summoned to his post on board the Rancocus, temporarily putting an end to his delightful interviews with Bridget. The lovers had made Anne their confidant, and she, well-meaning girl, seeing no sufficient reason why the son of one respectable physician should not be a suitable match for the daughter of another respectable physician, encouraged them in their vows of constancy, and pledges to become man and wife at a future, but an early day. To some persons all this may seem exceedingly improper, as well as extremely precocious; but the truth compels us to say, that its impropriety was by no means as obvious as its precocity. The latter it certainly was, though Mark had shot up early, and was a man at a time of life when lads, in less genial climates, scarcely get tails to their coats; but its impropriety must evidently be measured by the habits of the state of society in which the parties were brought up, and by the duties that had been inculcated. In America, then, as now, but little heed was taken by parents, more especially in what may be called the middle classes, concerning the connections thus formed by their children. So Long as the parties were moral, bore good characters, had nothing particular against them, and were of something near the same social station, little else was asked for; or, if more were actually required, it was usually when it was too late, and after the young people had got themselves too deeply in love to allow ordinary prudential reasons to have their due force.

Mark went to sea this time, dragging after him a "lengthening chain," but, nevertheless, filled with hope. His years forbade much despondency, and, while he remained as constant as if he had been a next-door neighbour, he was buoyant, and the life of the whole crew, after the first week out. This voyage was not direct to Canton, like the first; but the ship took a cargo of sugar to Amsterdam, and thence went to London, where she got a freight for Cadiz. The war of the French Revolution was now blazing in all the heat of its first fires, and American bottoms were obtaining a large portion of the carrying trade of the world. Captain Crutchely had orders to keep the ship in Europe, making the most of her, until a certain sum in Spanish dollars could be collected, when he was to fill up with provisions and water, and again make the best of his way to Canton. In obeying these instructions, he went from port to port; and, as a sort of consequence of having Quaker owners, turning his peaceful character to great profit, thus giving Mark many opportunities of seeing as much of what is called the world, as can be found in sea-ports. Great, indeed, is the difference between places that are merely the marts of commerce, and those that are really political capitals of large countries! No one can be aware of, or can fully appreciate the many points of difference that, in reality, exist between such places, who has not seen each,

17

and that sufficiently near to be familiar with both. Some places, of which London is the most remarkable example, enjoy both characters; and, when this occurs, the town gels to possess a tone that is even less provincial and narrow, if possible, than that which is to be found in a place that merely rejoices in a court. This it is which renders Naples, insignificant as its commerce comparatively is, superior to Vienna, and Genoa to Florence. While it would be folly to pretend that Mark, in his situation, obtained the most accurate notions imaginable of all he saw and heard, in his visits to Amsterdam, London, Cadiz, Bordeaux, Marseilles, Leghorn, Gibraltar, and two or three other ports that might be mentioned and to which he went, he did glean a good deal, some of which was useful to him in after-life. He lost no small portion of the provincial rust of home, moreover, and began to understand the vast difference between "seeing the world" and "going to meeting and going to mill."[3] In addition to these advantages, Mark was transferred from the forecastle to the cabin before the ship sailed for Canton. The practice of near two years had made him a very tolerable sailor, and his previous education made the study of navigation easy to him. In that day there was a scarcity of officers in America, and a young man of Mark's advantages, physical and moral, was certain to get on rapidly, provided he only behaved well. It is not at all surprising, therefore, that our young sailor got to be the second-mate of the Raucocus before he had quite completed his eighteenth year.

The voyage from London to Canton, and thence home to Philadelphia, consumed about ten months. The Rancocus was a fast vessel, but she could not impart her speed to the Chinamen. It followed that Mark wanted but a few weeks of being nineteen years old the day his ship passed Cape May, and, what was more, he had the promise of Captain Crutchely, of sailing with him, as his first officer, in the next voyage. With that promise in his mind, Mark hastened up the river to Bristol, as soon as he was clear of the vessel.

Bridget Yardley had now fairly budded, to pursue the figure with which we commenced the description of this blooming flower, and, if not actually expanded into perfect womanhood, was so near it as to show beyond all question that the promises of her childhood were to be very amply redeemed. Mark found her in black, however; or, in mourning for her mother. An only child, this serious loss had thrown her more than ever in the way of Anne, the parents on both sides winking at an association that could do no harm, and which might prove so useful. It was very different, however, with the young sailor. He had not been a fortnight at home, and getting to be intimate with the roof-tree of Doctor Yardley, before that person saw fit to pick a quarrel with him, and to forbid him his house. As the dispute was wholly gratuitous on the part of the Doctor, Mark behaving with perfect propriety on the occasion, it may be well to explain its real cause. The fact was, that Bridget was an heiress; if not on a very large scale, still an heiress, and, what was more, unalterably so in right of her mother; and the thought that a son of his competitor, Doctor Woolston, should profit by this fact, was utterly unsupportable to him. Accordingly he quarrelled with Mark, the instant he was apprised of the character of his attentions, and forbade him the house, To do Mark justice, he knew nothing of Bridget's worldly possessions. That she was beautiful, and warm-hearted, and frank, and sweet-tempered, and feminine, and affectionate, he both saw and felt; but beyond this he neither saw anything, nor cared about seeing anything. The young sailor was as profoundly ignorant that Bridget was the actual owner of certain three per cents, that brought twelve hundred a year, as if she did not own a 'copper,' as it was the fashion of that period to say,'*cents*' being then very little, if at all, used. Nor did he know anything of the farm she had inherited from her mother, or of the store in town, that brought three hundred and fifty more in rent. It is true that some allusions were made to these matters by Doctor Yardley, in his angry comments on the Woolston family generally, Anne always excepted, and in whose flavour he made a salvo, even in the height of his denunciations. Still, Mark thought so much of that which was really estimable and admirable in Bridget, and so little of anything mercenary, that even after these revelations he could not comprehend the causes of Doctor Yardley's harsh treatment of him. During the whole scene, which was purposely enacted in the presence of his wondering and trembling daughter, Mark behaved perfectly well. He had a respect for the Doctor's years, as well as for Bridget's father, and would not retort. After waiting as long as he conceived waiting could be of any use, he seized his hat, and left the room with an air of resentment that Bridget construed into the expression of an intention never to speak to any of them again. But Mark Woolston was governed by no such design, as the sequel will show.

Chapter II

> "She's not fourteen."
> "I'll lay fourteen of my teeth,
> And yet, to my teen be it spoken, I have but four, —
> She is not fourteen." —
>
> —Romeo and Juliet

Divine wisdom has commanded us to "Honour your father and your mother." Observant travellers affirm that less respect is paid to parents in America, than is usual in Christian nations-we say *Christian* nations; for many of the heathen, the Chinese for instance, worship them, though probably with an allegorical connection that we do not understand. That the parental tie is more loose in this country than in most others we believe, and there is a reason to be found for it in the migratory habits of the people, and in the general looseness in all the ties that connect men with the past. The laws on the subject of matrimony, moreover, are so very lax, intercourse is so simple and has so many facilities, and the young of the two sexes are left so much to themselves, that it is no wonder children form that connection so often without reflection and contrary to the wishes of their friends. Still, the law of God is there, and we are among those who believe that a neglect of its mandates is very apt to bring its punishment, even in this world, and we are inclined to think that much of that which Mark and Bridget subsequently suffered, was in consequence of acting directly in the face of the wishes and injunctions of their parents.

The scene which had taken place under the roof of Doctor Yardley was soon known under that of Doctor Woolston. Although the last individual was fully aware that Bridget was what was then esteemed rich, at Bristol, he cared not for her money. The girl he liked well enough, and in secret even admired her as much as he could find it in his heart to admire anything of Doctor Yardley's; but the indignity was one he was by no means inclined to overlook, and, in his turn, he forbade all intercourse between the girls. These two bitter pills, thus administered by the village doctors to their respective patients, made the young people very miserable. Bridget loved Anne almost as much as she loved Mark, and she began to pine and alter in her appearance, in a way to alarm her father. In order to divert her mind, he sent her to town, to the care of an aunt, altogether forgetting that Mark's ship lay at the wharves of Philadelphia, and that he could not have sent his daughter to any place, out of Bristol, where the young man would be so likely to find her. This danger the good doctor entirely overlooked, or, if he thought of it at all, he must have fancied that his sister would keep a sharp eye on the movements of the young sailor, and forbid him *her* house, too.

Everything turned out as the Doctor ought to have expected. When Mark joined his ship, of which he was now the first officer, he sought Bridget and found her. The aunt, however, administered to him the second potion of the same dose that her brother had originally dealt out, and gave him to understand that his presence in Front street was not desired. This irritated both the young people, Bridget being far less disposed to submit to her aunt than to her father, and they met clandestinely in the streets. A week or two of this intercourse brought matters to a crisis, and Bridget consented to a private marriage. The idea of again going to sea, leaving his betrothed entirely in the hands of those who disliked him for his father's sake, was intolerable to Mark, and it made him so miserable, that the tenderness of the deeply enamoured girl could not withstand his appeals. They agreed to get married, but to keep their union a secret until Mark should become of age, when it was hoped he would be in a condition, in every point of view, openly to claim his wife.

A thing of this sort, once decided on, is easily enough put in execution in America. Among Mark's college friends was one who was a few years older than himself, and who had entered the ministry. This young man was then acting as a sort of missionary among the seamen of the port, and he had fallen in the way of the young lover the very first day of his return to his ship. It was an easy matter to work on the good nature of this easy-minded man, who, on hearing of the ill treatment offered to his friend, was willing enough to perform the ceremony. Everything being previously arranged, Mark and Bridget were married, early one morning, during the time the latter was out, in company with a female friend of about her own age, to take what her aunt believed was her customary walk before breakfast. Philadelphia, in 1796, was not the town it is to-day. It then lay, almost entirely, on the shores of the Delaware, those of the Schuylkill being completely in the country. What was more, the best quarters were still near the river, and the distance between the Rancocus-meaning Mark's ship, and not the creek of that name-and the house of Bridget's aunt, was but trifling. The ceremony took place in the cabin of the vessel just named, which, now that the captain was ashore in his own house, Mark had all to himself, no second-mate having been shipped, and which was by no means an inappropriate place for the nuptials of a pair like that which our young people turned out to be, in the end.

The Rancocus, though not a large, was a very fine, Philadelphia-built ship, then the best vessels of the country. She was of a little less than four hundred tons in measurement, but she had a very neat and commodious poop-cabin. Captain Crutchely had a thrifty wife, who had contributed her full share to render her husband comfortable, and Bridget thought that the room in which she was united to Mark was one of the prettiest she had ever seen. The reader, however, is not to imagine it a cabin ornamented with marble columns, rose-wood, and the maples, as so often happens now-a-days. No such extravagance was dreamed of fifty years ago; but, as far as judicious arrangements, neat joiner's work, and appropriate furniture went, the cabin of the Rancocus was a very respectable little room. The circumstance that it was on deck, contributed largely to its appearance and comfort, sunken cabins, or those below decks, being necessarily much circumscribed in small ships, in consequence of being placed in a part of the vessel that is contracted in its dimensions under water, in order to help their sailing qualities.

The witnesses of the union of our hero and heroine were the female friend of Bridget named, the officiating clergyman, and one seaman who had sailed with the bridegroom in all his voyages, and who was now retained on board the vessel as a ship-keeper, intending to go out in her again as soon as she should be ready for sea. The name of this mariner was Betts, or Bob Betts as he was commonly called; and as he acts a conspicuous part in the events to be recorded, it may be well to say a word or two more of his history and character; Bob Betts was a Jerseyman; —or, as he would have pronounced the word himself, a Jarseyman-in the American meaning of the word, however, and not in the English. Bob was born in Cape May county, and in the *State* of New Jersey, United States of America. At the period of which we are now writing, he must have been about five-and-thirty, and seemingly a confirmed bachelor. The windows of Bob's father's house looked out upon the Atlantic Ocean, and he snuffed sea air from the hour of his birth. At eight years of age he was placed, as cabin-boy, on board a coaster; and from that time down to the moment when he witnessed the marriage ceremony between Mark and Bridget, he had been a sailor. Throughout the whole war of the revolution Bob had served in the navy, in some vessel or other, and with great good luck, never having been made a prisoner of war. In connection with this circumstance was one of the besetting weaknesses of his character. As often happens to men of no very great breadth of views, Bob had a notion that that which he had so successfully escaped, viz. captivity, other men too might have escaped had they been equally as clever. Thus it was that he had an ill-concealed, or only half-concealed contempt for such seamen as suffered themselves, at any time or under any circumstances, to fall into the enemies' hands. On all other subjects Bob was not only rational, but a very discreet and shrewd fellow, though on that he was often harsh, and sometimes absurd. But the best men have their weakness, and this was Bob Betts's.

Captain Crutchely had picked up Bob, just after the peace of 1783, and had kept him with him ever since. It was to Bob that he had committed the instruction of Mark, when the latter first joined the ship, and from Bob the youth had got his earliest notions of seamanship. In his calling Bob was full of resources, and, as often happens with the American sailor, he was even handy at a great many other things, and particularly so with whatever related to practical mechanics. Then he was of vast physical force, standing six feet two, in his stockings, and was round-built and solid. Bob had one sterling quality-he was as fast a friend as ever existed. In this respect he was a model of fidelity, never seeing a fault in those he loved, or a good quality in those he disliked. His attachment to Mark was signal, and he looked on the promotion of the young man much as he would have regarded preferment that befel himself. In the last voyage he had told the people in the forecastle "That young Mark Woolston would make a thorough sea-dog in time, and now he had got to be *Mr.* Woolston, he expected great things of him. The happiest day of my life will be that on which I can ship in a craft commanded by *Captain* Mark Woolston. I teached him, myself, how to break the first sea-biscuit he ever tasted, and next day he could do it as well as any on us! You see how handy and quick he is about a vessel's decks, shipmates; a ra'al rouser at a weather earin' —well, when he first come aboard here, and that was little more than two years ago, the smell of tar would almost make him swound away." The latter assertion was one of Bob's embellishments, for Mark was never either lackadaisical or very delicate. The young man cordially returned Bob's regard, and the two were sincere friends without any phrases on the subject.

Bob Betts was the only male witness of the marriage between Mark Woolston and Bridget Yardley, with the exception of the officiating clergyman; as Mary Bromley was the only female. Duplicate certificates, however, were given to the young couple, Mark placing his in his writing-desk, and Bridget hers in the bosom of her dress. Five minutes after the ceremony was ended, the whole party separated, the girls returning to their respective residences, and the clergyman going his way, leaving the mate and the ship-keeper together on the vessel's deck. The latter did not speak, so long as he saw the bridegroom's eyes fastened on the light form of the bride, as the latter went swiftly up the retired wharf where the ship was lying, on her way to Front street, accompanied by her young friend. But, no sooner had Bridget turned a corner, and Bob saw that the attraction was no longer in view, than he thought it becoming to put in a word.

"A trim-built and light-sailing craft, Mr. Woolston," he said, turning over the quid in his mouth; "one of these days she'll make a noble vessel to command."

"She is my captain, and ever will be, Bob," returned Mark. "But you'll be silent concerning what has passed."

"Ay, ay, sir. It is not my business to keep a log for all the women in the country to chatter about, like so many monkeys that have found a bag of nuts. But what was the meaning of the parson's saying, 'with all my worldly goods I thee endow' —does that make you any richer, or any poorer, sir?"

"Neither," answered Mark, smiling. "It leaves me just where I was, Bob, and where I am likely to be for some time to come, I fear."

"And has the young woman nothing herself, sir? Sometimes a body picks up a comfortable chest-full with these sort of things, as they tell me, sir."

"I believe Bridget is as poor as I am myself, Bob, and that is saying all that can be said on such a point. However, I've secured her now, and two years hence I'll claim her, if she has not a second gown to wear. I dare say the old man will be for turning her adrift with as little as possible."

All this was a proof of Mark's entire disinterestedness. He did not know that his young bride had quite thirty thousand dollars in reversion, or in one sense in possession, although she could derive no benefit from it until she was of age, or married, and past her eighteenth year. This fact her husband did not learn for several days after his marriage, when his bride communicated it to him, with a proposal that he should quit the sea and remain with her for life. Mark was very much in love, but this scheme scarce afforded him the satisfaction that one might have expected. He was attached to his profession, and scarce relished the thought of being dependent altogether on his wife for the means of subsistence. The struggle between love and pride was great, but Mark, at length, yielded to Bridget's blandishments, tenderness and tears. They could only meet at the house of Mary Bromley, the bride's-maid, but then the interviews between them were as frequent as Mark's duty would allow. The result was that Bridget prevailed, and the young husband went up to Bristol and candidly related all that had passed, thus revealing, in less than a week, a secret which it was intended should remain hid for at least two years.

Doctor Woolston was sorely displeased, at first; but the event had that about it which would be apt to console a parent. Bridget was not only young, and affectionate, and beautiful, and truthful; but, according to the standard of Bristol, she was rich. There was consolation in all this, notwithstanding professional rivalry and personal dislikes. We are not quite certain that he did not feel a slight gratification at the thought of his son's enjoying the fortune which his rival had received from his wife, and which, but for the will of the grandfather, would have been enjoyed by that rival himself. Nevertheless, the good Doctor did his duty in the premises. He communicated the news of the marriage to Doctor Yardley in a very civilly-worded note, which left a fair opening for a settlement of all difficulties, had the latter been so pleased. The latter did not so please, however, but exploded in a terrible burst of passion, which almost carried him off in a fit of apoplexy.

Escaping all physical dangers, in the end, Doctor Yardley went immediately to Philadelphia, and brought his daughter home. Both Mark and Bridget now felt that they had offended against one of the simplest commands of God. They had *not* honoured their father and their mother, and even thus early came the consciousness of their offence. It was in Mark's power, however, to go and claim his wife, and remove her to his father's house, notwithstanding his minority and that of Bridget. In this last respect, the law offered no obstacle; but the discretion of Doctor Woolston did. This gentleman, through the agency of a common friend, had an interview with his competitor, and they talked the matter over in a tolerably composed and reasonable temper. Both the parents, as medical men, agreed that it would be better that the young couple should not live together for two or three years, the very tender age of Bridget, in particular, rendering this humane, as well as discreet. Nothing was said of the fortune, which mollified Doctor Yardley a good deal, since he would be left to manage it, or at least to receive the income so long as no legal claimant interfered with his control. Elderly gentlemen submit very easily to this sort of influence. Then, Doctor Woolston was exceedingly polite, and spoke to his rival of a difficult case in his own practice, as if indirectly to ask an opinion of his competitor. All this contributed to render the interview more amicable than had been hoped, and the parties separated, if not friends, at least with an understanding on the subject of future proceedings.

It was decided that Mark should continue in the Rancocus for another voyage. It was known the ship was to proceed to some of the islands of the Pacific, in quest of a cargo of sandal-wood and bêche-le-mar, for the Chinese market, and that her next absence from home would be longer, even, than her last. By the time the vessel returned, Mark would be of age, and fit to command a ship himself, should it be thought expedient for him to continue in his profession. During the period the vessel still remained in port, Mark was to pay occasional visits to his wife, though not to live with her; but the young couple might correspond by letter, as often as they pleased. Such was an outline of the treaty made between the high contracting parties.

In making these arrangements, Doctor Yardley was partly influenced by a real paternal interest in the welfare of his daughter, who he thought altogether too young to enter on the duties and cares of the married life. Below the surface, however, existed an indefinite hope that something might yet occur to prevent the consummation of this most unfortunate union, as he deemed the marriage to be, and thus enable him to get rid of the hateful connection altogether. How this was to happen, the worthy doctor certainly did not know. This was because he lived in 1796, instead of in 1847. Now-a-days, nothing is easier than to separate a man from his wife, unless it be to obtain civic honours for a murderer. Doctor Yardley, at the present moment, would have coolly gone to work to get up a lamentable tale about his daughter's fortune, and youth, and her not knowing her own mind when she married, and a ship's cabin, and a few other embellishments of that sort, when the worthy and benevolent statesmen who compose the different legislatures of this vast Union would have been ready to break their necks, in order to pass a bill of divorce. Had there been a child or two, it would have made no great difference, for means would have been devised to give the custody of them to the mother. This would have been done, quite likely, for the first five years of the lives of the dear little things, because the children would naturally require a mother's care; and afterwards, because the precocious darlings, at the mature age of seven, would declare, in open court, that they really loved 'ma' more than they did 'pa'! To write a little plainly on a very important subject, we are of opinion that a new name ought to be adopted for the form of government which is so fast creeping into this country. New things require new names; and, were Solomon now living, we will venture to predict two things of him, viz. he would change his mind on the subject of novelties, and he would never go to congress. As for the new name, we would respectfully suggest that of Gossipian, in lieu of that of Republican, gossip fast becoming the lever that moves everything in the land. The newspapers, true to their instincts of consulting the ruling tastes, deal much more in gossip than they deal in reason; the courts admit it as evidence; the juries receive it as fact, as well as the law; and as for the legislatures, let a piteous tale but circulate freely in the lobbies, and bearded men, like Juliet when a child, as described by her nurse, will "stint and cry, ay!" In a word, principles and proof are in much less esteem than assertions and numbers, backed with enough of which, anything may be made to appear as legal, or even constitutional.

But neither of our doctors entered into all these matters. It was enough for them that the affair of the marriage was disposed of, for a time at least, and things were permitted to drop into their ancient channels. The intercourse between Bridget and Anne was renewed, just as if nothing had happened, and Mark's letters to his virgin bride were numerous, and filled with passion. The ship was 'taking in,' and he could only leave her late on Saturday afternoons, but each Sunday he contrived to pass in Bristol. On such occasions he saw his charming wife at church, and he walked with her in the fields, along with Anne and a favoured admirer of hers, of an afternoon, returning to town in season to be at his post on the opening of the hatches, of a Monday morning.

In less than a month after the premature marriage between Mark Woolston and Bridget Yardley, the Rancocus cleared for the Pacific and Canton. The bridegroom found one day to pass in Bristol, and Doctor Yardley so far pitied his daughter's distress, as to consent that the two girls should go to town, under his own care, and see the young man off. This concession was received with the deepest gratitude, and made the young people momentarily very happy. The doctor even consented to visit the ship, which Captain Crutchely, laughing, called St. Mark's chapel, in consequence of the religious rite which had been performed on board her. Mrs. Crutchely was there, on the occasion of this visit, attending to her husband's comforts, by fitting curtains to his berth, and looking after matters in general in the cabin; and divers jokes were ventured by the honest ship-master, in making his comments on, and in giving his opinion of the handy-work of his own consort. He made Bridget blush more than once, though her enduring tenderness in behalf of Mark induced her to sit out all the captain's wit, rather than shorten a visit so precious, one moment.

The final parting was an hour of bitter sorrow. Even Mark's young heart, manly, and much disposed to do his duty as he was, was near breaking: while Bridget almost dissolved in tears. They could not but think how long that separation was to last, though they did not anticipate by what great and mysterious events it was to be prolonged. It was enough for them, that they were to live asunder two whole years; and two whole years appear like an age to those who have not yet lived their four lustrums. But the final moment must and did arrive, and the young people were compelled to tear themselves asunder, though the parting was like that of soul and body. The bride hung on the bridegroom's neck, as the tendril clings to its support, until removed by gentle violence.

Bridget did not give up her hold upon Mark so long as even his vessel remained in sight. She went with Anne, in a carriage, as low as the Point, and saw the Rancocus pass swiftly down the river, on this its fourth voyage, bearing those in her who as little dreamed of their fate, as the unconscious woods and metals, themselves, of which the ship was constructed. Mark felt his heart beat, when he saw a woman's handkerchief waving to him from the shore, and a fresh burst of tenderness nearly unmanned him, when, by the aid of the glass, he recognised the sweet countenance and fairy figure of Bridget. Ten minutes later, distance and interposing objects separated that young couple for many a weary day!

A few days at sea restored the equanimity of Mark's feelings, while the poignant grief of Bridget did not fail to receive the solace which time brings to sorrows of every degree and nature. They thought of each other often, and tenderly; but, the pain of parting over, they both began to look forward to the joys of meeting, with the buoyancy and illusions that hope is so apt to impart to the bosoms of the young and inexperienced. Little did either dream of what was to occur before their eyes were to be again gladdened with the sight of their respective forms.

Mark found in his state-room —for, in the Rancocus, the cabin was fitted with four neat little state-rooms, one for the captain, and two for the mates, with a fourth for the supercargo-many proofs of Bridget's love and care. Mrs. Crutchely, herself, though so much longer experienced, had scarcely looked after the captain's comfort with more judgment, and certainly not with greater solicitude, than this youthful bride had expended on her bridegroom's room. In that day, artists were not very numerous in America, nor is it very probable that Doctor Yardley would have permitted his daughter to take so decided a step as to sit for her miniature for Mark's possession; but she had managed to get her profile cut, and to have it framed, and the mate discovered it placed carefully among his effects, when only a week out. From this profile Mark derived the greatest consolation. It was a good one, and Bridget happened to have a face that would tell in that sort of thing, so that the husband had no difficulty in recognising the wife, in this little image. There it was, with the very pretty slight turn of the head to one side, that in Bridget was both natural and graceful. Mark spent hours in gazing at and in admiring this inanimate shadow of his bride, which never failed to recall to him all her grace, and nature, and tenderness and love, though it could not convey any direct expression of her animation and spirit.

It is said ships have no Sundays. The meaning of this is merely that a vessel must perform her work, week-days and sabbaths, day and night, in fair or foul. The Rancocus formed no exception to the rule, and on she travelled, having a road before her that it would require months ere the end of it could be found. It is not our intention to dwell on the details of this long voyage, for two reasons. One is the fact that most voyages to the southern extremity of the American continent are marked by the same incidents; and the other is, that we have much other matter to relate, that must be given with great attention to minutiae, and which we think will have much more interest with the reader.

Captain Crutchely touched at Rio for supplies, as is customary; and, after passing a week in that most delightful of all havens, went his way. The passage round the Horn was remarkable neither way. It could not be called a very boisterous one, neither was the weather unusually mild. Ships do double this cape, occasionally, under their top-gallant-sails, and we have heard of one vessel that did not furl her royals for several days, while off that formidable head-land; but these cases form the exception and not the rule. The Rancocus was under close-reefed topsails for the better part of a fortnight, in beating to the southward and westward, it blowing very fresh the whole time; and she might have been twice as long struggling with the south-westerly gales, but for the fortunate circumstance of the winds veering so far to the southward as to permit her to lay her course, when she made a great run to the westward. When the wind again hauled, as haul it was almost certain to do, Captain Crutchely believed himself in a meridian that would admit of his running with an easy bowline, on the larboard tack. No one but a sailor can understand the effect of checking the weather-braces, if it be only for a few feet, and of getting a weather-leach to stand without 'swigging out' on its bowline. It has much the same influence on the progress of a ship, that an eloquent speech has on the practice of an advocate, a great cure or a skilful operation on that of a medical man, or a lucky hit in trade on the fortunes of the young merchant. Away all go alike, if not absolutely with flowing sheets, easily, swiftly, and with less of labour than was their wont. Thus did it now prove with the good ship Rancocus. Instead of struggling hard with the seas to get three knots ahead, she now made her six, and kept all, or nearly all, she made. When she saw the land again, it was found there was very little to spare, but that little sufficed. The vessel passed to windward of everything, and went on her way rejoicing, like any other that had been successful in a hard and severe struggle. A fortnight later, the ship touched at Valparaiso.

The voyage of the Rancocus may now be said to have commenced in earnest. Hitherto she had done little but make her way across the endless waste of waters; but now she had the real business before her to execute. A considerable amount of freight, which had been brought on account of the Spanish government, was discharged, and the vessel filled up her water. Certain supplies of food that was deemed useful in cases of scurvy, were obtained, and after a delay of less than a fortnight, the ship once more put to sea.

In the year 1796 the Pacific Ocean was by no means as familiar to navigators as it is to-day. Cooke had made his celebrated voyages less than twenty years before, and the accounts of them were then before the world; but even Cooke left a great deal to be ascertained, more especially in the way of details. The first inventor, or discoverer of anything, usually gains a great name, though it is those who come after him that turn his labours to account. Did we know no more of America to-day than was known to Columbus, our knowledge would be very limited, and the benefits of his vast enterprise still in their infancy.

Compared with its extent, perhaps, and keeping in view its ordinary weather, the Pacific can hardly be considered a dangerous sea; but he who will cast his eyes over its chart, will at once ascertain how much more numerous are its groups, islands, rocks, shoals and reefs, than those of the Atlantic. Still, the mariners unhesitatingly steered out into its vast waters, and none with less reluctance and fewer doubts than those of America.

For nearly two months did Captain Crutchely, after quitting Valparaiso, hold his way into the depths of that mighty sea, in search of the islands he had been directed to find. Sandal-wood was his aim, a branch of commerce, by the way, which ought never to be pursued by any Christian man, or Christian nation, if what we hear of its uses in China be true. There, it is said to be burned as incense before idols, and no higher offence can be committed by any human being than to be principal, or accessory, in any manner or way, to the substitution of any created thing for the ever-living God. In after-life Mark Woolston often thought of this, when reflection succeeded to action, and when he came to muse on the causes which may have led to his being the subject of the wonderful events that occurred in connection with his own fortunes. We have now reached a part of our narrative, however, when it becomes necessary to go into details, which we shall defer to the commencement of a new chapter.

Chapter III

> "God of the dark and heavy deep!
> The waves lie sleeping on the sands,
> Till the fierce trumpet of the storm
> Hath summon'd up their thundering bands;
> Then the white sails are clashed like foam,
> Or hurry trembling o'er the seas,
> Till calmed by thee, the sinking gale
> Serenely breathes, Depart in peace."
>
> —Peabody

The day that preceded the night of which we are about to speak, was misty, with the wind fresh at east-south-east. The Rancocus was running off, south-west, and consequently was going with the wind free. Captain Crutchely had one failing, and it was a very bad one for a ship-master; he would drink rather too much grog, at his dinner. At all other times he might have been called a sober man; out, at dinner, he would gulp down three or four glasses of rum and water. In that day rum was much used in America, far more than brandy; and every dinner-table, that had the smallest pretension to be above that of the mere labouring man, had at least a bottle of one of these liquors on it. Wine was not commonly seen at the cabin-table; or, if seen, it was in those vessels that had recently been in the vine-growing countries, and on special occasions. Captain Crutchely was fond of the pleasures of the table in another sense. His eating was on a level with his drinking; and for pigs, and poultry, and vegetables that would keep at sea, his ship was always a little remarkable.

On the day in question, it happened to be the birthday of Mrs. Crutchely, and the captain had drunk even a little more than common. Now, when a man is in the habit of drinking rather more than is good for him, an addition of a little more than common is very apt to upset him. Such, a sober truth, was the case with the commander of the Rancocus, when he left the dinner-table, at the time to which there is particular allusion. Mark, himself, was perfectly sober. The taste of rum was unpleasant to him, nor did his young blood and buoyant spirits crave its effects. If he touched it at all, it was in very small quantities, and greatly diluted with water. He saw the present condition of his superior, therefore, with regret; and this so much the more, from the circumstance that an unpleasant report was prevailing in the ship, that white water had been seen ahead, during a clear moment, by a man who had just come from aloft. This report the mate repeated to the captain, accompanying it with a suggestion that it might be well to shorten sail, round-to, and sound. But Captain Crutchely treated the report with no respect, swearing that the men were always fancying they were going ashore on coral, and that the voyage would last for ever, did he comply with all their conceits of this nature. Unfortunately, the second-mate was an old sea-dog, who owed his present inferior condition to his being a great deal addicted to the practice in which his captain indulged only a little, and he had been sharing largely in the hospitality of the cabin that afternoon, it being his watch below. This man supported the captain in his contempt for the rumours and notions of the crew, and between them Mark found himself silenced.

Our young officer felt very uneasy at the account of the sailor who had reported white water ahead, for he was one of the best men in the ship, and altogether unlikely to say that which was not true. It being now six o'clock in the evening, and the second-mate having taken charge of the watch, Mark went up into the fore-top-gallant cross-trees himself, in order to get the best look ahead that he could before the night set in. It wanted but half an hour, or so of sunset, when the young man took his station in the cross-trees, the royal not being set. At first, he could discern nothing ahead, at a distance greater than a mile, on account of the mist; but, just as the sun went below the waters it lighted up to the westward, and Mark then plainly saw what he was perfectly satisfied must be breakers, extending for several miles directly across the vessel's track!

Such a discovery required decision, and the young man shouted out —
"Breakers ahead!"

This cry, coming from his first officer, startled even Captain Crutchely, who was recovering a little from the effect of his potations, though it was still treated with contempt by the second-mate, who had never forgiven one as young as Mark, for getting a berth that he fancied due to his own greater age and experience. He laughed openly at this second report of breakers, at a point in the ocean where the chart laid down a clear sea; but the captain knew that the charts could only tell him what was known at the time they were made, and he felt disposed to treat his first officer, young as he was, with more respect than the second-mate. All hands were called in consequence, and sail was shortened. Mark came down to assist in this duty, while Captain Crutchely himself went aloft to look out for the breakers. They passed each other in the top, the latter desiring his mate to bring the ship by the wind, on the larboard tack, or with her head to the southward, as soon as he had the sail sufficiently reduced to do so with safety.

For a few minutes after he reached the deck, Mark was fully employed in executing his orders. Sail was shortened with great rapidity, the men working with zeal and alarm, for they believed their messmate when the captain had not. Although the vessel was under top-mast studding-sails when the command to take in the canvas was given, it was not long before Mark had her under her three topsails, and these with two reefs in them, and the ship on an easy bowline, with her head to the southward. When all this was done the young man felt a good deal of relief, for the danger he had seen was ahead, and this change of course brought it nearly abeam. It is true, the breakers were still to leeward, and insomuch most dangerously situated but the wind did not blow strong enough to prevent the ship from weathering them, provided time was taken by the forelock. The Rancocus was a good, weatherly ship, nor was there sufficient sea on to make it at all difficult for her to claw off a lee shore. Desperate indeed is the situation of the vessel that has rocks or sands under her lee, with the gale blowing in her teeth, and heavy seas sending her bodily, and surely, however slowly, on the very breakers she is struggling to avoid! Captain Crutchely had not been aloft five minutes before he hailed the deck, and ordered Mark to send Bob Betts up to the cross-trees. Bob had the reputation of being the brightest look-out in the vessel, and was usually employed when land was about to be approached, or a sail was expected to be made. He went up the fore-rigging like a squirrel, and was soon at the captain's side, both looking anxiously to leeward. A few minutes after the ship had hauled by the wind, both came down, stopping in the top, however, to take one more look to leeward.

The second-mate stood waiting the further descent of the captain, with a soft of leering look of contempt on his hard, well-dyed features, which seemed to anticipate that it would soon be known that Mark's white water had lost its colour, and become blue water once more. But Captain Crutchely did not go as far as this, when he got down. He admitted that he had seen nothing that he could very decidedly say was breakers, but that, once or twice, when it lighted up a little, there had been a gleaming along the western horizon which a good deal puzzled him. It might be white water, or it might be only the last rays of the setting sun tipping the combs of the regular seas. Bob Betts, too, was as much at fault as his captain, and a sarcastic remark or two of Hillson, the second-mate, were fast bringing Mark's breakers into discredit.

"Jest look at the chart, Captain Crutchely," put in Hillson —"a regular Tower Hill chart as ever was made, and you'll see there *can* be no white water hereabouts. If a man is to shorten sail and haul his wind, at every dead whale he falls in with, in these seas, his owners will have the balance on the wrong side of the book at the end of the v'y'ge!"

This told hard against Mark, and considerably in Hillson's favour.

"And could *you* see nothing of breakers ahead, Bob?" demanded Mark, with an emphasis on the '*you*' which pretty plainly implied that the young man was not so much surprised that the captain had not seen them.

"Not a bit of it, Mr. Woolston," answered Bob, hitching up his trowsers, "and I'd a pretty good look ahead, too."

This made still more against Mark, and Captain Crutchely sent for the chart. Over this map he and the second-mate pondered with a sort of muzzy sagacity, when they came to the conclusion that a clear sea *must* prevail around them, in all directions, for a distance exceeding a thousand miles. A great deal is determined in any case of a dilemma, when it is decided that this or that fact *must* be so. Captain Crutchely would not have arrived at this positive conclusion so easily, had not his reasoning powers been so much stimulated by his repeated draughts of rum and water, that afternoon; all taken, as he said and believed, not so much out of love for the beverage itself, as out of love for Mrs. John Crutchely. Nevertheless, our captain was accustomed to take care of a ship, and he was not yet in a condition to forget all his duties, in circumstances so critical. As Mark solemnly and steadily repeated his own belief that there were breakers ahead, he so far yielded to the opinions of his youthful chief-mate as to order the deep-sea up, and to prepare to sound.

This operation of casting the deep-sea lead is not done in a moment, but, on board a merchant vessel, usually occupies from a quarter of an hour to twenty minutes. The ship must first be hove-to, and her way ought to be as near lost as possible before the cast is made. Then the getting along of the line, the stationing of the men, and the sounding and hauling in again, occupy a good many minutes. By the time it was all over, on this occasion, it was getting to be night. The misty, drizzling weather threatened to make the darkness intense, and Mark felt more and more impressed with the danger in which the ship was placed.

The cast of the lead produced no other result than the certainty that bottom was not to be found with four hundred fathoms of line out. No one, however, not even the muzzy Hillson, attached much importance to this fact, inasmuch as it was known that the coral reefs often rise like perpendicular walls, in the ocean, having no bottom to be found within a cable's-length of them. Then Mark did not believe the ship to be within three leagues of the breakers he had seen, for they had seemed, both to him and to the seaman who had first reported them, to be several leagues distant. One on an elevation like that of the top-gallant cross-trees, could see a long way, and the white water had appeared to Mark to be on the very verge of the western horizon, even as seen from his lofty look-out.

After a further consultation with his officers, during which Hillson had not spared his hits at his less experienced superior, Captain Crutchely came to a decision, which might be termed semi-prudent. There is nothing that a seaman more dislikes than to be suspected of extra-nervousness on the subject of doubtful dangers of this sort. Seen and acknowledged, he has no scruples about doing his best to avoid them; but so long as there is an uncertainty connected with their existence at all, that miserable feeling of vanity which renders us all so desirous to be more than nature ever intended us for, inclines most men to appear indifferent even while they dread. The wisest thing Captain Crutchely could have done, placed in the circumstances in which he now found himself, would have been to stand off and on, under easy canvas, until the return of light, when he might have gone ahead on his course with some confidence, and a great deal more of safety. But there would have been an air of concession to the power of an unknown danger that conflicted with his pride, in such a course, and the old and well-tried ship-master did not like to give the 'uncertain' this advantage over him. He decided therefore to stand on, with his topsails reefed, keeping bright look-outs ahead, and having his courses in the brails, ready for getting the tacks down to claw off to windward, should it prove to be necessary. With this plan Mark was compelled to comply, there being no appeal from the decrees of the autocrat of the quarter deck.

As soon as the decision of Captain Crutchely was made, the helm was put up, and the ship kept off to her course. It was true, that under double-reefed topsails, and jib, which was all the canvas set, there was not half the danger there would have been under their former sail; and, when Mark took charge of the watch, as he did soon after, or eight o'clock, he was in hopes, by means of vigilance, still to escape the danger. The darkness, which was getting to be very intense, was now the greatest and most immediate source of his apprehensions. Could he only get a glimpse of the sea a cable's-length ahead, he would have felt vast relief; but even that small favour was denied him. By the time the captain and second-mate had turned in, which each did after going below and taking a stiff glass of rum and water in his turn, it was so dark our young mate could not discern the combing of the waves a hundred yards from the ship, in any direction. This obscurity was owing to the drizzle that filled the atmosphere, as well as to the clouds that covered the canopy above that lone and wandering ship.

As for Mark, he took his station between the knight-heads, where he remained most of the watch, nearly straining the eyes out of his head, in the effort to penetrate the gloom, and listening acutely to ascertain if he might not catch some warning roar of the breakers, that he felt so intimately persuaded must be getting nearer and nearer at each instant. As midnight approached, came the thought of Hillson's taking his place, drowsy and thick-headed as he knew he must be at that hour. At length Mark actually fancied he heard the dreaded sounds; the warning, however, was not ahead, but well on his starboard beam. This he thought an ample justification for departing from his instructions, and he instantly issued an order to put the helm hard a-starboard, so as to bring the vessel up to the wind, on the contrary tack. Unfortunately, as the result proved, it now became his imperative duty to report to Captain Crutchely what he had done. For a minute or two the young man thought of keeping silence, to stand on his present course, to omit calling the second-mate, and to say nothing about what he had done, keeping the deck himself until light should return. But reflection induced him to shrink from the execution of this plan, which would have involved him in a serious misunderstanding with both his brother officers, who could not fail to hear all that had occurred in the night, and who must certainly know, each in his respective sphere, that they themselves had been slighted. With a slow step, therefore, and a heavy heart, Mark went into the cabin to make his report, and to give the second-mate the customary call.

It was not an easy matter to awaken either of those, who slept under the influence of potations as deep as the night-caps taken by Captain Crutchely and Mr. Hillson. The latter, in particular, was like a man in a state of lethargy, and Mark had half a mind to leave him, and make his condition an excuse for not having persisted in the call. But he succeeded in arousing the captain, who soon found the means to bring the second-mate to a state of semi-consciousness.

"Well, sir," cried the captain, as soon as fairly awake himself, "what now?"

"I think I heard breakers abeam, sir, and I have hauled up to the southward."

A grunt succeeded, which Mark scarce knew how to interpret. It might mean dissatisfaction, or it might mean surprise. As the captain, however, was thoroughly awake, and was making his preparations to come out on deck, he thought that he had done all that duty required, and he returned to his own post. The after-part of the ship was now the best situation for watching, and Mark went up on the poop, in order to see and hear the better. No lower sail being in the way, he could look ahead almost as well from that position as if he were forward; and as for hearing, it was much the best place of the two, in consequence of there being no wash of the sea directly beneath him, as was the case when stationed between the knight-heads. To this post he soon summoned Bob Betts, who belonged to his watch, and with whom he had ever kept up as great an intimacy as the difference in their stations would allow.

"Bob, your ears are almost as good as your eyes," said Mark; "have you heard nothing of breakers?"

"I have, Mr. Woolston, and now own I did see something that may have been white water, this afternoon, while aloft; but the captain and second-mate seemed so awarse to believing in sich a thing, out here in the open Pacific, that I got to be awarse, too."

"It was a great fault in a look-out not to let what he had seen be known," said Mark, gravely.

"I own it, sir; I own how wrong I was, and have been sorry for it ever since. But it's going right in the wind's eye, Mr. Woolston, to go ag'in captain and dickey!"

"But, you now think you have *heard* breakers-where away?"

"Astarn first; then ahead; and, just as you called me up on the poop, sir, I fancied they sounded off here, on the weather bow."

"Are you serious, Bob?"

"As I ever was in my life, Mr. Mark. This oversight of the arternoon has made me somewhat conscientious, if I can be conscientious, and my sight and hearing are now both wide awake. It's my opinion, sir, that the ship is in the *midst* of breakers at this instant, and that we may go on 'em at any moment!"

"The devil it is!" exclaimed Captain Crutchely, who now appeared on the poop, and who caught the last part of Bob Betts's speech. "Well, for my part, I hear nothing out of the way, and I will swear the keenest-sighted man on earth can see nothing."

These words were scarcely out of the captain's mouth, and had been backed by a senseless, mocking laugh from Hillson, who was still muzzy, and quite as much asleep as awake, when the deep and near roar of breakers was most unequivocally heard. It came from to windward, too and abeam! This was proof that the ship was actually among the breakers when Mark hauled up, and that she was now passing a danger to leeward, that she must have previously gone by, in running down on her course. The captain, without waiting to consult with his cool and clear-headed young mate, now shouted for all hands to be called, and to "stand by to ware ship." These orders came out so fast, and in so peremptory a manner, that remonstrance was out of the question, and Mark set himself at work to obey them, in good earnest. *He* would have tacked in preference to waring, and it would have been much wiser to do so; but it was clearly expedient to get the ship on the other tack, and he lent all his present exertions to the attainment of that object. Waring is much easier done than tacking, certainly; when it does not blow too fresh, and there is not a dangerous sea on, no nautical manoeuvre can be more readily effected, though room is absolutely necessary to its success. This room was now wanting. Just as the ship had got dead before the wind, and was flying away to leeward, short as was the sail she was under, the atmosphere seemed to be suddenly filled with a strange light, the sea became white all around them, and a roar of tumbling waters arose, that resembled the sound of a small cataract. The ship was evidently in the midst of breakers, and the next moment she struck!

The intense darkness of the night added to the horrors of that awful moment. Nevertheless, the effect was to arouse all that there was of manliness and seamanship in Captain Crutchely, who from that instant appeared to be himself again. His orders were issued coolly, clearly and promptly, and they were obeyed as experienced mariners will work at an instant like that. The sails were all clewed up, and the heaviest of them were furled. Hillson was ordered to clear away an anchor, while Mark was attending to the canvas. In the mean time, the captain watched the movements of the ship. He had dropped a lead alongside, and by that he ascertained that they were still beating ahead. The thumps were not very hard, and the white water was soon left astern, none having washed on deck. All this was so much proof that the place on which they had struck must have had nearly water enough to float the vessel, a fact that the lead itself corroborated. Fifteen feet aft was all the Rancocus wanted, in her actual trim, and the lead showed a good three fathoms, at times. It was when the ship settled in the troughs of the sea that she felt the bottom. Satisfied that his vessel was likely to beat over the present difficulty, Captain Crutchely now gave all his attention to getting her anchored as near the reef and to leeward of it, as possible. The instant she went clear, a result he now expected every moment, he was determined to drop one of his bower anchors, and wait for daylight, before he took any further steps to extricate himself from the danger by which he was surrounded.

On the forecastle, the work went on badly, and thither Captain Crutchely proceeded. The second-mate scarce knew what he was about, and the captain took charge of the duty himself. At the same time he issued an order to Mark to get up tackles, and to clear away the launch, preparatory to getting that boat into the water. Hillson had bent the cable wrong, and much of the work had to be done over again. As soon as men get excited, as is apt to be the case when they find serious blunders made at critical moments, they are not always discreet. The precise manner in which Captain Crutchely met with the melancholy fate that befel him, was never known. It is certain that he jumped down on the anchor-stock, the anchor being a cock-bill, and that he ordered Mr. Hillson off of it. While thus employed, and at an instant when the cable was pronounced bent, and the men were in the act of getting inboard, the ship made a heavy roll, breakers again appeared all around her, the white foam rising nearly to the level of her rails. The captain was seen no more. There is little doubt that he was washed from the anchor stock, and carried away to leeward, in the midst of the darkness of that midnight hour.

Mark was soon apprised of the change that had occurred, and of the heavy responsibility that now rested on his young shoulders. A feeling of horror and of regret came over him, at first; but understanding the necessity of self-command, he aroused himself, at once, to his duty, and gave his orders coolly and with judgment. The first step was to endeavour to save the captain. The jolly-boat was lowered, and six men got in it, and passed ahead of the ship, with this benevolent design. Mark stood on the bowsprit, and saw them shoot past the bows of the vessel, and then, almost immediately, become lost to view in the gloomy darkness of the terrible scene. The men never reappeared, a common and an unknown fate thus sweeping away Captain Crutchely and six of his best men, and all, as it might be, in a single instant of time!

Notwithstanding these sudden and alarming losses, the work went on. Hillson seemed suddenly to become conscious of the necessity of exertion, and by giving his utmost attention to hoisting out the launch, that boat was got safely into the water. By this time the ship had beaten so far over the reef, as scarcely to touch at all, and Mark had everything ready for letting go his anchors, the instant he had reason to believe she was in water deep enough to float her. The thumps grew lighter and lighter, and the lead-line showed a considerable drift; so much so, indeed, as to require its being hauled in and cast anew every minute. Under all the circumstances, Mark expected each instant, to find himself in four fathoms' water, and he intended to let go the anchor the moment he was assured of that fact. In the mean time, he ordered the carpenter to sound the pumps. This was done, and the ship was reported with only the customary quantity of water in the well. As yet her bottom was not injured, materially at least.

While Mark stood with the lead-line in his hand, anxiously watching the drift of the vessel and the depth of water, Hillson was employed in placing provisions in the launch. There was a small amount of specie in the cabin, and this, too, was transferred to the launch; everything of that sort being done without Mark's knowledge, and by the second-mate's orders. The former was on the forecastle, waiting the proper moment to anchor; while all of the after-part of the ship was at the mercy of the second-mate, and a gang of the people, whom that officer had gathered around him.

At length Mark found, to his great delight, that there were four good fathoms of water under the ship's bows, though she still hung abaft. He ascertained this fact by means of Bob Betts, which true-hearted tar stood by him, with a lantern, by swinging which low enough, the marks were seen on the lead-line. Foot by foot the ship now surged ahead, the seas being so much reduced in size and power, by the manner in which they had been broken to windward, as not to lift the vessel more than an inch or two at a time. After waiting patiently 'a quarter' of an hour, Mark believed that the proper time had come, and he gave the order to 'let run.' The seaman stationed at the stopper obeyed, and down went the anchor. It happened, opportunely enough, that the anchor was thus dropped, just as the keel cleared the bottom, and the cable being secured at a short range, after forging ahead far enough to tighten the hitter, the vessel tended. In swinging to her anchor, a roller came down upon her, however; one that had crossed the reef without breaking, and broke on board her. Mark afterwards believed that the rush and weight of this sea, which did no serious harm, frightened the men into the launch, where Hillson was already in person, and that the boat either struck adrift under the power of the roller, or that the painter was imprudently cast off in the confusion of the moment. He had got in as far as the windlass himself, when the sea came aboard; and, as soon as he recovered his sight after the ducking he received, he caught a dim view of the launch, driving off to leeward, on the top of a wave. Hailing was useless, and he stood gazing at the helpless boat until it became lost, like everything else that was a hundred yards from the ship, in the gloom of night. Even then Mark was by no means conscious of the extent of the calamity that had befallen him. It was only when he had visited cabin, steerage and forecastle, and called the crew over by name, that he reached the grave fact that there was no one left on board the Rancocus but Bob Betts and himself!

As Mark did not know what land was to be found to leeward, he naturally enough hoped and expected that the people in both boats might reach the shore, and be recovered in the morning; but he had little expectation of ever seeing Captain Crutchely again. The circumstances, however, afforded him little time to reflect on these things, and he gave his whole attention, for the moment, to the preservation of the ship. Fortunately, the anchor held, and, as the wind, which had never blown very heavily, sensibly began to lessen, Mark was sanguine in the belief it would continue to hold. Captain Crutchely had taken the precaution to have the cable bitted at a short range with a view to keep it, as much as possible, off the bottom; coral being known to cut the hempen cables that were altogether in use, in that day, almost as readily as axes. In consequence of this bit of foresight, the Rancocus lay at a distance of less than forty fathoms from her anchor, which Mark knew had been dropped in four fathoms' water. He now sounded abreast of the main-mast, and ascertained that the ship itself was in nine fathoms. This was cheering intelligence, and when Bob Betts heard it, he gave it as his opinion that all might yet go well with them, could they only recover the six men who had gone to leeward in the jolly-boat. The launch had carried off nine of their crew, which, previously to this night, had consisted of nineteen, all told. This suggestion relieved Mark's mind of a load of care, and he lent himself to the measures necessary to the continued safety of the vessel, with renewed animation and vigour.

The pump-well was once more sounded, and found to be nearly empty. Owing to the nature of the bottom on which they had struck, the lightness of the thumps, or the strength of the ship herself, it was clear that the vessel had thus far escaped without any material injury. For this advantage Mark was deeply grateful, and could he only recover four or five of the people, and find his way out into open water, he might hope to live again to see America, and to be re-united to his youthful and charming bride.

The weather continued to grow more and more moderate, and some time before the day returned the clouds broke away, the drizzle ceased, and a permanent change was to be expected. Mark now found new ground for apprehensions, even in these favourable circumstances. He supposed that the ship must feel the influence of the tides, so near the land, and was afraid she might tail the other way, and thus be brought again over the reef. In order to obviate this difficulty, he and Bob set to work to get another cable bent, and another anchor clear for letting go. As all our readers may not be familiar with ships, it may be well to say that vessels, as soon as they quit a coast on a long voyage, unbend their cables and send them all below, out of the way, while, at the same time, they stow their anchors, as it is called; that is to say, get them from under the cat-heads, from which they are usually suspended when ready to let go, and where they are necessarily altogether on the outside of the vessel, to positions more inboard, where they are safer from the force of the waves, and better secured. As all the anchors of the Rancocus had been thus stowed, until Captain Crutchely got the one that was down, off the gunwale, and all the cables below, Mark and Bob had labour enough before them to occupy several hours, in the job thus undertaken.

Chapter IV

> "Deep in the wave is a coral grove,
> Where the purple mullet and gold fish rove,
> Where the sea-flower spreads its leaves of blues,
> That never are wet with falling dew,
> But in bright and changeful beauty shine,
> Far down in the green and grassy brine."
>
> —Percival

Our young mate, and his sole assistant, Bob Betts, had set about their work on the stream-cable and anchor, the lightest and most manageable of all the ground-tackle in the vessel. Both were strong and active, and both were expert in the use of blocks, purchases, and handspikes; but the day was seen lighting the eastern sky, and the anchor was barely off the gunwale, and ready to be stoppered in the meanwhile the ship still tended in the right direction, the wind had moderated to a mere royal-breeze, and the sea had so far gone down as nearly to leave the vessel without motion. As soon as perfectly convinced of the existence of this favourable state of things, and of its being likely to last, Mark ceased to work, in order to wait for day, telling Bob to discontinue his exertions also. It was fully time, for both of those vigorous and strong-handed men were thoroughly fatigued with the toil of that eventful morning.

The reader may easily imagine with what impatience our two mariners waited the slow return of light. Each minute seemed an hour, and it appeared to them as if the night was to last for ever. But the earth performed its usual revolution, and by degrees sufficient light was obtained to enable Mark and Bob to examine the state of things around them. In order to do this the better, each went into a top, looking abroad from those elevations on the face of the ocean, the different points of the reef, and all that was then and there to be seen. Mark went up forward, while Bob ascended into the main-top. The distance between them was so small, that there was no difficulty in conversing, which they continued to do, as was natural enough to men in their situation.

The first look that each of our mariners bestowed, after he was in his top, was to leeward, which being to the westward, was of course yet in the darkest point of the horizon. They expected to obtain a sight of at least one island, and that quite near to them, if not of a group. But no land appeared! It is true, that it was still too dark to be certain of a fact of this sort, though Mark felt quite assured that if land was finally seen, it must be of no great extent, and quite low. He called to Bob, to ascertain what *he* thought of appearances to leeward, his reputation as a look-out being so great.

"Wait a few minutes, sir, till we get a bit more day," answered his companion. "There is a look on the water, about a league off here on the larboard quarter, that seems as if something would come out of it. But, one thing can be seen plain enough, Mr. Mark, and that's the breakers. There's a precious line on 'em, and that too one within another, as makes it wonderful how we ever got through 'em as well as we did!"

This was true enough, the light on the ocean to windward being now sufficient to enable the men to see, in that direction, to a considerable distance. It was that solemn hour in the morning when objects first grow distinct, ere they are touched with the direct rays from the sun, and when everything appears as if coming to us fresh and renovated from the hands of the Creator. The sea had so far gone down as to render the breakers much less formidable to the eye, than when it was blowing more heavily; but this very circumstance made it impossible to mistake their positions. In the actual state of the ocean, it was certain that wherever water broke, there must be rocks or shoals beneath; whereas, in a blow, the combing of an ordinary sea might be mistaken for the white water of some hidden danger. Many of the rocks, however, lay so low, that the heavy, sluggish rollers that came undulating along, scarce did more than show faint, feathery lines of white, to indicate the character of the places across which they were passing. Such was now the case with the reef over which the ship had beaten, the position of which could hardly have been ascertained, or its danger discovered, at the distance of half a mile. Others again were of a very different character, the water still tumbling about them like so many little cataracts. This variety was owing to the greater depth at which some of the rocks lay than others.

As to the number of the reefs, and the difficulty in getting through them, Bob was right enough. It often happens that there is an inner and an outer reef to the islands of the Pacific, particularly to those of coral formation; but Mark began to doubt whether there was any coral at all in the place where the Rancocus lay, in consequence of the entire want of regularity in the position of these very breakers. They were visible in all directions; not in continuous lines, but in detached parts; one lying within another, as Bob had expressed it, until the eye could not reach their outer limits. How the ship had got so completely involved within their dangerous embraces, without going to pieces on a dozen of the reefs, was to him matter of wonder; though it sometimes happens at sea, that dangers are thus safely passed in darkness and fog, that no man would be bold enough to encounter in broad daylight, and with a full consciousness of their hazards. Such then had been the sort of miracle by which the Rancocus had escaped; though it was no more easy to see how she was to be got out of her present position, than it was to see how she had got into it. Bob was the first to make a remark on this particular part of the subject.

"It will need a reg'lar branch here, Mr. Mark, to carry the old Rancocus clear of all them breakers to sea again," he cried. "Our Delaware banks is just so many fools to 'em, sir!"

"It is a most serious position for a vessel to be in, Bob," answered Mark, sighing—"nor do I see how we *are* ever to get clear of it, even should we get back men enough to handle the ship."

"I'm quite of your mind, sir," answered Bob, taking out his tobacco-box, and helping himself to a quid. "Nor would I be at all surprised should there turn out to be a bit of land to leeward, if you and I was to Robinson Crusoe it for the rest of our days. My good mother was always most awarse to my following the seas on account of that very danger; most especially from a fear of the savages from the islands round about."

"We will look for our boats," Mark gravely replied, the image of Bridget, just at that instant, appearing before his mind with a painful distinctness.

Both now turned their eyes again to leeward, the first direct rays of the sun beginning to illumine the surface of the ocean in that quarter. Something like a misty cloud had been settled on the water, rather less than a league from the ship, in the western board, and had hitherto prevented a close examination in that part of the horizon. The power of the sun, however, almost instantly dispersed it, and then, for the first time, Bob fancied he did discover something like land. Mark, however, could not make it out, until he had gone up into the cross-trees, when he, too, got a glimpse of what, under all the circumstances, he did not doubt was either a portion of the reef that rose above the water, or was what might be termed a low, straggling island. Its distance from the ship, they estimated at rather more than two leagues.

Both Mark and Bob remained aloft near an hour longer, or until they had got the best possible view of which their position would allow, of everything around the ship. Bob went down, and took a glass up to his officer, Mark sweeping the whole horizon with it, in the anxious wish to make out something cheering in connection with the boats. The drift of these unfortunate craft must have been towards the land, and that he examined with the utmost care. Aided by the glass, and his elevation, he got a tolerable view of the spot, which certainly promised as little in the way of supplies as any other bit of naked reef he had ever seen. The distance, however, was so great as to prevent his obtaining any certain information on that point. One thing, however, he did ascertain, as he feared, with considerable accuracy. After passing the glass along the whole of that naked rock, he could see nothing on it in motion. Of birds there were a good many, more indeed than from the extent of the visible reef he might have expected; but no signs of man could be discovered. As the ocean, in all directions, was swept by the glass, and this single fragment of a reef, which was less than a mile in length, was the only thing that even resembled land, the melancholy conviction began to force itself on Mark and Bob, that all their shipmates had perished! They might have perished in one of several ways; as the naked reef did not lie precisely to leeward of the ship, the boats may have driven by it, in the deep darkness of the past night, and gone far away out of sight of the spot where they had left the vessel, long ere the return of day. There was just the possibility that the spars of the ship might be seen by the wanderers, if they were still living, and the faint hope of their regaining the vessel, in the course of the day, by means of their oars. It was, however, more probable that the boats had capsized in some of the numerous fragments of breakers, that were visible even in the present calm condition of the ocean, and that all in them had been drowned. The best swimmer must have hopelessly perished, in such a situation, and in such a night, unless carried by a providential interference to the naked rock to leeward. That no one was living on that reef, the glass pretty plainly proved.

Mark and Bob Betts descended to the deck, after passing a long time aloft making their observations. Both were pretty well assured that their situation was almost desperate, though each was too resolute, and too thoroughly imbued with the spirit of a seaman, to give up while there was the smallest shadow of hope. As it was now getting past the usual breakfast hour, some cold meat was got out, and, for the first time since Mark had been transferred to the cabin, they sat down on the windlass and ate the meal together. A little, however, satisfied men in their situation; Bob Betts fairly owning that he had no appetite, though so notorious at the ship's beef and a biscuit, as to be often the subject of his messmates' jokes. That morning even he could eat but little, though both felt it to be a duty they owed to themselves to take enough to sustain nature. It was while these two forlorn and desolate mariners sat there on the windlass, picking, as it might be, morsel by morsel, that they first entered into a full and frank communication with each other, touching the realities of their present situation. After a good deal had passed between them, Mark suddenly asked—

"Do you think it possible, Bob, for us two to take care of the ship, should we even manage to get her into deep water again?"

"Well, that is not so soon answered, Mr. Woolston," returned Bob. "We're both on us stout, and healthy, and of good courage, Mr. Mark; but 'twould be a desperate long way for two hands to carry a wessel of four hundred tons, to take the old 'Cocus from this here anchorage, all the way to the coast of America; and short of the coast there's no ra'al hope for us. However, sir, *that* is a subject that need give us no consarn."

"I do not see that, Bob; we shall have to do it, unless we fall in with something at sea, could we only once get the vessel; out from among these reefs."

"Ay, ay, sir-could' we get her out from among these reefs, indeed! There's the rub, Mr. Woolston; but I fear 't will never be 'rub and *go*.'"

"You think, then, we are too fairly in for it, ever to get the ship clear?"

"Such is just my notion, Mr. Woolston, on that subject, and I've no wish to keep it a secret. In my judgment, was poor Captain Crutchely alive and back at his post, and all hands just as they was this time twenty-four hours since, and the ship where she is now, that *here* she would have to stay. Nothing short of kedging can ever take the wessel clear of the reefs to windward on us, and man-of-war kedging could hardly do it, then."

"I am sorry to hear you say this," answered Mark, gloomily, "though I feared as much myself."

"Men is men, sir, and you can get no more out on 'em than is in 'em. I looked well at these reefs, sir, when aloft, and they're what I call as hopeless affairs as ever I laid eyes on. If they lay in any sort of way, a body might have some little chance of getting through 'em, but they don't lay, no how. 'T would be 'luff' and 'keep her away' every half minute or so, should we attempt to beat up among 'em; and who is there aboard here to brace up, and haul aft, and ease off, and to swing yards sich as our'n?"

"I was not altogether without the hope, Bob, of getting the ship into clear water: though I have thought it would be done with difficulty, I am still of opinion we had better try it, for the alternative is a very serious matter."

"I don't exactly understand what you mean by attorneytives, Mr. Mark; though it's little harm, or little good that any attorney can do the old 'Cocus, now! But, as for getting this craft through them reefs, to windward, and into clear water, it surpasses the power of man. Did you just notice the tide-ripples, Mr. Mark, when you was up in the cross-trees?"

"I saw them, Bob, and am fully aware of the difficulty of running as large a vessel as this among them, even with a full crew. But what will become of us, unless we get the ship into open water?"

"Sure enough, sir. I see no other hope for us, Mr. Mark, but to Robinson Crusoe it awhile, until our times come; or, till the Lord, in his marcy, shall see fit to have us picked up."

"Robinson Crusoe it!" repeated Mark, smiling at the quaintness of Bob's expression, which the well-meaning fellow uttered in all simplicity, and in perfect good faith —"where are we to find even an uninhabited island, on which to dwell after the mode of Robinson Crusoe?"

"There's a bit of a reef to-leeward, where I dare say a man might pick up a living, arter a fashion," answered Bob, coolly; "then, here is the ship."

"And how long would a hempen cable hold the ship in a place like this, where every time the vessel lifts to a sea, the clench is chafing on a rock? No, no, Bob-the ship cannot long remain where she is, depend on *that*. We must try and pass down to leeward, if we cannot beat the ship through the dangers to windward."

"Harkee, Mr. Mark; I thought this matter over in my mind, while we was aloft, and this is my idee as to what is best to be done, for a start. There's the dingui on the poop, in as good order as ever a boat was. She will easily carry two on us, and, on a pinch, she might carry half a dozen. Now, my notion is to get the dingui into the water, to put a breaker and some grub in her, and to pull, down to that bit of a reef, and have a survey of it. I'll take the sculls going down, and you can keep heaving the by way of finding out if there be sich a thang as a channel in that direction. If the ship is ever to be moved by us two, it must be by going to leeward, and not by attempting to turn up ag'in wind and tide among them 'ere rocks, out here to the eastward. No, sir; let us take the dingui, and surwey the reef, and look for our shipmates; a'ter which we can best tell what to undertake, with some little hope of succeeding. The weather seems settled, and the sooner we are off the better."

This proposal struck Mark's young mind as plausible, as well as discreet. To recover even a single man would be a great advantage, and he had lingering hopes that some of the people might yet be found on the reef. Then Bob's idea about getting the ship through the shoal water, by passing to leeward, in preference to making the attempt against the wind, was a sound one; and, on a little reflection, he was well enough disposed to acquiesce in it. Accordingly, when they quitted the windlass, they both set about putting this project in execution.

The dingui was no great matter of a boat, and they had not much difficulty in getting it into the water. First by slinging, it was swayed high enough to clear the rail, when Bob bore it over the side, and Mark lowered away. It was found to be tight, Captain Crutchely having kept it half full of water ever since they got into the Pacific, and in other respects it was in good order. It was even provided with a little sail, which did very well before the wind. While Bob saw to provisioning the boat, and filling its breakers with fresh water, Mark attended to another piece of duty that he conceived to be of the last importance. The Rancocus carried several guns, an armament prepared to repel the savages of the sandal-wood islands, and these guns were all mounted and in their places. There were two old-fashioned sixes, and eight twelve-pound carronades. The first made smart reports when properly loaded. Our young mate now got the keys of the magazine, opened it, and brought forth three cartridges, with which he loaded three of the guns. These guns he fired, with short intervals between them, in hopes that the reports would be carried to the ears of some of the missing people, and encourage them to make every effort to return. The roar of artillery sounded strangely enough in the midst of that vast solitude; and Bob Betts, who had often been in action, declared that he was much affected by it, As no immediate result was expected from the firing of these guns, Mark had no sooner discharged them, than he joined Betts, who by this time had everything ready, and prepared to quit the ship. Before he did this, however, he made an anxious and careful survey of the weather it being all-important to be certain no change in this respect was likely to occur in his absence. All the omens were favourable, and Bob reporting for the third time that everything was ready, the young man went over the side, and descended, with a reluctance he could not conceal, into the boat. Certainly, it was no trifling matter for men in the situation of our two mariners, to leave their vessel all alone, to be absent for a large portion of the day. It was to be done, however; though it was done reluctantly, and not without many misgivings, in spite of the favourable signs in the atmosphere.

When Mark had taken his seat in the dingui, Bob let go his hold of the ship, and set the sail. The breeze was light, and fair to go, though it was by no means so certain how it would serve them on the return. Previously to quitting the ship, Mark had taken a good look at the breakers to leeward, in order to have some general notion of the course best to steer, and he commenced his little voyage, but entirely without a plan for his own government. The breakers were quite as numerous to leeward as to windward, but the fact of there being so many of them made smooth water between them. A boat, or a ship, that was once fairly a league or so within the broken lines of rocks, was like a vessel embayed, the rollers of the open ocean expending their force on the outer reefs, and coming in much reduced in size and power. Still the uneasy ocean, even in its state of rest, is formidable at the points where its waters meet with rocks, or sands and the breakers that did exist, even as much embayed as was the dingui, were serious matters for so small a boat to encounter. It was necessary, consequently, to steer clear of them, lest they should capsize, or fill, this, the only craft of the sort that now belonged to the vessel, the loss of which would be a most serious matter indeed.

The dingui slid away from the ship with a very easy movement. There was just about as much wind as so small a craft needed, and Bob soon began to sound, Mark preferring to steer. It was, however, by no means easy to sound in so low a boat, while in such swift motion; and Bob was compelled to give it up. As they should be obliged to return with the oars, Mark observed that then he would feel his way back to the ship. Nevertheless, the few casts of the lead that did succeed, satisfied our mariners that there was much more than water enough for the Rancocus, between the reefs. *On* them, doubtless it would turn out to be different.

Mark met with more difficulty than he had anticipated in keeping the dingui out of the breakers. So very smooth was the sort of bay he was in —a bay by means of the reefs to windward, though no rock in that direction rose above the surface of the sea-so very smooth, then, was the sort of bay he was in, that the water did not break, in many places, except at long intervals; and then only when a roller heavier than common found its way in from the outer ocean. As a consequence, the breakers that did suddenly show themselves from a cause like this, were the heaviest of all, and the little dingui would have fared badly had it been caught on a reef, at the precise moment when such a sea tumbled over in foam. This accident was very near occurring once or twice, but it was escaped, more by providential interference than by any care or skill in the adventurers.

It is very easy to imagine the intense interest with which our two mariners drew near to the visible reef. Their observations from the cross-trees of the ship, had told them this was all the land anywhere very near them, and if they did not find their lost shipmates here, they ought not to expect to find them at all. Then this reef, or island, was of vast importance in other points of view. It might become their future home; perhaps for years, possibly for life. The appearances of the sunken reefs, over and among which he had just passed, had greatly shaken Mark's hope of ever getting the ship from among them, and he even doubted the possibility of bringing her down, before the wind, to the place where he was then going. All these considerations, which began to press more and more painfully on his mind, each foot as he advanced, served to increase the intensity of the interest with which he noted every appearance on, or about, the reef, or island, that he was now approaching. Bob had less feeling on the subject. He had less imagination, and foresaw consequences and effects less vividly than his officer, and was more accustomed to the vicissitudes of a seaman's life. Then he had left no virgin bride at home, to look for his return; and had moreover made up his mind that it was the will of Providence that he and Mark were to 'Robinson Crusoe it' awhile, on 'that bit of a reef.' Whether they should ever be rescued from so desolate a place, was a point on which he had not yet begun to ponder.

The appearances were anything but encouraging, as the dingui drew nearer and nearer to the naked part of the reef. The opinions formed of this place, by the examination made from the cross-trees, turned out to be tolerably accurate, in several particulars. It was just about a mile in length, while its breadth varied from half a mile to less than an eighth of a mile. On its shores, the rock along most of the reef rose but a very few feet above the surface of the water, though at its eastern, or the weather extremity, it might have been of more than twice the usual height; its length lay nearly east and west. In the centre of this island, however, there was a singular formation of the rock, which appeared to rise to an elevation of something like sixty or eighty feet, making a sort of a regular circular mound of that height, which occupied no small part of the widest portion of the island. Nothing like tree, shrub, or grass, was visible, as the boat drew near enough to render such things apparent. Of aquatic birds there were a good many: though even they did not appear in the numbers that are sometimes seen in the vicinity of uninhabited islands. About certain large naked rocks, at no great distance however from the principal reef, they were hovering in thousands.

At length the little dingui glided in quite near to the island. Mark was at first surprised to find so little surf beating against even its weather side, but this was accounted for by the great number of the reefs that lay for miles without it; and, particularly, by the fact that one line of rock stretched directly across this weather end, distant from it only two cables' lengths, forming a pretty little sheet of perfectly smooth water between it and the island. Of course, to do this, the line of reef just mentioned must come very near the surface; as in fact was the case, the rock rising so high as to be two or three feet out of water on the ebb, though usually submerged on the flood. The boat was obliged to pass round one end of this last-named reef, where there was deep water, and then to haul its wind a little in order to reach the shore.

It would be difficult to describe the sensations with which Mark first landed. In approaching the place, both he and Bob had strained their eyes in the hope of seeing some proof that their shipmates had been there; but no discovery rewarded their search. Nothing was seen, on or about the island, to furnish the smallest evidence that either of the boats had touched it. Mark found that he was treading on naked rock when he had landed, though the surface was tolerably smooth. The rock itself was of a sort to which he was unaccustomed; and he began to suspect, what in truth turned out on further investigation to be the fact, that instead of being on a reef of coral, he was on one of purely volcanic origin. The utter nakedness of the rock both surprised and grieved him. On the reefs, in every direction, considerable quantities of sea-weed had lodged, temporarily at least; but none of it appeared to have found its way to this particular place. Nakedness and dreariness were the two words which best described the island; the only interruption to its solitude and desolation being occasioned by the birds, which now came screaming and flying above the heads of the intruders, showing both by their boldness and their cries, that they were totally unacquainted with men.

The mound, in the centre of the reef, was an object too conspicuous to escape attention, and our adventurers approached it at once, with the expectation of getting a better look-out from its summit, than that they had on the lower level of the surface of the ordinary reef. Thither then they proceeded, accompanied by a large flight of the birds. Neither Mark nor Bob, however, had neglected to turn his eyes towards the now distant ship, which was apparently riding at its anchor, in exactly the condition in which it had been left, half an hour before. In that quarter all seemed right, and Mark led the way to the mount, with active and eager steps.

On reaching the foot of this singular elevation, our adventurers found it would not be so easy a matter as they had fancied, to ascend it. Unlike the rest of the reef which they had yet seen, it appeared to be composed of a crumbling rock, and this so smooth and perpendicular as to render it extremely difficult to get up. A place was found at length, however, and by lending each other a hand, Mark and Bob finally got on the summit. Here a surprise was ready for them, that drew an exclamation from each, the instant the sight broke upon him. Instead of finding an elevated bit of table-rock, as had been expected, a circular cavity existed within, that Mark at once recognised to be the extinct crater of a volcano! After the first astonishment was over, Mark made a close examination of the place.

The mound, or barrier of lava and scoriæ that composed the outer wall of this crater, was almost mathematically circular. Its inner precipice was in most places absolutely perpendicular, though overhanging in a few; there being but two or three spots where an active man could descend in safety. The area within might contain a hundred acres while the wall preserved a very even height of about sixty feet, falling a little below this at the leeward side, where there existed one narrow hole, or passage, on a level with the bottom of the crater; a sort of gateway, by which to enter and quit the cavity. This passage had no doubt been formed by the exit of lava, which centuries ago had doubtless broken through at this point, and contributed to form the visible reef beyond. The height of this hole was some twenty feet, having an arch above it, and its width may have been thirty. When Mark got to it, which he did by descending the wall of the crater, not without risk to his neck, he found the surface of the crater very even and unbroken, with the exception of its having a slight descent from its eastern to its western side; or from the side opposite to the outlet, or gateway, to the gateway itself. This inclination Mark fancied was owing to the circumstance that the water of the ocean had formerly entered at the hole, in uncommonly high tides and tempests, and washed the ashes which had once formed the bottom of the crater, towards the remote parts of the plain. These ashes had been converted by time into a soft, or friable rock, composing a stone that is called tufa. If there had ever been a cone in the crater, as was probably the case, it had totally disappeared under the action of time and the wear of the seasons. Rock, however, the bed of the crater could scarcely be yet considered, though it had a crust which bore the weight of a man very readily, in nearly every part of it. Once or twice Mark broke through, as one would fall through rotten ice, when he found his shoes covered with a light dust that much resembled ashes. In other places he broke this crust on purpose, always finding beneath it a considerable depth of ashes, mingled with some shells, and a few small stones.

That the water sometimes flowed into this crater was evident by a considerable deposit of salt, which marked the limits of the latest of these floods. This salt had probably prevented vegetation. The water, however, never could have entered from the sea, had not the lava which originally made the outlet left a sort of channel that was lower than the surface of the outer rocks. It might be nearer to the real character of the phenomenon were we to say, that the lava which had broken through the barrier at this point, and tumbled into the sea, had not quite filled the channel which it rather found than formed, when it ceased to flow. Cooling in that form, an irregular crevice was left, through which the element no doubt still occasionally entered, when the adjacent ocean got a sufficient elevation. Mark observed that, from some cause or other, the birds avoided the crater. It really seemed to him that their instincts warned them of the dangers that had once environed the place, and that, to use the language of sailors, "they gave it a wide berth," in consequence. Whatever may have been the cause, such was the fact; few even flying over it, though they were to be seen in hundreds, in the air all round it.

Chapter V

> "The king's son have I landed by himself;
> Whom I left cooling of the air with sighs
> In an odd angle of the isle, and sitting,
> His arms in this sad knot."
>
> —Tempest

Having completed this first examination of the crater, Mark and Bob next picked their way again to the summit of its wall, and took their seats directly over the arch. Here they enjoyed as good a look-out as the little island afforded, not only of its own surface, but of the surrounding ocean. Mark now began to comprehend the character of the singular geological formation, into the midst of which the Rancocus had been led, as it might almost be by the hand of Providence itself. He was at that moment seated on the topmost pinnacle of a submarine mountain of volcanic origin-submarine as to all its elevations, heights and spaces, with the exception of the crater where he had just taken his stand, and the little bit of visible and venerable lava, by which it was surrounded. It is true that this lava rose very near the surface of the ocean, in fifty places that he could see at no great distance, forming the numberless breakers that characterized the place; but, with the exception of Mark's Reef, as Bob named the principal island on the spot, two or three detached islets within a cable's-length of it, and a few little more remote, the particular haunts of birds, no other land was visible, far or near.

As Mark sat there, on that rock of concrete ashes, he speculated on the probable extent of the shoals and reefs by which he was surrounded. Judging by what he then saw, and recalling the particulars of the examination made from the cross-trees of the ship, he supposed that the dangers and difficulties of the navigation must extend, in an east and west direction, at least twelve marine leagues; while, in a north and south, the distance seemed to be a little, and a very little less. There was necessarily a good deal of conjecture in this estimate of the extent of the volcanic mountain which composed these extensive shoals; but, from what he saw, from the distance the ship was known to have run amid the dangers before she brought up, her present anchorage, the position of the island, and all the other materials before him to make his calculation on, Mark believed himself rather to have lessened than to have exaggerated the extent of these shoals. Had the throes of the earth, which produced this submerged rock, been a little more powerful, a beautiful and fertile island, of very respectable dimensions, would probably have been formed in its place.

From the time of reaching the reef, which is now to bear his name in all future time, our young seaman had begun to admit the bitter possibility of being compelled to pass the remainder of his days on it. How long he and his companion could find the means of subsistence in a place so barren, was merely matter of conjecture; but so long as Providence should furnish these means, was it highly probable that solitary and little-favoured spot was to be their home. It is unnecessary to state with what bitter regrets the young bridegroom admitted this painful idea; but Mark was too manly and resolute to abandon himself to despair, even at such a moment. He kept his sorrows pent up in the repository of his own bosom, and endeavoured to imitate the calm exterior of his companion. As for Bob, he was a good deal of a philosopher by nature and, having made up his mind that they were doomed to 'Robinson Crusoe it,' for a few years at least, he was already turning over in his thoughts the means of doing so to the best advantage. Under such circumstances, and with such feelings, it is not at all surprising that their present situation and their future prospects soon became the subject of discourse, between these two solitary seamen.

"We are fairly in for it, Mr. Mark," said Bob, "and differ from Robinson only in the fact that there are two of us; whereas he was obliged to set up for himself, and by himself, until he fell in with Friday!"

"I wish I could say *that* was the only difference in our conditions, Betts, but it is very far from being so. In the first place he had an island, while we have little more than a reef; he had soil, while we have naked rock; he had fresh water, and we have none; he had trees, while we have not even a spear of grass. All these circumstances make out a case most desperately against us."

"You speak truth, sir; yet is there light ahead. We have a ship, sound and tight as the day she sailed; while Robinson lost his craft under his feet. As long as there is a plank afloat, a true salt never gives up."

"Ay, Bob, I feel that, as strongly as you can yourself; nor do I mean to give up, so long as there is reason to think God has not entirely deserted us. But that ship is of no use, in the way of returning to our friends and home; or, of no use as a ship. The power of man could scarcely extricate her from the reefs around her."

"It's a bloody bad berth," said Bob, squirting the saliva of his tobacco half-way down the wall of the crater, "that I must allow. Howsomever, the ship will be of use in a great many ways, Mr. Mark, if we can keep her afloat, even where she is. The water that's in her will last us two a twelvemonth, if we are a little particular about it; and when the rainy season sets in, as the rainy season will be sure to do in this latitude, we can fill up for a fresh start. Then the ship will be a house for us to live in, and a capital good house, too. You can live aft, sir, and I'll take my swing in the forecastle, just as if nothing had happened."

"No, no, Bob; there is an end of all such distinctions now. Misery, like the grave, brings all upon a level. You and I commenced as messmates, and we are likely to end as messmates. There is a use to which the ship may be put, however, that you have not mentioned, and to which we must look forward as our best hope for this world. She may be broken up by us, and we may succeed in building a craft large enough to navigate these mild seas, and yet small enough to be taken through, or over the reefs. In *that* way, favoured by Divine Providence, we may live to see our friends again."

"Courage, Mr. Mark, courage, sir. I know it must be hard on the feelin's of a married man, like yourself, that has left a parfect pictur' behind him, to believe he is never to return to his home again. But I don't believe that such is to be our fate. I never heard of such an end to a Crusoe party. Even Robinson, himself, got off at last, and had a desperate hard journey of it, after he hauled his land-tacks aboard. I like that idee of the new craft 'specially well, and will lend a hand to help you through with it with all my heart. I'm not much of a carpenter, it's true; nor do I suppose you are anything wonderful with the broad-axe and adze; but two willing and stout men, who has got their lives to save, can turn their hands to almost anything. For my part, sir, since I *was* to be wrecked and to Robinson it awhile, I'm gratefully thankful that I've got you for a companion, that's all!"

Mark smiled at this oblique compliment, but he felt well assured that Bob meant all for the best. After a short pause, he resumed the discourse by saying—

"I have been thinking, Bob, of the possibility of getting the ship safely down as far as this island. Could we but place her to leeward of that last reef off the weather end of the island, she might lie there years, or until she fell to pieces by decay. If we are to attempt building a decked boat, or anything large enough to ride out a gale in, we shall want more room than the ship's decks to set it up in. Besides, we could never get a craft of those dimensions off the ship's decks, and must, of necessity, build it in some place where it may be launched. Our dingui would never do to be moving backward and forward, so great a distance, for it will carry little more than ourselves. All things considered, therefore, I am of opinion we can do nothing better to begin with, than to try to get the ship down here, where we have room, and may carry out our plans to some advantage."

Bob assented at once to this scheme, and suggested one or two ideas in approbation of it, that were new even to Mark. Thus, it was evident to both, that if the ship herself were ever to get clear of the reef, it must be by passing out to leeward; and by bringing her down to the island so much would be gained on the indispensable course. Thus, added Bob, she might be securely moored in the little bay to windward of the island; and, in the course of time it was possible that by a thorough examination of the channels to the westward, and by the use of buoys, a passage might be found, after all, that would carry them out to sea. Mark had little hope of ever getting the Rancocus extricated from the maze of rocks into which she had so blindly entered, and where she probably never could have come but by driving over some of them; but he saw many advantages in this plan of removing the ship, that increased in number and magnitude the more he thought on the subject. Security to the fresh water was one great object to be attained. Should it come on to blow, and the ship drift down upon the rocks to leeward of her, she would probably go to pieces in an hour or two, when not only all the other ample stores that she contained, but every drop of sweet water at the command of the two seamen, would inevitably be lost. So important did it appear to Mark to make sure of a portion of this great essential, at least, that he would have proposed towing down to the reef, or island, a few casks, had the dingui been heavy enough to render such a project practicable. After talking over these several points still more at large, Mark and Bob descended from the summit of the crater, made half of its circuit, and returned to their boat.

As the day continued calm, Mark was in no hurry, but passed half an hour in sounding the little bay that was formed by the sunken rocks that lay off the eastern, or weather end of the Crater Reef, as, in a spirit of humility, he insisted on calling that which everybody else now calls Mark's Reef. Here he not only found abundance of water for all he wanted, but to his surprise he also found a sandy bottom, formed no doubt by the particles washed from the surrounding rocks under the never-ceasing abrasion of the waves. On the submerged reef there were only a few inches of water, and our mariners saw clearly that it was possible to secure the ship in this basin, in a very effectual manner, could they only have a sufficiency of good weather in which to do it.

After surveying the basin, itself, with sufficient care, Bob pulled the dingui back towards the ship, Mark sounding as they proceeded. But two difficulties were found between the points that it was so desirable to bring in communication with each other. One of these difficulties consisted in a passage between two lines of reef, that ran nearly parallel for a quarter of a mile, and which were only half a cable's-length asunder. There was abundance of water between these reefs, but the difficulty was in the course, and in the narrowness of the passage. Mark passed through the latter four several times, sounding it, as it might be, foot by foot, and examining the bottom with the eye; for, in that pellucid water, with the sun near the zenith, it was possible to see two or three fathoms down, and nowhere did he find any other obstacle than this just mentioned. Nor was any buoy necessary, the water breaking over the southern end of the outer, and over the northern end of the inner ledge, and nowhere else near by, thus distinctly noting the very two points where it would be necessary to alter the course.

The second obstacle was much more serious than that just described. It was a reef with a good deal of water over most of it; so much, indeed, that the sea did not break unless in heavy gales, but not enough to carry a ship like the Rancocus over, except in one, and that a very contracted pass, of less than a hundred feet in width. This channel it would be indispensably necessary to buoy, since a variation from the true course of only a few fathoms would infallibly produce the loss of the ship. All the rest of the distance was easily enough made by a vessel standing down, by simply taking care not to run into visible breakers.

Mark and Bob did not get back to the Rancocus until near three o'clock. They found everything as they had left it, and the pigs, poultry and goat, glad enough to see them, and beginning to want their victuals and drink. The two first are to be found on board of every ship, but the last is not quite so usual. Captain Crutchely had brought one along to supply milk for his tea, a beverage that, oddly enough, stood second only to grog in his favour. After Bob had attended to the wants of the brute animals, he and Mark, again sat down on the windlass to make another cold repast on broken meat-as yet, they had not the hearts to cook anything. As soon as this homely meal was taken Mark placed a couple of buoys in the dingui, with the pig-iron that was necessary to anchor them, and proceeded to the spot on the reef, where it was proposed to place them.

Our mariners were quite an hour in searching for the channel, and near another in anchoring the buoys in a way to render the passage perfectly safe. As soon as this was done, Bob pulled back to the ship, which was less than a mile distant, as fast as he could, for there was every appearance of a change of weather. The moment was one, now, that demanded great coolness and decision. Not more than an hour of day remained, and the question was whether to attempt to move the ship that night, when the channel and its marks were all fresh in the minds of the two seamen, and before the foul weather came, or to trust to the cable that was down to ride out any blow that might happen. Mark, young as he was, thought justly on most professional subjects. He knew that heavy rollers would come in across the reef where the vessel then lay, and was fearful that the cable would chafe and part, should it come on to blow hard for four-and-twenty hours continually. These rollers, he also knew by the observation of that day, were completely broken and dispersed on the rocks, before they got down to the island, and he believed the chances of safety much greater by moving the ship at once, than by trying the fortune of another night, out where she then lay. Bob submitted to this decision precisely as if Mark was still his officer, and no sooner got his orders than he sprang from sail to sail, and rope to rope, like a cat playing among the branches of some tree. In that day, spensers were unknown, staysails doing their duty. Thus Bob loosed the jib, main-topmast and mizen-staysails, and saw the spanker clear for setting. While he was thus busied, Mark was looking to the stopper and shank-painter of the sheet-anchor, which had been got ready to let go, before Captain Crutchely was lost. He even succeeded in getting that heavy piece of metal a cock-bill, without calling on Bob for assistance.

It was indeed time for them to be in a hurry; for the wind began to come in puffs, the sun was sinking into a bank of clouds, and all along the horizon to windward the sky looked dark and menacing. Once Mark changed his mind, determining to hold on, and let go the sheet-anchor where he was, should it become necessary; but a lull tempted him to proceed. Bob shouted out that all was ready, and Mark lifted the axe with which he was armed, and struck a heavy blow on the cable. That settled the matter; an entire strand was separated, and three or four more blows released the ship from her anchor. Mark now sprang to the jib-halliards, assisting Bob to hoist the sail. This was no sooner done than he went aft to the wheel, where he arrived in time to help the ship to fall off. The spanker was next got out as well as two men could do it in a hurry, and then Bob went forward to tend the jib-sheet, and to look out for the buoys.

It was indispensable in such a navigation to make no mistake, and Mark enjoined the utmost vigilance on his friend. Twenty times did he hail to inquire if the buoys were to be seen, and at last he was gratified by an answer in the affirmative.

"Keep her away, Mr. Mark-keep her away, you may, sir; we are well to windward of the channel. Ay, that'll do, Mr. Woolston-that's your beauty, sir. Can't you get a sight of them b'ys yourself, sir?"

"Not just yet, Bob, and so much the greater need that you should look out the sharper. Give the ship plenty of room, and I'll let her run down for the passage, square for the channel."

Bob now ran aft, telling the mate he had better go on the forecastle himself and conn the ship through the passage, which was a place he did not like. Mark was vexed that the change should be made just at that critical instant, but bounding forward, he was between the knight-heads in half a minute, looking out for the buoys. At first, he could not see them; and then he most felt the imprudence of Bob's quitting his post in such a critical instant. In another minute, however, he found one; and presently the other came in sight, fearfully close, as, it now appeared to our young mariner, to its neighbour. The position of the ship, nevertheless, was sufficiently to windward, leaving plenty of room to keep off in. As soon as the ship was far enough ahead, Mark called out to Bob to put his helm hard up. This was done, and away the Rancocus went, Mark watching her with the utmost vigilance, lest she should sheer a little too much to the one side or to the other. He hardly breathed as the vessel glided down upon these two black sentinels, and, for an instant, he fancied the wind or the current had interfered with their positions. It was now too late, however, to attempt any change, and Mark saw the ship surging onward on the swells of the ocean, which made their way thus far within the reefs, with a greater intensity of anxiety than he had ever before experienced in his life. Away went the ship, and each time she settled in the water, our young man expected to hear her keel grating on the bottom, but it did not touch. Presently the buoys were on her quarters, and then Mark knew that the danger of this one spot was passed!

The next step was to find the southern end of the outer ledge that formed the succeeding passage. This was not done until the ship was close aboard of it. A change had come over the spot within the last few hours, in consequence of the increase of wind, the water breaking all along the ledge, instead of on its end only; but Mark cared not for this, once certain he had found that end. He was now half-way between his former anchorage and the crater, and he could distinguish the latter quite plainly. But sail was necessary to carry the ship safely through the channel ahead, and Mark called to Bob to lash the helm a-midships after luffing up to his course, and to spring to the main-topmast staysail halliards, and help him hoist the sail. This was soon done, and the new sail was got up, and the sheet hauled aft. Next followed the mizen staysail, which was spread in the same manner. Bob then flew to the wheel, and Mark to his knight-heads again. Contrary to Mark's apprehensions, he saw that the ship was luffing up close to the weather ledge, leaving little danger of her going on to it. As soon as met by the helm, however, she fell off, and Mark no longer had any doubt of weathering the northern end of the inner ledge of this passage. The wind coming in fresher puffs, this was soon done, when the ship was kept dead away for the crater. There was the northern end of the reef, which formed the inner basin of all, to double, when that which remained to do was merely to range far enough within the reef to get a cover, and to drop the anchor. In order to do this with success, Mark now commenced hauling down the jib. By the time he had that sail well in, the ship was off the end of the sunken reef, when Bob put his helm a-starboard and rounded it. Down came the main-topmast staysail, and Mark jumped on the forecastle, while he called out to Bob to lash the helm a-lee. In an instant Bob was at the young man's side, and both waited for the ship to luff into the wind, and to forge as near as possible to the reef. This was successfully done also, and Mark let go the stopper within twenty feet of the wall of the sunken reef, just as the ship began to drive astern. The canvas was rolled up and secured, the cable payed out, until the ship lay just mid-channel between the island and the sea-wall without, and the whole secured. Then Bob took off his tarpaulin and gave three cheers, while Mark walked aft, silently returning thanks to God for the complete success of this important movement.

Important most truly was this change. Not only was the ship anchored, with her heaviest anchor down, and her best cable out, in good holding ground, and in a basin where very little swell ever penetrated, and that entering laterally and diminished in force; but there she was within a hundred and fifty feet of the island, at all times accessible by means of the dingui, a boat that it would not do to trust in the water at all outside when it blew in the least fresh. In short, it was scarcely possible to have a vessel in a safer berth, so long as her spars and hull were exposed to the gales of the ocean, or one that was more convenient to those who used the island. By getting down her spars and other hamper, the power of the winds would be much lessened, though Mark felt little apprehension of the winds at that season of the year, so long as the sea could not make a long rake against the vessel. He believed the ship safe for the present, and felt the hope of still finding a passage, through the reef to leeward, reviving in his breast.

Well might Mark and Bob rejoice in the great feat they had just performed. That night it blew so heavily as to leave little doubt that the ship never could have been kept at her anchor, outside; and had she struck adrift in the darkness nothing could have saved them from almost immediate destruction. The rollers came down in tremendous billows, breaking and roaring on all sides of the island, rendering the sea white with their foam, even at midnight; but, on reaching the massive, natural wall that protected the Rancocus, they dashed themselves into spray against it, wetting the vessel from her truck down, but doing her no injury. Mark remained on deck until past twelve o'clock, when finding that the gale was already breaking, he turned in and slept soundly until morning. As for Bob, he had taken his watch below early in the evening, and there he remained undisturbed until the appearance of day, when he turned out of his own accord.

Mark took another look at the sea, reefs and islands, from the main-topmast cross-trees of the ship, as she lay in her new berth. Of course, the range of his vision was somewhat altered by this change of position, and especially did he see a greater distance to the westward, or towards the lee side of the reefs. Nothing encouraging was made out, however; the young man rather inclining more to the opinion than he had ever done before, that the vessel could not be extricated from the rocks which surrounded her. With this conviction strongly renewed, he descended to the deck, to share in the breakfast Bob had set about preparing, the moment he quitted his cat-tails; for Bob insisted on sleeping in the forecastle, though Mark had pressed him to take one of the cabin state-rooms. This time the meal, which included some very respectable ship's coffee, was taken on the cabin-table, the day being cloudless, and the sun's rays possessing a power that made it unpleasant to sit long anywhere out of a shade. While the meal was taken, another conversation was held touching their situation.

"By the manner in which it blew last night," Mark observed, "I doubt if we should have had this comfortable cabin to eat in this morning, and these good articles to consume, had we left the ship outside until morning,"

"I look upon it as a good job well done, Mr. Mark," answered Bob. "I must own I had no great hopes of our ever getting here, but was willing to try it; for them rollers didn't mind half-a-dozen reefs, but came tumbling in over them, in a way to threaten the old 'Cocus with being ground into powder. For my part, sir, I thank God, from the bottom of my heart, that we are here."

"You have reason to do so, Bob; and while we may both regret the misfortune that has befallen us, we had need remember how much better off we are than our shipmates, poor fellows! —or how much better we are off than many a poor mariner who loses his vessel altogether."

"Yes, the saving of the ship is a great thing for us. We can hardly call this a shipwreck, Mr. Mark, though we have been ashore once; it is more like being docked, than anything else!"

"I have heard, before, of vessels being carried over reefs, and bars of rivers, into berths they could not quit," answered Mark. "But, reflect a moment, Bob, how much better our condition is, than if we had been washed down on this naked reef, with only such articles to comfort us, as could be picked up along shore from the wreck!"

"I'm glad to hear you talk in this rational way, Mr. Mark; for it's a sign you do not give up, or take things too deeply to heart. I was afeard that you might be thinking too much of Miss Bridget, and make yourself more unhappy than is necessary for a man who has things so comfortable around him."

"The separation from my wife causes me much pain, Betts, but I trust in God. It has been in his pleasure to place us in this extraordinary situation, and I hope that something good will come of it."

"That's the right sentiments, sir-only keep such feelings uppermost, and we shall do right down well. Why, we have water, in plenty, until after the rainy season shall be along, when we can catch a fresh supply. Then, there is beef and pork enough betwixt decks to last you and me five or six years; and bread and flour in good quantities, to say nothing of lots of small stores, both forward and aft."

"The ship is well found, and, as you say, we might live a long time, years certainly, on the food she contains. There is, however, one thing to be dreaded, and to provide against which shall be my first care. We are now fifty days on salted provisions, and fifty more will give us both the scurvy."

"The Lord in his mercy protect me from that disease!" exclaimed Bob. "I had it once, in an old v'y'ge round the Horn, and have no wish to try it ag'in, But there must be fish in plenty among these rocks, Mr. Mark, and we have a good stock of bread. By dropping the beef and pork, for a few days at a time, might we not get shut of the danger?"

"Fish will help us, and turtle would be a great resource, could we meet with any of *that*. But, man requires mixed food, meats and vegetables, to keep him healthy; and nothing is so good for the scurvy as the last. The worst of our situation is a want of soil, to grow any vegetables in. I did not see so much as a rush, or the coarsest sea-plant, when we were on the island yesterday. If we had soil, there is seed in plenty on board, and this climate would bring forward vegetation at a rapid rate."

"Ay, ay, sir, and I'll tell you what I've got in the way of seeds, myself. You may remember the delicious musk and watermelons we fell in with last v'y'ge, in the east. Well, sir, I saved some of the seed, thinking to give it to my brother, who is a Jarsey farmer, you know, sir; and, sailor-like, I forgot it altogether, when in port. If a fellow could get but a bit of earth to put them melon-seeds in, we might be eating our fruit like gentlemen, two months hence, or three months, at the latest."

"That is a good thought, Betts, and we will turn it over in our minds. If such a thing is to be done at all, the sooner it is done the better, that the melons maybe getting ahead while we are busy with the other matters. This is just the season to put seed into the ground, and I think we might make soil enough to sustain a few hills of melons. If I remember right, too, there are some of the sweet potatoes left."

Bob assented, and during the rest of the meal they did nothing but pursue this plan of endeavouring to obtain half-a-dozen or a dozen hills of melons. As Mark felt all the importance of doing everything that lay in his power to ward off the scurvy, and knew that time was not to be lost, he determined that the very first thing he would now attend to, would be to get all the seed into as much ground as he could contrive to make. Accordingly, as soon as the breakfast was ended, Mark went to collect his seeds Bob set the breakfast things aside, after properly cleaning them.

There were four shoats on board, which had been kept in the launch, until that boat was put into the water, the night the Rancocus ran upon the rocks. Since that time they had been left to run about the decks, producing a good deal of dirt, and some confusion. These shoats Bob now caught, and dropped into the bay, knowing that their instinct would induce them to swim for the nearest land. All this turned out as was expected, and the pigs were soon seen on the island, snuffing around on the rocks, and trying to root. A small quantity of the excrement of these animals still lay on the deck, where it had been placed when the launch was cleaned for service, no one thinking at such a moment of cleaning the decks. It had been washed by the sea that came aboard quite across the deck, but still formed a pile, and most of it was preserved. This manure Mark was about to put in a half-barrel, in order to carry it ashore, for the purpose of converting it into soil, when Bob suddenly put an end to what he was about, by telling him that he knew where a manure worth two of that was to be found. An explanation was asked and given. Bob, who had been several voyages on the western coast of America, told Mark that the Peruvians and Chilians made great use of the dung of aquatic birds, as a manure, and which they found on the rocks that lined their coast. Now two or three rocks lay near the reef, that were covered with this deposit, the birds still hovering about them, and he proposed to take the dingui, and go in quest of a little of that fertilizing manure. A very little, he said, would suffice, the Spaniards using it in small quantities, but applying it at different stages in the growth of the plant. It is scarcely necessary to say that Bob had fallen on a knowledge of the use of the article which is now so extensively known under the name of guano, in the course of his wanderings, and was enabled to communicate the fact to his companion. Mark knew that Betts was a man of severe truth, and he was so much the more disposed to listen to his suggestion. While our young mate was getting the boat ready, therefore, Bob collected his tools, provided himself with a bucket, passed the half-barrel, into which Mark had thrown the sweepings of the decks, into the dingui, and descended himself and took the sculls. The two then proceeded to Bob's rock, where, amid the screams of a thousand sea-birds, the honest fellow filled his bucket with as good guano as was ever found on the coast of Peru.

While the boat was at the rock, Mark saw that the pigs had run round to the western end of the island, snuffing at everything that came in their way, and trying in vain to root wherever one of them could insert his nose. As a hog is a particularly sagacious animal, Mark kept his eyes on them while Bob was picking out his guano, in the faint hope that they might discover fresh water, by means of their instinct. In this way he saw them enter the gate way of the crater, pigs being pretty certain to run their noses into any such place as that.

On landing, Mark took a part of the tools and the bucket of guano, while Bob shouldered the remainder, and they went up to the hole, and entered the crater together, having landed as near to the gate-way as they could get, with that object. To Mark's great delight he found that the pigs were now actually rooting with some success, so far as stirring the surface was concerned, though getting absolutely nothing for their pains. There were spots on the plain of the crater, however, where it was possible, by breaking a sort of crust, to get down into coarse ashes that were not entirely without some of the essentials of soil. Exposure to the air and water, with mixing up with sea-weed and such other waste materials as he could collect, the young man fancied would enable him to obtain a sufficiency of earthy substances to sustain the growth of plants. While on the summit of the crater-wall, he had seen two or three places where it had struck him sweet-potatoes and beans might be made to grow, and he determined to ascend to those spots, and make his essay there, as being the most removed from the inroads of the pigs. Could he only succeed in obtaining two or three hundred melons, he felt that a great deal would be done in providing the means of checking any disposition to scurvy that might appear in Bob or himself. In this thoughtful manner did one so young look ahead, and make provision for the future.

Chapter VI

> "—that done, partake
> The season, prime for sweetest scents and airs;
> Then commune how that day they best may ply
> Their growing work; for much their work outgrew
> The hands dispatch of two gard'ning so wide."
>
> —Milton

Our two mariners had come ashore well provided with the means of carrying out their plans. The Rancocus was far better provided with tools suited to the uses of the land, than was common for ships, her voyage contemplating a long stay among the islands she was to visit. Thus, axes and picks were not wanting, Captain Crutchely having had an eye to the possible necessity of fortifying himself against savages. Mark now ascended the crater-wall with a pick on his shoulder, and a part of a coil of ratlin-stuff around his neck. As he went up, he used the pick to make steps, and did so much in that way, in the course of ten minutes, as greatly to facilitate the ascent and descent at the particular place he had selected. Once on the summit, he found a part of the rock that overhung its base, and dropped one end of his line into the crater. To this Bob attached the bucket, which Mark hauled up and emptied. In this manner everything was transferred to the top of the crater-wall that was needed there, when Bob went down to the dingui to roll up the half-barrel of sweepings that had been brought from the ship.

Mark next looked about for the places which had seemed to him, on his previous visit, to have most of the character of soil. He found a plenty of these spots, mostly in detached cavities of no great extent, where the crust had not yet formed; or, having once formed, had been disturbed by the action of the elements. These places he first picked to pieces with his pick; then he stirred them well up with a hoe, scattering a little guano in the heaps, according to the directions of Betts. When this was done, he sent down the bucket, and hauled up the sweepings of the deck, which Bob had ready for him, below. Nor was this all Bob had done, during the hour Mark was at work, in the sun, on the summit of the crater. He had found a large deposit of sea-weed, on a rock near the island, and had made two or three trips with the dingui, back and forth, to transfer some of it to the crater. After all his toil and trouble, the worthy fellow did not get more than a hogshead full of this new material, but Mark thought it well worth while to haul it up, and to endeavour to mix it with his compost. This was done by making it up in bundles, as one would roll up hay, of a size that the young man could manage.

Bob now joined his friend on the crater-wall, and assisted in carrying the sea-weed to the places prepared to receive it, when both of the mariners next set about mixing it up with the other ingredients of the intended soil. After working for another hour in this manner, they were of opinion that they might make the experiment of putting in the seed. Melons, of both sorts, and of the very best quality, were now put into the ground, as were also beans peas, and Indian-corn, or maize. A few cucumber-seeds, and some onions were also tried, Captain Crutchely having brought with him a considerable quantity of the common garden seeds, as a benefit conferred on the natives of the islands he intended to visit, and through them on future navigators. This care proceeded from his owners, who were what is called 'Friends,' and who somewhat oddly blended benevolence with the practices of worldly gain.

Mark certainly knew very little of gardening, but Bob could turn his hand to almost anything. Several mistakes were made, notwithstanding, more particularly in the use of the seed, with which they were not particularly acquainted. Mark's Reef lay just within the tropics, it is true (in 21° south latitude), but the constant sea-breeze rendered its climate much cooler than would otherwise have been the case. Thus the peas, and beans, and even the onions, did better, perhaps, on the top of the crater, than they would have done in it; but the ochre, egg-plants, melons, and two or three other seeds that they used, would probably have succeeded better had they been placed in the warmest spots which could be found. In one respect Mark made a good gardener. He knew that moisture was indispensable to the growth of most plants, and had taken care to put all his seeds into cavities, where the rain that fell (and he had no reason to suppose that the dry season had yet set in) would not run off and be wasted. On this point he manifested a good deal of judgment, using his hoe in a way to avoid equally the danger of having too much or too little water.

It was dinner-time before Mark and Betts were ready to quit the 'Summit,' as they now began to term the only height in their solitary domains. Bob had foreseen the necessity of a shade, and had thrown an old royal into the boat. With this, and two or three light spars, he contrived to make a sort of canopy, down in the crater, beneath which he and Mark dined, and took their siestas. While resting on a spare studding-sail that had also been brought along, the mariners talked over what they had done, and what it might be best to undertake next.

Thus far Mark had been working under a species of excitement, that was probably natural enough to his situation, but which wanted the coolness and discretion that are necessary to render our efforts the most profitable to ourselves, or to others. Now, that the feverish feeling which set him at work so early to make a provision against wants which, at the worst, were merely problematical, had subsided, Mark began to see that there remained many things to do, which were of even more pressing necessity than anything yet done. Among the first of these there was the perfect security of the ship. So long as she rode at a single anchor, she could not be considered as absolutely safe; for a shift of wind would cause her to swing against the 'sea-wall,' as he called the natural breakwater outside of her, where, if not absolutely wrecked, she might receive material damage. Prudence required, therefore, that the ship should be moored, as well as anchored. Nevertheless, there was a good deal of truth in what Mark had said touching the plants growing while he and Bob were busy at other matters; and this thought, of itself, formed a sufficient justification for what he had just done, much as it had been done under present excitement. As they under the shade of the royal, our mariners discussed these matters, and matured some plans for the future.

At two o'clock Mark and Bob resumed their work. The latter suggested the necessity of getting food and water ashore for the pigs, as an act that humanity imperiously demanded of them; not humanity in the sense of feeling for our kind, but in the sense in which we all ought to feel for animal suffering, whether endured by man or beast. Mark assented as to the food, but was of opinion a thunder shower was about to pass over the reef. The weather certainly did wear this aspect, and Bob was content to wait the result, in order to save himself unnecessary trouble. As for the pigs, they were still in the crater rooting, as it might be for life or death, though nothing edible had as yet rewarded them for their toil. Perhaps they found it pleasant to be thrusting their noses into something that resembled soil, after so long a confinement to the planks of a ship. Seeing them at work in this manner, suggested to Mark to try another experiment, which certainly looked far enough ahead, as if he had no great hopes of getting off the island for years to come. Among the seeds of Captain Crutchely were those of oranges, lemons, limes, shaddocks, figs, and grapes; all plants well enough suited to the place, if there were only soil to nourish them. Now, one of the hogs had been rooting, as best he might, just under the wall, on the northern side of the crater, making a long row of little hillocks, of earthy ashes, at unequal distances it is true, but well enough disposed for the nature of the different fruits, could they only be got to grow. Along this irregular row of hillocks did Mark bury his seeds, willing to try an experiment which might possibly benefit some other human being, if it never did any good to himself. When this was done, he and Betts left the crater, driving the hogs out before them.

Having made his plantation, Mark felt a natural desire to preserve it. He got the royal, therefore, and succeeded in fastening it up as a substitute for a gate, in their natural gate-way. Had the pigs met with any success in rooting, it is not probable this slight obstacle would have prevented their finding their way, again, into the cavity of the crater; but, as it was, it proved all-sufficient, and the sail was permitted to hang before the hole, until a more secure gate was suspended in its stead.

The appearances of the thunder-shower were so much increased by this time, that our mariners hastened back to the ship in order to escape a ducking. They had hardly got on board before the gust came, a good deal of water falling, though not in the torrents in which one sometimes sees it stream down within the tropics. In an hour it was all over, the sun coming out bright and scorching, after the passage of the gust. One thing occurred, however, which at first caused both of the seamen a good deal of uneasiness, and again showed them the necessity there was for mooring the ship. The wind shifted from the ordinary direction of the trades, during the squall, to a current of air that was nearly at right angles to the customary course. This caused the ship to swing, and brought her so near the sea-wall, that once or twice her side actually rubbed against it. Mark was aware, by his previous sounding, that this wall rather impended over its base, being a part of an old crater, beyond a question, and that there was little danger of the vessel's hitting the bottom, or taking harm in any other way than by friction against the upper part; but this friction might become too rude, and finally endanger the safety of the vessel.

As soon as the weather became fine, however, the trades returned, and the ship swung round to her old berth. Bob now suggested the expediency of carrying out their heaviest kedge ashore, of planting it in the rocks, and of running out to it two or three parts of a hawser, to which a line of planks might be lashed, and thus give them the means of entering and quitting the ship, without having recourse to the dingui. Mark approved of this plan, and, it requiring a raft to carry ashore the kedge, the dingui being so light they were afraid to trust it, it was decided to commence that work in the morning. For the rest of the present day nothing further was done, beyond light and necessary jobs, and continuing the examination of the island. Mark was curious to look at the effect of the shower, both in reference to his plantations, and to the quantity of fresh water that might have lodged on the reef. It was determined, therefore, to pass an hour or two ashore before the night shut in again.

Previously to quitting the ship, Bob spoke of the poultry. There were but six hens, a cock, and five ducks, left. They were all as low in flesh and spirits, as it was usual to find birds that have been at sea fifty days, and the honest tar proposed turning them all adrift on the reef, to make their own living in the best way they could. Now and then a little food might be put in their way, but let them have a chance for their lives. Mark assented at once, and the coops were opened. Each fowl was carried to the taffrail, and tossed into the air, when it flew down upon the reef, a distance of a couple of hundred feet, almost as a matter of course. Glad enough were the poor things to be thus liberated. To Mark's surprise, no sooner did they reach the reef, than to work they went, and commenced picking up something with the greatest avidity, as if let loose in the best supplied poultry-yard. Confident there was nothing for even a hen to glean on the rocks when he left there, the young man could not account for this, until turning his eyes inboard, he saw the ducks doing the same thing on deck. Examining the food of these last-mentioned animals, he found there were a great number of minute mucilaginous particles on the deck, which no doubt had descended with the late rain, and which all the birds, as well as the hogs, seemed eager to devour. Here, then, was a supply, though a short-lived one, of a manna suited to those creatures, which might render them happy for a few hours, at least. Bob caught the ducks, and tossed them overboard, when they floundered about and enjoyed themselves in a way that communicated a certain pleasure even to the desolate and shipwrecked men who had set them at liberty. Nothing with life now remained in the ship but the goat, and Mark thought it best not to turn her ashore until they had greater facilities for getting the necessary food to her than the dingui afforded. As she was not likely to breed, there was no great use in keeping this animal at all, to say nothing of the means of feeding her, for any length of time; but Mark was unwilling to take her life, since Providence had brought them all to that place in company. Then he thought she might be a pretty object leaping about the cliffs of the crater, giving the island a more lively and inhabited appearance, though he foresaw she might prove very destructive to his plantations, did his vegetables grow. As there was time enough to decide on her final fate, it was finally settled she should be put ashore, and have a comfortable fortnight, even though condemned to die at the end of that brief period.

On landing, every hole in the face of the cliff was found filled with fresh water. Betts was of opinion that the water-casks might all be filled with the water which was thus collected, the fluid having seemingly all flowed into these receptacles, while little had gone into the sea. This was encouraging for the future, at any rate; the want of water, previously to this shower, appearing to Mark to be a more probable occurrence than the want of food. The sea might furnish the last, on an emergency, while it could do nothing with the first. But the manner in which the ducks were enjoying themselves, in these fresh pools, can scarcely be imagined! As Mark stood looking at them, a doubt first suggested itself to his mind concerning the propriety of men's doing anything that ran counter to their instincts, with any of the creatures of God. Pet-birds in cages, birds that were created to fly, had always been disagreeable to him; nor did he conceive it to be any answer to say that they were born in cages, and had never known liberty. They were created with an instinct for flight, and intense must be their longings to indulge in the power which nature had bestowed on them. In the cage in which he now found himself, though he could run, walk, leap, swim, or do aught that nature designed him to do, in the way of mere animal exploits, young Mark felt how bitter were the privations he was condemned to suffer.

The rain had certainly done no harm, as yet, to the planting. All the hills were entire, as Mark and Bob had left them, though well saturated with water. In a few, there might be even too much of the element, perhaps, but Mark observed that a tropical sun would soon remove that objection. His great apprehension was that he had commenced his gardening too late, and that the dry weather might set in too soon for the good of his vegetables; if any of them, indeed, ever came up at all. Here was one good soaking secured, at all events; and, knowing the power of a tropical sun, Mark was of opinion that the fate of the great experiment he had tried would soon be known. Could he succeed in producing vegetation among the *débris* of the crater, he and Bob might find the means of subsistence during their natural lives; but, should that resource fail them, all their hopes would depend on being able to effect their escape in a craft of their own construction. In no case, however, but that of the direst necessity, did Mark contemplate the abandonment of his plan for getting back to the inhabited world, his country, and his bride!

That night our mariners had a sounder sleep than they had yet been blest with since the loss of their shipmates, and the accident to the vessel itself. The two following days they passed in securing the ship. Bob actually made a very respectable catamaran, or raft, out of the spare spars, sawing the topmasts and lower yards in two, for that purpose, and fastening them together with ingenuity and strength, by means of lashings. But Mark hit upon an expedient for getting the two kedges ashore, that prevented the necessity of having recourse to the raft on that occasion. These kedges lay on the poop, where they were habitually kept, and two men had no great difficulty in getting them over the stern, suspended by stoppers. Now Mark had ascertained that the rock of the Reef rose like a wall, being volcanic, like all the rest of the formation, and that the ship could float almost anywhere alongside of it. Aided by the rake of the stern of an old-fashioned Philadelphia-built ship, nothing was easier than to veer upon the cable, let the vessel drop in to the island, until the kedges actually hung over the rocks, and then lower the last down. All this was done, and the raft was reserved for other purposes. Notwithstanding the facility with which the kedges were got ashore, it took Mark and Bob quite half a day to plant them in the rock precisely where they were wanted. When this was accomplished, however, it was so effectually done as to render the hold even greater than that of the sheet-anchor. The stocks were not used at all, but the kedges were laid flat on the rock, quite near to each other, and in such a manner that the flukes were buried in crevices of the lava, giving a most secure hold, while the shanks came out through natural grooves, leading straight towards the ship. Six parts of a hawser were bent to the kedges, three to each, and these parts were held at equal distances by pieces of spars ingeniously placed between them, the whole being kept in its place by regular stretchers that were lashed along the hawsers at distances of ten feet, giving all the parts of the ropes the same level. Before these stretchers were secured, the ship was hove ahead by her cable, and the several parts of the hawser brought to an equal strain. This left the vessel about a hundred feet from the island, a convenient, and if the anchor held, a *safe* position; though Mark felt little fear of losing the ship against rocks that were so perpendicular and smooth. On the stretchers planks were next laid and lashed, thus making a clear passage between the vessel and the shore, that might be used at all times, without recourse to the dingui; besides mooring the ship head and stern, thereby keeping her always in the same place, and in the same position.

The business of securing the ship occupied nearly two days, and was not got through with until about the middle of the afternoon of the second day. It was Saturday, and Mark had determined to make a good beginning, and keep all their Sabbaths, in future, as holy times, set apart for the special service of the Creator. He had been born and educated an Episcopalian, but Bob claimed to be a Quaker, and what was more he was a little stiff in some of his notions on the opinion of his sect. The part of New Jersey in which Betts was born, had many persons of this religious persuasion, and he was not only born, but, in one sense, educated in their midst; though the early age at which he went to sea had very much unsettled his practice, much the most material part of the tenets of these good persons. When the two knocked off work, Saturday afternoon, therefore, it was with an understanding that the next day was to be one of rest in the sense of Christians, and, from that time henceforth, that the Sabbath was to be kept as a holy day. Mark had ever been inclined to soberness of thought on such subjects. His early engagement to Bridget had kept him from falling into the ways of most mariners, and, time and again, had a future state of being been the subject of discourse between him and his betrothed. As the seasons of adversity are those in which men are the most apt to bethink them of their duties to God, it is not at all surprising that one of this disposition, thus situated, felt renewed demands on his gratitude and repentance.

While Mark, in this frame of mind, went rambling around his narrow domains, Bob got the dingui, and proceeded with his fishing-tackle towards some of the naked rocks, that lifted their caps above the surface of the sea, in a north-westerly direction from the crater. Of these naked rocks there were nearly twenty, all within a mile of the crater, and the largest of them not containing more than six or eight acres of dry surface. Some were less than a hundred feet in diameter. The great extent and irregular formation of the reefs all around the island, kept the water smooth, for some distance, on all sides of it; and it was only when the rollers were sent in by heavy gales, that the dingui could not move about, in this its proper sphere, in safety.

Betts was very fond of fishing, and could pass whole days, at a time, in that quiet amusement, provided he had a sufficient supply of tobacco. Indeed, one of the greatest consolations this man possessed, under the present misfortune, was the ample store of this weed which was to be found in the ship. Every man on board the Rancocus, Mark alone excepted, made use of tobacco; and, for so long a voyage, the provision laid in had been very abundant. On this occasion, Bob enjoyed his two favourite occupations to satiety, masticating the weed while he fished.

With Mark it was very different. He was fond of his fowling-piece, but of little use was that weapon in his present situation. Of all the birds that frequented the adjacent rocks, not one was of a sort that would be eaten, unless in cases of famine. As he walked over the island, that afternoon, his companion was the goat, which had been driven ashore on the new gangway, and was enjoying its liberty almost as much as the ducks. As the animal frisked about him, accompanying him everywhere in his walks. Mark was reminded of the goats of Crusoe, and his mind naturally adverted to the different accounts of shipwrecks of which he had read, and to a comparison between his own condition and those of other mariners who had been obliged to make their homes, for a time, on otherwise uninhabited islands.

In this comparison, Mark saw that many things made greatly against him, on the one hand; while, on the other, there were many others for which he had every reason to be profoundly grateful. In the first place, this island was, as yet, totally without vegetation of every kind. It had neither plant, shrub, nor tree. In this he suffered a great privation, and it even remained to be proved by actual experiment, whether he was master of what might be considered the elements of soil. It occurred to him that something like vegetation must have shown itself, in or about the crater, did its *débris* contain the fertilizing principle, Mark not being sufficiently versed in the new science of chemical agriculture, to understand that the admixtures of certain elements might bring to life forces that then were dormant. Then the Reef had no water. This was a very, very great privation, the most serious of all, and might prove to be a terrible calamity. It is true that, just at that moment, there was a shower every day, and sometimes two or three of them; but it was then spring, and there could be little reason to doubt that droughts would come in the hot and dry season. As a last objection, the Reef had no great extent, and no variety, the eye taking it all in at a glance, while the crater was its sole relief against the dullest monotony. Nor was there a bit of wood, or fuel of any sort to cook with, after the supply now in the ship should be exhausted. Such were the leading disadvantages of the situation in which our mariners were placed, as compared with those into which most other shipwrecked seamen had been thrown.

The advantages, on the other hand, Mark, in humble gratitude to God, admitted to be very great. In the first place, the ship and all she contained was preserved, giving them a dwelling, clothes, food and water, as well as fuel, for a long time to come; possibly, aided by what might be gleaned on even that naked reef, sufficient to meet all their wants for the duration of a human life. The cargo of the Rancocus was of no great extent, and of little value in a civilized country; but Mark knew that it included many articles that would be of vast service where he was. The beads and coarse trinkets with which it had been intended to trade with the savages, were of no use whatever, it is true; but the ship's owners were pains-taking and thoughtful Quakers, as has been already intimated, who blended with great shrewdness in the management of their worldly affairs, a certain regard to benevolence in general, and a desire to benefit their species. On this principle, they had caused a portion of their cargo to be made up, sending, in addition to all the ruder and commoner tools, that could be used by a people without domestic animals, a small supply of rugs, coarse clothes, coarse earthen-ware, and a hundred similar things, that would be very serviceable to any who knew how to use them. Most of the seeds came from these thoughtful merchants.

If fresh water were absolutely wanting on the reef, it rained a good deal; in the rainy season it must rain for a few weeks almost incessantly, and the numerous cavities in the ancient lava, formed natural cisterns of great capacity. By taking the precaution of filling up the water-casks of the ship, periodically, there was little danger of suffering for the want of this great requisite. It is true, the sweet, cool, grateful draught, that was to be got from the gushing spring, must be forgotten; but rain-water collected in clean rock, and preserved in well-sweetened casks, was very tolerable drinking for seamen. Captain Crutchely, moreover, had a filterer for the cabin, and through it all the water used there was habitually passed.

In striking the balance between the advantages and disadvantages of his own situation, as compared with that of other shipwrecked mariners, Mark confessed that he had quite as much reason to be grateful as to repine. The last he was resolved not to do, if possible; and he pursued his walk in a more calm and resigned mood than he had been in since the ship entered among the shoals.

Mark, naturally enough, cast his eyes around him, and asked himself the question what was to be done with the domestic animals they had now all landed. The hogs might, or might not be of the greatest importance to them as their residence on the island was or was not protracted, and as they found the means of feeding them. There was still food enough in the ship to keep these creatures for some months, and food that had been especially laid in for that purpose; but that food would serve equally well for the fowls, and our young man was of opinion, that eggs would be of more importance to himself and Betts, than hog's flesh. Then there was the goat; she would soon cease to be of any use at all, and green food was not to be had for her. A little hay, however, remained; and Mark was fully determined that Kitty, as the playful little thing was called, should live at least as long as that lasted. She was fortunate in being content with a nourishment that no other animal wanted.

Mark could see absolutely nothing on the rocks for a bird to live on, yet were the fowls constantly picking up something. They probably found insects that escaped his sight; while it was certain that the ducks were revelling in the pools of fresh water, of which there might, at that moment, have been a hundred on the reef. As all these creatures were, as yet, regularly fed from the supplies in the ship, each seemed to be filled with the joy of existence; and Mark, as he walked among them, felt how profound ought to be his own gratitude, since he was still in a state of being which admitted of a consciousness of happiness so much beyond anything that was known to the inferior animals of creation. He had his mind, with all its stores gathered from study and observation, his love for God, and his hopes of a blessed future, ever at command. Even his love for Bridget had its sweets, as well as its sorrows. It was grateful to think of her tenderness to himself, her beauty, her constancy, of which he would not for a moment doubt, and of all the innocent and delightful converse they had had during a courtship that occupied so much of their brief lives.

Just as the sun was setting, Bob returned from his fishing excursion. To Mark's surprise, he saw that the dingui floated almost with her gunwale-to, and he hastened down to meet his friend, who came ashore in a little bay, quite near the gate-way, and in which the rock did not rise as much like a wall as it did on most of the exterior of the reef. Bob had caught about a dozen fish, some of which were of considerable size, though all were of either species or varieties that were unknown to them both. Selecting two of the most promising-looking, for their own use, he threw the others on the rocks, where the pigs and poultry might give them a trial. Nor was it long before these creatures were hard at work on them, disregarding the scales and fins. At first the hens were a little delicate, probably from having found animal food enough for their present wants in the insects; but, long before the game was demolished, they had come in for their full share. This experiment satisfied the mariners that there would be no difficulty in furnishing plenty of food for all their stock, and for any length of time, Kitty excepted. It is true, the pork and the poultry would be somewhat fishy; but that would be a novelty, and should it prove disagreeable on tasting it, a little clean feeding, at the proper moment, would correct the flavour.

But the principal cargo of the dingui was not the dozen fish mentioned. Bob had nearly filled the boat with a sort of vegetable loam, that he had found lodged in the cavity of one of the largest rocks, and which, from the signs around the place, he supposed to have been formed by deposits of sea-weed. By an accident of nature, this cavity in the rock received a current, which carried large quantities of floating weed *into* it, while every storm probably had added to its stores since the mass had risen above the common level of the sea, by throwing fresh materials on to the pile, by means of the waves, nothing quitting it. Bob reported that there were no signs of vegetation around the rock, which circumstance, however, was easily enough accounted for by the salt water that was incessantly moistening the surface, and which, while it took with it the principle of future, was certain to destroy all present, vegetable life; or, all but that which belongs exclusively to aquatic plants.

"How much of this muck do you suppose is to be found on your rock, Bob?" asked Mark, after he had examined the dingui's cargo, by sight, taste, and smell. "If is surprisingly like a rich earth, if it be not actually so."

"Lord bless you, Mr. Mark, there is enough on't to fill the old 'Cocus, ag'in and ag'in. How deep it is, I don't pretend to know; but it's a good hundred paces across it, and the spot is as round as that there chimbly, that you call a cr'ature."

"If that be the case, we will try our hands at it next week, and see what can be done with an importation. I do not give up the blessed hope of the boat, Bob-that you will always bear in mind-but it is best to keep an eye on the means of living, should it please God to prevent our getting to sea again."

"To sea, Mr. Mark, neither you nor I, nor any mortal man will ever get, in the old 'Cocus ag'in, as I know by the looks of things outside of us. 'Twill never do to plant in my patch, however, for the salt water must wash it whenever it blows; though a very little work, too, might keep it out, when I come to think on it. Sparrow-grass would grow there, as it is, desperately well; and Friend Abraham White had both seeds and roots put up for the use of the savages, if a body only know'd whereabouts to look for them, among the lot of rubbish of that sort, that he sent aboard."

"All the seeds and roots are in two or three boxes, in the steerage," answered Mark. "I'll just step up to the crater and bring a shovel, to throw this loam out of the boat with, while you can clean the fish and cook the supper. A little fresh food, after so much salt, will be both pleasant and good for us."

Bob assented, and each went his way. Mark threw the loam into a wheelbarrow, of which Friend Abraham had put no less than three in the ship, as presents to the savages, and he wheeled it, at two or three loads, into the crater, where he threw it down in a pile, intending to make a compost heap of all the materials of the sort he could lay his hands on.

As for Bob he cleaned both fish, taking them on board the ship to do so. He put the largest and coarsest into the coppers, after cutting it up, mixing with it onions, pork, and ship's bread, intending to start a fire beneath it early in the morning, and cook a sort of chowder. The other he fried, Mark and he making a most grateful meal on it, that evening.

Chapter VII

> "Be thou at peace! —Th' all-seeing eye,
> Pervading earth, and air, and sky,
> The searching glance which none may flee,
> Is still, in mercy, turn'd on thee."
>
> —Mrs. Hemans

The Sabbath ever dawns on the piously-inclined, with hope and a devout gratitude to the Creator for all his mercies. This is more apt to be the case in genial seasons, and rural abodes, perhaps, than amidst the haunts of men, and when the thoughts are diverted from the proper channels by the presence of persons around us. Still greater is the influence of absolute solitude, and that increased by the knowledge of a direct and visible dependence on the Providence of God, for the means of even prolonging existence. In the world, men lose sight of this dependence, fancying themselves and their powers of more account than the truth would warrant, and even forgetting whence these very boasted powers are derived; but man, when alone, and in critical circumstances, is made to feel that he is not sufficient for his own wants, and turns with humility and hope to the divine hand that upholds him.

With feelings of this character, did Mark and Betts keep their first Sabbath on the reef. The former read the morning service, from beginning to end, while the latter sat by, an attentive listener. The only proof given of any difference in religious faith between our mariners, was of so singular a nature as to merit notice. Notwithstanding Bob's early familiarity with Mark, his greater age, and the sort of community of feeling and interest created by their common misfortune, the former had not ceased to treat the last with the respect due to his office. This deference never deserted him, and he had riot once since the ship was embayed, entered the cabin without pulling off his hat As soon as church commenced, however, Bob resumed his tarpaulin, as a sort of sign of his own orthodoxy in the faith of his fathers; making it a point to do as they had done in meeting, and slightly concerned lest his companion might fall into the error of supposing he was a man likely to be converted. Mark also observed that, in the course of that Sabbath, Bob used the pronouns 'thee' and 'thou,' on two or three occasions, sounding oddly enough in the mouth of the old salt.

Well did both our mariners prove the efficacy of the divine provision of a day of rest, in a spiritual sense, on the occasion of this their first Sabbath on the reef. Mark felt far more resigned to his fate than he could have believed possible, while Betts declared that he should be absolutely happy, had he only a better boat than the dingui; not that the dingui was at all a bad craft of its kind, but it wanted size. After the religious services, for which both our mariners had shaved and dressed, they took a walk together, on the reef, conversing of their situation and future proceedings. Bob then told Mark, for the first time, that, in his opinion, there was the frame and the other materials of a pinnace, or a large boat, somewhere in the hold, which it was intended to put together, when the ship reached the islands, as a convenience for cruising about among them to trade with the savages, and to transport sandal-wood. The mate had never heard of this boat, but acknowledged that a part of the hold-had been stowed while he was up at Bristol, and it might have been taken in then. Bob confessed that he had never seen it, though he had worked in the stevedore's gang; but was confident he had heard Friend Abraham White and Captain Crutchely talking of its dimensions and uses. According to his recollection it was to be a boat considerably larger than the launch, and to be fitted with masts and sails, and to have a half-deck. Mark listened to ah1 this patiently, though he firmly believed that the honest fellow was deceiving himself the whole time. Such a craft could scarcely be in the ship, and he not hear of it, if he did not actually see it; though he thought it possible that the captain and owners may have had some such plan in contemplation, and conversed together on it, in Betts's presence. As there were plenty of tools on board, however, by using stuff of one sort or another, that was to be found in the ship, Mark had strong hopes of their being able, between them, to construct, in the course of time-though he believed a long time might be necessary—a craft of some sort, that should be of sufficient stability to withstand the billows of that ordinarily mild sea, and enable them to return to their homes and friends. In conversing of things of this sort, in religious observances, and in speculating on the probable fate of their shipmates, did our mariners pass this holy day. Bob was sensibly impressed with the pause in their ordinary pursuits, and lent himself to the proper feelings of the occasion with a zeal and simplicity that gave Mark great satisfaction; for, hitherto, while aware that his friend was as honest a fellow as ever lived, in the common acceptation of such a phrase, he had not supposed him in the least susceptible of religious impressions. But the world had suddenly lost its hold on Betts, the barrier offered by the vast waters of the Pacific, being almost as impassable, in his actual circumstances, as that of the grave; and the human heart turns to God in its direst distress, as to the only being who can administer relief. It is when men are prosperous that they vainly imagine they are sufficient for their own wants, and are most apt to neglect the hand that alone can give durable support.

The following morning our mariners resumed their more worldly duties with renewed powers. While the kettle was boiling for their tea, they rolled ashore a couple of empty water-casks, and filled them with fresh water, at one of the largest natural reservoirs on the reef; it having rained hard in the night. After breakfast, Mark walked round to examine his piles of loam, in the crater, while Bob pulled away in the dingui, to catch a few fish, and to get a new cargo of the earth; it being the intention of Mark to join him at the next trip, with the raft, which required some little arranging, however, previously to its being used for such a purpose. The rain of the past night had thoroughly, washed the pile of earth, and, on tasting it. Mark was convinced that much of the salt it contained had been carried off. This encouraged him to persevere in his gardening projects. As yet, the spring had only just commenced, and he was in hopes of being able to prepare one bed, at least, in time to obtain useful vegetables from it.

The Rancocus had a great many planks and boards in her hold, a part of the ample provision made by her owners for the peculiar voyage on which she had been sent. Of real cargo, indeed, she had very little, the commerce between the civilized man and the savage being ordinarily on those great principles of Free Trade, of which so much is said of late years, while so little is understood, and which usually give the lion's share of the profit to them who need it least. With some of these planks, Mark made a staging for his raft. By the time he was ready, Bob returned with a load of loam, and, on the next outward voyage, the raft was taken as well as the dingui. Mark had fitted pins and grummets, by which the raft was rowed, he and Bob impelling it, when light, very easily at the rate of two miles in the hour.

Mark found Betts's deposit of decayed vegetable matter even larger and more accessible than he had hoped for. A hundred loads might be got without even using a wheelbarrow; and to all appearances there was enough of it to give a heavy dressing to many acres, possibly to the whole area of the crater. The first thing the young man did was to choose a suitable place, dig it well up, mixing a sufficiency of guano with it, agreeably to Betts's directions, and then to put in some of his asparagus roots. After this he scattered a quantity of the seed, raking the ground well after sowing. By the time this was done, Bob had both dingui and raft loaded, when they pulled the last back to the reef, towing the boat. In this manner our two mariners continued to work most of the time, for the next fortnight, making, daily, more or less trips to the 'loam-rock,' as they called the place where this precious deposit had been made; though they neglected none of their other necessary duties. As the distance was short, they could come and go many times in a day, transporting at each trip about as much of the loam as would make an ordinary American cart-load of manure. In the whole, by Mark's computation, they got across about fifty of these cargoes, in the course of their twelve days' work. The entire day, however, was on no occasion given up wholly to this pursuit. On the contrary, many little odd tasks were completed, which were set by their necessities, or by fore thought and prudence. All the empty water-casks, for one thing, were rolled ashore, and filled at the largest pool; the frequency of the rains admonishing them of the wisdom of making a provision for the dry season. The Rancocus had a good deal of water still left in her, some of it being excellent Delaware river water, though she had filled up at Valparaiso, after passing the Horn. Mark counted the full casks, and allowing ten gallons a day for Bob and himself, a good deal more than could be wanted, there remained in the ship fresh water enough to last them two years. It is true, it was not such water as the palate often craved of a warm day; but they were accustomed to it, and it was sweet. By keeping it altogether between decks, the sun had no power on it, and it was even more palatable than might have been supposed. Mark occasionally longed for one good drink at some gushing spring that he remembered at home, it is true; and Bob was a little in the habit of extolling a particular well that, it would seem, his family were reputed to have used for several generations. Notwithstanding these little natural backslidings on this subject, our mariners might be thought well off on the score of water, having it in great abundance, and with no reasonable fear of ever losing it altogether. The casks taken ashore were filled for their preservation, as well as for convenience, an old sail being spread over them, after they were rolled together and chocked. As yet, no water was given to any of the stock, all the animals finding it in abundance, in the cavities of the lava.

Some of the time, moreover, Betts passed in fishing, supplying not only Mark and himself, but the pigs and the poultry, with as much food as was desired. Several of the fish caught turned out to be delicious, while others were of a quality that caused them to be thrown into the compost heap. A cargo of guano was also imported, the rich manure being mixed up in liberal quantities with the loam. At the end of the first week of these voyages to 'loam-rock,' Betts went out to fish in a new direction, passing to windward of the 'sea-wall,' as they called the reef that protected the ship, and pulling towards a bit of naked rock a short distance beyond it, where he fancied he might find a particular sort of little fish, that greatly resembled the Norfolk Hog-fish, one of the most delicious little creatures for the pan that is to be found in all the finny tribe. He had been gone a couple of hours, when Mark, who was at work within the crater, picking up the encrusted ashes that formed its surface, heard Bob's shout outside, as if he wished assistance. Throwing down the pick, our young man ran out, and was not a little surprised to see the sort of cargo with which Bob was returning to port. It would seem that a great collection of sea-weed had formed to windward of the rock where Bob had gone to fish, at which spot it ordinarily gathered in a pile until the heap became too large to lodge any longer, when, owing to the form of the rock, it invariably broke adrift, and passed to the southward of the Reef, floating to leeward, to fetch up on some other rock, or island, in that direction. Bob had managed to get this raft round a particular point in the reef, when the wind and current carried it, as near as might be, directly towards the crater. He was calling to Mark to come to his assistance, to help get the raft into a sort of bay, ahead of him, where it might be lodged; else would there be the danger of its drifting past the Reef, after all his pains. Our young man saw, at once, what was wanted, got a line, succeeded in throwing it to Bob, and by hauling upon it brought the whole mass ashore in the very spot Betts wished to see it landed.

This sea-weed proved to be a great acquisition on more accounts than one. There was as much of it in quantity as would have made two good-sized loads of hay. Then, many small shell-fish were found among it, which the pigs and poultry ate with avidity. It also contained seeds, that the fowls picked up as readily as if it had been corn. The hogs moreover masticated a good deal of the weed, and poor Kitty, the only one of the domestic animals on the Reef that was not now living to its heart's content, nibbled at it, with a species of half-doubting faith in its salubrity. Although it was getting to be late in the afternoon, Mark and Bob got two of Friend Abraham White's pitchforks (for the worthy Quaker had sent these, among other implements of husbandry, as a peace-offering to the Fejee savages), and went to work with a hearty good-will, landed all this weed, loaded it up, and wheeled it into the crater, leaving just enough outside to satisfy the pigs and the poultry. This task concluded the first week of the labour already mentioned.

At the termination of the second week, Mark and Betts held a council on the subject of their future proceedings. At this consultation it was decided that it would be better to finish the picking up of a considerable plot of ground, one of at least half an acre in extent, that was already commenced, within the crater, scatter their compost over it, and spade all up together, and plant, mixing in as much of the sea-weed as they could conveniently spade under. Nothwithstanding their success in finding the loam, and this last discovery of a means of getting sea-weed in large supplies to the Reef, Mark was not very sanguine of success in his gardening. The loam appeared to him to be cold and sour, as well as salt, though a good deal freshened by the rain since it was put in the crater; and he knew nothing of the effects of guano, except through the somewhat confused accounts of Bob. Then the plain of the crater offered nothing beside a coarse and shelly ashes. These ashes were deep enough for any agricultural purpose, it is true, for Mark could work a crowbar down into them its entire length; but they appeared to him to be totally wanting in the fertilizing principle. Nor could he account for the absence of everything like vegetation, on or about the reef, if the elements of plants of any sort were to be found in the substances of which it was composed. He had read, however, that the territory around active volcanoes, and which was far enough removed from the vent to escape from the destruction caused by lava, scoriæ and heat, was usually highly fertile, in consequence of the ashes and impalpable dust that was scattered in the air; but seeing no proofs of any such fertility here, he supposed that the adjacent sea had swallowed up whatever there might have been of these bountiful gifts. With these impressions, it is not surprising that Mark was disposed to satisfy himself with a moderate beginning, in preference to throwing away time and labour in endeavouring to produce resources which after all would fail them.

Mark's plan, as laid before his companion, on the occasion of the council mentioned, was briefly this:—He proposed to pass the next month in preparing the half-acre they had commenced upon, and in getting in seed; after which they could do no more than trust their husbandry to Providence and the seasons. As soon as done with the tillage, it was his idea that they ought to overhaul the ship thoroughly, ascertain what was actually in her, and, if the materials of the boat mentioned by Betts were really to be found, to set that craft up as soon as possible, and to get it into the water. Should they not find the frame and planks of the pinnace, as Betts seemed to think they would, they must go to work and get out the best frame they could themselves, and construct such a craft as their own skill could contrive. After building such a boat, it was Mark's opinion that he and Bob could navigate her across that tranquil ocean, until they reached the coast of South America, or some of the islands that were known to be friendly to the white man; for, fifty yearns ago, it will be remembered, we did not possess the same knowledge of the Pacific that we possess to-day, and mariners did not trust themselves always with confidence among the natives of its islands. With this plan pretty well sketched out, then, our mariners saw the first month of their captivity among the unknown reefs of this remote quarter of the world, draw to its close.

Mark was a little surprised by a proposal that he received from Bob, next morning, which was the Sabbath, of course. "Friends have monthly meetings," Betts observed, "and he thought they ought to set up some such day on the Reef. He was willing to keep Christmas, if Mark saw fit, but rather wished to pay proper respect to all the festivals and observances of Friends." Mark was secretly amused with this proposition, even while it pleased him. The monthly meeting of the Quakers was for the secular part of church business, as much as for the purposes of religious worship; and Bob having all those concerns in his own hands, it was not so easy to see how a stated day was to aid him any in carrying out his church government. But Mark understood the feeling which dictated this request, and was disposed to deal gently by it. Betts was becoming daily more and more conscious of his dependence on a Divine Providence, in the situation in which he was thrown; and his mind, as well as his feelings, naturally enough reverted to early impressions and habits, in their search for present relief. Bob had not the clearest notions of either the theory or practice of his sect, but he remembered much of the last, and believed he should be acting right by conforming as closely as possible to the 'usages of Friends,' Mark promised to take the matter into consideration, and to come to some decision on it, at an early day.

The following Monday it rained nearly the whole morning, confining our mariners to the ship. They took that occasion to overhaul the "twixt-deck' more thoroughly than had yet been done, and particularly to give the seed-boxes a close examination. Much of the lumber, and most of the tools too, were stowed on this deck, and something like a survey was also made of them. The frame and other materials of the pinnace were looked for, in addition, but without any success. If in the ship at all, they were certainly not betwixt decks. Mark was still of opinion no such articles would ever be found; but Betts insisted on the conversation he had overheard, and on his having rightly understood it. The provision of tools was very ample, and, in some respects, a little exaggerated in the way of Friend White's expectations of civilizing the people of Fejee. It may be well, here, to say a word concerning the reason that the Rancocus contained so many of these tributes to civilization. The voyage of the ship, it will be remembered, was in quest of sandal-wood. This sandal-wood was to be carried to Canton and sold, and a cargo of teas taken in with the avails. Now, sandal-wood was supposed to be used for the purposes of idolatry, being said to be burned before the gods of that heathenish people, Idolatry being one of the chiefest of all sins, Friend Abraham White had many compunctions and misgivings of conscience touching the propriety of embarking in the trade at all. It was true, that our knowledge of the Chinese customs did not extend far enough to render it certain that the wood was used for the purpose of burning before idols, some pretending it was made into ornamental furniture; but Friend Abraham White had heard the first, and was disposed to provide a set-off, in the event of the report's being true, by endeavouring to do something towards the civilization of the heathen. Had he been a Presbyterian merchant, of a religious turn, it is probable a quantity of tracts would have been made to answer the purpose; but, belonging to a sect whose practice was generally as perfect as its theory is imperfect, Friend Abraham White's conscience was not to be satisfied with any such shallow contrivance. It is true that he expected to make many thousands of dollars by the voyage, and doubtless would so have done, had not the accident befallen the ship, or had poor Captain Crutchely drank less in honour of his wedding-day; but the investment in tools, seeds, pigs, wheelbarrows, and other matters, honestly intended to better the condition of the natives of Vanua Levu and Viti Levu, did not amount to a single cent less than one thousand dollars, lawful money of the republic.

In looking over the packages, Mark found white clover seed, and Timothy seed, among other things, in sufficient quantity to cover most of the mount of the crater. The weather temporarily clearing off, he called to Bob, and they went ashore together, Mark carrying some of the grass seed in a pail, while. Betts followed with a vessel to hold guano. Providing a quantity of the last from a barrel that had been previously filled with it, and covered to protect it from the rain, they clambered up the side of the crater. This was the first time either had ascended since the day they finished planting there, and Mark approached his hills with a good deal of freshly-revived interest in their fate. From *them* he expected very little, having had no loam to mix with the ashes; but, by dwelling so much of late on the subject of tillage, he was not without faint hopes of meeting with some little reward for the pains he had taken. The reader will judge of the rapture then, as well as of the surprise, with which he first saw a hill of melons, already in the fourth leaf. Here, then, was the great problem successfully solved. Vegetation had actually commenced on that hitherto barren mount, and the spot which had lain-how long, Mark knew not, but probably for a thousand years, if not for thousands of years, in its nakedness-was about to be covered with verdure, and blest with fruitfulness. The inert principles which, brought to act together; had produced this sudden change from barrenness to fertility, had probably been near neighbours to each other all that time, but had failed of bringing forth their fruits, for the want of absolute contact. So Mark reasoned, for he nothing doubted that it was Betts's guano that had stimulated the otherwise barren deposit of the volcano, and caused his seed to germinate. The tillage may have aided, as well as the admission of air, light and water; but something more than this, our young gardener fancied, was wanting to success. That something the manure of birds, meliorated and altered by time, had supplied, and lo! the glorious results were before his eyes.

It would not be easy to portray to the reader all the delight which these specks of incipient verdure conveyed to the mind of Mark Woolston. It far exceeded the joy that would be apt to be awakened by a relief from an apprehension of wanting food at a distant day, for it resembled something of the character of a new creation. He went from hill to hill, and everywhere did he discover plants, some just peeping through the ashes, others already in leaf, and all seemingly growing and thriving. Fortunately, Kitty had not been on the mount for the last fortnight, her acquired habits, and the total nakedness of the hills, having kept her below with the other animals, since her first visits. Mark saw the necessity of keeping her off the elevation, which she would certainly climb the instant anything like verdure caught her eyes from below. He determined, therefore, to confine her to the ship, until he had taken the precautions necessary to prevent her ascending the mount. This last was easily enough done. On the exterior of the hills there were but three places where even a goat could get up. This was owing to the circumstance that the base of the ascent rose like a wall, for some ten or twelve feet, everywhere but at the three points mentioned. It appeared to Mark as if the sea had formerly washed around the crater, giving this form to its bottom for so wall-like was the rock for these ten or twelve feet, that it would have defied the efforts of a man for a long time, to overcome the difficulties of the ascent. At two of the places where the *débris* had made a rough footing, half an hour's work would remove the material, and leave these spots as impassable as the others. At the third point, it might require a good deal of labor to effect the object. At this last place, Mark told Betts it would be necessary, for the moment, to make some sort of a fence. Within the crater, it was equally difficult to ascend, except at one or two places; but these ascents our mariners thought of improving, by making steps, as the animals were effectually excluded from the plain within by means of the sail which served for a curtain at the gateway, or hole of entrance.

As soon as Mark had recovered a little from his first surprise, he sent Bob below to bring up some buckets filled with the earth brought from Loam Rock, or island. This soil was laid carefully around each of the plants, the two working alternately at the task, until a bucket-full had been laid in each hill. Mark did not know it at the time, but subsequent experience gave him reason to suspect, that this forethought saved most of his favourites from premature deaths. Seed might germinate, and the plants shoot luxuriantly from out of the ashes of the volcano, under the united influence of the sun and rains, in that low latitude, but it was questionable whether the nourishment to be derived from such a soil, if soil it could yet be called, would prove to be sufficient to sustain the plants when they got to be of an age and size to demand all the support they wanted. So convinced did Mark become, as the season advanced, of the prudence of what he then did out of a mere impulse, that he passed hours, subsequently, in raising loam to the summit of the mount, in order to place it in the different hills. For this purpose, Bob rigged a little derrick, and fitted a whip, so that the buckets were whipped up, sailor-fashion, after two or three experiments made in lugging them up by hand had suggested to the honest fellow that there might be a cheaper mode of obtaining their wishes.

When Mark was temporarily satisfied with gazing at his new-found treasures, he went to work to scatter the grass stood over the summit and sides of the crater. Inside, there was not much motive for sowing anything, the rock being so nearly perpendicular; but on the outside of the hill, or 'mountain,' as Bob invariably called it, the first ten or twelve feet excepted, there could be no obstacle to the seeds taking; though from the want of soil much of it, Mark knew, must be lost; but, if it only took in spots, and gave him a few green patches for the eye to rest on, he felt he should be amply rewarded for his trouble. Bob scattered guano wherever he scattered grass-seed, and in this way they walked entirely round the crater, Mark using up at least half of Friend Abraham White's provision in behalf of the savages of Fejee, in the way of the grasses. A gentle soft rain soon came to moisten this seed, and to embed it with whatever there was of soil on the surface, giving it every chance to take root that circumstances would allow.

This preliminary step taken towards covering the face of the mount with verdure, our mariners went to work to lay out their garden, regularly, within the crater. Mark manifested a good deal of ingenuity in this matter. With occasional exceptions the surface of the plain, or the bottom of the crater, was an even crust of no great thickness, compared of concrete ashes, scoriæ &c., but which might have borne the weight of a loaded wagon. This crust once broken, which it was not very difficult to do by means of pick and crows, the materials beneath were found loose enough for the purposes of agriculture, almost without using the spade. Now, space being abundant, Mark drew lines, in fanciful and winding paths, leaving the crust for his walks, and only breaking into the loose materials beneath, wherever he wished to form a bed. This variety served to amuse him and Betts, and they worked with so much the greater zeal, as their labours produced objects that were agreeable to the eye, and which amused them now, while they promised to benefit them hereafter. As each bed, whether oval, winding or straight, was dug, the loam and sea-weed was mixed up in it, in great abundance, after which it was sown, or planted.

Mark was fully aware that many of Friend Abraham White's seeds, if they grew and brought their fruits to maturity, would necessarily change their properties in that climate; some for the worse, and others for the better. From the Irish potato, the cabbage, and most of the more northern vegetables, he did not expect much, under any circumstances; but, he thought he would try all, and having several regularly assorted boxes of garden-seeds, just as they had been purchased out of the shops of Philadelphia, his garden scarce wanted any plant that was then known to the kitchens of America.

Our mariners were quite a fortnight preparing, manuring, and sowing their *parterre*, which, when complete, occupied fully half an acre in the very centre of the crater, Mark intending it for the nucleus of future similar works, that might convert the whole hundred acres into a garden. By the time the work was done, the rains were less frequent, though it still came in showers, and those that were still more favourable to vegetation. In that fortnight the plants on the mount had made great advances, showing the exuberance and growth of a tropical climate. It sometimes, nay, it often happens, that when the sun is the most genial for vegetation, moisture is wanting to aid its power, and, in some respects, to counteract its influence. These long and periodical droughts, however, are not so much owing to heat as to other and local causes, Mark now began to hope, as the spring advanced, that his little territory was to be exempt, in a great measure, from the curse of droughts, the trades, and some other causes that to him were unknown, bringing clouds so often that not only shed their rain upon his garden, but which served in a great measure to mitigate a heat that, without shade of some sort or other, would be really intolerable.

With a view to the approaching summer, our mariners turned their attention to the constructing of a tent within the crater. They got some old sails and some spars ashore, and soon had a spacious, as well as a comfortable habitation of this sort erected. Not only did they spread a spacious tent for themselves, within the crater, but they erected another, or a sort of canopy rather, on its outside, for the use of the animals, which took refuge beneath it, during the heats of the day, with an avidity that proved how welcome it was. This outside shed, or canopy, required a good deal of care in its construction, to resist the wind, while that inside scarce ever felt the breeze. This want of wind, or of air in motion, indeed, formed the most serious objection to the crater, as a place of residence, in the hot months; and the want of breeze that was suffered in the tent, set Mark to work to devise expedients for building some sort of tent, or habitation, on the in net itself, where it would be always cool, provided one could get a protection from the fierce rays of the sun.

After a good deal of search, Mark selected a spot on the 'Summit,' as he began to term the place, and pitched his tent on, it. Holes were made in the soft rocks, and pieces of spars were inserted, to answer for posts. With a commencement as solid as this, it was not difficult to make the walls of the tent (or marquee would be the better word, since both habitations had nearly upright sides) by means of an old fore-course. In order to get the canvas up there, however, it was found necessary to cut out the pieces below, when, by means of the purchase at the derrick, it was all hoisted to the Summit.

These several arrangements occupied Mark and Bob another fortnight, completing the first quarter of a year they had passed on the Reef. By this time they had got accustomed to their situation, and had fallen into regular courses of duty, though the increasing heats admonished both of the prudence of not exposing themselves too much beneath the fiery sun at noon-day.

Chapter VIII

> "Now from the full-grown day a beamy shower
> Gleams on the lake, and gilds each glossy flower,
> Gay insects sparkle in the genial blaze,
> Various as light, and countless as its rays —
> Now, from yon range of rocks, strong rays rebound,
> Doubling the day on flowery plains around."
>
> —Savage

After the tent on the Summit was erected, Mark passed much of his leisure time there. Thither he conveyed many of his books, of which he had a very respectable collection, his flute, and a portion of his writing materials. There he could sit and watch the growth of the different vegetables he was cultivating. As for Bob, he fished a good deal, both in the way of supplies and for his amusement. The pigs and poultry fared well, and everything seemed to thrive but poor Kitty. She loved to follow Mark, and cast many a longing look up at the Summit, whenever she saw him strolling about among his plants.

The vegetables on the Summit, or those first put into the ground, flourished surprisingly. Loam had been added repeatedly, and they wanted for nothing that could bring forward vegetation. The melons soon began to run, as did the cucumbers, squashes, and pumpkins; and by the end of the next month, there were a dozen large patches on the mount that were covered by a dense verdure. Nor was this all; Mark making a discovery about this time, that afforded him almost as, much happiness as when he first saw his melons in leaf. He was seated one day, with the walls of his tent brailed up, in order to allow the wind to blow through, when something dark on the rock caught his eye. This spot was some little distance from him, and going to it, he found that large quantities of his grass-seed had actually taken! Now he might hope to convert that barren-looking, and often glaring rock, into a beautiful grassy hill, and render that which was sometimes painful to the eyes, a pleasure to look upon. The young man understood the laws of vegetation well enough to be certain that could the roots of grasses once insinuate themselves into the almost invisible crevices of the crust that coveted the place, they would of themselves let in light, air and water enough for their own wants, and thus increase the very fertility on which they subsisted. He did not fail, however, to aid nature, by scattering a fresh supply of guano all over the hill.

While Mark was thus employed at home, Bob rowed out to the reef, bringing in his fish in such quantities that it occurred to Mark to convert them also into manure. A fresh half-acre was accordingly broken up, within the crater, the cool of the mornings and of the evenings being taken for the toil; and, as soon as a bed was picked over, quantities of fish were buried in it, and left there to decay. Nor did Betts neglect the sea-weed the while. On several occasions he floated large bodies of it in, from the outer reefs, which were all safely landed and wheeled into the crater, where a long pile of it was formed, mingled with loam from Loam Island, and guano. This work, however, gradually ceased, as the season advanced, and summer came in earnest. That season, however, did not prove by any means as formidable as Mark had anticipated, the sea-breezes keeping the place cool and refreshed. Our mariners now missed the rain, which was by no means as frequent a it had been, though it fell in larger quantities when it did come. The stock had to be watered for several weeks, the power of the sun causing all the water that lodged it the cavities of the rocks to evaporate almost immediately.

During the time it was too warm to venture out in the dingui, except for half an hour of a morning, or for as long a period of an evening, Mark turned his attention to the ship again. Seizing suitable moments, each sail was loosened, thoroughly dried, unbent, and got below. An awning was got out, and spread, and the decks were wet down, morning and evening, both for the purposes of cleanliness, and to keep them from cheeking. The hold was now entered, and overhauled, for the first time since the accident. A great many useful things were found in it, and among other articles two barrels of good sharp vinegar, which Friend Abraham White had caused to be put on board to be used with anything that could be pickled, as an anti-scorbutic. The onions and cucumbers both promising so well, Mark rejoiced at this discovery, determining at once to use some of the vinegar on a part of his expected crop of those two vegetables.

One day as Bob was rummaging about in the hold, and Mark was looking on, that being the coolest place on the whole reef, the former got hold of a piece of wood, and began to tug at it to draw it out from among a pile that lay in a dark corner. After several efforts, the stick came, when Mark, struck with a glimpse he got of its form, bade Bob bring it under the light of the hatchway. The instant he got a good look at it, Woolston knew that Bob's 'foolish, crooked stick, which was fit to stow nowhere,' as the honest fellow had described it when it gave him so much trouble, was neither more nor less than one of the ribs of a boat of larger size than common.

"This is providential, truly!" exclaimed Mark. "Your crooked stick, Bob, is a part of the frame of the pinnace of which you spoke, and which we had given up, as a thing not to be found on board!"

"You're right, Mr. Mark, you're right!" answered Bob —"and I most have been oncommon stupid not to have thought of it, when it came so hard. And if there's one of the boat's bones stowed in that place, there must be more to be found in the same latitude."

This was true enough. After working in that dark corner of the hold for several hours, all the materials of the intended craft were found and collected in the steerage. Neither Mark nor Betts was a boat-builder, or a shipwright; but each had a certain amount of knowledge on the subject, and each well knew where every piece was intended to be put. What a revolution this discovery made in the feelings of our young husband! He had never totally despaired of seeing Bridget again, for that would scarce have comported with his youth and sanguine temperament; but the hope had, of late, become so very dim, as to survive only as that feeling will endure in the bosoms of the youthful and inexperienced Mark had lived a long time for his years; had seen more and performed far more than usually falls to persons of his age, and he was, by character, prudent and practical; but it would have been impossible for one who had lived as long and as well as himself, to give up every expectation of being restored to his bride, even in circumstances more discouraging than those in which he was actually placed. Still, he had been slowly accustoming himself to the idea of a protracted separation, and had never lost sight of the expediency of making his preparations for passing his entire life in the solitary place where he and Betts had been cast by a mysterious and unexpected dispensation of a Divine Providence. When Bob, from time to-time, insisted on his account of the materials for the pinnace being in the ship, Mark had listened incredulously, unconscious himself how much his mind had been occupied by Bridget when this part of the cargo had been taken in, and unwilling to believe such an acquisition could have been made without his knowledge. Now that he saw it, however, a tumultuous rushing of all the blood in his body towards his heart, almost overpowered him, and the future entirely changed its aspects. He did not doubt an instant, of the ability of Bob and himself to put these blessed materials together, or of their success in navigating the mild sea around them, for any necessary distance, in a craft of the size this must turn out to be. A bright vista, with Bridget's brighter countenance at its termination, glowed before his imagination, and a great deal of wholesome philosophy and Christian submission were unsettled, as it might be, in the twinkling of an eye, by this all-important discovery. Mark had never abandoned the thought of constructing a little vessel with materials torn from the ship; but that would nave been a most laborious, as well as a doubtful experiment, while here was the problem solved, with a certainty and precision almost equal to one in mathematics!

The agitation and revulsion of feeling produced in Mark by the discovery of the materials of the pinnace, were so great as to prevent him from maturing any plan for several days. During that time he could perceive in himself an alteration that amounted almost to an entire change of character. The vines on the Summit were now in full leaf, and they covered broad patches of the rock with their luxuriant vegetation, while the grass could actually be seen from the ship, converting the drab-coloured concretions of the mount into slopes and acclivities of verdure. But, all this delighted him no longer. Home and Bridget met him even in the fanciful and now thriving beds within the crater, where everything appeared to push forward with a luxuriance and promise of return, far exceeding what had once been his fondest expectations. He could see nothing, anticipate nothing, talk of nothing, think of nothing, but these new-found means of quitting the Reef, and of returning to the abodes of men, and to the arms of his young wife.

Betts took things more philosophically. He had made up his mind to 'Robinson Crusoe it' a few years, and, though he had often expressed a wish that the dingui was of twice its actual size, he would have been quite as well content with this new boat could it be cut down to one-fourth of its real dimensions. He submitted to Mark's superior information, however; and when the latter told him that he could wait no longer for the return of cooler weather, or for the heat of the sun to become less intense before he began to set up the frame of his craft, as had been the first intention, Bob acquiesced in the change of plan, without remonstrance, bent on taking things as they came, in humility and cheerfulness.

Nevertheless, it was far easier bravely to determine in this matter, than to execute. The heat was now so intense for the greater part of the day, that it would have far exceeded the power of our two mariners to support it, on a naked rock, and without shade of any sort. The frame of the pinnace must be set up somewhere near the water, regular ways being necessary to launch her; and nowhere, on the shore, was the smallest shade to be found, without recourse to artificial means of procuring it. As Mark's impatience would no longer brook delay, this artificial shade, therefore, was the first thing to be attended to.

The leeward end of the reef was chosen for the new ship-yard. Although this choice imposed a good deal of additional labour on the two workmen, by compelling them to transport all the materials rather more than a mile, reflection and examination induced Mark to select the spot he did. The formation of the rock was more favourable there, he fancied, than in any other place he could find; offering greater facilities for launching. This was one motive; but the principal inducement was connected with an apprehension of floods. By the wall-like appearance of the exterior base of the mount, by the smoothness of the surface of the Reef in general, which, while it had many inequalities, wore the appearance of being semi-polished by the washing of water over it; and by the certain signs that were, to be found on most of the lower half of the plain of the crater itself, Mark thought it apparent that the entire reef the crater excepted, had been often covered with the water of the ocean, and that at no very distant day. The winter months were usually the tempestuous months in that latitude, though hurricanes might at any time occur. Now, the winter was yet an untried experiment with our two 'reefers,' as Bob sometimes laughingly called himself and Mark, and hurricanes were things that often raised the seas in their neighbourhood several feet in an hour or two. Should the water be actually driven upon the Reef, so as to admit of a current to wash across it, or the waves to roll along its surface, the pinnace would be in the greatest danger of being carried off before it could be even launched. All these things Mark bore in mind, and he chose the spot he did, with an eye to these floods, altogether. It might be six or eight months before they could be ready to get the pinnace into the water, and it now wanted but six to the stormy season. At the western, or leeward, extremity of the island, the little craft would be under the lee of the crater, which would form a sort of breakwater, and might be the means of preventing it from being washed away. Then the rock, just at that spot, was three or four feet higher than at any other point, sufficiently near the sea to admit of launching with ease; and the two advantages united, induced our young 'reefer' to incur the labour of transporting the materials the distance named, in reference to foregoing them. The raft, however, was put in requisition, and the entire frame, with a few of the planks necessary for a commencement, was carried round at one load.

Previously to laying the keel of the pinnace, Mark named it the Neshamony, after a creek that was nearly opposite to the Rancocus, another inlet of the Delaware, that had given its name to the ship from the circumstance that Friend Abraham White had been born on its low banks. The means of averting the pains and penalties of working in the sun, were also attended to, as indeed the great preliminary measure in this new enterprise. To this end, the raft was again put in requisition; an old main-course was got out of the sail-room, and lowered upon the raft; spare spars were cut to the necessary length, and thrown into the water, to be towed down in company; ropes, &c., were provided, and Bob sailed anew on this voyage. It was a work of a good deal of labour to get the raft to windward, towing having been resorted to as the easiest process, but a trip to leeward was soon made. In twenty minutes after this cargo had left the ship, it reached its point of destination.

The only time when our men could work at even their awning, were two hours early in the morning, and as many after the sun had got very low, or had absolutely set. Eight holes had to be drilled into the lava, to a depth of two feet each. Gunpowder, in very small quantities, was used, or these holes could not have been made in a twelvemonth. But by drilling with a crowbar a foot or two into the rock, and charging the cavity with a very small portion of powder, the lava was cracked, when the stones rather easily were raised by means of the picks and crows. Some idea may be formed of the amount of labour that was expended on this, the first step in the new task, by the circumstance that a month was passed in setting those eight awning-posts alone. When up, however, they perfectly answered the purpose, everything having been done in a thorough, seaman-like manner. At the top of each post, itself a portion of solid spar, a watch-tackle was lashed, by means of which the sail was bowsed up to its place. To prevent the bagging unavoidable, in an awning of that size, several uprights were set in the centre, on end, answering their purpose sufficiently without boring into the rocks.

Bob was in raptures with the new 'ship-yard.' It was as large as the mainsail of a ship of four hundred tons, was complete as to shade, with the advantage of letting the breeze circulate, and had a reasonable chance of escaping from the calamities of a flood. Mark, too, was satisfied with the result, and the very next day after this task was completed, our shipwrights set to work to lay their keel. That day was memorable on another account. Bob had gone to the Summit in quest of a tool left there, in fitting up the boat of Mark, and while on the mount, he ascertained the important fact that the melons were beginning to ripen. He brought down three or four of these delicious fruits, and Mark had the gratification of tasting some of the bounties of Providence, which had been bestowed, as a reward of his own industry and forethought. It was necessary to eat of these melons in moderation, however; but it was a great relief to get them at all, after subsisting for so long a time on salted meats, principally, with no other vegetables but such as were dry, and had been long in the ship. It was not the melons alone, however, that were getting to be ripe; for, on examining himself, among the vines which now covered fully an acre of the Summit, Mark found squashes, cucumbers, onions, sweet-potatoes, tomatoes, string-beans, and two or three other vegetables, all equally fit to be used. From that time, some of these plants were put into the pot daily, and certain slight apprehensions which Woolston had begun again to entertain on the subject of scurvy, were soon dissipated. As for the garden within the crater, which was much the most extensive and artistical, it was somewhat behind that on the Summit, having been later tilled; but everything, there, looked equally promising, and Mark saw that one acre, well worked, would produce more than he and Betts could consume in a twelvemonth.

It was an important day on the Reef when the keel of the pinnace was laid. On examining his materials, Mark ascertained that the boat-builders had marked and numbered each portion of the frame, each plank, and everything else that belonged to the pinnace. Holes were bored, and everything had been done in the boat-yard that could be useful to those who, it was expected, were to put the work together in a distant part of the world. This greatly facilitated our new boat-builders' labours in the way of skill, besides having done so much of the actual toil to their hands. As soon as the keel was laid, Mark set up the frame, which came together with very little trouble. The wailes were then got out, and were fitted, each piece being bolted in its allotted place. As the work had already been put together, there was little or no dubbing necessary. Aware that the parts had once been accurately fitted to each other, Mark was careful not to disturb their arrangement by an unnecessary use of the adze, or broad-axe, experimenting and altering the positions of the timbers and planks; but, whenever he met with any obstacle, in preference to cutting and changing the materials themselves, he persevered until the parts came together as had been contemplated. By observing this caution, the whole frame was set up, the wailes were fitted and bolted, and the garboard-streak got on and secured, without taking off a particle of the wood, though a week was necessary to effect these desired objects.

Our mariners now measured their new frame. The keel was just four-and-twenty feet long, the distance between the knight-heads and the taffrail being six feet greater; the beam, from outside to outside, was nine feet, and the hold might be computed at five feet in depth. This gave something like a measurement of eleven tons; the pinnace having been intended for a craft a trifle smaller than this. As a vessel of eleven tons might make very good weather in a sea-way, if properly handled, the result gave great satisfaction, Mark cheering Bob with accounts of crafts, of much smaller dimensions, that had navigated the more stormy seas, with entire safety, on various occasions.

The planking of the Neshamony was no great matter, being completed the week it was commenced. The caulking, however, gave more trouble, though Bob had done a good deal of that sort of work in his day. It took a fortnight for the honest fellow to do the caulking to his own mind, and before it was finished another great discovery was made by rummaging in the ship's hold, in quest of some of the fastenings which had not at first been found. A quantity of old sheet-copper, that had run its time on a vessel's bottom, was brought to light, marked "copper for the pinnace." Friend Abraham White had bethought him of the worms of the low latitudes, and had sent out enough of the refuse copper of a vessel that had been broken up to cover the bottom of this little craft fairly up to her bends. To work, then, Mark and Bob went to put on the sheathing-paper and copper that had thus bountifully been provided for them, as soon as the seams were well payed. This done, and it was no great job, the paint-brush was set to work, and the hull was completed! In all, Mark and Betts were eight weeks, hard at work, putting their pinnace together. When she was painted, the summer was more than half gone. The laying of the deck had given more trouble than any other portion of the work on the boat, and this because it was not a plain, full deck, or one that covered the whole of the vessel, but left small stern-sheets aft, which was absolutely necessary to the comfort and safety of those she was to carry. The whole was got together, however, leaving Mark and Bob to rejoice in their success thus far, and to puzzle their heads about the means of getting their craft into the water, now she was built. In a word, it was far easier to put together a vessel often tons, that had been thus ready fitted to their hands, than it was to launch her.

As each of our mariners had necessarily seen many vessels in their cradles, each had some idea of what it was now necessary to do. Mark had laid the keel as near the water as he could get it, and by this precaution had saved himself a good deal of labour. It was very easy to find materials for the ways, many heavy planks still remaining; but the difficulty was to lay them so that they would not spread. Here the awning-posts were found of good service, plank being set on their edges against them, which, in their turn, were made to sustain the props of the ways. In order to save materials in the cradle, the ways themselves were laid on blocks, and they were secured as well as the skill of our self-formed shipwrights could do it. They had some trouble in making the cradle, and had once to undo all they had done, in consequence of a mistake. At length Mark was of opinion they had taken all the necessary precautions, and told Betts that he thought they might venture to attempt launching the next day. But Bob made a suggestion which changed this plan, and caused a delay that was attended with very serious consequences.

The weather had become cloudy, and a little menacing, for the last, few days, and Bob proposed that they should lower the awning, get up shears on the rock, and step the mast of the pinnace before they launched her, as a means of saving some labour. The spar was not very heavy, it was true, and it might be stepped by crossing a couple of the oars in the boat itself; but a couple of light spars-top-gallant studding-sail booms for instance-would enable them to do it much more readily, before the craft was put into the water, than it could be done afterwards. Mark listened to the suggestion, and acquiesced. The awning was consequently lowered, and got out of the way. To prevent the hogs from tearing the sail, it was placed on two of the wheelbarrows and wheeled up into the crater, whither those animals had never yet found their way. Then the shears were got up, and the mast was stepped and rigged; the boat's sails were found and bent. Mark now thought enough had been done, and that, the next day, they might undertake the launch. But another suggestion of Bob's delayed the proceedings.

The weather still continued clouded and menacing. Betts was of opinion, therefore, that it might be well to stow the provisions and water they intended to use in the pinnace, while she was on the stocks, as they could work round her so much the more easily then than afterwards. Accordingly, the breakers were got out, on board the ship, and filled with fresh water. They were then stuck into the raft. A barrel of beef, and one of pork followed, with a quantity of bread. At two trips the raft carried all the provisions and stores that were wanted, and the cargoes were landed, rolled up to the side of the pinnace, hoisted on board of her, by means of the throat-halliard, and properly stowed. Two grapnels, or rather one grapnel, and a small kedge, were found among the pinnace's materials, everything belonging to her having been stowed in the same part of the ship. These, too, were carried round to the ship-yard, got on board, and their hawsers bent. In a word, every preparation was made that might be necessary to make sail on the pinnace, and to proceed to sea in her, at once.

It was rather late in the afternoon of the third clouded day, that Betts himself admitted no more could be done to the Neshamony, previously to putting her into the water When our two mariners ceased the business of the day, therefore, it was with the understanding that they would turn out early in the morning, wedge up, and launch. An hour of daylight remaining, Mark went up to the Summit to select a few melons, and to take a look at the state of the plantations and gardens. Before ascending the hill, the young man walked through his garden in the crater, where everything was flourishing and doing well. Many of the vegetables were by this time fit to eat, and there was every prospect of there being a sufficient quantity raised to meet the wants of two or three persons for a long period ahead. The sight of these fruits of his toil, and the luxuriance of the different plants, caused a momentary feeling of regret in Mark at the thought of being about to quit the place for ever. He even fancied he should have a certain pleasure in returning to the Reef; and once a faint outline of a plan came over his mind, in which he fancied that he might bring Bridget to this place, and pass the rest of his life with her, in the midst of its peace and tranquillity. This was but a passing thought, however, and was soon forgotten in the pictures that crowded on his mind, in connection with the great anticipated event of the next day.

While strolling about the little walks of his garden, the appearance of verdure along the edge of the crater, or immediately beneath the cliff, caught Mark's eye. Going hastily to the spot, he found that there was a long row of plants of a new sort, not only appearing above the ground, but already in leaf, and rising several inches in height. These were the results of the seeds of the oranges, lemons, limes, shaddocks, figs, and other fruits of the tropics, that he had planted there as an experiment, and forgotten. While his mind was occupied with other things, these seeds had sent forth their shoots, and the several trees were growing with the rapidity and luxuriance that distinguish vegetation within the tropics. As Mark's imagination pictured what might be the effects of cultivation and care on that singular spot, a sigh of regret mingled with his hopes for the future, as he recollected he was so soon to abandon the place for ever; while on the Summit, too, this feeling of regret was increased, rather than diminished. So much of the grass-seed had taken, and the roots had already so far extended, that acres were beginning to look verdant and smiling. Two or three months had brought everything forward prodigiously, and the frequency of the rains in showers, added to the genial warmth of the sun, gave to vegetation a quickness and force that surprised, as much as it delighted our young man.

That night Mark and Betts both slept in the ship. They had a fancy it might be the last in which they could ever have any chance of doing so, and attachment to the vessel induced both to return to their old berths; for latterly they had slept in hammocks, swung beneath the ship-yard awning, in order to be near their work. Mark was awoke at a very early hour, by the howling of a gale among the rigging and spars of the Rancocus, sounds that he had not heard for many a day, and which, at first, were actually pleasant to his ears. Throwing on his clothes, and going out on the quarter-deck, he found that a tempest was upon them. The storm far exceeded anything that he had ever before witnessed in the Pacific. The ocean was violently agitated, and the rollers came in over the reef, to windward, with a force and majesty that seemed to disregard the presence of the rocks. It was just light, and Mark called Bob, in alarm. The aspect of things was really serious, and, at first, our mariners had great apprehensions for the safety of the ship. It was true, the sea-wall resisted every shock of the rollers that reached it, but even the billows after they were broken by this obstacle, came down upon the vessel with a violence that brought a powerful strain on every rope-yarn in the sheet-cable. Fortunately, the ground-tackle, on which the safety of the vessel depended, was of the very best quality, and the anchor was known to have an excellent hold. Then, the preservation of the ship was no longer a motive of the first consideration with them; that of the pinnace being the thing now most to be regarded. It might grieve them both to see the Rancocus thrown upon the rocks, and broken up; but of far greater account was it to their future prospects that the Neshamony should not be injured. Nor were the signs of the danger that menaced the boat to be disregarded. The water of the ocean appeared to be piling in among these reefs, the rocks of which resisted its passage to leeward, and already was washing up on the surface of the Reef, in places, threatening them with a general inundation. It was necessary to look after the security of various articles that were scattered about on the outer plain, and our mariners went ashore to do so.

Although intending so soon to abandon the Reef altogether, a sense of caution induced Mark to take everything he could within the crater. All the lower portions of the outer plain were already covered with water, and those sagacious creatures, the hogs, showed by their snuffing and disturbed manner of running about, that they had internal as well as external warnings of danger. Mark pulled aside the curtain, and let all the animals into the crater. Poor Kitty was delighted to get on the Summit, whither she soon found her way, by ascending the steps commonly used by her masters. Fortunately for the plants, the grass was in too great abundance, and too grateful to her, not to be her choice in preference to any other food. As for the pigs, they got at work in a pile of sea-weed, and overlooked the garden, which was at some distance, until fairly glutted, and ready to lie down.

In the meanwhile the tempest increased in violence, the sea continued to pile among the rocks, and the water actually covered the whole of the outer plain of the Reef. Now it was that Mark comprehended how the base of the crater had been worn by water, the waves washing past it with tremendous violence. There was actually a strong current running over the whole of the reef, without the crater; the water rushing to leeward, as if glad to get past the obstacle of the island on any terms, in order to hasten away before the tempest. Mark was fully half an hour engaged in looking to his marquee and its contents, all of which were exposed, more or less, to the power of the gale. After securing his books, furniture, &c., and seeing that the stays of the marquee itself were likely to hold out, he cast an eye to the ship, which was on that side of the island, also. The staunch old 'Cocus, as Bob called her, was rising and falling with the waves that now disturbed her usually placid basin; but, as yet, her cable and anchor held her, and no harm was done. Fortunately, our mariners, when they unbent the sails, had sent down all the upper and lighter spars, and had lowered the fore and main yards on the gunwale, measures of precaution that greatly lessened the strain on her ground-tackle. The top-gallant-masts had also been lowered, and the vessel was what seamen usually term 'snug.' Mark would have been very, very sorry to see her lost, even though he did expect to have very little more use out of her; for he loved the craft from habit.

After taking this look at the ship, our mate passed round the Summit, having two or three tumbles on his way in consequence of puffs of wind, until he reached the point over the gate-way, which was that nearest to the ship-yard. It now occurred to him that possibly it might become necessary to look a little to the security of the Neshamony, for by this time the water on the reef was two or three feet deep. To his surprise, on looking round for Bob, whom he thought to be at work securing property near the gateway, he ascertained that the honest fellow had waded down to the ship-yard, and clambered on board the pinnace, with a view to take care of her. The distance between the point where Mark now stood and the Neshamony exceeded half a mile, and communication with the voice would have been next to impossible, had the wind not blown as it did. With the roaring of the seas, and the howling of the gale, it was of course entirely out of the question. Mark, however, could see his friend, and see that he was gesticulating, in the most earnest manner, for himself to join him. Then it was he first perceived that the pinnace was in motion, seeming to move on her ways. Presently the blockings were washed from under her, and the boat went astern half her length at a single surge. Mark made a bound down the hill, intending to throw himself into the racing surf, and to swim off to the aid of Betts; but, pausing an instant to choose a spot at which to get down the steep, he looked towards the ship-yard, and saw the pinnace lifted on a sea, and washed fairly clear of the land!

Chapter IX

> "Man's rich with little, were his judgments true;
> Nature is frugal, and her wants are few;
> These few wants answered bring sincere delights,
> But fools create themselves new appetites."
>
> —Young

It would have been madness in Mark to pursue his intention. A boat, or craft of any sort, once adrift in such a gale, could not have been overtaken by even one of those islanders who are known to pass half their lives in the water; and the young man sunk down on the rock, almost gasping for breath in the intensity of his distress. He felt more for Bob than he did for himself, for escape with life appeared to him to be a forlorn hope for his friend. Nevertheless, the sturdy old sea-dog who was cast adrift, amid the raging of the elements, comported himself in a way to do credit to his training. There was nothing like despair in his manner of proceeding; but so coolly and intelligently did he set about taking care of his craft, that Mark soon found himself a curious and interested observer of all he did, feeling quite as much of admiration for Bob's steadiness and skill, as concern for his danger.

Betts knew too well the uselessness of throwing over his kedge to attempt anchoring. Nor was it safe to keep the boat in the trough of the sea, his wisest course being to run before the gale until he was clear of the rocks, when he might endeavour to lie-to, if his craft would bear it. In driving off the Reef the Neshamony had gone stern foremost, almost as a matter of course, vessels usually being laid down with their bows towards the land. No sooner did the honest old salt find he was fairly adrift, therefore, than he jumped into the stern-sheets and put the helm down. With stern-way on her, this caused the bows of the craft to fall off; and, as she came broadside to the gale, Mark thought she would fall over, also. Some idea could be formed of the power of the wind, in the fact that this sloop-rigged craft, without a rag of sail set, and with scarce any hamper aloft, no sooner caught the currents of air abeam, than she lay down to it, as one commonly sees such craft do under their canvas in stiff breezes.

It was a proof that the Neshamony was well modelled, that she began to draw ahead as soon as the wind took her fairly on her broadside, when Betts shifted the helm, and the pinnace fell slowly off. When she had got nearly before the wind, she came up and rolled to-windward like a ship, and Mark scarce breathed as he saw her plunging down upon the reefs, like a frantic steed that knows not whither he is rushing in his terror. From the elevated position he occupied, Mark could see the ocean as far as the spray, which filled the atmosphere, would allow of anything being seen at all. Places which were usually white with the foam of breakers, could not now be distinguished from any of the raging cauldron around them, and it was evident that Bob must run at hazard. Twenty times did Mark expect to see the pinnace disappear in the foaming waves, as it drove furiously onward; but, in each instance, the light and buoyant boat came up from cavities where our young man fancied it must be dashed to pieces, scudding away to leeward like the sea-fowl that makes its flight with wings nearly dipping. Mark now began to hope that his friend might pass over the many reefs that lay in his track, and gain the open water to leeward. The rise in the ocean favoured such an expectation, and no doubt was the reason why the Neshamony was not dashed to pieces within the first five minutes after she was washed off her ways. Once to leeward of the vast shoals that surrounded the crater, there was the probability of Bob's finding smoother water, and the chance of his riding out the tempest by bringing his little sloop up head to sea. The water through which the boat was then running was more like a cauldron, bubbling and boiling under some intense heat produced by subterranean fires, than the regular, rolling billows of the ocean when piled up by gales. Under the lee of the shoals this cauldron would disappear, while the mountain waves of the open ocean could not rise until a certain distance from the shallow water enabled them to 'get up,' as sailors express it. Mark saw the Neshamony for about a quarter of an hour after she was adrift, though long before the expiration of even that brief period she was invisible for many moments at a time, in consequence of the distance, her want of sail, her lowness in the water, and the troubled state of the element through which she was driving. The last look he got of her was at an instant when the spray was filling the atmosphere like a passing cloud; when it had driven away, the boat could no longer be seen!

Here was a sudden and a most unexpected change for the worse in the situation of Mark Woolston! Not only had he lost the means of getting off the island, but he had lost his friend and companion. It was true, Bob was a rough and an uncultivated associate; but he was honest as human frailty could leave a human being, true as steel in his attachments, strong in body, and of great professional skill. So great, indeed, was the last, that our young man was not without the hope he would be able to keep under the lee of the shoals until the gale broke, and then beat up through them, and still come to his rescue. There was one point, in particular, on which Mark felt unusual concern. Bob knew nothing whatever of navigation. It was impossible to teach him anything on that subject. He knew the points of the compass, but had no notion of the variations, of latitude or longitude, or of anything belonging to the purely mathematical part of the business. Twenty times had he asked Mark to give him the latitude and longitude of the crater; twenty times had he been told what they were, and just as often had he forgotten them. When questioned by his young friend, twenty-four hours after a lesson of this sort, if he remembered the figures at all, he was apt to give the latitude for the longitude, or the longitude for the latitude, the degrees for the minutes, or the minutes for the degrees. Ordinarily, however, he forgot all about the numbers themselves. Mark had in vain endeavoured to impress on his mind the single fact that any number which exceeded ninety must necessarily refer to longitude, and not to latitude; for Bob could not be made to remember even this simple distinction. He was just as likely to believe the Reef lay in the hundred and twentieth degree of latitude, as he was to fancy it lay in the twentieth. With such a head, therefore, it was but little to be expected Bob could give the information to others necessary to find the reef, even in the almost hopeless event of his ever being placed in circumstances to do so. Still, while so completely ignorant of mathematics and arithmetic, in all their details, few mariners could find their way better than Bob Betts by the simple signs of the ocean. He understood the compass perfectly, the variations excepted; and his eye was as true as that of the most experienced artist could be, when it became necessary to judge of the colour of the water. On many occasions had Mark known him intimate that the ship was in a current, and had a weatherly or a lee set, when the fact had escaped not only the officers, but the manufacturers of the charts. He judged by ripples, and sea-weed, and the other familiar signs of the seas, and these seldom failed him. While, therefore, there was not a seaman living less likely to find the Reef again, when driven off from its vicinity, by means of observations and the charts, there was not a seaman living more likely to find it, by resorting to the other helps of the navigator. On this last peculiarity Mark hung all his hopes of seeing his friend again, when the gale should abate.

Since the moment when all the charge of the ship fell upon his shoulders, by the loss of Captain Crutchely, Mark had never felt so desolate, as when he lost sight of Bob and the Neshamony. Then, indeed, did he truly feel himself to be alone, with none between him and his God with whom to commune. It is not surprising, therefore, that one so much disposed to cherish his intercourse with the Divine Spirit, knelt on the naked rock and prayed. After this act of duty and devotion, the young man arose, and endeavoured to turn his attention to the state of things around him.

The gale still continued with unabated fury. Each instant the water rose higher and higher on the Reef, until it began to enter within the crater, by means of the gutters that had been worn in the lava, covering two or three acres of the lower part of its plain. As for the Rancocus, though occasionally pitching more heavily than our young man could have believed possible behind the sea-wall, her anchor still held, and no harm had yet come to her. Finding it impossible to do any more, Mark descended into the crater, where it was a perfect lull, though the wind fairly howled on every side, and got into one of the South American hammocks, of which there had been two or three in the ship, and of which he had caused one to be suspended beneath the sort of tent he and poor Bob had erected near the garden. Here Mark remained all the rest of that day, and during the whole of the succeeding night. But for what he had himself previously seen, the roar of the ocean on the other side of his rocky shelter, and the scuffling of the winds about the Summit, he might not have been made conscious of the violence of the tempest that was raging so near him. Once and awhile, however, a puff of air would pass over him; but, on the whole, he was little affected by the storm, until near morning, when it rained violently. Fortunately, Mark had taken the precaution to give a low ridge to all his awnings and tent-coverings, which turned the water perfectly. When, therefore, he heard the pattering of the drops on the canvas, he did not rise, but remained in his hammock until the day returned. Previously to that moment, however, he dropped into a deep sleep, in which he lay several hours.

When consciousness returned to Mark, he lay half a minute trying to recall the past. Then he listened for the sounds of the tempest. All was still without, and, rising, he found that the sun was shining, and that a perfect calm reigned in the outer world. Water was lying in spots, in holes on the surface of the crater, where the pigs were drinking and the ducks bathing. Kitty stood in sight, on the topmost knoll of the Summit, cropping the young sweet grass that had so lately been refreshed by rain, disliking it none the less, probably, from the circumstance that a few particles of salt were to be found among it, the deposit of the spray. The garden looked smiling, the plants refreshed, and nothing as yet touched in it, by the visitors who had necessarily been introduced.

Our young man washed himself in one of the pools, and then crossed the plain to drive out the pigs and poultry, the necessity of husbanding his stores pressing even painfully on his mind. As he approached the gate-way, he saw that the sea had retired; and, certain that the animals would take care of themselves, he drove them through the hole, and dropped the sail before it. Then he sought one of the ascents, and was soon on the top of the hill. The trades had returned, but scarce blew in zephyrs; the sea was calm; the points in the reefs were easily to be seen; the ship was at rest and seemingly uninjured, and the whole view was one of the sweetest tranquillity and security. Already had the pent and piled waters diffused themselves, leaving the Reef as before, with the exception that those cavities which contained rain-water, during most of the year, now contained that which was not quite so palatable. This was a great temporary inconvenience, though the heavy showers of the past night had done a good deal towards sweetening the face of the rock, and had reduced most of the pools to a liquid that was brackish rather than salt. A great many fish lay scattered about, on the island, and Mark hastened down to examine their qualities.

The pigs and poultry were already at work on the game that was so liberally thrown in their way, and Mark felt indebted to these scavengers for aiding him in what he perceived was now a task indispensable to his comfort. After going to the ship, and breaking his fast, he returned to the crater, obtained a wheelbarrow, and set to work in earnest to collect the fish, which a very few hours' exposure to the sun of that climate would render so offensive as to make the island next to intolerable. Never in his life did our young friend work harder than he did all that morning. Each load of fish, as it was wheeled into the crater, was thrown into a trench already prepared for that purpose, and the ashes were hauled over it, by means of the hoe. Feeling the necessity of occupation to lessen his sorrow, as well as that of getting rid of pestilence, which he seriously apprehended from this inroad of animal substances, Mark toiled two whole days at this work, until fairly driven from it by the intolerable effluvium which arose, notwithstanding all he had done, on every side of the island. It is impossible to say what would have been consequences had not the birds come, in thousands, to his relief. They made quick work of it, clearing off the fish in numbers that would be nearly incredible. As it was, however, our young hermit was driven into the ship, where-he passed a whole week, the steadiness of the trades driving the disagreeable odours to leeward. At the end of that time he ventured ashore, where he found it possible to remain, though the Reef did not get purified for more than a month. Finding a great many fish still remaining that neither hog nor bird would touch, Mark made a couple of voyages to Loam Island, whence he brought two cargoes of the deposit, and landed at the usual place.

This he wheeled about the Reef, throwing two or three-shovels full on each offensive creature, thus getting rid of the effluvium and preparing a considerable store of excellent manure for his future husbandry. It may be as well said here, that, at odd times, he threw these little deposits into large heaps, and subsequently wheeled them into the crater, where they were mixed with the principal pile of compost that had now been, for months, collecting there.

It is a proof of the waywardness of human nature that we bear great misfortunes better than small ones. So it proved with Mark, on this occasion; for, much as he really regarded Bob, and serious as was the loss of his friend to himself, the effects of the inundation occupied his thoughts, and disturbed him more, just at that time, than the disappearance of the Neshamony. Nevertheless, our young man had not forgotten to look out for the missing boat, in readiness to hail its return with joy. He passed much of the week he was shut up in the ship in her topmast-cross-trees, vainly examining the sea to leeward, in the hope of catching a distant view of the pinnace endeavouring to bear up through the reefs. Several times he actually fancied he saw her; but it always turned out to be the wing of some gull, or the cap of a distant breaker. It was when Mark had come ashore again, and commenced the toil of covering the decayed fish, and of gathering them into piles, that these smaller matters supplanted the deep griefs of his solitude.

One of the annoyances to which our solitary man found himself most subject, was the glare produced by a burning sun on rocks and ashes of the drab colour of the crater. The spots of verdure that he had succeeded in producing on the Summit, not only relieved and refreshed his eyes, but they were truly delightful as aids to the view, as well as grateful to Kitty, which poor creature had, by this time, cropped them down to a pretty short herbage. This Mark knew, however, was an advantage to the grass, making it finer, and causing it to thicken at the roots. The success of this experiment, the annoyance to his eyes, and a feverish desire to be doing, which succeeded the disappearance of Botts, set Mark upon the project of sowing grass-seed over as much of the plain of the crater as he thought he should not have occasion to use for the purposes of tillage. To work he went then, scattering the seed in as much profusion as the quantity to be found in the ship would justify. Friend Abraham White had provided two barrels of the seed, and this went a good way. While thus employed a heavy shower fell, and thinking the rain a most favourable time to commit his grass-seeds to the earth, Mark worked through the whole of it, or for several hours, perspiring with the warmth and exercise.

This done, a look at the garden, with a free use of the hoe, was the next thing undertaken. That night Mark slept in his hammock, under the crater-awning, and when he awoke in the morning it was to experience a weight, like that of lead in his forehead, a raging thirst, and a burning fever. Now it was that our poor solitary hermit felt the magnitude of his imprudence and the weight of the evils of his peculiar situation. That he was about to be seriously ill he knew, and it behoved him to improve the time that remained to him, to the utmost. Everything useful to him was in the ship, and thither it became indispensable for him to repair, if he wished to retain even a chance for life. Opening an umbrella, then, and supporting his tottering legs by a cane, Mark commenced a walk of very near a mile, under an almost perpendicular sun, at the hottest season of the year. Twenty times did the young man think he should be compelled to sink on the bare rock, where there is little question he would soon have expired, under the united influence of the fever within and the burning heat without. Despair urged him on, and, after pausing often to rest, he succeeded in entering the cabin, at the end of the most perilous hour he had ever yet passed.

No words of ours can describe the grateful sense of coolness, in spite of the boiling blood in his veins, that Mark Woolston experienced when he stepped beneath the shade of the poop-deck of the Rancocus. The young man knew that he was about to be seriously ill and his life might depend on the use he made of the next hour, or half-hour, even. He threw himself on a settee, to get a little rest, and while there he endeavoured to reflect on his situation, and to remember what he ought to do. The medicine-chest always stood in the cabin, and he had used its contents too often among the crew, not to have some knowledge of their general nature and uses. Potions were kept prepared in that depository, and he staggered to the table, opened the chest, took a ready-mixed dose of the sort he believed best for him, poured water on it from the filterer, and swallowed it. Our mate ever afterwards believed that draught saved his life. It soon made him deadly sick, and produced an action in his whole system. For an hour he was under its influence, when he was enabled to get into his berth, exhausted and literally unable any longer to stand. How long he remained in that berth, or near it rather-for he was conscious of having crawled from it in quest of water, and for other purposes, on several occasions-but, how long he was confined to his cabin, Mark Woolston never knew. The period was certainly to be measured by days, and he sometimes fancied by weeks. The first probably was the truth, though it might have been a fortnight. Most of that time his head was light with fever, though there were intervals when reason was, at least partially, restored to him, and he became painfully conscious of the horrors of his situation. Of food and water he had a sufficiency, the filterer and a bread-bag being quite near him, and he helped himself often from the first, in particular; a single mouthful of the ship's biscuit commonly proving more than he could swallow, even after it was softened in the water. At length he found himself indisposed to rise at all, and he certainly remained eight-and-forty hours in his berth, without quitting it, and almost without sleeping, though most of the time in a sort of doze.

At length the fever abated in its violence, though it began to assume, what for a man in Mark Woolston's situation was perhaps more dangerous, a character of a low type, lingering in his system and killing him by inches. Mark was aware of his condition, and though: of the means of relief. The ship had some good Philadelphia porter in her, and a bottle of it stood on a shelf over his berth. This object caught his eye, and he actually longed for a draught of that porter. He had sufficient strength to raise himself high enough to reach it, but it far exceeded his powers to draw the cork, even had the ordinary means been at hand, which they were not. There was a hammer on the shelf, however, and with that instrument he did succeed in making a hole in the side of the bottle, and in filling a tumbler. This liquor he swallowed at a single draught. It tasted deliciously to him, and he took a second tumbler full, when he lay down, uncertain as to the consequences. That his head was affected by these two glasses of porter, Mark himself was soon aware, and shortly after drowsiness followed. After lying in an uneasy slumber for half an hour, his whole person was covered with a gentle perspiration, in which condition, after drawing the sheet around him, the sick man fell asleep.

Our patient never knew how long he slept, on this all-important occasion. The period certainly included part of two days and one entire night; but, afterwards, when Mark endeavoured to correct his calendar, and to regain something, like a record of the time, he was inclined to think he must have lain there two nights with the intervening day. When he awoke, Mark was immediately sensible that he was free from disease. He was not immediately sensible, nevertheless, how extremely feeble disease had left him. At first, he fancied he had only to rise, take nourishment, and go about his ordinary pursuits. But the sight of his emaciated limbs, and the first effort he made to get up, convinced him that he had a long state of probation to go through, before he became the man he had been a week or two before. It was well, perhaps, that his head was so clear, and his judgment so unobscured at this, his first return to consciousness.

Mark deemed it a good symptom that he felt disposed to eat. How many days he had been altogether without nourishment he could not say, but they must have been several; nor had he received more than could be obtained from a single ship's biscuit since his attack. All this came to his mind, with a distinct recollection that he must be his own physician and nurse. For a few minutes he lay still, during which he addressed himself to God, with thanks for having spared his life until reason was restored. Then he bethought him, well as his feeble state would allow, of the course he ought to pursue. On a table in the cabin, and in sight of his berth, through the state-room door, was a liquor-case, containing wines, brandy, and gin. Our sick man thought all might yet go well, could he get a few spoonsfull of an excellent port wine which that case, contained, and which had been provided expressly for cases of sickness. To do this, however, it was necessary to obtain the key, to open the case, and to pour out the liquor; three things, of which he distrusted his powers to perform that which was the least difficult.

The key of the liquor-case was in the draw of an open secretary, which, fortunately, stood between him and the table. Another effort was made to rise, which so far succeeded as to enable the invalid to sit up in his bed. The cool breeze which aired the cabin revived him a little, and he was able to stretch out a hand and turn the cock of the filterer, which he had himself drawn near his berth, while under the excitement of fever, in order to obtain easy access to water. Accidentally this filterer stood in a draught, and the quart or two of water that had not yet evaporated was cool and palatable; that is, cool for a ship and such a climate. One swallow of the water was all Mark ventured on, but it revived him more than he could believe possible. Near the glass into which he had drawn the water, lay a small piece of pilot bread, and this he dropped into the tumbler. Then he ventured to try his feet, when he found a dizziness come over him, that compelled him to fall back on his berth. Recovering from this in a minute or two, a second attempt succeeded better, and the poor fellow, by supporting himself against the bulkheads, and by leaning on chairs, was enabled to reach the desk. The key was easily obtained, and the table was next reached. Here Mark sunk into a chair, as much exhausted as he would have been, previously to his illness, by a desperate effort to defend life.

The invalid was in his shirt, and the cool sea-breeze had the effect of an air-bath on him. It revived him in a little while, when he applied the key, opened the case, got out the bottle by using both hands, though it was nearly empty, and poured out a wine-glass of the liquor. With these little exertions he was so much exhausted as almost to faint. Nothing saved him, probably, but a sip of the wine which he took from the glass as it stood on the table. It has been much the fashion, of late years, to decry wine, and this because it is a gift of Providence that has been greatly abused. In Mark Woolston's instance it proved, what it was designed to be, a blessing instead of a curse. That single sip of wine produced an effect on him like that of magic. It enabled him soon to obtain his tumbler of water, into which he poured the remainder of the liquor. With the tumbler in his hand, the invalid next essayed to cross the cabin, and to reach the berth in the other state-room. He was two or three minutes in making this passage, sustained by a chair, into which he sunk not less than three times, and revived by a few more sips of the wine and water. In this state-room was a bed with clean cool linen, that had been prepared for Bob, but which that worthy fellow had pertinaciously refused to use, out of respect to his officer. On these sheets Mark now sank, almost exhausted. He had made a happy exchange, however, the freshness and sweetness of the new bed, of itself, acting as delicious restoratives.

After resting a few minutes, the solitary invalid formed a new plan of proceeding. He knew the importance of not over-exerting himself, but he also knew the importance of cleanliness and of a renovation of his strength. By this time the biscuit had got to be softened in the wine and water, and he took a piece, and after masticating it well, swallowed it. This was positively the first food the sick and desolate young man had received in a week. Fully aware of this, he abstained from taking a second mouthful, though sorely pressed to it by hunger. So strong was the temptation, and so sweet did that morse taste, that Mark felt he might not refrain unless he had something to occupy his mind for a few minutes. Taking a small swallow of the wine and water, he again got on his feet, and staggered to the drawer in which poor Captain Crutchely had kept his linen. Here he got a shirt, and tottered on as far as the quarter-deck. Beneath the awning Mark had kept the section of a hogshead, as a bathing-tub, and for the purpose of catching the rain-water that ran from the awning, Kitty often visiting the ship and drinking from this reservoir.

The invalid found the tub full of fresh and sweet water, and throwing aside the shirt in which he had lain so long, he rather fell than seated himself in the water. After remaining a sufficient, time to recover his breath, Mark washed his head, and long matted beard, and all parts of his frame, as well as his strength would allow. He must have remained in the water several minutes, when he managed to tear himself from it, as fearful of excess from this indulgence as from eating. The invalid now felt like a new man! It is scarcely possible to express the change that came over his feelings, when he found himself purified from the effects of so long a confinement in a feverish bed, without change, or nursing of any sort. After drying himself as well as he could with a towel, though the breeze and the climate did that office for him pretty effectually, Mark put on the clean, fresh shirt, and tottered back to his own berth, where he fell on the mattress, nearly exhausted. It was half-an-hour before he moved again, though all that time experiencing the benefits of the nourishment taken, and the purification undergone. The bath, moreover, had acted as a tonic, giving a stimulus to the whole system. At the end of the half hour, the young man took another mouthful of the biscuit, half emptied the tumbler, fell back on his pillow, and was soon in a sweet sleep.

It was near sunset when Mark lost his consciousness on this occasion, nor did he recover it until the light of day was once more cheering the cabin. He had slept profoundly twelve hours, and this so much the more readily from the circumstance that he had previously refreshed himself with a bath and clean linen. The first consciousness of his situation was accompanied with the bleat of poor Kitty. That gentle animal, intended by nature to mix with herds, had visited the cabin daily, and had been at the sick man's side, when his fever was at its height; and had now come again, as if to inquire after his night's rest. Mark held out his hand, and spoke to his companion, for such she was, and thought she was rejoiced to hear his voice again, and to be allowed to lick his hand. There was great consolation in this mute intercourse, poor Mark feeling the want of sympathy so much as to find a deep pleasure in this proof of affection even in a brute.

Mark now arose, and found himself sensibly improved by his night's rest, the washing, and the nourishment received, little as the last had been. His first step was to empty the tumbler, bread and all. Then he took another bath, the last doing quite as much good, he fancied, as his breakfast. All that day, the young man managed his case with the same self-denial and prudence, consuming a ship's biscuit in the course of the next twenty-four hours, and taking two or three glasses of the wine, mixed with water and sweetened with sugar. In the afternoon he endeavoured to shave, but the first effort convinced him he was getting well too fast.

It was thrice twenty-four hours after his first bath, before Mark Woolston had sufficient strength to reach the galley and light a fire. In this he then succeeded, and he treated himself to a cup of good warm tea. He concocted some dishes of arrow-root and cocoa, too, in the course of that and the next day, continuing his baths, and changing his linen repeatedly. On the fifth day, he got off his beard, which was a vast relief to him, and by the end of the week he actually crawled up on the poop, where he could get a sight of his domains.

The Summit was fast getting to be really green in considerable patches, for the whole rock was now covered with grass. Kitty was feeding quietly enough on the hillside, the gentle creature having learned to pass the curtain at the gate, and go up and down the ascents at pleasure. Mark scarce dared to look for his hogs, but there they were rooting and grunting about the Reef, actually fat and contented. He knew that this foreboded evil to his garden, for the creatures must have died for want of food during his illness, had not some such relief been found. As yet, his strength would not allow him to go ashore, and he was obliged to content himself with this distant view of his estate. The poultry appeared to be well, and the invalid fancied he saw chickens running at the side of one of the hens.

It was a week later before Mark ventured to go as far as the crater. On entering it, he found that his conjectures concerning the garden were true. Two-thirds of it had been dug over by the snouts of his pigs, quite as effectually as he could have done it, in his vigour, with the spade. Tops and roots had been demolished alike, and about as much wasted as had been consumed, Kitty was found, *flagrante delictu*, nibbling at the beans, which, by this time, were dead ripe. The peas, and beans, and Indian corn had made good picking for the poultry; and everything possessing life had actually been living in abundance, while the sick man had lain unconscious of even his own, existence, in a state as near death as life.

Mark found his awning standing, and was glad to rest an hour or two in his hammock, after looking at the garden. While there the hogs entered the crater, and made a meal before his eyes. To his surprise, the sow was followed by ten little creatures, that were already getting to be of the proper size for eating. A ravenous appetite was now Mark's greatest torment, and the coarse food of the ship was rather too heavy for him. He had exhausted his wit in contriving dishes of flour, and pined for something more grateful than salted beef, or pork. Although he somewhat distrusted his strength, yet longing induced him to make an experiment. A fowling-piece, loaded with ball, was under the awning; and freshening the priming, the young man watched his opportunity when one of the grunters was in a good position, and shot it in the head. Then cutting its throat with a knife, he allowed it to bleed, when he cleaned, and *skinned it*. This last operation was not very artistical, but it was necessary in the situation of our invalid. With the carcase of this pig, which was quite as much as he could even then carry back to the ship, though the animal was not yet six weeks old, Mark made certain savoury and nourishing dishes, that contributed essentially to the restoration of his strength. In the course of the ensuing month three more of the pigs shared the same fate, as did half-a-dozen of the brood of chickens already mentioned, though the last were not yet half-grown. But Mark felt, now, as if he could eat the crater, though as yet he had not been able to clamber to the Summit.

Chapter X

> "Yea! long as nature's humblest child
> Hath kept her temple undefiled
> By sinful sacrifice,
> Earth's fairest scenes are all his own,
> He is a monarch, and his throne
> Is built amid the skies."
>
> —Wilson

Our youthful hermit was quite two months in regaining his strength, though, by the end of one he was able to look about him, and turn his hand to many little necessary jobs. The first thing he undertook was to set up a gate that would keep the animals on the outside of the crater. The pigs had not only consumed much the largest portion of his garden truck, but they had taken a fancy to break up the crust of that part of the crater where the grass was showing itself, and to this inroad upon his meadows, Mark had no disposition to submit. He had now ascertained that the surface of the plain, though of a rocky appearance, was so far shelly and porous that the seeds had taken very generally; and as soon as their roots worked their way into the minute crevices, he felt certain they would of themselves convert the whole surface into a soil sufficiently rich to nourish the plants he wished to produce there. Under such circumstances he did not desire the assistance of the hogs. As yet, however, the animals had done good, rather than harm to the garden, by stirring the soil up, and mixing the sea-weed and decayed fish with it; but among the grass they threatened to be more destructive; than useful. In most places the crust of the plain was just thick enough to bear the weight of a man, and Mark, no geologist, by the way, came to the conclusion that it existed at all more through the agency of the salt deposited in ancient floods, than from any other cause. According to the great general law of the earth, soil should have been formed from rock, and not rock from soil: though there certainly are cases in which the earths indurate, as well as become disintegrated. As we are not professing to give a scientific account of these matters, we shall simply state the facts, leaving better scholars than ourselves to account for their existence.

Mark made his gate out of the fife-rail, at the foot of the mainmast, sawing off the stanchions for that purpose. With a little alteration it answered perfectly, being made to swing from a post that was wedged into the arch, by cutting it to the proper length. As this was the first attack upon the Rancocus that had yet been made, by axe or saw, it made the young man melancholy; and it was only with great reluctance that he could prevail on himself to begin what appeared like the commencement of breaking up the good craft. It was done, however, and the gate was hung, thereby saving the rest of the crop. It was high time; the hogs and poultry, to say nothing of Kitty, having already got their full share. The inroads of the first, however, were of use in more ways than one, since they taught our young cultivator a process by which he could get his garden turned up at a cheap rate. They also suggested to him an idea that he subsequently turned to good account. Having dug his roots so early, it occurred to Mark that, in so low a climate, and with such a store of manure, he might raise two crops in a year, those which came in the cooler months varying a little in their properties from those which came in the warmer. On this hint he endeavoured to improve, commencing anew beds that, without it, would probably have lain fallow some months longer.

In this way did our young man employ-himself until he found his strength perfectly restored. But the severe illness he had gone through, with the sad views it had given him of some future day, when he might be compelled to give up life itself, without a friendly hand to smooth his pillow, or to close his eyes, led him to think far more seriously than he had done before, on the subject of the true character of our probationary condition here on earth, and on the unknown and awful future to which it leads us. Mark had been carefully educated on the subject of religion, and was well enough disposed to enter into the inquiry in a suitable spirit of humility; but, the grave circumstances in which he was now placed, contributed largely to the clearness of his views of the necessity of preparing for the final change. Cut off, as he was, from all communion with his kind; cast on what was, when he first knew it, literally a barren rock in the midst of the vast Pacific Ocean, Mark found himself, by a very natural operation of causes, in much closer communion with his Creator, than he might have been in the haunts of the world. On the Reef, there was little to divert his thoughts from their true course; and the very ills that pressed upon him, became so many guides to his gratitude by showing, through the contrasts, the many blessings which had been left him by the mercy of the hand that had struck him. The nights in that climate and season were much the pleasantest portions of the four-and-twenty hours. There were no exhalations from decayed vegetable substances or stagnant pools, to create miasma, but the air was as pure and little to be feared under a placid moon as under a noon-day sun. The first hours of night, therefore, were those in which our solitary man chose to take most of his exercise, previously to his complete restoration to strength; and then it was that he naturally fell into an obvious and healthful communion with the stars.

So far as the human mind has as yet been able to penetrate the mysteries of our condition here on-earth, with the double connection between the past and the future, all its just inferences tend to the belief in an existence of a vast and beneficent design. We have somewhere heard, or read, that the gipsies believe that men are the fallen angels, oiling their way backward on the fatal path along which hey formerly rushed to perdition. This may not be, probably is not true in its special detail; but that men are placed here to prepare themselves for a future and higher condition of existence, is not only agreeable to our consciousness, but is in harmony with revelation. Among the many things that have been revealed to us, where so many are hid, we are told that our information is to increase, as we draw nearer to the millennium, until "The whole earth shall be filled with the knowledge of the Lord, as the waters cover the sea." We may be far from that blessed day; probably are; but he has lived in vain, who has dwelt his half century in the midst of the civilization of this our own age, and does not see around him the thousand proofs of the tendency of things to the fulfilment of the decrees, announced to us ages ago by the pens of holy men. Rome, Greece, Egypt, and all that we know of the past, which comes purely of man and his passions; empires, dynasties, heresies and novelties, come and go like the changes of the seasons; while the only thing that can be termed stable, is the slow but sure progress of prophecy. The agencies that have been employed to bring about the great ends foretold so many centuries since, are so very natural, that we often lose sight of the mighty truth in its seeming simplicity. But, the signs of the times are not to be mistaken. Let any man of fifty, for instance, turn his eyes toward the East, the land of Judea, and compare its condition, its promises of to-day, with those that existed in his own youth, and ask himself how the change has been produced. That which the Richards and Sts. Louis of the middle ages could not effect with their armed hosts, is about to happen as a consequence of causes so obvious and simple that they are actually overlooked by the multitude. The Ottoman power and Ottoman prejudices are melting away, as it might be under the heat of divine truth, which is clearing for itself a path that will lead to the fulfilment of its own predictions.

Among the agents that are to be employed, in impressing the human race with a sense of the power and benevolence of the Deity, we think the science of astronomy, with its mechanical auxiliaries, is to act its full share. The more deeply we penetrate into the arcana of nature, the stronger becomes the proofs of design; and a deity thus obviously, tangibly admitted, the more profound will become the reverence for his character and power. In Mark Woolston's youth, the great progress which has since been made in astronomy, more especially in the way of its details through observations, had but just commenced. A vast deal, it is true, had been accomplished in the way of pure science, though but little that came home to the understandings and feelings of the mass. Mark's education had given him an outline of what Herschel and his contemporaries had been about, however; and when he sat on the Summit, communing with the stars, and through those distant and still unknown worlds, with their Divine First Cause, it was with as much familiarity with the subject as usually belongs to the liberally educated, without carrying a particular branch of learning into its recesses. He had increased his school acquisitions a little, by the study and practice of Navigation, and had several works that he was fond of reading, which may have made him a somewhat more accurate astronomer than those who get only leading ideas on the subject. Hours at a time did Mark linger on the Summit, studying the stars in the clear, transparent atmosphere of the tropics, his spirit struggling the while to get into closer communion with that dread Being which had produced all these mighty results; among which the existence of the earth, its revolutions, its heats and colds, its misery and happiness, are but specks in the incidents of a universe. Previously to this period, he had looked into these things from curiosity and a love of science; now, they impressed him with the deepest sense of the power and wisdom of the Deity, and caused him the better to understand his own position in the scale of created beings.

Not only did our young hermit study the stars with his own eyes, but he had the aid of instruments. The ship had two very good spy-glasses, and Mark himself was the owner of a very neat reflecting telescope, which he had purchased with his wages, and had brought with him as a source of amusement and instruction. To this telescope there was a brass stand, and he conveyed it to the tent on the Summit, where it was kept for use. Aided by this instrument, Mark could see the satellites of Jupiter and Saturn, the ring of the latter, the belts of the former, and many of the phenomena of the moon. Of course, the spherical forms of all the nearer planets, then known to astronomers, were plainly to be seen by the assistance of this instrument; and there is no one familiar fact connected with our observations of the heavenly bodies, that strikes the human mind, through the senses, as forcibly as this. For near a month, Mark almost passed the nights' gazing at the stars, and reflecting on their origin and uses. He had no expectations of making discoveries, or of even adding to his own stores of knowledge: but his thoughts were brought nearer to his Divine Creator by investigations of this sort; for where a zealous mathematician might have merely exulted in the confirmation of some theory by means of a fact, he saw the hand of God instead of the solution of a problem. Thrice happy would it be for the man of science, could he ever thus hold his powers in subjection to the great object for which they were brought into existence; and, instead of exulting in, and quarrelling about the pride of human reason, be brought to humble himself and his utmost learning, at the feet of Infinite Knowledge and power, and wisdom, as they are thus to be traced in the path of the Ancient of Days!

By the time his strength returned, Mark had given up, altogether, the hope of ever seeing Betts again. It was just possible that the poor fellow might fall in with a ship, or find his way to some of the islands; but, if he did so, it would be the result of chance and not of calculations. The pinnace was well provisioned, had plenty of water, and, tempests excepted, was quite equal to navigating the Pacific; and there was a faint hope that Bob might continue his course to the eastward, with a certainty of reaching some part of South America in time. If he should lake this course, and succeed, what would be the consequence? Who would put sufficient faith in the story of a simple seaman, like Robert Betts, and send a ship to look for Mark Woolston? In these later times, the government would doubtless despatch a vessel of war on such an errand, did no other means of rescuing the man offer; but, at the close of the last century, government did not exercise that much of power. It scarcely protected its seamen from the English press-gang and the Algerine slave-driver; much less did it think of rescuing a solitary individual from a rock in the midst of the Pacific. American vessels did then roam over that distant ocean, but it was comparatively in small numbers, and under circumstances that promised but little to the hopes of the hermit. It was a subject he did not like to dwell on, and he kept his thoughts as much diverted from it as it was in his power so to do.

The season had now advanced into as much of autumn as could be found within the tropics, and on land so low. Everything in the garden had ripened, and much had been thrown out to the pigs and poultry, in anticipation of its decay. Mark saw that it was time to re-commence his beds, selecting such seed as would best support the winter of that climate, if winter it could be called. In looking around him, he made a regular survey of all his possessions, inquiring into the state of each plant he had put into the ground, as well as into that of the ground itself. First, then, as respects the plants.

The growth of the oranges, lemons, cocoa-nuts, limes, figs, &c., placed in rows beneath the cliffs, had been prodigious. The water had run off the adjacent rocks and kept them well moistened most of the season, though a want of rain was seldom known on the Reef. Of the two, too much, rather than too little water fell; a circumstance that was of great service, however, in preserving the stock, which had used little beside that it found in the pools, for the last ten months. The shrubs, or little trees, were quite a foot high, and of an excellent colour. Mark gave each of them a dressing with the hoe, and manured all with a sufficient quantity of the guano. About half he transplanted to spots more favourable, putting the cocoa-nuts, in particular, as near the sea as he could get them.

With respect to the other plants, it was found that each had flourished precisely in proportion to its adaptation to the climate. The products of some were increased in size, while those of others had dwindled. Mark took note of these facts, determining to cultivate those most which succeeded best. The melons of both sorts, the tomatoes, the egg-plants, the peppers, cucumbers, onions, beans, corn, sweet-potatoes, &c. &c., had all flourished; while the Irish potato, in particular, had scarce produced a tuber at all.

As for the soil, on examination Mark found it had been greatly improved by the manure, tillage and water it had received. The hogs were again let in to turn it over with their snouts, and this they did most effectually in the course of two or three days. By this time, in addition to the three grown porkers our young man possessed, there were no less than nine young ones. This number was getting to be formidable, and he saw the necessity of killing off, in order to keep them within reasonable limits. One of the fattest and best he converted into pickled pork, not from any want of that article, there being still enough left in the ship to last him several years, but because he preferred it corned to that which had been in the salt so long a time. He saw the mistake he had made in allowing the pigs to get to be so large, since the meat would spoil long before he could consume even the smallest-sized shoats. For their own good, however, he was compelled to shoot no less than five, and these he buried entire, in deep places in his garden, having heard that earth which had imbibed animal substances, in this way, was converted into excellent manure.

Mark now made a voyage to Loam Island, in quest of a cargo, using the raft, and towing the dingui. It was on this occasion that our young man was made to feel how much he had lost, in the way of labour, in being deprived of the assistance of Bob. He succeeded in loading his raft, however, and was just about to sail for home again, when it occurred to him that possibly the seeds and roots of the asparagus he had put into a corner of the deposit might have come to something. Sure enough, on going to the spot, Mark found that the seed had taken well, and hundreds of young plants were growing flourishingly, while plants fit to eat had pushed their tops through the loam, from the roots. This was an important discovery, asparagus being a vegetable of which Mark was exceedingly fond, and one easily cultivated. In that climate, and in a soil sufficiently rich, it might be made to send up new shoots the entire year; and there was little fear of scurvy so long as he could obtain plenty of this plant to eat. The melons and other vegetables, however, had removed all Mark's dread of that formidable disease; more especially as he had now eggs, chickens, and fresh fish, the latter in quantities that were almost oppressive. In a word, the means of subsistence now gave the young man no concern whatever. When he first found himself on a barren rock, indeed, the idea had almost struck terror into his mind; but, now that he had ascertained that his crater could be cultivated, and promised, like most other extinct volcanoes, unbounded fertility, he could no longer apprehend a disease which is commonly owing to salted provisions.

When Mark found his health completely re-established, he sat down and drew up a regular plan of dividing his time between work, contemplation, and amusement. Fortunately, perhaps, for one who lived in a climate where vegetation was so luxuriant when it could be produced at all, work was pressed into his service as an amusement. Of the last, there was certainly very little, in the common acceptation of the word; but our hermit was not without it altogether. He studied the habits of the sea-birds that congregated in thousands around so many of the rocks of the Reef, though so few scarce ever ventured on the crater island. He made voyages to and fro, usually connecting business with pleasure. Taking favourable times for such purposes, he floated several cargoes of loam to the Reef, as well as two enormous rafts of sea-weed. Mark was quite a month in getting these materials into his compost heap, which he intended should lie in a pile during the winter, in order that it might be ready for spading in the spring. We use these terms by way of distinguishing the seasons, though of winter, strictly speaking, there was none. Of the two, the grass grew better at mid-winter than at mid-summer, the absence of the burning heat of the last being favourable to its growth. As the season advanced, Mark saw his grass very sensibly increase, not only in surface, but in thickness. There were now spots of some size, where a turf was forming, nature performing all her tasks in that genial climate, in about a fourth of the time it would take to effect the same object in the temperate zone. On examining these places, Mark came to the conclusion that the roots of his grasses acted as cultivators, by working their way into the almost insensible crevices of the crust, letting in air and water to places whence they had hitherto been excluded. This seemed, in particular, to be the case with the grass that grew within the crater, which had increased so much in the course of what may be termed the winter, that it was really fast converting a plain of a light drab colour, that was often painful to the eyes, into a plot of as lovely verdure as ever adorned the meadows of a Swiss cottage. It became desirable to keep this grass down, and Kitty being unable to crop a meadow of so many acres, Mark was compelled to admit his pigs and poultry again. This he did at stated times only, however; or when he was at work himself in the garden, and could prevent their depredations on his beds. The rooting gave him the most trouble; but this he contrived in a great measure to prevent, by admitting his hogs only when they were eager for grass, and turning them out as soon as they began to generalize, like an epicure picking his nuts after dinner.

It was somewhere near mid-winter, by Mark's calculations, when the young man commenced a new task that was of great importance to his comfort, and which *might* affect his future life. He had long determined to lay down a boat, one of sufficient size to explore the whole reef in, if not large enough to carry him out to sea. The dingui was altogether too small for labour; though exceedingly useful in its way, and capable of being managed even in pretty rough water by a skilful hand, it wanted both weight and room. It was difficult to float in, even a raft of sea-weed, with so light a boat; and as for towing the raft, it was next to impossible. But the raft was unwieldy, and when loaded down, besides carrying very little for its great weight, it was very much at the mercy of the currents and waves. Then the construction of a boat was having an important purpose in view, and, in that sense, was a desirable undertaking.

Mark had learned so much in putting the pinnace together, that he believed himself equal to this new undertaking. Materials enough remained in the ship to make half-a-dozen boats, and in tumbling over the lumber he had found a quantity of stuff that had evidently been taken in with a view to repair boats, if not absolutely to construct them. A ship's hold is such an omnium gatherum, stowage being necessarily so close, that it usually requires time for who does not know where to put his hand on everything, to ascertain how much or how little is to be found in it. Such was the fact with Mark, whose courtship and marriage had made a considerable inroad on his duties as a mate. As he overhauled the hold, he daily found fresh reasons for believing that Friend Abraham White had made provisions, of one sort and another, of which he was profoundly ignorant, but which, as the voyage had terminated, proved to be of the greatest utility. Thus it was, that just as he was about to commence getting out these great requisites from new planks, he came across a stem, stern-frame, and keel of a boat, that was intended to be eighteen feet long. Of course our young man profited by this discovery, getting the materials of all sorts, including these, round to the ship-yard by means of the raft.

For the next two months, or until he had reason to believe spring had fairly set in, Mark toiled faithfully at his boat. Portions of his work gave him a great deal of trouble; some of it on account of ignorance of the craft, and some on account of his being alone. Getting the awning up anew cost poor Mark the toil of several days, and this because his single strength was not sufficient to hoist the corners of that heavy course, even when aided by watch-tackles. He was compelled to rig a crab, with which he effected his purpose, reserving the machine to aid him on other occasions. Then the model of the boat cost him a great deal of time and labour. Mark knew a good bottom when he saw it, but that was a very different thing from knowing how to make one. Of the rules of draughting he was altogether ignorant, and his eye was his only guide. He adopted a plan that was sufficiently ingenious, though it would never do to build a navy on the same principle.

Having a great plenty of deal, Mark got out in the rough about twice as many timbers for one side of his boat as would be required, in this thin stuff, when he set them up in their places. Aided by this beginning, the young man began to dub and cut away, until he got each piece into something very near the shape his eye told him it ought to be. Even after he had got as far as this, our boat-builder passed a week in shaving, and planing, and squinting, and in otherwise reducing his lines to fair proportions. Satisfied, at length, with the bottom he had thus fashioned, Mark took out just one half of his pieces, leaving the other half standing. After these moulds did he saw and cut his boat's timbers, making, in each instance, duplicates. When the ribs and floors of his craft were ready, he set them up in the vacancies, and secured them, after making an accurate fit with the pieces left standing. On knocking away the deal portions of his work, Mark had the frame of his boat complete. This was much the most troublesome part of the whole job; nor was it finished, when the young man was obliged, by the progress of the seasons, to quit the ship-yard for the garden.

Mark had adopted a system of diet and a care of his person, that kept him in perfect health, illness being the evil that he most dreaded. His food was more than half vegetable, several plants having come forward even in the winter; and the asparagus, in particular, yielding at a rate that would have made the fortune of a London gardener. The size of the plants he cut was really astounding, a dozen stems actually making a meal. The hens laid all winter, and eggs were never wanting. The corned pork gave substance, as well as a relish, to all the dishes the young man cooked; and the tea, sugar and coffee, promising to hold out years longer, the table still gave him little concern. Once in a month, or so, he treated himself to a bean-soup, or a pea-soup, using the stores of the Rancocus for that purpose, foreseeing that the salted meats would spoil after a time, and the dried vegetables get to be worthless, by means of insects and worms. By this time, however, there were fresh crops of both those vegetables, which grew better in the winter than they could in the summer, in that hot climate. Fish, too, were used as a change, whenever the young man had an inclination for that sort of food, which was as often as three or four times a week; the little pan-fish already mentioned, being of a sort of which one would scarcely ever tire.

It being a matter of some moment to save unnecessary labour, Mark seldom cooked more than once in twenty-four hours, and then barely enough to last for that day. In consequence of this rule, he soon learned how little was really necessary for the wants of one person, it being his opinion that a quarter of an acre of such soil as that which now composed his garden, would more than furnish all the vegetables he could consume. The soil, it is true, was of a very superior quality. Although it had lain so long unproductive and seemingly barren, now that it had been stirred, and air and water were admitted, and guano, and sea-weed, and loam, and dead fish had been applied, and all in quantities that would have been deemed very ample in the best wrought gardens of christendom, the acre he had under tillage might be said to have been brought to the highest stage of fertility. It wanted a little in consistency, perhaps; but the compost heap was very large, containing enough of all the materials just mentioned to give the garden another good dressing. As for the grass, Mark was convinced the guano was all-sufficient for that, and this he took care to apply as often as once in two or three months.

Our young man was never tired, indeed, with feasting his eyes with the manner in which the grass had spread over the mount. It is true, that he had scattered seed, at odd and favourable moments, over most of it, by this time; but he was persuaded the roots of those first sown would have extended themselves, in the course of a year or two, over the whole Summit. Nor were these grasses thin and sickly, threatening as early an extinction as they had been quick in coming to maturity. On the contrary, after breaking what might be called the crust of the rock with their vigorous though nearly invisible roots, they made a bed for themselves, on which they promised to repose for ages. The great frequency of the rains favoured their growth, and Mark was of opinion after the experience of one summer, that his little mountain might be green the year round.

We have called the mount of the crater little, but the term ought not to be used in reference to such a hill, when the extent of the island itself was considered. By actual measurement, Mark had ascertained that there was one knoll on the Summit which was just seventy-two feet above the level of the rock. The average height, however, might be given as somewhat less than fifty. Of surface, the rocky barrier of the crater had almost as much as the plain within it, though it was so broken and uneven as not to appear near as large. Kitty had long since determined that the hill was more than large enough for all her wants; and glad enough did she seem when Mark succeeded, after a great deal of difficulty, in driving the hogs up a flight of steps he had made within the crater, to help her crop the herbage. As for the rooting of the last, so long as they were on the Summit, it was so much the better; since, in that climate, it was next to impossible to kill grass that was once fairly in growth, and the more the crust of the ashes was broken, the more rapid and abundant would be the vegetation.

Mark had, of course, abandoned the idea of continuing to cultivate his melons, or any other vegetables, on the Summit, or he never would have driven his hogs there. He was unwilling, notwithstanding, to lose the benefit of the deposits of soil and manure which he and Bob had made there with so much labour to themselves. After reflecting what he could do with them, he came to the conclusion that he would make small enclosures around some fifteen or twenty of the places, and transplant some of the fig-trees, orange-trees, limes, lemons, &c., which still stood rather too thick within the crater to ripen their fruits to advantage. In order to make these little enclosures, Mark merely drove into the earth short posts, passing around them old rope, of which there was a superabundance on board the ship. This arrangement suggested the idea of fencing in the garden, by the same means, in order to admit the pigs to eat the grass, when he was not watching them. By the time these dispositions were made, it was necessary to begin again to put in the seeds.

On this occasion Mark determined to have a succession of crops, and not to bring on everything at once, as he had done the first year of his tillage. Accordingly, he would manure and break up a bed, and plant or sow it, waiting a few days before he began another. Experience had told him that there was never an end to vegetation in that climate, and he saw no use in pushing his labours faster than he might require their fruits. It was true, certain plants did better if permitted to come to maturity in particular periods, but the season was so long as very well to allow of the arrangement just mentioned. As this distribution of his time gave the young man a good deal of leisure, he employed it in the ship-yard. Thus the boat and the garden were made to advance together, and when the last was sown and planted, the first was planked. When the last bed was got in, moreover, those first set in order were already giving forth their increase. Mark had abundance of delicious salad, young onions, radishes that seemed to grow like mushrooms, young peas, beans, &c., in quantities that enabled him to turn the hogs out on the Reef, and keep them well on the refuse of his garden, assisted a little by what was always to be picked up on the rocks.

By this time Mark had settled on a system which he thought to pursue. There was no use in his raising more pigs than he could use. Taking care to preserve the breed, therefore, he killed off the pigs, of which he had fresh litters, from time to time; and when he found the old hogs getting to be troublesome, as swine will become with years, he just shot them, and buried their bodies in his compost heap, or in his garden, where one common-sized hog would render highly fertile several yards square of earth, or ashes. This practice he continued ever after, extending it to his fowls and ducks, the latter of which produced a great many eggs. By rigidly observing this rule, Mark avoided an evil which is very common even in inhabited countries, that of keeping more stock than is good for their owner. Six or eight hens laid more eggs than he could consume, and there was always a sufficient supply of chickens for his wants. In short, our hermit had everything he actually required, and most things that could contribute to his living in great abundance. The necessity of cooking for himself, and the want of pure, cold spring water, were the two greatest physical hardships he endured. There were moments, indeed, when Mark would have gladly yielded one-half of the advantages he actually possessed, to have a good spring of living water. Then he quelled the repinings of his spirit at this privation, by endeavouring to recall how many blessings were left at his command, compared to the wants and sufferings of many another shipwrecked mariner of whom he had read or heard.

The spring passed as pleasantly as thoughts of home and Bridget would allow, and his beds and plantations flourished to a degree that surprised him. As for the grass, as soon as it once got root, it became a most beneficial assistant to his plans of husbandry. Nor was it grass alone that rewarded Mark's labours and forethought in his meadows and pastures. Various flowers appeared in the herbage; and he was delighted at finding a little patch of the common wild strawberry, the seed of which had doubtless got mixed with those of the grasses. Instead of indulging his palate with a taste of this delicious and most salubrious fruit, Mark carefully collected it all, made a bed in his garden, and included the cultivation of this among his other plants. He would not disturb a single root of the twenty or thirty different shoots that he found, all being together, and coming from the same cast of his hand while sowing, lest it might die; but, with the seed of the fruit, he was less chary. One thing struck Mark as singular. Thus far his garden was absolutely free from weeds of every sort. The seed that he put into the ground came up, and nothing else. This greatly simplified his toil, though he had no doubt that, in the course of time, he should meet with intruders in his beds. He could only account for this circumstance by the facts, that the ashes of the volcano contained of themselves no combination of the elements necessary to produce plants, and that the manures he used, in their nature, were free from weeds.

Chapter XI

> "The globe around earth's hollow surface shakes,
> And is the ceiling of her sleeping sons:
> O'er devastation we blind revels keep;
> While buried towns support the dancer's heel."
>
> —Young

It was again mid-summer ere Mark Woolston had his boat ready for launching. He had taken things leisurely, and completed his work in all its parts, before he thought of putting the craft into the water. Afraid of worms, he used some of the old copper on this boat, too; and he painted her, inside and out, not only with fidelity, but with taste. Although there was no one but Kitty to talk to, he did not forget to paint the name which he had given to his new vessel, in her stern-sheets, where he could always see it. She was called the "Bridget Yardley;" and, notwithstanding the unfavourable circumstances in which she had been put together, Mark thought she did no discredit to her beautiful namesake, when completed. When he had everything finished, even to mast and sails, of the last of which he fitted her with mainsail and jib, the young man set about his preparations for getting his vessel afloat.

There was no process by which one man could move a boat of the size of the Bridget, while out of its proper element, but to launch it by means of regular ways. With a view to this contingency, the keel had been laid between the ways of the Neshamony, which were now all ready to be used. Of course it was no great job to make a cradle for a boat, and our boat-builder had 'wedged up,' and got the keel of his craft off the 'blocks,' within eight-and-forty hours after he had begun upon that part of his task. It only remained to knock away the spur-shores and start the boat. Until that instant, Mark had pursued his work on the Bridget as mechanically and steadily as if hired by the day When, however, he perceived that he was so near his goal, a flood of sensations came over the young man, and his limbs trembled to a degree that compelled him to be seated. Who could tell the consequences to which that boat might lead? Who knew but the 'Bridget' might prove the means of carrying him to his own Bridget, and restoring him to civilized life? At that instant, if appeared to Mark as if his existence depended on the launching of his boat, and he was fearful some unforeseen accident might prevent it. He was obliged to wait several minutes in order to recover his self-possession.

At length Mark succeeded in subduing this feeling, and he resumed his work with most of his former self-command. Everything being ready, he knocked away the spur-shores, and, finding the boat did not start, he gave it a blow with a mawl. This set the mass in motion, and the little craft slid down the ways without any interruption, until it became water-born, when it shot out from the Reef like a duck. Mark was delighted with his new vessel, now that it was fairly afloat, and saw that it sat on an even keel, according to his best hopes. Of course he had not neglected to secure it with a line, by which he hauled it in towards the rock, securing it in a natural basin which was just large enough for such a purpose. So great, indeed, were his apprehensions of losing his boat, which now seemed so precious to him, that he had worked some ringbolts out of the ship and let them into the rock, where he had secured them by means of melted lead, in order to make fast to.

The Bridget was not more than a fourth of the size of the Neshamony, though rather more than half as long. Nevertheless, she was a good boat; and Mark, knowing that he must depend on sails principally to move her, had built a short deck forward to prevent the seas from breaking aboard her, as well as to give him a place in which he might stow away various articles, under cover from the rain. Her ballast was breakers, filled with fresh water, of which there still remained several in the ship. All these, as well as her masts, sails, oars, &c., were in her when she was launched; and that important event having taken place early in the morning, Mark could not restrain his impatience for a cruise, but determined to go out on the reef at once, further than he had ever yet ventured in the dingui, in order to explore the seas around him. Accordingly, he put some food on board, loosened his fasts, and made sail.

The instant the boat moved ahead, and began to obey her helm, Mark felt as if he had found a new companion. Hitherto Kitty had, in a measure, filled this place; but a boat had been the young man's delight on the Delaware, in his boyhood, and he had not tacked his present craft more than two or three times, before he caught himself talking to it, and commending it, as he would a human being. As the wind usually blew in the same direction, and generally a good stiff breeze, Mark beat up between the Reef and Guano Island, working round the weather end of the former, until he came out at the anchorage of the Rancocus. After beating about in that basin a little while, as if merely to show off the Bridget to the ship, Mark put the former close by the wind, and stood off in the channel by which he and Bob had brought the latter into her present berth.

It was easy enough to avoid all such breakers as would be dangerous to a boat, by simply keeping out of white water; but the Bridget could pass over most of the reefs with impunity, on account of the depth of the sea on them. Mark beat up, on short tacks, therefore, until he found the two buoys between which he had brought the ship, and passing to windward of them, he stood off in the direction where he expected to find the reef over which the Rancocus had beaten. He was not long in making this discovery. There still floated the buoy of the bower, watching as faithfully as the seaman on his look-out! Mark ran the boat up to this well-tried sentinel, and caught the lanyard, holding on by it, after lowering his sails.

The boat was now moored by the buoy-rope of the ship's anchor, and it occurred to our young man that a certain use might be made of this melancholy memorial of the calamity that had befallen the Rancocus. The anchor lay quite near a reef, on it indeed in one sense; and it was in such places that fish most abounded. Fishing-tackle was in the boat, and Mark let down a line. His success was prodigious. The fish were hauled in almost as fast as he could bait and lower his hook, and what was more they proved to be larger and finer than those taken at the old fishing-grounds. By the experience of the half hour he passed at the spot, Mark felt certain that he could fill his boat there in a day's fishing. After hauling in some twenty or thirty, however, he cast off from the lanyard, hoisted his sails, and crossed the reef, still working to windward.

It was Mark's wish to learn something of the nature and extent of the shoals in this direction. With this object in view, he continued beating up, sometimes passing boldly through shallow water, at others going about to avoid that which he thought might be dangerous, until he believed himself to be about ten miles to windward of the island. The ship's masts were his beacon, for the crater had sunk below the horizon, or if visible at all, it was only at intervals, as the boat was lifted on a swell, when it appeared a low hummock, nearly awash. It was with difficulty that the naked spars could be seen at that distance; nor could they be, except at moments, and that because the compass told the young man exactly where to look for them.

As for the appearance of the reefs, no naked rock was anywhere to be seen in this direction, though there were abundant evidences of the existence of shoals. As well as he could judge, Mark was of opinion that these shoals extended at least twenty miles in this direction, he having turned up fully five leagues without getting clear of them. At that distance from his solitary home, and out of sight of everything like land, did the young man eat his frugal, but good and nourishing dinner, with his jib-sheet to windward and the boat hove-to. The freshness of the breeze had induced him to reef, and under that short sail, he found the Bridget everything he could wish. It was now about the middle of the afternoon, and Mark thought it prudent to turn out his reef, and run down for the crater. In half an hour he caught a sight of the spars of the ship; and ten minutes later, the Summit appeared above the horizon.

It had been the intention of our young sailor to stay out all night, had the weather been promising. His wish was to ascertain how he might manage the boat, single-handed, while he slept, and also to learn the extent of the shoals. As the extraordinary fertility of the crater superseded the necessity of his labouring much to keep himself supplied with food, he had formed a plan of cruising off the shoals, for days at a time, in the hope of falling in with something that was passing, and which might carry him back to the haunts of men. No vessel would or could come in sight of the crater, so long as the existence of the reefs was known; but the course steered by the Rancocus was a proof that ships did occasionally pass in that quarter of the Pacific. Mark had indulged in no visionary hopes on this subject, for he knew he might keep in the offing a twelvemonth and see nothing; but an additional twenty-four hours might realize all his hopes.

The weather, however on this his first experiment, did not encourage him to remain out the whole night. On the contrary, by the time the crater was in sight, Mark thought he had not seen a more portentous-looking sky since he had been on the Reef. There was a fiery redness in the atmosphere that alarmed him, and he would have rejoiced to be at home, in order to secure his stock within the crater. From the appearances, he anticipated another tempest with its flood. It is true, it was not the season when the last occurred, but the climate might admit of these changes. The difference between summer and winter was very trifling on that reef, and a hurricane, or a gale, was as likely to occur in the one as in the other.

Just as the Bridget was passing the two buoys by which the ship-channel had been marked, her sail flapped. This was a bad omen, for it betokened a shift of wind, which rarely happened, unless it might be from six months to six months, without being the precursor of some sort of a storm. Mark was still two miles from the Reef, and the little wind there was soon came ahead. Luckily, it was smooth water, and very little air sufficed to force that light craft ahead, while there was usually a current setting from that point towards the crater. The birds, moreover, seemed uneasy, the air being filled with them, thousands flying over the boat, around which they wheeled, screaming and apparently terrified. At first Mark ascribed this unusual behaviour of his feathered neighbours to the circumstance of their now seeing a boat for the commencement of such an acquaintance; but, recollecting how often he had passed their haunts, in the dingui, when they would hardly get out of the way, he soon felt certain there must be another reason for this singular conduct.

The sun went down in a bank of lurid fire, and the Bridget was still a mile from the ship. A new apprehension now came over our hermit. Should a tempest bring the wind violently from the westward, as was very likely to be the case under actual circumstances, he might be driven out to sea, and, did the little craft resist the waves, forced so far off as to make him lose the Reef altogether. Then it was that Mark deeply felt how much had been left him, by casting his lot on that beautiful and luxuriant crater, instead of reducing him to those dregs of misery which so many shipwrecked mariners are compelled to swallow! How much, or how many of the blessings that he enjoyed on the Reef, would he not have been willing to part with, that evening, in order to secure a safe arrival at the side of the Rancocus! By the utmost care to profit by every puff of air, and by handling the boat with the greatest skill, this happy result was obtained, however, without any sacrifice.

About nine o'clock, and not sooner, the boat was well secured, and Mark went into his cabin. Here he knelt and returned thanks to God, for his safe return to a place that was getting to be as precious to him as the love of life could render it. After this, tired with his day's work, the young man got into his berth and endeavoured to sleep.

The fatigue of the day, notwithstanding the invigorating freshness of the breeze, acted as an anodyne, and our young man soon forgot his adventures and his boat, in profound slumbers. It was many hours ere Mark awoke, and when he did, it was with a sense of suffocation. At first he thought the ship had taken fire, a lurid light gleaming in at the open door of the cabin, and he sprang to his feet in recollection of the danger he ran from the magazine, as well as from being burned. But no cracking of flames reaching his ears, he dressed hastily and went out on the poop. He had just reached this deck, when he felt the whole ship tremble from her truck to her keel, and a rushing of water was heard on all sides of him, as if a flood were coming. Hissing sounds were heard, and streams of fire, and gleams of lurid light were seen in the air. It was a terrible moment, and one that might well induce any man to imagine that time was drawing to its close.

Mark Woolston now comprehended his situation, notwithstanding the intense darkness which prevailed, except in those brief intervals of lurid light. He had felt the shock of an earthquake, and the volcano had suddenly become active. Smoke and ashes certainly filled the air, and our poor hermit instinctively looked towards his crater, already so verdant and lively, in the expectation of seeing it vomit flames. Everything there was tranquil; the danger, if danger there was, was assuredly more remote. But the murky vapour which rendered breathing exceedingly difficult, also obstructed the view, and prevented his seeing where the explosion really was. For a brief space our young man fancied he must certainly be suffocated; but a shift of wind came, and blew away the oppressive vapour, clearing the atmosphere of its sulphurous and most offensive gases and odours. Never did feverish tongue enjoy the cooling and healthful draught, more than Mark rejoiced in this change. The wind had got back to its old quarter, and the air he respired soon became pure and refreshing. Had the impure atmosphere lasted ten minutes longer, Mark felt persuaded he could not have breathed it with any safety.

The light was now most impatiently expected by our young man. The minutes seemed to drag; but, at length, the usual signs of returning day became apparent to him, and he got on the bowsprit of the ship, as if to meet it in its approach. There he stood looking to the eastward, eager to have ray after ray shoot into the firmament, when he was suddenly struck with a change in that quarter of the ocean, which at once proclaimed the power of the effort which the earth had made in its subterranean throes. Naked rocks appeared in places where Mark was certain water in abundance had existed a few hours before. The sea-wall, directly ahead of the ship, and which never showed itself above the surface more than two or three inches, in any part of it, and that only at exceedingly neap tides, was now not only bare for a long distance, but parts rose ten and fifteen feet above the surrounding sea. This proved, at once, that the earthquake had thrust upward a vast surface of the reef, completely altering the whole appearance of the shoal! In a word, nature had made another effort, and islands had been created, as it might be in the twinkling of an eye.

Mark was no sooner assured of this stupendous fact, than he hurried on to the poop, in order to ascertain what changes had occurred in and about the crater. It had been pushed upward, in common with all the rocks for miles on every side of it, though without disturbing its surface! By the computation of our young man, the Reef, which previously lay about six feet above the level of the ocean, was now fully twenty, so many cubits having been, by one single but mighty effort of nature, added to its stature. The planks which led from the stern of the vessel to the shore, and which had formed a descent, were now nearly level, so much water having left the basin as to produce this change. Still the ship floated, enough remaining to keep her keel clear of the bottom.

Impatient to learn all, Mark ran ashore, for by this time it was broad daylight, and hastened into the crater, with an intention to ascend at once to the Summit. As he passed along, he could detect no change whatever on the surface of the Reef; everything lying just as it had been left, and the pigs and poultry were at their usual business of providing for their own wants. Ashes, however, were strewn over the rocks to a depth that left his footprints as distinct as they could have been made in a light snow. Within the crater the same appearances were observed, fully an inch of ashes covering its verdant pastures and the whole garden. This gave Mark very little concern, for he knew that the first rain would wash this drab-looking mantle into the earth, where it would answer all the purposes of a rich dressing of manure.

On reaching the Summit, our young man was enabled to form a better opinion of the vast changes which had been wrought around him, by this sudden elevation of the earth's crust. Everywhere sea seemed to be converted into land, or, at least, into rock. All the white water had disappeared, and in its place arose islands of rock, or mud, or sand. A good deal of the last was to be seen, and some quite near the Reef, as we shall still continue to call the island of the crater. Island, however, it could now hardly be termed. It is true that ribands of water approached it on all sides, resembling creeks, and rivers and small sounds; but, as Mark stood there on the Summit, it seemed to him that it was now possible to walk for leagues, in every direction, commencing at the crater and following the lines of reefs, and rocks, and sands, that had been laid bare by the late upheaving. The extent of this change gave him confidence in its permanency, and the young man had hopes that what had thus been produced by the Providence of God would be permitted to remain, to answer his own benevolent purposes. It certainly made an immense difference in his own situation. The boat could still be used, but it was now possible for him to ramble for hours, if not for days, along the necks, and banks, and hummocks, and swales that had been formed, and that with a dry foot. His limits were so much enlarged as to offer something like a new world to his enterprise and curiosity.

The crater, nevertheless, was apparently about the centre of this new creation. To the south, it is true, the eye could not penetrate more than two or three leagues. A vast, dun-looking cloud, still covered the sea in that direction, veiling its surface far and wide, and mingling with the vapours of the upper atmosphere. Somewhere within this cloud, how far or how near from him he knew not, Mark made no doubt a new outlet to the pent forces of the inner earth was to be found, forming another and an active crater for the exit of the fires beneath. Geology was a science that had not made its present progress in the day of Mark Woolston, but his education had been too good to leave him totally without a theory for what had happened. He supposed that the internal fires had produced so much gas, just beneath this spot, as to open crevices at the bottom of the ocean, through which water had flowed in sufficient quantities to create a vast body of steam, which steam had been the immediate agent of lifting so much of the rock and land, and of causing the earthquake. At the same time, the internal fires had acted in concert; and following an opening, they had got so near the surface as to force a chimney for their own exit, in the form of this new crater, of the existence of which, from all the signs to the southward, Mark did not entertain the smallest doubt.

This theory may have been true, in whole or in part, or it may have been altogether erroneous. Such speculations seldom turn out to be minutely accurate. So many unknown causes exist in so many unexpected forms, as to render precise estimates of their effects, in cases of physical phenomena, almost as uncertain as those which follow similar attempts at any analysis of human motives and human conduct. The man who has been much the subject of the conjectures and opinions of his fellow-creatures, in this way, must have many occasions to wonder, and some to smile, when he sees how completely those around him misjudge his wishes and impulses. Although formed of the same substance, influenced by the same selfishness, and governed by the same passions, in nothing do men oftener err than in this portion of the exercise of their intellects. The errors arise from one man's rigidly judging his fellow by himself, and that which he would do he fancies others would do also. This rule would be pretty safe, could we always penetrate into the wants and longings of others, which quite as often fail to correspond closely with our own, as do their characters, fortunes, and hopes.

At first sight, Mark had a good deal of difficulty in understanding the predominant nature of the very many bodies of water that were to be seen on every side of him. On the whole, there still remained almost as much of one element as of the other, in the view; which of itself, however, was a vast change from what had previously been the condition of the shoals. There were large bodies of water, little lakes in extent, which it was obvious enough must disappear under the process of evaporation, no communication existing between them and the open ocean. But, on the other hand, many of these sheets were sounds, or arms of the sea, that must always continue, since they might be traced, far as eye could reach, towards the mighty Pacific. Such, Mark was induced to believe, was the fact with the belt of water that still surrounded, or nearly surrounded the Reef; for, placed where he was, the young man was unable to ascertain whether the latter had, or had not, at a particular point, any land communication with an extensive range of naked rock, sand, mud, and deposit, that stretched away to the westward, for leagues. In obvious connection with this broad reach of what might be termed bare ground, were Guano and Loam Islands; neither of which was an island any longer, except as it was a part of the whole formation around it. Nevertheless, our young man was not sorry to see that the channel around the Reef still washed the bases of both those important places of deposit, leaving it in his power to transport their valuable manures by means of the raft, or boat.

The situation of the ship next became the matter of Mark's most curious and interested investigation. She was clearly afloat, and the basin in which she rode had a communication on each side, of it, with the sound, or inlet, that still encircled the Reef. Descending to the shore, our young mariner got into the dingui, and pulled out round the vessel, to make a more minute examination. So very limpid was the water of that sea, it was easy enough to discern a bright object on the bottom, at a depth of several fathoms. There were no streams in that part of the world to pour their deposits into the ocean, and air itself is scarce more transparent than the pure water of the ocean, when unpolluted with any foreign substances. All it wants is light, to enable the eye to reach into it's mysteries for a long way. Mark could very distinctly perceive the sand beneath the Rancocus' keel, and saw that the ship still floated two or three feet clear of the bottom. It was near high water, however; and there being usually a tide of about twenty inches, it was plain enough that, on certain winds, the good old craft would come in pretty close contact with the bottom. All expectation of ever getting the vessel out of the basin must now be certainly abandoned, since she lay in a sort of cavity, where the water was six or eight feet deeper than it was within a hundred yards on each side of her.

Having ascertained these facts, Mark provided himself with a fowling-piece, provisions, &c., and set out to explore his newly acquired territories on foot. His steps were first directed to the point where it appeared to the eye, that the vast range of dry land to the westward, extending both north and south, had become connected with the Reef. If such connection existed at all, it was by two very narrow necks of rock, of equal height, both of which had come up out of the water under the late action, which action had considerably altered and extended the shores of Crater Island. Sand appeared in various places along these shores, now; whereas, previously to the earthquake, they had everywhere been nearly perpendicular rocks.

Mark was walking, with an impatient step, towards the neck just mentioned, and which was at no great distance from the ship-yard, when his eye was attracted towards a sandy beach of several acres in extent, that spread itself along the margin of the rocks, as clear from every impurity as it was a few hours before, when it had been raised from out of the bosom of the ocean. To him, it appeared that water was trickling through this sand, coming from beneath the lava of the Reef. At first, he supposed it was merely the remains of some small portion of the ocean that had penetrated to a cavity within, and which was now trickling back through the crevices of the rocks, to find its level, under the great law of nature. But it looked so pleasant to see once more water of any sort coming upwards from the earth, that the young man jumped down upon the sands, and hastened to the spot for further inquiry. Scooping up a little of the water in the hollow of his hand, he found it sweet, soft, and deliciously cool. Here was a discovery, indeed! The physical comfort for which he most pined was thus presented to him, as by a direct gift from heaven; and no miser who had found a hoard of hidden gold, could have felt so great pleasure, or a tenth part of the gratitude, of our young hermit, if hermit we may call one who did not voluntarily seek his seclusion from the world, and who worshipped God less as a penance than from love and adoration.

Before quitting this new-found treasure, Mark opened a cavity in the sand to receive the water, placing stone around it to make a convenient and clean little basin. In ten minutes this place was filled with water almost as limpid as air, and every way as delicious as the palate of man could require. The young man could scarce tear himself away from the spot, but fearful of drinking too much he did so, after a time. Before quitting the spring, however, he placed a stone of some size at a gap in the rock, a precaution that completely prevented the hogs, should they stroll that way, from descending to the beach and defiling the limpid basin. As soon as he had leisure, Mark resolved to sink a barrel in the sand, and to build a fence around it; after which the stock might descend and drink at a pool he should form below, at pleasure.

Mark proceeded. On reaching the narrowest part of the 'Neck,' he found that the rocks did not meet, but the Reef still remained an island. The channel that separated the two points of rock was only about twenty feet wide, however, though it was of fully twice that depth. The young man found it necessary to go back to the ship-yard (no great distance, by the way), and to bring a plank with which to make a bridge. This done, he passed on to the newly emerged territory. As might have been expected, the rocks were found tolerably well furnished with fish, which had got caught in pools and crevices when the water flowed into the sea; and what was of still more importance, another and a much larger spring of fresh water was found quite near the bridge, gushing through a deposit of sand of some fifteen or twenty acres in extent. The water of this spring had run down into a cavity, where it had already formed a little lake of some two acres in surface, and whence it was already running into the sea, by overflowing its banks. These two discoveries induced Mark to return to the Reef again, in quest of the stock. After laying another-plank at his bridge, he called every creature he had over into the new territory; for so great was the command he had obtained over even the ducks, that all came willingly at his call. As for Kitty, she was never more happy than when trotting at his side, accompanying him in his walks, like a dog.

Glad enough were the pigs, in particular, to obtain this new range. Here was everything they could want; food in thousands, sand to root on, fresh water to drink, pools to wallow in, and a range for their migratory propensities. Mark had no sooner set them at work on the sea-weed and shell-fish that abounded there, for the time being at least, than he foresaw he should have to erect a gate at his bridge, and keep the hogs here most of the time. With such a range, and the deposits of the tides alone, would have no great difficulty in making their own living. This would enable him to increase the number kept, which he had hitherto been obliged to keep down with the most rigid attention to the increase.

Mark now set out, in earnest, on his travels. He was absent from the Reef the entire day. At one time, he thought he was quite two leagues in a straight line from the ship, though he had been compelled to walk four to get there. Everywhere he found large sheets of salt water, that had been left on the rocks, in consequence of the cavities in the latter. In several instances, these little lakes were near a mile in length, having the most beautifully undulating outlines. None of them were deep, of course, though their bottoms varied. Some of these bottoms were clean rock; others contained large deposits of mud; and others, again, were of a clean, dark-coloured sand. One, and one only, had a bottom of a bright, light-coloured sand. As a matter of course, these lakes, or pools, must shortly evaporate, leaving their bottoms bare, or encrusted with salt. One thing gave the young man great satisfaction. He had kept along the margin of the channel that communicated with the water that surrounded the Reef, and, when at the greatest distance from the crater, he ascended a rock that must have had an elevation of a hundred feet above the sea. Of course most of this rock had been above water previously to the late eruption, and Mark had often seen it at a distance, though he had never ventured through the white water near so far, in the dingui. When on its apex, Mark got an extensive view of the scene around him. In the first place, he traced the channel just mentioned, quite into open water, which now appeared distinctly not many leagues further, towards the north-west. There were a great many other channels, some mere ribands of water, others narrow sounds, and many resembling broad, deep, serpenting creeks, which last was their true character, being strictly inlets from the sea. The lakes or pools, could be seen in hundreds, creating some confusion in the view; but all these must soon disappear, in that climate.

Towards the southward, however, Mark found the objects of his greatest wonder and admiration. By the time he reached the apex of the rock, the smoke in that quarter of the horizon had, in a great measure, risen from the sea; though a column of it continued to ascend towards a vast, dun-coloured cloud that overhung the place. To Mark's astonishment he had seen some dark, dense body first looming through the rising vapour. When the last was sufficiently removed, a high, ragged mountain became distinctly visible. He thought it arose at least a thousand feet above the ocean, and that it could not be less than a league in extent. This exhibition of the power of nature filled the young man's soul with adoration and reverence for the mighty Being that could set such elements at work. It did not alarm him, but rather tended to quiet his longings to quit the place; for he who lives amid such scenes feels that he is so much nearer to the arm of God than those who dwell in uniform security, as to think less of ordinary advantages than is common.

Mark knew that there must have been a dislocation of the rocks, to produce such a change as that he saw to the southward. It was well for him it occurred there at a distance, as he then thought, of ten or fifteen miles from the Reef, though in truth it was at quite fifty, instead of happening beneath him. It was possible, however, for one to have been on the top of that mountain, and to have lived through the late change, could the lungs of man have breathed the atmosphere. Not far from this mountain a column of smoke rose out of the sea, and Mark fancied that, at moments, he could discern the summit of an active crater at its base.

After gazing at these astonishing changes for a long time, our young man descended from the height and retraced his steps homeward. Kitty gladly preceded him, and some time after the sun had set, they regained the Reef. About a mile short of home, Mark passed all the hogs, snugly deposited in a bed of mud, where they had esconced themselves for the night, as one draws himself beneath his blanket.

Chapter XII

> "All things in common nature should produce
> Without sweat or endeavour: treason, felony,
> Sword, pike, gun, or need of any engine
> Would I not have; but nature should bring forth
> Of its own kind, all foizen, all abundance
> To feed my innocent people."
>
> —Tempest

For the next ten days Mark Woolston did little but explore. By crossing the channel around the Reef, which he had named the 'Armlet' (the young man often talked to himself), he reached the sea-wall, and, once there, he made a long excursion to the eastward. He now walked dryshod over those very reefs among which he had so recently sailed in the Bridget, though the ship-channel through which he and Bob had brought in the Rancocus still remained. The two buoys that had marked the narrow passage were found, high and dry; and the anchor of the ship, that by which she rode after beating over the rocks into deep water, was to be seen so near the surface, that the stock could be reached by the hand.

There was little difference in character between the newly-made land to windward and that which Mark had found in the opposite direction. Large pools, or lakes, of salt water, deposits of mud and sand, some of which were of considerable extent and thickness, sounds, creeks, and arms of the sea, with here and there a hummock of rock that rose fifteen or twenty feet above the face of the main body, were the distinguishing peculiarities. For two days Mark explored in this direction, or to windward, reaching as far by his estimate of the distance, as the place where he had bore up in his cruise in the Bridget. Finding a great many obstacles in the way, channels, mud, &c., he determined, on the afternoon of the second day, to return home, get a stock of supplies, and come out in the boat, in order to ascertain if he could not now reach the open water to windward.

On the morning of the fourth day after the earthquake, and the occurrence of the mighty change that had altered the whole face of the scene around him, the young man got under way in the Bridget. He shaped his course to windward, beating out of the Armlet by a narrow passage, that carried him into a reach that stretched away for several miles, to the northward and eastward, in nearly a straight line. This passage, or sound, was about half a mile in width, and there was water enough in nearly all parts of it to float the largest sized vessel. By this passage the poor hermit, small as was his chance of ever seeing such an event occur, hoped it might be possible to come to the very side of the Reef in a ship.

When about three leagues from the crater, the 'Hope Channel,' as Mark named this long and direct passage, divided into two, one trending still more to the northward, running nearly due north, indeed, while the other might be followed in a south-easterly direction, far as the eye could reach. Mark named the rock at the junction 'Point Fork,' and chose the latter passage, which appeared the most promising, and the wind permitting him to lay through it. The Bridget tacked in the Forks, therefore, and stood away to the south-east, pretty close to the wind. Various other channels communicated with this main passage, or the Hope; and, about noon, Mark tacked into one of them, heading about north-east, when trimmed up sharp to do so. The water was deep, and at first the passage was half a mile in width; but after standing along it for a mile or two, it seemed all at once to terminate in an oval basin, that might have been a mile in its largest diameter, and which was bounded to the eastward by a belt of rock that rose some twenty feet above the water. The bottom of this basin was a clear beautiful sand, and its depth of water, on sounding, Mark found was uniformly about eight fathoms. A more safe or convenient basin for the anchorage of ships could not have been formed by the art of man, had there been an entrance to it, and any inducement for them to come there.

Mark had beaten about 'Oval Harbour,' as he named the place, for half an hour, before he was struck by the circumstance that the even character of its surface appeared to be a little disturbed by a slight undulation which seemed to come from its north-eastern extremity. Tacking the Bridget, he stood in that direction, and on reaching the place, found that there was a passage through the rock of about a hundred yards in width. The wind permitting, the boat shot through this passage, and was immediately heaving and setting in the long swells of the open ocean. At first Mark was startled by the roar of the waves that plunged into the caverns of the rocks, and trembled lest his boat might be hove up against that hard and iron-bound coast, where one toss would shatter his little craft into splinters. Too steady a seaman, however, to abandon his object unnecessarily, he stood on, and soon found he could weather the rocks under his lee, tacking in time. After two or three short stretches were made, Mark found himself half a mile to windward of a long line, or coast, of dark rock, that rose from twenty to twenty-five feet above the level of the water, and beyond all question in the open ocean. He hove-to to sound, and let forty fathoms of line out without reaching bottom. But everywhere to leeward of him was land, or rock; while everywhere to windward, as well as ahead and astern, it was clear water. This, then, was the eastern limit of the old shoals, now converted into dry land. Here the Rancocus had, unknown to her officers, first run into the midst of these shoals, by which she had ever since been environed.

It was not easy to compute the precise distance from the outlet or inlet of Oval Harbour, to the crater. Mark thought it might be five-and-twenty miles, in a straight line, judging equally by the eye, and the time he had been in running it. The Summit was not to be seen, however, any more than the masts of the ship; though the distant Peak, and the column of dark smoke, remained in sight, as eternal land-marks. The young man might have been an hour in the open sea, gradually hauling off the land, in order to keep clear of the coast, when he bethought him of returning. It required a good deal of nerve to run in towards those rocks, under all the circumstances of the case. The wind blew fresh, so much indeed as to induce Mark to reef, but there must always be a heavy swell rolling in upon that iron-bound shore. The shock of such waves expending their whole force on perpendicular rocks may be imagined better than it can be described. There was an undying roar all along that coast, produced by these incessant collisions of the elements; and occasionally, when a sea entered a cavern, in a way suddenly to expel its air, the sound resembled that which some huge animal might be supposed to utter in its agony, or its anger. Of course, the spray was flying high, and the entire line of black rocks was white with its particles.

Mark had unwittingly omitted to take any land-marks to his inlet, or strait. He had no other means of finding it, therefore, than to discover a spot in which the line of white was broken. This inlet, however, he remembered did not open at right angles to the coast, but obliquely; and it was very possible to be within a hundred yards of it, and not see it. This fact, our young sailor was not long in ascertaining; for standing in towards the point where he expected to find the entrance, and going as close to the shore as he dared, he could see nothing of the desired passage. For an hour did he search, passing to and fro, but without success. The idea of remaining out in the open sea for the night, and to windward of such an inhospitable coast, was anything but pleasant to Mark, and he determined to stand to the northward, now, while it was day, and look for some other entrance.

For four hours did Mark Woolston run along those dark rocks, whitened only by the spray of the wide ocean, without perceiving a point at which a boat might even land. As he was now running off the wind, and had turned out his reef, he supposed he must have gone at least five-and-twenty miles, if not thirty, in that time; and thus had he some means of judging of the extent of his new territories. About five in the afternoon a cape, or headland, was reached, when the coast suddenly trended to the westward. This, then, was the north-eastern angle of the entire formation, and Mark named it Cape North-East. The boat was now jibed, and ran off west, a little northerly, for another hour, keeping quite close in to the coast, which was no longer dangerous as soon as the Cape was doubled. The seas broke upon the rocks, as a matter of course; but there being a lee, it was only under the power of the ceaseless undulations of the ocean. Even the force of the wind was now much less felt, the Bridget carrying whole sail when hauled up, as Mark placed her several times, in order to examine apparent inlets.

It was getting to be too late to think of reaching home that night, for running in those unknown channels after dark was not a desirable course for an explorer to adopt. Our young man, therefore, limited his search to some place where he might lie until the return of light. It is true, the lee formed by the rocks was now such as to enable him to remain outside, with safety, until morning; but he preferred greatly to get within the islands, if possible, to trusting himself, while asleep, to the mercy of the open ocean. Just as the sun was setting, leaving the evening cool and pleasant, after the warmth of an exceedingly hot day, the boat doubled a piece of low headland; and Mark had half made up his mind to get under its lee, and heave a grapnel ashore in order to ride by his cable during the approaching night, when an opening in the coast greeted his eyes. It was just as he doubled the cape. This opening appeared to be a quarter of a mile in width, and it had perfectly smooth water, a half-gunshot within its mouth. The helm was put down, the sheets hauled aft, and the Bridget luffed into this creek, estuary, sound, or harbour, whichever it might prove to be. For twenty minutes did Mark stand on through this passage, when suddenly it expanded into a basin, or bay, of considerable extent. This was at a distance of about a league within the coast. This bay was a league long, and half a league in width, the boat entering it close to its weather side. A long and wide sandy beach offered on that side, and the young man stood along it a short distance, until the sight of a spring induced him to put his helm down. The boat luffed short round, and came gently upon the beach. A grapnel was thrown on the sands, and Mark leaped ashore.

The water proved to be sweet, cool, and every way delicious. This was at least the twentieth spring which had been seen that day, though it was the first of which the waters had been tasted. This new-born beach had every appearance of having been exposed to the air a thousand years. The sand was perfectly clean, and of a bright golden colour, and it was well strewed with shells of the most magnificent colours and size. The odour of their late tenants alone proclaimed the fact of their recent shipwreck. This, however, was an evil that a single month would repair; and our sailor determined to make another voyage to this bay, which he called Shell Bay, in order to procure some of its treasures. It was true he could not place them before the delighted eyes of Bridget, but he might arrange them in his cabin, and fancy that she was gazing at their beauties. After drinking at the spring, and supping on the rocks above, Mark arranged a mattress, provided for that purpose, in the boat, and went to sleep.

Early next morning the Bridget was again under way, but not until her owner had both bathed and broken his fast. Bathe he did every morning throughout the year, and occasionally at night also. A day of exertion usually ended with a bath, as did a night of sweet repose also. In all these respects no one could be more fortunate. From the first, food had been abundant; and now he possessed it in superfluity, including the wants of all dependent on him. Of clothes, also, he had an inexhaustible supply, a small portion of the cargo consisting of coarse cotton jackets and trousers, with which to purchase sandal-wood. To these means, delicious water was now added in inexhaustible quantities. The late changes had given to Mark's possession territory sufficient to occupy him months, even in exploring it thoroughly, as it was his purpose to do. God was there, also, as he is everywhere. This our secluded man found to be a most precious consolation. Again and again, each day, was he now in the practice of communing in spirit, directly with his Creator; not in cold and unmeaning forms and commonplaces, but with such yearning of the soul, and such feelings of love and reverence, as an active and living faith can alone, by the aid of the Divine Spirit, awaken in the human breast.

After crossing Shell Bay, the Bridget continued on for a couple of hours, running south, westerly, through a passage of a good width, until it met another channel, at a point which Mark at once recognized as the Forks. When at Point Fork, he had only to follow the track he had come the previous day, in order to arrive at the Reef. The crater could be seen from the Forks, and there was consequently a beacon in sight, to direct the adventurer, had he wanted such assistance; which he did not, however, since he now recognized objects perfectly well as he advanced, About ten o'clock he ran alongside of the ship, where he found everything, as he had left it. Lighting the fire, he put on food sufficient to last him for another cruise, and then went up into the cross-trees in order to take a better look than he had yet obtained, of the state of things to the southward.

By this time the vast, murky cloud that had so long overhung the new outlet of the volcano, was dispersed. It was succeeded by one of ordinary size, in which the thread of smoke that arose from the crater, terminated. Of course the surrounding atmosphere was clear, and nothing but distance obstructed the view. The Peak was indeed a sublime sight, issuing, as it did, from the ocean without any relief. Mark now began to think he had miscalculated its height, and that it might be *two* thousand feet, instead of one, above the water. There it was, in all its glory, blue and misty, but ragged and noble. The crater was clearly many miles beyond it, the young man being satisfied, after this look, that he had not yet seen its summit. He also increased his distance from Vulcan's Peak, as he named the mountain, to ten leagues, at least. After sitting in the cross-trees for fully an hour, gazing at this height with as much pleasure as the connoisseur ever studied picture, or statue, the young man determined to attempt a voyage to that place, in the Bridget. To him, such an expedition had the charm of the novelty and change which a journey from country to town could bring to the wearied worldling, who sighed for the enjoyment of his old haunts, after a season passed in the ennui of his country-house. It is true, great novelties had been presented to our solitary youth, by the great changes wrought immediately in his neighbourhood, and they had now kept him for a week in a condition of high excitement; but nothing they presented could equal the interest he felt in that distant mountain, which had arisen so suddenly in a horizon that he had been accustomed to see bare of any object but clouds, for near eighteen months.

That afternoon Mark made all his preparations for a voyage that he felt might be one of great moment to him. All the symptoms of convulsions in the earth, however, had ceased; even the rumbling sounds which he had heard, or imagined, in the stillness of the night, being no longer audible. From that source, therefore, he had no great apprehensions of danger; though there was a sort of dread majesty in the exhibition of the power of nature that he had so lately witnessed, which disposed him to approach the scene of its greatest effort with secret awe. So much did he think of the morrow and its possible consequences, that he did not get asleep for two or three hours, though he awoke in the morning unconscious of any want of rest. An hour later, he was in his boat, and under way.

Mark had now to steer in an entirely new direction, believing, from what he had seen while aloft the day before, that he could make his way out into the open ocean by proceeding a due south course. In order to do this, and to get into the most promising-looking channel in that direction, he was obliged to pass through the narrow strait that separated the Reef from the large range of rock over which he had roamed the day succeeding the earthquake. Of course, the bridge was removed, in order to allow the boat's mast to pass; but for this, Mark did not care. He had seen his stock the previous evening, and saw that it wanted for nothing. Even the fowls had gone across to the new territory, on exploring expeditions; and Kitty herself had left her sweet pastures on the Summit, to see of what the world was made beyond her old range. It is true she had made one journey in that quarter, in the company, of her master; but, one journey no more satisfied her than it would have satisfied the curiosity of any other female.

After passing the bridge, the boat entered a long narrow reach, that extended at least two leagues, in nearly a direct line towards Vulcan's Peak. As it approached the end of this piece of water, Mark saw that he must enter a bay of considerable extent; one, indeed, that was much larger than any he had yet seen in his island, or, to speak more accurately, his group of islands. On one side of this bay appeared a large piece of level land, or a plain, which Mark supposed, might cover one or two thousand acres. Its colour was so different from anything he had yet seen, that our young man was induced to land, and to walk a short distance to examine it. On reaching its margin, it was found to be a very shallow basin, of which the bottom was mud, with a foot or two of salt water still remaining, and in which sea weed, some ten or twelve inches in thickness, was floating. It was almost possible for Mark to walk on this weed, the green appearance of which induced him to name the place the Prairie. Such a collection of weed could only have been owing to the currents, which must have brought it into this basin, where it was probably retained even previously to the late eruption. The presence of the deposit of mud, as well as the height of the surrounding rocks, many of which were doubtless out of water previously to the phenomenon, went to corroborate this opinion.

After working her way through a great many channels, some wide and some narrow, some true and some false, the Bridget reached the southern verge of the group, about noon. Mark then supposed himself to be quite twenty miles from the Reef, and the Peak appeared very little nearer than when he left it. This startled him on the score of distance; and, after meditating on all his chances, the young man determined to pass the remainder of that day where he was, in order to put to sea with as much daylight before him as possible. He desired also to explore the coast and islands in that vicinity, in order to complete his survey of the cluster. He looked for a convenient place to anchor his boat, accordingly, ate his dinner, and set out on foot to explore, armed as usual with a fowling-piece.

In the first place, an outlet to the sea very different from that on the eastern side of the group, was found here, on its southern. The channel opened into a bay of some size, with an arm of rock reaching well off on the weather side, so that no broken water was encountered in passing into or out of it, provided one kept sufficiently clear of the point itself. As there was abundance of room, Mark saw he should have no difficulty in getting out into open water, here, or in getting back again. What was more, the arm, or promontory of rock just mentioned, had a hummock near a hundred feet in height on its extremity, that answered admirably for a land-mark. Most of this hummock must have been above water previously to the late eruption, though it appeared to our explorer, that all the visible land, as he proceeded south, was lifted higher and on a gradually-increasing scale, as if the eruption had exerted its force at a certain point, the new crater for instance, and raised the earth to the northward of that point, on an inclined plane. This might account, in a measure, for the altitude of the Peak, which was near the great crevice that must have been left somewhere, unless materials on its opposite side had fallen to fill it up again. Most of these views were merely speculative, though the fact of the greater elevation of all the rocks, in this part of the group, over those further north, was beyond dispute. Thus the coast, here, was generally fifty or eighty feet high; whereas, at the Reef, even now, the surface of the common rock was not much more than twenty feet above the water. The rise seemed to be gradual, moreover, which certainly favoured this theory.

As a great deal of sand and mud had been brought up by the eruption, there was no want of fresh water. Mark found even a little brook, of as perfectly sweet a stream as he had ever tasted in America, running into the little harbour where he had secured the boat. He followed this stream two miles, ere he reached its source, or sources; for it came from at least, a dozen copious springs, that poured their tribute from a bed of clean sand several miles in length, and which had every sign of having been bare for ages. In saying this, however, it is not to be supposed that the signs, as to time, were very apparent anywhere. Lava, known to have been ejected from the bowels of the earth thousands of years, has just as fresh an appearance, to the ordinary observer, as that which was thrown out ten years ago; and, had it not been for the deposits of moist mud, the remains of fish, sea-weed that was still undecayed, pools of salt water, and a few other peculiarities of the same sort, Mark would have been puzzled to find any difference between the rocks recently thrown up, and those which were formerly exposed to the air. Even the mud was fast changing its appearance, cracking and drying under the sun of the tropics. In a month or two, should as much rain as usual fall, it was probable the sea-weed would be far gone in decay.

It was still early when our adventurer kneeled on the sand, near his boat, to hold his last direct communication with his Creator, ere he slept. Those communications were now quite frequent with Mark, it being no unusual thing for him to hold them when sailing in his boat, on the deck of the ship, or in the soft salubrious air of the Summit. He slept none the less soundly for having commended his soul to God, asking support against temptations, and forgiveness for past sins. These prayers were usually very short. More than half the time they were expressed in the compendious and beautiful words given to man by Christ himself, the model and substance of all petitions of this nature. But the words were devoutly uttered, the heart keeping even pace with them, and the soul fully submitting to their influence.

Mark arose, next morning, two hours before the light appeared, and at once left the group. Time, was now important to him; for, while he anticipated the possibility of remaining under the lee of the mountain during the succeeding night, he also anticipated the possibility of being compelled to return. In a favourable time, with the wind a little free, five knots in the hour was about the maximum of the boat's rate of sailing, though it was affected by the greater or less height of the sea that was on. When the waves ran heavily, the Bridget's low sails got becalmed in the troughs, and she consequently lost much of her way. On the whole, however, five knots might be set down as her average speed, under the pressure of the ordinary trades, and with whole canvas, and a little off the wind. Close-hauled, she scarcely made more than three; while, with the wind on the quarter, she often went seven, especially in smooth water.

The course steered was about a point to the westward of south, the boat running altogether by compass, for the first two hours. At the end of that time day returned and the dark, frowning Peak itself became visible. The sun had no sooner risen, than Mark felt satisfied with his boat's performance. Objects began to come out of the mass of the mountain, which no longer appeared a pile of dark outline, without detail. He expected this, and was even disappointed that his eyes could not command more, for he now saw that he had materially underrated the distance between the crater and the Peak, which must be nearer sixty than fifty miles. The channel between the group and this isolated mass was, at least, twelve leagues in width. These twelve leagues were now to be run, and our young navigator thought he had made fully three of them, when light returned.

From that moment every mile made a sensible difference in the face of the mountain. Light and shadow first became visible; then ravines, cliffs, and colours, came into the view. Each league that he advanced increased Mark's admiration and awe; and by the time that the boat was on the last of those leagues which had appeared so long, he began to have a more accurate idea of the sublime nature of the phenomenon that had been wrought so near him. Vulcan's Peak, as an island, could not be less than eight or nine miles in length, though its breadth did not much exceed two. Running north and south, it offered its narrow side to the group of the crater, which had deceived its solitary observer. Yes! of the millions on earth, Mark Woolston, alone, had been so situated as to become a witness of this grand display of the powers of the elements. Yet, what was this in comparison with the thousand vast globes that were rolling about in space, objects so familiar as to be seen daily and nightly without raising a thought, in the minds of many, from the created to the creator? Even these globes come and go, and men remain indifferent to the mighty change!

The wind had been fresh in crossing the strait, and Mark was not sorry when his pigmy boat came under the shadow of the vast cliffs which formed the northern extremity of the Peak. When still a mile distant, he thought he was close on the rocks; nor did he get a perfectly true idea of the scale on which this rare mountain had been formed until running along at its base, within a hundred yards of its rocks. Coming in to leeward, as a matter of course, Mark found comparatively smooth water, though the unceasing heaving and setting of the ocean rendered it a little hazardous to go nearer to the shore. For some time our explorer was fearful he should not be able to land at all; and he was actually thinking of putting about, to make the best of his way back, while light remained to do so, when he came off a place that seemed fitted by art, rather than by nature, to meet his wishes. A narrow opening appeared between two cliffs, of about equal height, or some hundred feet in elevation, one of which extended further into the ocean than its neighbour. The water being quite smooth in this inlet, Mark ventured to enter it, the wind favouring his advance. On passing this gateway, he found himself nearly becalmed, in a basin that might be a hundred yards in diameter, which was not only surrounded by a sandy beach, but which had also a sandy bottom. The water was several fathoms deep, and it was very easy to run the bows of the boat anywhere on the beach. This was done, the sails were furled, and Mark sprang ashore, taking the grapnel with him. Like Columbus, he knelt on the sands, and returned his thanks to God.

Not only did a ravine open from this basin, winding its way up the entire ascent, but a copious stream of water ran through it, foaming and roaring amid its glens. At first, Mark supposed this was sea-water, still finding its way from some lake on the Peak; but, on tasting it, he found it was perfectly sweet. Provided with his gun, and carrying his pack, our young man entered this ravine, and following the course of the brook, he at once commenced an ascent. The route was difficult only in the labour of moving upwards, and by no means as difficult in that as he had expected to find it. It was, nevertheless, fortunate that this climbing was to be done in the shade, the sun seldom penetrating into those cool and somewhat damp crevices through which the brook found its way.

Notwithstanding his great activity, Mark Woolston was just an hour in ascending to the Peak. In no place had he found the path difficult, though almost always upward; but he believed he had walked more than two miles before he came out on level ground. When he had got up about three-fourths of the way, the appearances of things around him suddenly changed. Although the rock itself looked no older than that below, it had, occasionally, a covering that clearly could never have emerged from the sea within the last few days. From that point everything denoted an older existence in the air, from which our young man inferred that the summit of Vulcan's Peak had been an island long prior to the late eruption. Every foot he advanced confirmed this opinion, and the conclusion was that the ancient island had lain too low to be visible to one on the Reef.

An exclamation of delight escaped from our explorer, as he suddenly came out on the broken plain of the Peak. It was not absolutely covered, but was richly garnished with wood; cocoa-nut, bread-fruits, and other tropical trees; and it was delightfully verdant with young grasses. The latter were still wet with a recent shower that Mark had seen pass over the mountain, while standing for the island; and on examining them more closely, the traces of the former shower of volcanic ashes were yet to be seen. The warmth in the sun, after so sharp a walk, caused the young man to plunge into the nearest grove, where he had no difficulty in helping himself to as many cocoa-nuts, fresh from the trees, as a thousand men could have consumed. Every one has heard of the delicious beverage that the milk of the cocoa-nut, and of the delicious food that its pulp furnishes, when each is taken from the fruit before it hardens. How these trees came there, Mark did not know. The common theory is that birds convey the seeds from island to island; though some suppose that the earth contains the elements of all vegetation, and that this or that is quickened, as particular influences are brought to bear by means of climate and other agents.

After resting himself for an hour in that delicious grove, Mark began to roam around the plain, to get an idea of its beauties and extent. The former were inexhaustible, offering every variety of landscape, from the bold and magnificent to the soft and bewitching. There were birds innumerable, of the most brilliant plumage, and some that Mark imagined must be good to eat. In particular did he observe an immense number of a very small sort that were constantly pecking at a wild fig, of which there was a grove of considerable extent. The fig itself, he did not find as palatable as he had hoped, though it was refreshing, and served to vary the diet; but the bird struck him to be of the same kind as the celebrated reed-bird, of the Philadelphia market, which we suppose to be much the same as the *becca fichi* of Italy. Being provided with mustard-seed shot, Mark loaded his piece properly, and killed at least twenty of these little creatures at one discharge. After cleaning them, he struck a light by means of the pan and some powder, and kindled a fire. Here was wood, too, in any quantity, an article of which he had feared in time he might be in want, and which he had already begun to husband, though used only in his simple cookery. Spitting half-a-dozen of the birds, they were soon roasted. At the same time he roasted a bunch of plantain, and, being provided with pepper and salt in his pack, as well as with some pilot-bread, and a pint-bottle of rum, we are almost ashamed to relate how our young explorer dined. Nothing was wanting to such a meal but the sweets of social converse. Mark fancied, as he sat enjoying that solitary repast, so delicious of itself, and which was just enough sweetened with toil to render it every way acceptable, that he could gladly give up all the rest of the world, for the enjoyment of a paradise like that before him, with Bridget for his Eve.

The elevation of the mountain rendered the air far more grateful and cool than he was accustomed to find it, at mid-summer, down on the Reef, and the young man was in a sort of gentle intoxication while breathing it. Then it was that he most longed for a companion, though little did he imagine how near he was to some of his species, at that very moment; and how soon that, the dearest wish of his heart, was to be met by an adventure altogether so unexpected to him, that we must commence a new chapter, in order to relate it.

Chapter XIII

> "The merry homes of England!
> Around their hearths by night,
> What gladsome looks of household love
> Meet in the ruddy light!
> There woman's voice flows forth in song,
> Or childhood's tale is told,
> Or lips move tunefully along
> Some glorious page of old."
>
> —Mrs. Hemans

The peak, or highest part of the island, was at its northern extremity, and within two miles of the grove in which Mark Woolston had eaten his dinner. Unlike most of the plain, it had no woods whatever, but rising somewhat abruptly to a considerable elevation, it was naked of everything but grass. On the peak itself, there was very little of the last even, and it was obvious that it must command a full view of the whole plain of the island, as well as of the surrounding sea, for a wide distance. Resuming his pack, our young adventurer, greatly refreshed by the delicious repast he had just made, left the pleasant grove in which he had first rested, to undertake this somewhat sharp acclivity. He was not long in effecting it, however, standing on the highest point of his new discovery within an hour after he had commenced its ascent.

Here, Mark found all his expectations realized touching the character of the view. The whole plain of the island, with the exceptions of the covers made by intervening woods, lay spread before him like a map. All its beauties, its shades, its fruits, and its verdant glades, were placed beneath his eye, as if purposely to delight him with their glories. A more enchanting rural scene the young man had never beheld, the island having so much the air of cultivation and art about it, that he expected, at each instant, to see bodies of men running across its surface. He carried the best glass of the Rancocus with him, in all his excursions, not knowing at what moment Providence might bring a vessel in sight, and he had it now slung from his shoulders. With this glass, therefore, was every part of the visible surface of the island swept, in anxious and almost alarmed search for the abodes of inhabitants. Nothing of this sort, however, could be discovered. The island was unquestionably without a human being, our young man alone excepted. Nor could he see any trace of beast, reptile, or of any animal but birds. Creatures gifted with wings had been able to reach that little paradise; but to all others, since it first arose from the sea, had it probably been unapproached, if not unapproachable, until that day. It appeared to be the very Elysium of Birds!

Mark next examined the peak itself. There was a vast deposit of very ancient guano on it, the washings of which for ages, had doubtless largely contributed to the great fertility of the plain below. A stream of more size than one would expect to find on so small an island, meandered through the plain, and could be traced to a very copious spring that burst from the earth at the base of the peak. Ample as this spring was, however, it could never of itself have supplied the water of the brook, or rivulet, which received the contributions of some fifty other springs, that reached it in rills, as it wound its way down the gently inclined plane of the island. At one point, about two leagues from the Peak, there was actually a little lake visible, and Mark could even trace its outlet, winding its way beyond it. He supposed that the surplus tumbled into the sea in a cascade.

It will readily be imagined that our young man turned his glass to the northward, in search of the group he had left that morning, with a most lively interest. It was easy enough to see it from the great elevation at which he was now placed. There it lay, stretched far and wide, extending nearly a degree of latitude, north and south, and another of longitude, east and west, most truly resembling a vast dark-looking map, spread upon the face of the waters for his special examination. It reminded Mark of the moon, with its ragged outlines of imaginary continents, as seen by the naked eye, while the island he was now on, bore a fancied resemblance to the same object viewed through a telescope; not that it had the look of molten silver which is observed in the earth's satellite, but that it appeared gloriously bright and brilliant. Mark could easily see many of the sheets of water that were to be found among the rocks, though his naked eye could distinguish neither crater nor ship. By the aid of the glass, however, the first was to be seen, though the distance was too great to leave the poor deserted Rancocus visible, even with the assistance of magnifying-glasses.

When he had taken a good look at his old possessions, Mark made a sweep of the horizon with the glass, in order to ascertain if any other land were visible, from the great elevation on which he now stood. While arranging the focus of the instrument, an object first met his eye that caused his heart almost to leap into his mouth. Land was looming up, in the western board, so distinctly as to admit of no cavil about its presence. It was an island, mountainous, and Mark supposed it must be fully a hundred miles distant. Still it was land, and strange land, and might prove to be the abode of human beings. The glass told him very little more than his eye, though he could discern a mountainous form through it, and saw that it was an island of no great size. Beyond this mountain, again, the young man fancied that he could detect the haze of more land; but, if he did, it was too low, too distant, and too indistinct, to be certain of it. It is not easy to give a clear idea of the tumult of feeling with which Mark Woolston beheld these unknown regions, though it might best be compared with the emotions of the astronomer who discovers a new planet. It would scarce exceed the truth to say that he regarded that dim, blue mountain, which arose in the midst of a watery waste, with as much of admiration, mysterious awe and gratification united, as Herschel may have been supposed to feel when he established the character of Uranus. It was fully an hour before our hermit could turn his eyes in any other direction.

And when our young mariner did look aside, it was more with the intention of relieving eyes that had grown dim with gazing, than of not returning to the same objects again, as soon as restored to their power. It was while walking to and fro on the peak, with this intent, that a new subject of interest caused him almost to leap into the air, and to shout aloud. He saw a sail! For the first time since Betts disappeared from his anxious looks, his eyes now surely rested on a vessel. What was more, it was quite near the island he was on, and seemed to be beating up to get under its lee. It appeared but a speck on the blue waves of the ocean, seen from that height, it is true; but Mark was too well practised in his craft to be mistaken. It was a vessel, under more or less canvas, how much he could not then tell, or even see-but it was most decidedly a vessel. Mark's limbs trembled so much that he was compelled to throw himself upon the earth to find the support he wanted. There he lay several minutes, mentally returning thanks to God for this unexpected favour; and when his strength revived, these signs of gratitude were renewed on his knees. Then he arose, almost in terror lest the vessel should have disappeared, or it should turn out that he was the subject of a cruel illusion.

There was no error. There was the little white speck, and he levelled the glass to get a better look at it. An exclamation now clearly broke from his lips, and for a minute or two the young man actually appeared to be out of his senses. "The pinnace," "the Neshamony," however, were words that escaped him, and, had there been a witness, might have given an insight into this extraordinary conduct. Mark had, in fact, ascertained that the sail beneath the peak was no other than the little craft that had been swept away, as already described, with Betts in it. Fourteen months had elapsed since that occurrence, and here it was again, seemingly endeavouring to return to the place where it had been launched! Mark adopted perhaps the best expedient in his power to attract attention to himself, and to let his presence be known. He fired both barrels of his fowling-piece, and repeated the discharges several times, or until a flag was shown on board the sloop, which was now just beneath the cliff, a certain sign that he had succeeded. A musket was also fired from the vessel.

Our young man rather flew than ran to the ravine, down which he went at a pace that several times placed his neck in jeopardy. It was a very different thing to descend from ascending such a mountain. In less than a quarter of an hour the half-distracted hermit was in his boat, nearly crazy with the apprehension that he might yet not meet with his friend; for, that it was Bob looking for the Reef and himself, he did not now entertain the least doubt. The most plausible course for him to adopt was precisely that which he followed. He pushed off in the Bridget, making sail on the boat, and getting out of the cove in the shortest time he could. On quitting his little haven, and coming out clear of all the rocks, another shout burst out of his very soul, when he saw the Neshamony, beyond all cavil, within a hundred fathoms of him, running along the shore in search of a place to land. That shout was returned, and Mark and Bob recognised each other at the next instant. As for the last, he just off tarpaulin, and gave three hearty cheers, while the former sank on a seat, literally unable to stand. The sheet of the sail got away from him, nor could he be said to know what he was about, until some little time after he was in the arms of his friend, and on board the pinnace.

It was half-an-hour before Mark was master of himself again. At length tears relieved him; nor was he ashamed to indulge in them, when he saw his old companion not only alive and well, but restored to him. He perceived another in the boat; but as he was of a dark skin, he naturally inferred this second person was a native of some neighbouring island where Bob had been, and who had consented to come with him in this, his search after the shipwrecked mariner. At length Bob began to converse.

"Well, Mr. Mark, the sight of you is the pleasantest prospect that has met my eyes this many a day," exclaimed the honest fellow. "It was with fear and trembling that I set out on the search, and little did I hope to fall in with you so early in the cruise."

"Thank you, thank you, Bob, and God be praised for this great mercy! You have been to some other island, I see, by your companion; but the miraculous part of all is, that you should find your way back to the Reef, since you are no navigator."

"The Reef! If this here mountain is the Reef, the country has greatly altered since I left it," answered Bob. Mark then briefly explained the great change that had actually occurred, and told his own story touching his boat and his late voyages of discovery. Betts listened with the greatest attention, casting occasional glances upward at the immense mass that had been so suddenly lifted out of the sea, as well as turning his head to regard the smoke of the more distant volcano.

"Well, this explains our 'arthquake," he answered, as soon as Mark was done. "I must have been as good as a hundred and fifty leagues from this very spot at the time you mention, and we had tremblings there that would scarce let a body stand on his feet. A ship came in two days arterwards, that must have been a hundred leagues further to the nor'ard when it happened, and her people reported that they thought heaven and 'arth was a coming together, out there in open water."

"It has been a mighty earthquake-must have been, to have wrought these vast changes; though I had supposed that Providence had confined a knowledge of its existence to myself. But, you spoke of a ship, Bob-surely we are not in the neighbourhood of vessels."

"Sartain-but, I may as well tell you my adventures at once, Mr. Mark; though I own I should like to land first, as it is a long story, and take a look at this island that you praise so much, and taste them reed-birds of which you give so good an account. I'm Jarsey-born and bred, and know what the little things be."

Mark was dying to hear Bob's story, more especially since he understood a ship was connected with it, but he could not refuse his friend's demand for sweet water and a dinner. The entrance of the cove was quite near and the boats entered that harbour and were secured; after which the three men commenced the ascent, Mark picking up by the way the spy-glass, fowling-piece, and other articles that he had dropped in the haste of his descent. While going up this sharp acclivity, but little was said; but, when they reached the summit, or the plain rather, exclamations of delight burst from the mouths of both of Mark's companions. To the young man's great surprise, those which came from Bob's dark-skinned associate were in English, as well as those which came from Bob himself. This induced him to take a good look at the man, when he discovered a face that he knew!

"How is this, Bob?" cried Mark, almost gasping for breath —"whom have you here? Is not this Socrates?"

"Ay, ay, sir; that's Soc; and Dido, his wife, is within a hundred miles of you."

This answer, simple as it was, nearly overcame our young man again. Socrates and Dido had been the slaves of Bridget, when he left home; a part of the estate she had received from her grandmother. They dwelt in the house with her, and uniformly called her mistress. Mark knew them both very well, as a matter of course; and Dido, with the archness of a favourite domestic, was often in the habit of calling him her 'young master.' A flood of expectations, conjectures and apprehensions came over our hero, and he refrained from putting any questions immediately, out of pure astonishment. He was almost afraid indeed to ask any.

Nearly unconscious of what he was about, he led the way to the grove where he had dined two or three hours before, and where the remainder of the reed-birds were suspended from the branch of a tree. The embers of the fire were ready, and in a few minutes Socrates handed Betts his dinner.

Bob ate and drank heartily. He loved a tin-pot of rum and-water, or grog, as it used to be called-though even the word is getting to be obsolete in these temperance times-and he liked good eating. It was not epicurism, however, or a love of the stomach, that induced him to defer his explanations on the present occasion. He saw that Mark must hear what he had to relate gradually, and was not sorry that the recognition of the negro had prepared him to expect something wonderful. Wonderful it was, indeed; and at last Betts, having finished his dinner, and given half-a-dozen preparatory hints, in order to lessen the intensity of his young friend's feelings, yielded to an appeal from the other's eyes, and commenced his narrative. Bob told his story, as a matter of course, with a great deal of circumlocution, and in his own language. There was a good deal of unnecessary prolixity in it, and some irrelative digressions touching currents, and the trades, and the weather; but, on the whole, it was given intelligibly, and with sufficient brevity for one who devoured every syllable he uttered. The reader, however, would most probably prefer to hear an abridgement of the tale in our own words.

When Robert Betts was driven off the Reef, by the hurricane of the preceding year, he had no choice but to let the Neshamony drive to leeward with him. As soon as he could, he got the pinnace before the wind, and, whenever he saw broken water ahead, he endeavoured to steer clear of it. This he sometimes succeeded in effecting; while at others he passed through it, or over it, at the mercy of the tempest. Fortunately the wind had piled up the element in such a way as to carry the craft clear of the rocks, and in three hours after the Neshamony was lifted out of her cradle, she was in the open ocean, to leeward of all the dangers. It blew too hard, however, to make sail on her, and Bob was obliged to scud until the gale broke. Then, indeed, he passed a week in endeavouring to beat back and rejoin his friend, but without success, 'losing all he made in the day, while asleep at night.' Such, at least, was Bob's account of his failure to find the Reef again; though Mark thought it probable that he was a little out in his reckoning, and did not look in exactly the right place for it.

At the end of this week high land was made to leeward, and Betts ran down for it, in the hope of finding inhabitants. In this last expectation, however, he did not succeed. It was a volcanic mountain, of a good many resources, and of a character not unlike that of Vulcan's Peak, but entirely unpeopled. He named it after his old ship, and passed several days on it. On describing its appearance, and its bearings from the place where they then were, Mark had no doubt it was the island that was visible from the peak near them, and at which he had been gazing that very afternoon, for fully an hour with longing eyes. On describing its form to Bob, the latter coincided in this opinion, which was in fact the true one.

From the highest point of Rancocus Island, land was to be seen to the northward and westward, and Bob now determined to make the best of his way in that direction, in the hope of falling in with some vessel after sandal-wood or bêche-le-mar. He fell in with a group of low islands, of a coral formation, about a hundred leagues from his volcanic mountain, and on them he found inhabitants. These people were accustomed to see white men, and turned out to be exceedingly mild and just. It is probable that they connected the sudden appearance of a vessel like the Neshamony, having but one man in it, with some miraculous interposition of their gods, for they paid Bob the highest honours, and when he landed, solemnly tabooed his sloop. Bob was a long-headed fellow in the main, and was not slow to perceive the advantage of such a ceremony, and encouraged it. He also formed a great intimacy with the chief, exchanging names and rubbing noses with him. This chief was styled Betto, after the exchange, and Bob was called Ooroony by the natives. Ooroony stayed a month with Betto, when he undertook a voyage with him in a large canoe, to another group, that was distant two or three hundred miles, still further to the northward, and where Bob was told he should find a ship. This account proved to be true, the ship turning out to be a Spaniard, from South America, engaged in the pearl fishery, and on the eve of sailing for her port. From some misunderstanding with the Spanish captain, that Bob never comprehended and of course could not explain, and which he did not attempt to explain, Betto left the group in haste, and without taking leave of his new friend, though he sent him a message of apology, one-half of which was lost on Bob, in consequence of not understanding the language. The result was, however, to satisfy the latter that his friend was quite as sorry to abandon *him*, as he was glad to get away from the Spanish captain.

This desertion left Betts no choice between remaining on the pearl island, or of sailing in the brig, which went to sea next day. He decided to do the last. In due time he was landed at Panama, whence he made his way across the isthmus, actually reaching Philadelphia in less than five months after he was driven off the Reef. In all this he was much favoured by circumstances; though an old salt, like Bob, will usually make his way where a landsman would be brought up.

The owners of the Rancocus gave up their ship, as soon as Betts had told his story, manifesting no disposition to send good money after bad. They looked to the underwriters, and got Bob to make oath to the loss of the vessel; which said oath, by the way, was the ground-work of a law-suit that lasted Friend Abraham White as long as he lived. Bob next sought Bridget with his tale. The young wife received the poor fellow with floods of tears, and the most eager attention to his story, as indeed did our hero's sister Anne. It would seem that Betts's arrival was most opportune. In consequence of the non-arrival of the ship, which was then past due two or three months, Doctor Yardley had endeavoured to persuade his daughter that she was a widow, if indeed, as he had of late been somewhat disposed to maintain, she had ever been legally married at all. The truth was, that the medical war in Bristol had broken out afresh, in consequence of certain cases that had been transferred to that village, during one of the fever-seasons in Philadelphia. Greater cleanliness, and the free use of fresh water, appear to have now arrested the course of this formidable disease, in the northern cities of America; but, in that day, it was of very frequent occurrence. Theories prevailed among the doctors concerning it, which were bitterly antagonistical to each other; and Doctor Woolston headed one party in Bucks, while Doctor Yardley headed another. Which was right, or whether either was right, is more than we shall pretend to say, though we think it probable that both were wrong. Anne Woolston had been married to a young physician but a short time, when this new outbreak concerning yellow fever occurred. Her husband, whose name was Heaton, unfortunately took the side of this grave question that was opposed to his father-in-law, for a reason no better than that he believed in the truth of the opposing theory, and this occasioned another breach. Doctor Yardley could not, and did not wholly agree with Doctor Heaton, because the latter was Doctor Woolston's son-in-law, and he altered his theory a little to create a respectable point of disagreement; while Doctor. Woolston could not pardon a disaffection that took place, as it might be, in the height of a war. About this time too, Mrs. Yardley died.

All these occurrences, united to the protracted absence of Mark, made Bridget and Anne extremely unhappy. To increase this unhappiness, Doctor Yardley took it into his head to dispute the legality of a marriage that had been solemnized on board a ship. This was an entirely new legal crotchet, but the federal government was then young, and jurisdictions had not been determined as clearly as has since been the case. Had it been the fortune of Doctor Yardley to live in these later times, he would not have given himself the trouble to put violent constructions on anything; but, getting a few female friends to go before the necessary judge, with tears in their eye's, anything would be granted to their requests, very much as a matter of course. Failing of this, moreover, there is always the resource of the legislature, which will usually pass a law taking away a man's wife, or his children, and sometimes his estate, if a pretty pathetic appeal can be made to it, in the way of gossip. We have certainly made great progress in this country, within the last twenty years; but whether it has been in a direction towards the summit of human perfection, or one downward towards the destruction of all principles, the next generation will probably be better able to say than this. Even the government is getting to be gossipian.

In the case of Bridget, however, public sympathy was with her, as it always will be with a pretty woman. Nevertheless, her father had great influence in Bucks county, more especially with the federalists and the anti-depletionists, and it was in his power to give his daughter great uneasiness, if not absolutely to divorce her. So violent did he become, that he actually caused proceedings to be commenced in Bridget's name, to effect a legal separation, taking the grounds that the marriage had never been consummated, that the ceremony had occurred on board a ship, that the wife was of tender years, and lastly, that she was an heiress. Some persons thought the Doctor's proceedings were instigated by the circumstance that another relative had just died, and left Bridget five thousand dollars, which were to be paid to her the day she was eighteen, the period of a female's reaching her majority, according to popular notions. The possession of this money, which Bridget received and, placed in the hands of a friend in town, almost made her father frantic for the divorce, or a decree against the marriage, he contending there was no marriage, and that a divorce was unnecessary. The young wife had not abandoned the hope of seeing her husband return, all this time, although uneasiness concerning the fate of the ship, was extending from her owners into the families of those who had sailed in her. She wished to meet Mark with a sum of money that would enable him, at once, to commence life respectably, and place him above the necessity of following the seas.

Betts reached Bristol the very day that a decision was made, on a preliminary point, in the case of Yardley versus Woolson, that greatly encouraged the father in his hopes of final success, and as greatly terrified his daughter. It was, in fact, a mere question of practice, and had no real connection with the merits of the matter at issue; but it frightened Bridget and her friend Anna enormously. In point of fact, there was not the smallest danger of the marriage being declared void, should any one oppose the decision; but this was more than any one of the parties then knew, and Doctor Yardley seemed so much in earnest, that Bridget and Anne got into the most serious state of alarm on the subject. To increase their distress, a suitor for the hand of the former appeared in the person of a student of medicine, of very fair expectations and who supported every one of Doctor Yardley's theories, in all their niceties and distinctions; and what is more, would have supported them, had they been ten times as untenable as they actually were, in reason.

Had the situation of Doctor Heaton been more pleasant than it was, it is probable that the step taken by himself, his wife, and Bridget, would never have been thought of. But it was highly unpleasant. He was poor, and dependent altogether on his practice for a support. Now, it was in Doctor Woolston's power to be of great service to the young couple, by introducing the son-in-law to his own patients, but this he could not think of doing with a depletionist; and John, as Anne affectionately styled her husband, was left to starve on his system of depletion. Such was the state of things when Bob appeared in Bristol, to announce to the young wife not only the existence but the deserted and lone condition of her husband. The honest fellow knew there was something clandestine about the marriage, and he used proper precautions not to betray his presence to the wrong persons. By means of a little management he saw Bridget privately, and told his story. As Bob had been present at the wedding, and was known to stand high in Mark's favour, he was believed, quite as a matter of course, and questioned in a thousand ways, until the poor fellow had not really another syllable to communicate.

The sisters shed floods of tears at the thought of poor Mark's situation. For several days they did little besides weep and pray. Then Bridget suddenly dried her tears, and announced an intention to go in person to the rescue of her husband. Not only was she determined on this, but, as a means of giving a death-blow to all expectations of a separation and to the hopes of her new suitor, she was resolved to go in a way that should enable her to remain on the Reef with Mark, and, if necessary, to pass the remainder of her days there. Bob had given a very glowing description of the charms of the residence, as well as of the climate, the latter quite justly, and declared his readiness to accompany this faithful wife in the pursuit of her lost partner. The whole affair was communicated to Doctor and Mrs. Heaton, who not only came into the scheme, but enlisted in its execution in person. The idea pleased the former in particular, who had a love of adventure, and a desire to see other lands, while Anne was as ready to follow her husband to the ends of the earth, as Bridget was to go to the same place in quest of Mark. In a word, the whole project was deliberately framed, and ingeniously carried out.

Doctor Heaton had a brother, a resident of New York, and often visited him. Bridget was permitted to accompany Anne to that place, whither her money was transferred to her. A vessel was found that was about to sail for the North-west Coast, and passages were privately engaged. A great many useful necessaries were laid in, and, at the proper time, letters of leave-taking were sent to Bristol, and the whole party sailed. Previously to the embarkation, Bob appeared to accompany the adventurers. He was attended by Socrates, and Dido, and Juno, who had stolen away by order of their young mistress, as well as by a certain Friend Martha Waters, who had stood up in 'meeting' with Friend Robert Betts, and had become "bone of his bone and flesh of his flesh;" and her maiden sister, Joan Waters, who was to share their fortunes. In a word, Bob had brought an early attachment to the test of matrimony.

So well had the necessary combinations been made, that the ship sailed with our adventurers, nine in number, without meeting with the slightest obstacle. Once at sea, of course nothing but that caused by the elements was to be anticipated. Cape Horn was doubled in due time, are Doctor Heaton, with all under his care, was landed at Panama, just five months, to a day, after leaving New York. Here passages were taken in the same brig that Bob had returned in, which was again bound out, on a pearl-fishing voyage. Previously to quitting Panama, however, a recruit was engaged in the person of a young American shipwright, of the name of Bigelow, who had run from his ship a twelvemonth before, to marry a Spanish girl, and who had become heartily tired of his life in Panama. He and his wife and child joined the party, engaging to serve the Heatons, for a stipulated sum, for the term of two years.

The voyage from Panama to, the pearl islands was a long one, but far from unpleasant. Sixty days after leaving port the adventurers were safely landed, with all their effects. These included two cows, with a young bull, two yearling colts, several goats obtained in South America, and various implements of husbandry that it had not entered into the views of Friend Abraham White to send to even the people of Fejee. With the natives of the pearl island, Bob, already known to them and a favourite, had no difficulty in negotiating. He had brought them suitable and ample presents, and soon effected an arrangement, by which they agreed to transport him and all his stores, the animals included, to Betto's Islands, a distance of fully three hundred miles. The horses and cows were taken on a species of catamaran, or large raft, that is much used in those mild seas, and which sail reasonably well a little off the wind, and not very badly on. At Betto's Islands a new bargain was struck, and the whole party proceeded to Rancocus Island, Bob making his land-fall without any difficulty, from having observed the course steered in coming from it.

At Betto's group, however, Bob found the Neshamony, covered with mats, and tabooed, precisely as he had left her to a rope-yarn. Not a human hand had touched anything belonging to the boat, or a human foot approached it, during the whole time of his absence. Ooroony, or Betto, was rewarded for his fidelity by the present of a musket and some ammunition, articles that were really of the last importance to his dignity and power. They were as good as a standing army to him, actually deciding summarily a point of disputed authority, that had long been in controversy between himself and another chief, in his favour. The voyage between Betto's group and Rancocus Island was made in the Neshamony, so far as the human portion of the freight was concerned, The catamarans and canoes, however, came on with the other animals, and all the utensils and stores.

The appearance of Rancocus Island created quite as much astonishment among the native mariners, as had that of the horses, cows, &c. Until they saw it, not one of them had any notion of its existence, or of a mountain at all. They dwelt themselves on low coral islands, and quite beyond the volcanic formation, and a hill was a thing scarcely known to them. At this island Heaton and Betts deemed it prudent to dismiss their attendants, not wishing them to know anything of the Reef, as they were not sure what sort of neighbours they, might prove, on a longer acquaintance. The mountain, however, possessed so many advantages over the Reef, as the latter was when Bob left it, that the honest fellow frankly admitted its general superiority, and suggested the possibility of its becoming their permanent residence. In some respects it was not equal to the Reef, as a residence, however, the fishing in particular turning out to be infinitely inferior. But it had trees and fruits, being very much of the same character as Vulcan's Peak, in this respect. Nevertheless, there was no comparison between the two islands as places of residence, the last having infinitely the most advantages. It was larger, had more and better fruits, better water, and richer grasses. It had also a more even surface, and a more accessible plain. Rancocus Island was higher and more broken, and, while it might be a pleasanter place of residence than the Reef during the warm months, it never could be a place as pleasant as the plain of the Peak.

Bob found it necessary to leave his friends, and most of his stores, at Rancocus Island; Mrs. Heaton becoming a mother two days after their arrival at it, and the cows both increasing their families in the course of the same week. It was, moreover, impossible to transport everybody and everything in the Neshamony, at the same time. As Doctor Heaton would not leave Anne at such a moment, and Bridget was of the same way of thinking, it was thought best to improve the time by sending out Betts to explore. It will be remembered that he was uncertain where the Reef was to be found exactly, though convinced it was to windward, and within a hundred miles of him. While roaming over the rocks of Rancocus, however, Vulcan's Peak had been seen, as much to Bob's surprise as to his delight. To his surprise, inasmuch as he had no notion of the great physical change that had recently been wrought by the earthquake, yet could scarce believe he had overlooked such an object in his former examinations; and to his delight, because he was now satisfied that the Reef must be to the northward of that strange mountain, and a long distance from it, because no such peak had been visible from the former when he left it. It was a good place to steer for, nevertheless, on this new voyage, since it carried him a hundred miles to wind ward; and when Bob, with Socrates for a companion, left Rancocus to look for the Reef, he steered as near the course for the Peak as the wind would permit. He had made the island from the boat, after a run of ten hours; and, at the same time, he made the crater of the active volcano. For the latter, he stood that night, actually going within a mile of it, and, next morning, he altered his course, and beat up for the strange island. When Mark first discovered him, he had nearly made the circuit of Vulcan's Peak, in a vain endeavour to land, and he would actually have gone on his way, had it not been for the firing of the fowling-piece, the report of which he heard, and the smoke of which he saw.

Chapter XIV

> "Compell the hawke to sit, that is unmanned,
> Or make the hound, untaught, to draw the deere,
> Or bring the free, against his will, in band,
> Or move the sad, a pleasant tale to heere,
> Your time is lost, and you no whit the neere!
> So love ne learnes, of force, the heart to knit:
> She serves but those, that feels sweet fancie's fit."
>
> *—Churchyard,*

We leave the reader to imagine with what feelings Mark heard these facts. Bridget, for whom his tenderness was unabated; Bridget, who had been the subject of so many of his thoughts since his shipwreck, had shown herself worthy to be thus loved, and was now on an island that he might easily reach in a run of a few hours! The young man retired further within the grove, leaving Bob and Socrates behind, and endeavoured to regain his composure by himself. Before rejoining his companions, he knelt and returned thanks to God for this instance of his great kindness. It was a long time, notwithstanding before he could become accustomed to the idea of having associates, at all. Time and again, within the next month or two, did he *dream* that all this fancied happiness was only a *dream*, and awoke under a sense of having been the subject of an agreeable illusion. It took months perfectly to restore the tone of his mind in this respect, and to bring it back into the placid current of habitual happiness. The deep sense of gratitude to God he never lost; but the recollection of what he had suffered, and from what he had been relieved by the Divine mercy, remained indelibly impressed on his heart, and influenced his future life to a degree that increased the favour a thousand-fold.

The mode of proceeding was next discussed, in the course of doing which Mark communicated to Bob, somewhat in detail, the circumstance of the recent convulsion, and the changes which it had produced. After talking the matter over, both agreed it would be every way desirable to bring the whole party, and as much of the property as could be easily moved, up to windward at once. Now, that the natives knew of the existence of Rancocus Island, their visits might be often expected, and nothing was more uncertain than their policy and friendship. Once on Rancocus Island the Peak could be seen, and from the Peak the Reef was visible. In this way, then, there was every reason to believe that the existence of their little colony would soon become known, and the property they possessed the object of cupidity and violence. Against such consequences it would be necessary to guard with the strictest care, and the first step should be to get everything of value up to windward, with the least possible delay. The natives often went a long distance, in their canoes and on their rafts, with the wind abeam, but it was not often they undertook to go directly to windward. Then the activity of the volcano might be counted on as something in favour of the colonists, since those uninstructed children of nature would be almost certain to set the phenomenon down to the credit of some god, or some demon, neither of whom would be likely to permit his special domains to be trespassed on with impunity.

While Mark and Bob were talking these matters over, Socrates had been shooting and cleaning a few dozen more of the reed-birds. This provision of the delicacy was made, because Betts affirmed no such delicious little creature was to be met with on Rancocus, though they were to be found on Vulcan's Peak literally in tens of thousands. This difference could be accounted for in no other way, than by supposing that some of the birds had originally found their way to the latter, favoured by accidental circumstances, driven by a hurricane, transported on sea-weed, or attending the drift of some plants, and that the same, or similar circumstances, had never contributed to carry them the additional hundred miles to leeward.

It was near sunset when the Neshamony left Snug Cove, as Mark had named his little haven, at the foot of the ravine, which, by the way, he called the Stairs, and put to sea, on her way to Rancocus Island. The bearings of the last had been accurately taken, and our mariners were just as able to run by night as by day. It may as well be said here, moreover, that the black was a capital boatman, and a good fresh-water sailor in general, a proficiency that he had acquired in consequence of having been born and brought up on the banks of the Delaware. But it would have been very possible to run from one of these islands to the other, by observing the direction of the wind alone, since it blew very steadily in the same quarter, and changes in the course were always to be noted by changes in the violence or freshness of the breeze. In that quarter of the ocean the trades blew with very little variation from the south-east, though in general the Pacific Trades are from the south-west.

Mark was delighted with the performances of the Neshamony. Bob gave a good account of her qualities, and said he should not hesitate to make sail in her for either of the continents, in a case of necessity. Accustomed, as he had been of late, to the little Bridget, the pinnace appeared a considerable craft to Mark, and he greatly exalted in this acquisition. No seaman could hesitate about passing from the Reef to the islands, at any time when it did not absolutely blow a gale, in a boat of this size and of such qualities; and, even in a gale, it might be possible to make pretty good weather of it. Away she now went, leaving the Bridget moored in Snug Cove, to await their return. Of course, Mark and Bob had much discourse, while running down before the wind that night, in which each communicated to the other many things that still remained to be said. Mark was never tired of asking questions about Bridget; her looks, her smiles, her tears, her hopes, her fears, her health, her spirits, and her resolution, being themes of which he never got weary. A watch was set, nevertheless, and each person in the pinnace had his turn of sleep, if sleep he could.

At the rising of the sun Mark was awake. Springing to his feet, he saw that Rancocus Island was plainly in view. In the course of the ten hours she had been out, the Neshamony had run about seventy miles, having a square-sail set, in addition to her jib and mainsail. This brought the mountain for which she was steering within ten leagues, and directly to leeward. A little impatience was betrayed by the young husband, but, on the whole, he behaved reasonably well. Mark had never neglected his person, notwithstanding his solitude. Daily baths, and the most scrupulous attention to his attire, so far as neatness went, had kept him not only in health, but in spirits, the frame of the mind depending most intimately on the condition of the body. Among other habits, he preserved that of shaving daily. The cutting of his hair gave him the most trouble, and he had half a mind to get Bob to act as barber on the present occasion. Then he remembered having seen Bridget once cut the hair of a child, and he could not but fancy how pleasant it would be to have her moving about him, in the performance of the same office on himself. He decided, consequently, to remain as he was, as regarded his looks, until his charming bride could act as his hair-dresser. The toilette, however, was not neglected, and, on the whole, there was no reason to complain of the young man's appearance. The ship furnished him clothes at will, and the climate rendered so few necessary, that even a much smaller stock than he possessed, would probably have supplied him for life.

When about a league from the northern end of Rancocus Island, Bob set a little flag at his mast-head, the signal, previously arranged, of his having been successful. Among the stores brought by the party from America, were three regular tents, or marquees, which Heaton purchased at a sale of old military stores, and had prudently brought with him, to be used as occasion might demand. These marquees were now pitched on a broad piece of low land, that lay between the cliffs and the beach, and where the colony had temporarily established itself. Mark's heart beat violently as Bob pointed out these little canvas dwellings to him. They were the abodes of his friends, including his young wife. Next the cows appeared, quietly grazing near by, with a pleasant home look, and the goats and colts were not far off, cropping the grass. Altogether our young man was profoundly overcome again, and it was some time ere he could regain his self-command. On a point that proved to be the landing-place, stood a solitary female figure. As the boat drew nearer she extended her arms, and then, as if unable to stand, she sunk on a rock which had served her for a seat ever since the distant sail was visible. In two more minutes Mark Woolston had his charming young bride encircled in his arms. The delicacy which kept the others aloof from this meeting, was imitated by Bob, who, merely causing the boat, to brush near the rock, so as to allow of Mark's jumping ashore, passed on to a distant landing, where he was met by most of his party, including 'Friend Martha,' who rejoiced not a little in the safe return of Friend Robert Betts. In half-an-hour Mark and Bridget came up to the marquees, when the former made the acquaintance of his brother-in-law, and had the happiness of embracing his sister. It was a morning of the purest joy, and deepest gratitude. On the one side, the solitary man found himself restored to the delights of social life, in the persons of those on earth whom he most loved and, on the other hand, the numberless apprehensions of those who looked for him, and his place of retirement, had all their anxiety rewarded by complete success. Little was done that day but to ask and answer questions. Mark had to recount all that had happened since Bob was taken from him, and not trifling was the trepidation created among his female listeners, when he related the history of the earthquake. Their fears, however, were somewhat appeased by his assurances of security; the circumstance that a volcano was in activity near by, being almost a pledge that no very extensive convulsions could follow.

The colonists remained a week at Rancocus Island, being actually too happy to give themselves the disturbance of a removal. At the end of that time, however, Anne was so far recovered that they began to talk of a voyage, Bridget, in particular, dying to see the place where Mark had passed so many solitary hours; and, as he had assured her more than once, where her image had scarcely ever been absent from his thoughts an hour at a time. As it would be impossible to embark all the effects at once, in the Neshamony, some method was to be observed in the removal. The transportation of the cows and horses was the most serious part of the undertaking, the pinnace not being constructed to receive such animals. Room, nevertheless, could be made for one at a time, and still leave sufficient space in the stern-sheets for the accommodation of five or six persons. It was very desirable to get the females away first, lest the rumour of the mountain, hitherto unknown, should spread among the islands, and bring them visitors who might prove to be troublesome, if not dangerous. Parties existed in Betto's group, as we believe they exist everywhere else; and Bob knew very well that nothing but the ascendancy of his friend, the chief, Ooroony, had been the means of his escaping as well as he did, in the land-fall among them that he had made. The smallest reverse of fortune might put Betto down, and some bitter foe up, and then there was the certainty that war canoes might come off in quest of the mountain, at any time, without asking the leave of the friendly chief, even while he remained in power. On the whole, therefore, it was determined to freight the pinnace with the most valuable of the effects, put all the females on board, and send her off under the care of Mark, Heaton, and Socrates, leaving Bob and Bigelow to look after the stock and the rest of the property. It was supposed the boat might be absent a week. This was done accordingly, Bob, on taking leave of Friend Martha, particularly recommending to her attention the Vulcan's Peak reed-birds, throwing in a hint that he should be glad to find a string of them in the pinnace, on her return.

The voyage to windward was a much more serious business than the run to leeward. By Bob's advice Mark reefed his mainsail, and took the bonnet off the jib. Following the same instructions, he stood away to the southward, letting the boat go through the water freely, intending to tack when he came near the volcano, and not before. This was what Bob himself had done, and that which had turned out so well with him, he fancied might succeed with his friend. The Neshamony left Rancocus Island just at sunset. Next morning Mark saw the smoke of the Volcano, and stood for it. After making two stretches he came up within a league of this spot, when he tacked and stood to the northward and eastward, Vulcan's Peak having been in plain view the entire day. As respects the volcano, it was in a comparatively quiet state, though rumbling sounds were heard, and stones were cast into the air in considerable quantities, while the boat was nearest in. One thing, moreover, Mark ascertained, which greatly increased his confidence in the permanency of the changes that had lately occurred in the physical formation of all that region. He found himself in comparatively shoal water, when fully a league from this new crater. Shoal in a seaman's sense, though not in shallow water; the soundings being from fifteen to twenty fathoms, with a rocky bottom.

Between the volcano and Vulcan's Peak it blew quite fresh, and Mark had a good occasion to ascertain the qualities of the pinnace. A long, heavy swell came rolling through the passage, which was near sixty miles in width, seemingly with a sweep that extended to the Southern Ocean. Notwithstanding all this, the little craft did wonders, struggling along in a way one would hardly have expected from so small a vessel. She made fully two knots' headway in the worst of it, and in general her rate of sailing, close on a wind and under pretty short canvas, was about three. The night was very dark, and there was nothing to steer by but the wind, which gave some little embarrassment; but finding himself in much smoothe water than he had been all the previous day, about midnight, our young man felt satisfied that he was under the lee of the island, and at no great distance from it. He made short tacks until daylight, when the huge mass hove up out of the departing darkness, within a mile of the boat. It only remained to run along the land for two or three miles, and to enter the haven of Snug Cove. Mark had been telling his companions what a secret place this haven was to conceal a vessel in, when he had a practical confirmation of the truth of his statement that caused him to be well laughed at. For ten minutes he could not discover the entrance himself, having neglected to take the proper land-marks, that he might have no difficulty in running for his port. After a time, however, he caught sight of an object that he remembered, and found his way into the cove. Here lay the little namesake of his pretty wife, just as he had left her, the true Bridget smiling and blushing as the young husband pointed out the poor substitute he had been compelled to receive for herself, only ten days earlier.

Mark, and Socrates, and Dido, and Teresa, Bigelow's wife, all carried up heavy loads; while Heaton had as much as he could do to help Anne and the child up the sharp acclivity. Bridget, with her light active step, and great eagerness to behold a scene that Mark had described with so much eloquence, was the first, by a quarter of an hour, on the plain. When the others reached the top, they saw the charming young thing running about in the nearest grove, that in which her husband had dined, collecting fruit, and apparently as enchanted as a child. Mark paused as he gained the height, to gaze on this sight, so agreeable in his eyes, and which rendered the place so very different from what it had been so recently, while he was in possession of its glorious beauties, a solitary man. Then, he had several times likened himself to Adam in the garden of Eden, before woman was given to him for a companion. Now, now he could feast his eyes on an Eve, who would have been highly attractive in any part of the world.

The articles brought up on the plain, at this first trip, comprised all that was necessary to prepare and to partake of a breakfast in comfort. A fire was soon blazing, the kettle on, and the bread-fruit baking. It was almost painful to destroy the reed-birds, or *becca fichi* so numerous were they, and so confiding. One discharge from each barrel of the fowling-piece had enabled Heaton to bring in enough for the whole party, and these were soon roasting. Mark had brought with him from the Reef a basket of fresh eggs, and they had been Bridget's load, in ascending the mountain. He had promised her an American breakfast, and these eggs, boiled, did serve to remind everybody of a distant home, that was still remembered with melancholy pleasure. A heartier, or a happier meal, notwithstanding, was never made than was that breakfast. The mountain air, invigorating though bland, the exercise, the absence of care, the excellence of the food, which comprised fresh figs, a tree or two of tolerable sweetness having been found, the milk of the cocoa-nut, the birds, the eggs, the bread-fruit, &c., all contributed their share to render the meal memorable.

The men, and the three labouring women, were employed two days in getting the cargo of the Neshamony up on the plain; or to Eden, as Bridget named the spot, unconscious how often she herself had been likened to a lovely Eve, in the mind of her young husband. Two of the marquees had been brought, and were properly erected, having board floors, and everything comfortably arranged within and without them. A roof, however, was scarcely necessary in that delicious climate, where one could get into the shade of a grove; and a thatched shed was easily prepared for a dwelling for the others. By the end of the third day the whole party in Eden was comfortably established, and Mark took a short leave of his bride, to sail for Rancocus again, Bridget shed fears at this separation short as it was intended to be; and numberless were the injunctions to be wary of the natives, should the latter have visited Betts, in the time intervening between the departure of the Neshamony and her return.

The voyage between the two islands lost something of its gravity each time it was made. Mark learned a little every trip, of the courses to be steered, the peculiarities of the currents, and the height of the seas. He ran down to Rancocus, on this occasion, in three hours less time than he had done it before, sailing at dusk, and reaching port next day at noon. Nothing had occurred, and to work the men went at once, to load the pinnace. Room was left for one of the cows and its calf: and Bob being seriously impressed with the importance of improving every moment, the little sloop put to sea again, the evening of the very day on which it had arrived.

Bridget was standing on a rock, by the side of the limpid water of the cove, when the Neshamony shot through its entrance into the little haven, and her hand was in Mark's the instant he landed. Tears gushed into the eyes of the young man as he recalled his year of solitude, and felt how different was such a welcome from his many melancholy arrivals and departures, previously to the recent events.

It was rather a troublesome matter to get the cow and calf up the mountain. The first did not see enough that was attractive in naked rocks, to induce her to mount in the best of humours. She drank freely, however, at the brook, appearing to relish its waters particularly well. At length the plan was adopted of carrying the calf up a good distance, the cries of the little thing inducing its mother immediately to follow. In this way both were got up into Eden, in the course of an hour. And well did the poor cow vindicate the name, when she got a look at the broad glades of the sweetest grasses, that were stretched before her. So strongly was her imagination struck with the view-for we suppose that some cows have even more imagination than many men-that she actually kicked up her heels, and away she went, head down and tail erect, scampering athwart the sward like a colt. It was not long, however, before she began to graze, the voyage having been made on a somewhat short allowance of both food and water. If there ever was a happy animal, it was that cow! Her troubles were all over. Sea-sickness, dry food, short allowances of water, narrow lodgings, and hard beds, were all, doubtless, forgotten, as she roamed at pleasure over boundless fields, on which the grass was perennial, seeming never to be longer or shorter than was necessary to give a good bite; and among which numberless rills of the purest waters were sparkling like crystal. The great difficulty in possessing a dairy, in a warm climate, is the want of pasture, the droughts usually being so long in the summer months. At Vulcan's Peak, however, and indeed in all of that fine region, it rained occasionally, throughout the year; more in winter than in summer, and that was the sole distinction in the seasons, after allowing for a trifling change in the temperature. These peculiarities appear to have been owing to the direction of the prevalent winds, which not only brought frequent showers, but which preserved a reasonable degree of freshness in the atmosphere. *Within* the crater, Mark had often found the beat oppressive, even in the shade; but, *without*, scarcely ever, provided his body was not directly exposed to the sun's rays. Nor was the difference in the temperature between the Reef and the Peak, as marked as might have been expected from the great elevation of the last. This was owing to the circumstance that the sea air, and that usually in swift motion, entered so intimately into the composition of the atmosphere down on that low range of rocks, imparting its customary freshness to everything it passed over.

Mark did not make the next trip to Rancocus. By this time Anne passed half the day in the open air, and was so fast regaining her strength that Heaton did not hesitate to leave her. The doctor had left many things behind him that he much wished to see embarked in person, and he volunteered to be the companion of Socrates, on this occasion, leaving the bridegroom behind, with his bride. By this time Heaton himself was a reasonably good sailor, and to him Mark confided the instructions as to the course to be steered, and the distance to be run. All resulted favourably, the Neshamony making the trip in very good time, bringing into the cove, the fourth day after she had sailed, not only the remaining cow, and her calf, but several of the goats. Convinced he might now depend on Heaton and Socrates to sail the pinnace, and Anne expressing a perfect willingness to remain on the Peak, in company with Teresa and Dido, Mark resolved to proceed to the crater with his two Bridgets, feeling the propriety of no longer neglecting the property in that quarter of his dominions. There was nothing to excite apprehension, and the women had all acquired a certain amount of resolution that more properly belonged to their situation than to their sex or nature. Anne's great object of concern was the baby. As long as that was safe, everything with her was going on well; and Dido being a renowned baby doctor, and all the simples for a child's ailings being in the possession of the young mother, she raised no objection whatever to her brother's quitting her.

Bridget had great impatience to make this voyage, for she longed to see the spot where her husband had passed so many days in solitude. Everything he had mentioned, in their many conferences on this subject, was already familiar to her in imagination; but, she wished to become more intimately acquainted with each and all. For Kitty she really entertained a decided fondness, and even the pigs, as Mark's companions, had a certain romantic value in her eyes.

The morning was taken for the departure, and just as the little craft got out from under the lee of the Peak, and began to feel the true breeze, the sun rose gloriously out of the eastern waves, lighting the whole of the blue waters with his brilliant rays. Never did Vulcan's Peak appear more grand or more soft-for grandeur or sublimity, blended with softness, make the principal charm of noble tropical scenery-than it did that morning; and Bridget looked up at the dark, overhanging cliffs, with a smile, as she said —

"We may love the Reef, dear Mark, for what it did for you in your distress, but I foresee that this Eden will eventually become our home."

"There are many things to render this mountain preferable to the Reef; though, now we are seriously thinking of a colony, it may be well to keep both. Even Rancocus would be of great value to us, as a pasture for goats, and a range for cattle. It may be long before the space will be wanted by human beings, for actual cultivation; but each of our present possessions is now, and long will continue to be, of great use to us as assistants. We shall live principally on the Peak, I think myself; but we must fish, get our salt, and obtain most of our vegetables from the Reef."

"Oh! that Reef, that Reef-how long will it be, Mark, before we see it?"

The enamoured young husband laughed, and kissed his charming wife, and told her to restrain her impatience. Several hours must elapse before they could even come in sight of the rocks. These hours did pass, and with the occurrence of no event worthy of being recorded. The Trades usually blew fresh in that quarter of the ocean, but it was seldom that they brought tempests. Occasionally squalls did occur, it is true; but a prudent and experienced mariner could ordinarily guard against their consequences, while the hurricane seldom failed, like most other great physical phenomena, to have its precursors, that were easily seen and understood. On the present occasion, the boat ran across the passage in very good time, making the crater in about five hours, and the ship's masts in six. Mark made a good land-fall coming in to leeward of the cape, or low promontory already mentioned-Cape South he called it-while there still remained several hours of day. Bridget was greatly struck with the vast difference she could not help finding between the appearance of these low, dark, and so often naked rocks, and that of the Eden she had just left. Tears came into her eyes, as she pictured her husband a solitary wanderer over these wastes, with no water, even, but that which fell from the clouds, or which came from the casks of the ship. When, however, she gave utterance to this feeling, one so natural to her situation, Mark told her to have patience until they reached the crater, when she would see that he had possessed a variety of blessings, for which he had every reason to be grateful to God.

There was no difficulty in getting into the proper channel, when the boat fairly flew along the rocks that lined the passages. So long as she was in rough water, the sails of so small a craft were necessarily becalmed a good deal of the time; but, now that there was nothing to intercept the breeze, she caught it all, and made the most of it. To Mark's surprise, as they passed the Prairie, he saw all of his swine on it, now, including two half-unconsumed litters of well-grown pigs, some seventeen in number. These animals had actually found their way along the rocks, a distance of at least twenty miles from home, and by the crooked path they had taken, probable one much greater. They all appeared full, and contented. So much of the water had already evaporated as to make it tolerable walking on the sea-weed; and Mark, stopping to examine the progress of things, prognosticated that another year, in that climate, would convert the whole of that wide plain into dry land. In many places, the hogs had already found their way down, through the sea-weed, into the mud; and there was one particular spot, quite near the channel, where the water was all gone, and where the pigs had rooted over so much of the surface, as to convert two or three acres into a sort of half-tilled field, in which the sea-weed was nearly turned under the mud. Nothing but drenching rains were wanting to render such a place highly productive, and it was certain those rains would come at the end of the season.

About the middle of the day, Mark ran the beat alongside of the Reef, at the usual landing, and welcomed Bridget to his and her home, with a kiss. Everything was in its place, and a glance sufficed to show that no human foot had been there, during the weeks of his absence. Kitty was browsing on the Summit, and no spaniel could have played more antics than she did, at the sight of her master. At first, Mark had thought of transferring this gentle and playful young goat to the Peak, and to place her in the little flock collected there; but he had been induced to change his mind, by recollecting how much she contributed to the beauty of the Summit, by keeping down the grass. He had therefore brought her a companion, which had no sooner been landed on the Reef, than it bounded off to make acquaintance with the stranger on the elevation.

Bridget was almost overcome when she got on board the ship. There was even a certain sublimity in the solitude that reigned over everything, that impressed her imagination, and she wondered that any human being could so long have dwelt there alone, uncheered by the hope of deliverance. In the cabin of that vessel she had plighted her faith to Mark, and a flood of recollections burst upon her as she entered it. Mark was obliged to allow her to seek relief in tears. But, half an hour brought her round again, and then she set about putting things in order, and making this very important abode submit to the influence of woman's love of comfort and order. By the time Mark came back from his garden, whither he had gone to ascertain its condition, Bridget had his supper ready for him, prepared with a neatness and method to which he had long been a stranger. That was a very delicious meal to both. The husband had lighted a fire in the galley, where the wife had cooked the meal, which consisted principally of some pan-fish, taken in the narrow channels between the rocks, and which had been cleaned by Mark himself, as they sailed along. It was, indeed, a great point of solicitude with this young husband to prevent his charming wife from performing duties for which she was unfitted by education, while the wife herself was only too solicitous to make herself useful. In one sense, Bridget was a very knowing person about a household. She knew how to prepare many savoury compounds, and had the whole culinary art at her fingers' ends, in the way of giving directions. It was no wonder, then, that Mark found everything she touched, or prepared, good, as everything she said sounded pleasant and reasonable. The last is a highly important ingredient in matrimonial life, but the first has its merit. And Bridget Woolston was both pleasant and reasonable. Though a little romantic, and inclined to hazard all for feeling, and what she conceived to be duty, at the bottom of all ran a vein of excellent sense, which had been reasonably attended to. Her temper was sweetness itself, and that is one of the greatest requisites in married happiness. To this great quality must be added affection, for she was devoted to Mark, and nothing he wished would she hesitate about striving to obtain, even at painful sacrifices to herself. One as generous-minded and manly as her husband, could not fail to discover and appreciate such a disposition, which entered very largely into the composition of their future happiness.

Our young couple did not visit the crater and the Summit until the sun had lost most of its power. Then Mark introduced his wife into his garden, and to his lawn. Exclamations of delight escaped the last, at nearly every step; for, in addition to the accidental peculiarities of such a place, the vegetation had advanced, as vegetation only can advance within the tropics, favoured by frequent rains and a rich soil. The radishes were half as large as Bridget's wrists, and as tender as her heart. The lettuce was already heading; the beans were fit to pull; the onions large enough to boil, and the peas even too old. On the Summit Mark cut a couple of melons, which were of a flavour surpassing any he had ever before tasted. With that spot Bridget was especially delighted. It was, just then, as green as grass could be, and Kitty had found its plants so very sweet, that she had scarce descended once to trespass on the garden. Here and there the imprint of her little hoof was to be traced on a bed, it is true, but she appeared to have gone there more to look after the condition of the garden than to gratify her appetite.

While on the Summit, Mark pointed out to his wife the fowls, now increased to something like fifty. Two or three broods of chickens had come within the last month, making their living on the reef that was separated from that of the crater by means of the bridge of planks. As two or three flew across the narrow pass, however, he was aware that the state of his garden must be owing to the fact that they still found a plenty on those rocks for their support. In returning to the ship, he visited a half-barrel prepared for that purpose, and, as he expected, found a nest containing a dozen eggs. These he took the liberty of appropriating to his own use, telling Bridget that they could eat some of them for their breakfast.

But food never had been an interest to give our solitary man much uneasiness. From the hour when he found muck, and sea-weed, and guano, he felt assured of the means of subsistence; being in truth, though he may not have known it himself, more in danger of falling behind hand, in consequence of the indisposition to activity that almost ever accompanies the abundance of a warm climate, than from the absolute want of the means of advancing. That night Mark and Bridget knelt, side by side, and returned thanks to God for all his mercies. How sweet the former found it to see the light form of his beautiful companion moving about the spacious cabin, giving it an air of home and happiness, no one can fully appreciate who has not been cut off from these accustomed joys, and then been suddenly restored to them.

Chapter XV

> "I beg, good Heaven, with just desires,
> What need, not luxury, requires;
> Give me, with sparing hands, but moderate wealth,
> A little honour, and enough of health;
> Free from the busy city life,
> Near shady groves and purling streams confined,
> A faithful friend, a pleasing wife;
> And give me all in one, give a contented mind."
>
> —Anonymous

Mark and Bridget remained at the Reef a week, entirely alone. To them the time seemed but a single day; and so completely were they engrossed with each other, and their present happiness, that they almost dreaded the hour of return. Everything was visited, however, even to the abandoned anchor, and Mark made a trip to the eastward, carrying his wife out into the open water, in that direction. But the ship and the crater gave Bridget the greatest happiness. Of these she never tired, though the first gave her the most pleasure. A ship was associated with all her earliest impressions of Mark; on board that very ship she had been married; and now it formed her home, temporarily, if not permanently. Bridget had been living so long beneath a tent, and in savage huts, that the accommodations of the Rancocus appeared like those of a palace. They were not inelegant even, though it was not usual, in that period of the republic, to fit up vessels with a magnificence little short of royal yachts, as is done at present. In the way of convenience, however, our ship could boast of a great deal. Her cabins were on deck, or under a poop, and consequently enjoyed every advantage of light and air. Beneath were store-rooms, still well supplied with many articles of luxury, though time was beginning to make its usual inroads on their qualities. The bread was not quite as sound as it was once, nor did the teas retain all their strength and flavour. But the sugar was just as sweet as the day it was shipped, and in the coffee there was no apparent change. Of the butter, we do not choose to say anything. Bridget, in the prettiest manner imaginable, declared that as soon as she could set Dido at work the store-rooms should be closely examined, and thoroughly cleaned. Then the galley made such a convenient and airy kitchen! Mark had removed the house, the awning answering every purpose, and his wife declared that it was a pleasure to cook a meal for him, in so pleasant a place.

The first dish Bridget ever literally cooked for Mark, with her own hands, or indeed for any one else, was a mess of 'grass,' as it was the custom of even the most polished people of America then to call asparagus. They had gone together to the asparagus bed on Loam Island, and had found the plant absolutely luxuriating in its favourite soil. The want of butter was the greatest defect in this mess, for, to say the truth, Bridget refused the ship's butter on this occasion, but luckily, enough oil remained to furnish a tolerable substitute. Mark declared he had never tasted anything in his life half so good!

At the end of the week, the governor, as Heaton had styled Mark, and as Bridget had begun playfully to term him, gave the opinion that it was necessary for them to tear themselves away from their paradise. Never before, most certainly, had the Reef appeared to the young husband a spot as delightful as he now found it, and it did seem to him very possible for one to pass a whole life on it without murmuring. His wife again and again assured him she had never before been half as happy, and that, much as she loved Anne and the baby, she could remain a month longer, without being in the least wearied. But it was prudent to return to the Peak, for Mark had never felt his former security against foreign invasion, since he was acquainted with the proximity of peopled islands.

The passage was prosperous, and it gave the scene an air of civilization and life, to fall in with the Neshamony off the cove. She was coming in from Rancocus, on her last trip for the stores, having brought everything away but two of the goats. These had been driven up into the mountains, and there left. Bigelow had come away, and the whole party of colonists were now assembled at Vulcan's Peak. But Betts had a communication to make that gave the governor a good deal of concern. He reported that after they had got the pinnace loaded, and were only waiting for the proper time of day to quit Rancocus, they discovered a fleet of canoes and catamarans, approaching the island from the direction of the Group, as they familiarly termed the cluster of islands that was known to be nearest to them, to the northward and westward. By means of a glass, Betts had ascertained that a certain Waally was on board the leading canoe, and he regarded this as an evil omen. Waally was Ooroony's most formidable rival and most bitter foe; and the circumstance that he was leading such a flotilla, of itself, Bob thought, was an indication that he had prevailed over honest Betto, in some recent encounter, and was now abroad, bent on further mischief. Indeed, it seemed scarcely possible that men like the natives should hear of the existence of such a mountain as that of Rancocus Island, in their vicinity, and not wish to explore, if not to possess it.

Betts had pushed off, and made sail, as soon as assured of this fact. He knew the pinnace could outsail anything the islanders possessed, more especially on a wind, and he manoeuvred about the flotilla for an hour, making his observations, before he left it. This was clearly a war party, and Bob thought there were white men in it. At least, he saw two individuals who appeared to him to be white sailors, attired in a semi-savage way, and who were in the same canoe with the terrible Waally. It was nothing out of the way for seamen to get adrift on the islands scattered about in the Pacific, there being scarcely a group in which more or less of them are not to be found. The presence of these men, too, Bob regarded as another evil omen, and he felt the necessity of throwing all the dust he could into their eyes. When the pinnace left the flotilla, therefore, instead of passing out to windward of the island, as was her true course, she steered in an almost contrary direction, keeping off well to leeward of the land, in order not to get becalmed under the heights, for Bob well knew the canoes, with paddles, would soon overhaul him, should he lose the wind.

It was the practice of our colonists to quit Rancocus just before the sun set, and to stand all night on a south-east course. This invariably brought them in sight of the smoke of the volcano by morning, and shortly after they made the Peak. All of the day that succeeded, was commonly passed in beating up to the volcano, or as near to it as it was thought prudent to go; and tacking to the northward and eastward, about sunset of the second day, it was found on the following morning, that the Neshamony was drawing near to the cliffs of Vulcan's Peak, if she were not already beneath them. As a matter of course, then, Bob had not far to go, before night shut in, and left him at liberty to steer in whatever direction he pleased. Fortunately, that night had no moon, though there was not much danger of so small a craft as the Neshamony being seen at any great distance on the water, even by moonlight. Bob consequently determined to beat up off the north end of the island, or Low Cape, as it was named by the colonists, from the circumstance of its having a mile or two of low land around it, before the mountains commenced. Once off the cape again, and reasonably well in, he might possibly make discoveries that would be of use.

It took two or three hours to regain the lost ground, by beating to windward. By eleven o'clock, however, the Neshamony was not only off the cape, but quite close in with the landing. The climate rendering fires altogether unnecessary at that season, and indeed at nearly all seasons, except for cooking, Bob could not trace the encampment of the savages, by that means. Still, he obtained all the information he desired. This was not done, however, without great risk, and by a most daring step on his part. He lowered the sails of the boat and went alongside of the rock, where the pinnace usually came to, the canoes, &c., having made another, and a less eligible harbour. Bob then landed in person, and stole along the shore in the direction of the sleeping savages. Unknown to himself, he was watched, and was just crouching under some bushes, in order to get a little nearer, when he felt a hand on his shoulder. There was a moment when blood was in danger of being shed, but Betts's hand was stayed by hearing, in good English, the words —

"Where are you bound, shipmate?"

This question was asked in a guarded, under-tone, a circumstance that reassured Bob, quite as much as the language. He at once perceived that the two men whom he had, rightly enough, taken for seamen, were in these bushes, where it would seem they had long been on the watch, observing the movements of the pinnace. They told Bob to have no apprehensions, as all the savages were asleep, at some little distance, and accompanied him back to the Neshamony. Here, to the surprise and joy of all parties, Bigelow recognised both the sailors, who had not only been his former shipmates, but were actually his townsmen in America, the whole three having been born within a mile of each other. The history of these three wanderers from home was very much alike. They had come to the Pacific in a whaler, with a drunken captain, and had, in succession, left the ship. Bigelow found his way to Panama, where he was caught by the dark eyes of Theresa, as has been related. Peters had fallen in with Jones, in the course of his wanderings, and they had been for the last two years among the pearl islands, undecided what to do with themselves, when Waally ordered both to accompany him in the present expedition. They had gathered enough in hints given by different chiefs, to understand that a party of Christians was to be massacred, or enslaved, and plundered of course. They had heard of the 'canoe' that had been tabooed for twelve moons, but were at a loss to comprehend one-half of the story, and were left to the most anxious conjectures. They were not permitted to pass on to the islands under the control of Ooroony, but were jealously detained in Waally's part of the group, and consequently had not been in a situation to learn all the particulars of the singular party of colonists who had gone to the southward. Thus much did Peters relate, in substance, when a call among the savages notified the whole of the whites of the necessity of coming to some conclusion concerning the future. Jones and Peters acknowledged it would not be safe to remain any longer, though the last gave his opinion with an obvious reluctance. As it afterwards appeared, Peters had married an Indian wife, to whom he was much attached, and he did not like the idea of abandoning her. There was but a moment for reflection, however, and almost without knowing it himself, when he found the pinnace about to make sail in order to get off the land, he followed Jones into her, and was half a mile from the shore before he had time to reflect much on her he had left behind him. His companion consoled him by telling him that an opportunity might occur of sending a message to Petrina, as they had named the pretty young savage, who would not fail to find her way to Rancocus, sooner or later.

With these important accessions to his forces, Bob did not hesitate about putting to sea, leaving Waally to make what discoveries he might. Should the natives ascend to the higher parts of the mountain, they could hardly fail to see both the smoke of the volcano and the Peak, though it would luckily not be in their power to see the Reef, or any part of that low group of rocks. It was very possible they might attempt to cross the passage between the two mountains, though the circumstance that Vulcan's Peak lay so directly to windward of Rancocus offered a very serious obstacle to their succeeding. Had the two sailors remained with them, *they*, indeed, might have taught the Indians to overcome the winds and waves; but these very men were of opinion, from what they had seen of the natives and of their enterprises, that it rather exceeded their skill and perseverance, to work their canoes a hundred miles dead to windward, and against the sea that was usually on in that quarter of the Pacific.

The colonists, generally, gave the two recruits a very welcome reception. Bridget smiled when Mark suggested that Jones, who was a well-looking lad enough, would make a very proper husband for Joan, and that he doubted not his being called on, in his character of magistrate, to unite them in the course of the next six months. The designs of the savages, however, caused the party to think of anything but weddings, just at that moment, and a council was held to devise a plan for their future government. As Mark was considered the head of the colony, and had every way the most experience, his opinion swayed those of his companions, and all his recommendations were adopted. There were on board the ship eight carronades, then quite a new gun, and mounted on trucks. They were of the bore of twelve-pounders, but light and manageable, There was also abundance of ammunition in the vessel's magazine, no ship coming to the Fejees to trade without a proper regard to the armament. Mark proposed going over to the Reef with the Neshamony, the very next day, in order to transport two of the guns, with a proper supply of powder and shot, to the Peak. Now there was one place on the path, or Stairs, where it would be easy to defend the last against an army, the rocks, which were absolutely perpendicular on each side of it, coming so close together, as to render it practicable to close the passage by a narrow gate. This gate Mark did not purpose to erect now, for he thought it unnecessary. All he intended was to plant the two guns at this pass; one on a piece of level rock directly over it, and a little on one side, which would command the entrance of the cove, and the cove itself, as well as the whole of the path beneath, and the other on another natural platform, a short distance above, where it could not only command the pass, but, by using the last as a sort of embrasure, by firing through it, could not only sweep the ravine for some distance down, but could also rake the entrance of the cove, and quite half of the little basin itself.

Bob greatly approved of this arrangement, though all the seamen were too much accustomed to obey their officers to raise the smallest objections to anything that Mark proposed. Betts was the only person who had made the circuit of the Peak; but he, and Mark, and Heaton, who had been a good deal round the cliffs, on the side of the water, all agreed in saying they did not believe it possible for a human being to reach the plain, unless the ascent was made by the Stairs. This, of course, rendered the fortifying of the last a matter of so much the greater importance, since it converted the whole island into a second Gibraltar. It was true, the Reef would remain exposed to depredations; though Mark was of opinion that, by leaving a portion of their force in the ship, with two or three of the guns at command, it would not be difficult to beat off five hundred natives. As for the crater, it might very easily be made impregnable.

At this meeting Heaton proposed the establishment of some sort of government and authority, which they should all solemnly swear to support. The idea was favourably received, and Mark was unanimously chosen governor for life, the law being the rule of right, with such special enactments as might, from time to time, issue from a council of three, who were also elected for life. This council consisted of the governor, Heaton, and Setts. Human society has little difficulty in establishing itself on just principles, when the wants are few and interests simple. It is the bias given by these last that perverts it from the true direction. In our island community, most of its citizens were accustomed to think that education and practice gave a man certain claims to control, and, as yet, demagogueism had no place with them. A few necessary rules, that were connected with their particular situation, were enacted by the council and promulgated, when the meeting adjourned. Happily they were as yet far, very far from that favourite sophism of the day, which would teach the inexperienced to fancy it an advantage to a legislator to commence his career as low as possible on the scale of ignorance, in order that he might be what it is the fashion, to term "a self-made man."

Mark now took the command, and issued his orders with a show of authority. His attention was first turned to rendering the Peak impregnable. There were a plenty of muskets and fowling-pieces already there, Heaton having come well provided with arms and ammunition. As respects the last, Peters and Jones were set to work to clear out a sort of cavern in the rock, that was not only of a convenient size, but which was conveniently placed for such a purpose, at no great distance from the head of the Stairs, to receive the powder, &c. The cavity was perfectly dry, an indispensable requisite, and it was equally well protected against the admission of water.

The next thing was to collect a large pile of dry wood on the naked height of the Peak. This was to be lighted, at night, in the event of the canoes appearing while he was absent, Mark being of opinion that he could see such a beacon-fire from the Reef, whither he was about to proceed. Having made these arrangements, the governor set sail with Betts, Bigelow, and Socrates for his companions; leaving Heaton, with Peters and Jones, to take care of most of the females. We say of most, since Dido and Juno went along, in order to cook, and to wash all the clothes of the whole colony, a part of which were sent in the pinnace, but most of which were on hoard the ship. This was a portion of his duty, when a solitary man, to which Mark was exceedingly averse, and having shirts almost *ad libitum,* Bridget had found nearly a hundred ready for the 'buck-basket.' There was no danger, therefore, that the 'wash' would be too small.

Betts was deeply impressed with the change that he found in the rocks. There, where he had left, water over which he had often floated his raft, appeared dry land. Nor was he much less struck with the appearance of the crater. It was now a hill of a bright, lively verdure, Kitty and her new friend keeping it quite as closely cropped as was desirable. The interior, too, struck him forcibly; for there, in addition to the garden, now flourishing, though a little in want of the hoe, was a meadow of acres in extent, in which the grass was fit to cut. Mark had observed this circumstance when last at the crater, and Socrates had brought his scythe and forks, to cut and cure the hay.

The morning after the arrival, everybody went to work. The women set up their tubs, under an awning spread for that purpose, near the spring, and were soon up to their elbows in suds. The scythe was set in motion, and the pinnace was taken round to the ship. Three active seamen soon hoisted out the carronades, and stowed them in the little sloop. The ammunition followed, and half-a-dozen barrels of the beef and pork were, put in the Neshamony also. Mark scarcely ever touched this food now, the fish, eggs, chickens, and pigs, keeping his larder sufficiently well supplied. But some of the men pined for *ship's* provisions, beef and pork that had now been packed more than two years, and the governor thought it might be well enough to indulge them. The empty barrels would be convenient on the Peak, and the salt would be acceptable, after being dried and pulverized.

The day was passed in loading the Neshamony, and in looking after various interests on the Reef. The hogs had all come in, and were fed. Mark shot one, and had it dressed, putting most of its meat into the pinnace. He also sent Bob out to his old place of resort, near Loam Island, whence he brought back near a hundred hog-fish. These were divided, also, some being given to Dido's mess, and the rest put in the pinnace, after taking out enough for a good supper. About ten at night the Neshamony sailed, Mark carrying her out into the open water, when he placed Bob at the helm. Bigelow had remained in the ship, to overhaul the lumber, of which there were still large piles both betwixt decks and in the lower hold, as did the whole of the Socrates family, who were yet occupied with the hay harvest and the 'wash.' Before he lay down to catch his nap, Mark took a good look to the southward, in quest of the beacon, but it was not burning, a sign the savages had not appeared in the course of the day. With this assurance he fell asleep, and slept until informed by Bob that the pinnace was running in beneath the cliffs. Betts called him, because the honest fellow was absolutely at a loss to know where to find the entrance of the cove. So closely did the rocks lap, that this mouth of the harbour was most effectually concealed from all but those who happened to get quite close in with the cliffs, and in a particular position. Mark, himself, had caught a glimpse of this narrow entrance accidentally, on his first voyage, else might he have been obliged to abandon the hope of getting on the heights; for subsequent examination showed that there was but that one spot, on the whole circuit of Vulcan's Peak, where man could ascend to the plain, without having recourse to engineering and the labour of months, if not of years.

Bob had brought along one of the two swivels of the ship, as an armament for the Neshamony, and he fired it under the cliffs, as a signal of her return. This brought down all the men, who, with their united strength, dragged the carronades up the Stairs, and placed them in position. With a view to scale the guns, the governor now had each loaded, with a round shot and a case of canister. The gun just above the pass, he pointed himself, at the entrance of the cove, and touched it off. The whole of the missiles went into the passage, making the water fairly foam again. The other gun was depressed so as to sweep the Stairs and, on examination, it was found that its shot had raked the path most effectually for a distance exceeding a hundred yards. Small magazines were made in the rocks, near each guy, when the most important part of the arangements for defence were considered to be satisfactorily made for the present. The remainder of the cargo was discharged, and got up the mountain, though it took three days to effect the last. The provisions were opened below and overhauled, quite one-half of the pork being consigned to the soap-fat, though the beef proved to be still sound and sweet. Such as was thought fit to be consumed was carried up in baskets, and re-packed on the mountain, the labour of rolling up the barrels satisfying everybody, after one experiment. This difficulty set Mark to work with his wits, and he found a shelf that overhung the landing, at a height of fully a hundred yards above it, where there was a natural platform of rock, that would suffice for the parade of a regiment of men. Here he determined to rig a derrick, for there was an easy ascent and descent to this 'platform,' as the place was called, and down which a cart might go without any difficulty, if a cart was to be had. The 'platform' might also be used for musketeers, in an action, and on examining it, Mark determined to bring over one of the two long sixes, and mount it there, with a view to command the offing. From that height a shot could be thrown in any direction, for more than a mile, outside of the harbour.

Heaton had seen no signs of the canoes, nor could Mark, at any time during the next four clays after his return, though he was each day on the Peak itself, to examine the ocean. On the fifth day, therefore, he and Bob crossed over to the Reef again, taking Bridget along this time. The latter delighted in the ship, the cabins of which were so much more agreeable and comfortable than the tents, and which had so long been her husband's solitary abode.

On reaching the Reef, the governor was greatly surprised to find that Bigelow had the frame of a boat even larger than the pinnace set up, one that measured fourteen tons, though modelled to carry, rather than to sail. In overhauling the 'stuff' in the ship, he had found not only all the materials for this craft, but those necessary for a boat a little larger than the Bridget, which, it seems, had been sent for the ordinary service of the ship, should anything occur to occasion the loss of the two she commonly used, in addition to the dingui. These were treasures, indeed, vessels of this size being of the utmost use to the colonists. For the next month, several hands were kept at work on these two boats, when both were got into the water, rigged, and turned over for duty. The largest boat of the little fleet, which had no deck at all, not even forward, and which was not only lighter-built but lighter-rigged, having one large sprit-sail that brailed, was called the Mary, in honour of Heaton's mother; while the jolly-boat carried joy to the hearts of the house of Socrates, by being named the Dido. As she was painted black as a crow, this appellation was not altogether inappropriate, Soc declaring, "dat 'e boat did a good deal favour his ole woman."

While these things were in progress, the Neshamony was not idle. She made six voyages between the Reef and the Peak in that month, carrying to the last, fish, fresh pork, various necessaries from the ship, as well as eggs and salt. Some of the fowls were caught and transferred to the Peak, as well as half-a-dozen of the porkers. The return cargo consisted of reed-birds, in large quantities, several other varieties of birds, bread-fruits, bananas, yams, cocoa-nuts, and a fruit that Heaton discovered, which was of a most delicious flavour, resembling strawberries and cream, and which was afterwards ascertained to be the charra-moya, the fruit that, of all others, when good, is thought to surpass everything else of that nature. Bridget also picked a basket of famously large wild strawberries on the Summit, and sent them to Anne. In return. Anne sent her sister, not only cream and milk, by each passage, but a little fresh butter. The calves had been weaned, and the two cows were now giving their largest quantity of milk, furnishing almost as much butter as was wanted.

At the crater, Socrates put everything in order. He mowed the grass, and made a neat stack of it, in the centre of the meadow. He cleaned the garden thoroughly, and made some arrangements for enlarging it, though the yield, now, was quite as great as all the colonists could consume; for, no sooner was one vegetable dug, or cut, than another was put in its place. On the Peak, Peters, who was half a farmer, dug over an acre or two of rich loam, and made a fence of brush, with a view of having a garden in Eden. Really, it almost seemed superfluous; though those who had been accustomed to salads, and beans, and beets, and onions, and cucumbers, and all the other common vegetables of a civilized kitchen, soon began to weary of the more luscious fruits of the tropics. With the wild figs, however, Heaton, who was a capital horticulturist, fancied he could do something. He picked out three or four thriving young trees of that class, which bore fruit a little better flavoured than most around them, and cut away all their neighbours, letting in the sun and air freely. He also trimmed their branches, and dug around the roots, which he refreshed with guano; the use of which had been imparted by Mark to his fellow-colonists, though Bigelow knew all about it from having lived in Peru, and Bob had early let the governor himself into the secret.

The governor and his lady, as the community now began to term Mr. and Mrs. Mark Woolston, were on the point of embarking in the Neshamony, to visit Vulcan's Peak, after a residence on the Reef of more than a month, when the orders for sailing were countermanded, in consequence of certain signs in the atmosphere, which indicated something like another hurricane. The tempest came, and in good earnest, but without any of the disastrous consequences which had attended that of the previous year. It blew fearfully, and the water was driven into all the sounds, creeks, channels and bays of the group, bringing many of the islands, isthmuses, peninsulas, and plains of rock, what the seamen call 'awash,' though no material portion was actually overflowed. At the Reef itself, the water rose a fathom, but it did not reach the surface of the island by several feet, and all passed off without any other consequences than giving the new colonists a taste of the climate.

Mark, on this occasion, for the first time, noted a change that was gradually taking place on the surface of the Reef, without the crater. Most of its cavities were collecting deposits, that were derived from various sources. Sea-weed, offals, refuse stuff of all kinds, the remains of the deluge of fish that occurred the past year, and all the indescribable atoms that ever contribute to form soil in the neighbourhood of man. There were many spots on the Reef, of acres in extent, that formed shallow basins, in which the surface might be two or three inches lower than the surrounding rocks, and, in these spots in particular, the accumulations of an incipient earthy matter were plainly visible. As these cavities collected and retained the moisture, usually from rain to rain, Mark had some of Friend Abraham White's grass-seed sown over them, in order to aid nature in working out her own benevolent designs. In less than a month, patches of green began to appear on the dusky rocks, and there was good reason to hope that a few years would convert the whole Reef into a smiling, verdant plain. It was true, the soil could not soon obtain any useful depth, except in limited spots; but, in that climate, where warmth and moisture united to push vegetation to the utmost, it was an easy thing to obtain a bottom for grasses of almost all kinds.

Nor did Mark's provident care limit itself to this one instance of forethought. Socrates was sent in the dinghy to the prairie, over which the hogs had now been rooting for fully two months, mixing together mud and sea-weed, somewhat loosely it is true, but very extensively; and there he scattered Timothy-seed in tolerable profusion. Socrates was a long-headed, as well as a long-footed fellow, and he brought back from this expedition a report that was of material importance to the future husbandry of the colonists. According to his statement, this large deposit of mud and sea-weed lay on a peninsula, that might be barricaded against the inroads of hogs, cattle, &c., by a fence of some two or three rods in length. This was a very favourable circumstance, where wood was to be imported for many years to come, if not for ever; though the black had brought the seeds of certain timbers, from the Peak, and put them into the ground in a hundred places on the Reef, where the depth of deposit, and other circumstances, seemed favourable to their growth. As for the Prairie, could it be made to grow grasses, it would be a treasure to the colony, inasmuch as its extent reached fully to a thousand acres. The examination of Socrates was flattering in other respects. The mud was already dry, and the deposit of salt did riot seem to be very great; little water having been left there after the eruption, or lifting of the earth's crust. The rains had done much, and certain coarse, natural grasses, were beginning to show themselves in various parts of the field. As the hogs would not be likely to root over the same spot twice, it was not proposed to exclude them, but they were permitted to range over the field at pleasure, in the hope that they would add to its fertility by mixing the materials for soil. In such a climate, every change of a vegetable character was extremely rapid, and now that no one thought of abandoning the settlement, it was very desirable to obtain the different benefits of civilization as soon as possible.

All the blacks remained at the Reef, where Mark himself passed a good deal of his time. In their next visit to the Peak, they found things flourishing, and the garden looking particularly well. The Vulcanists had their melons in any quantity, as well as most vegetables without limits. It was determined to divide the cows, leaving one on the Peak, and sending the other to the crater, where there was now sufficient grass to keep two or three such animals. With a view to this arrangement, Bob had been directed to fence in the garden and stack, by means of ropes and stanchions let into the ground. When the Anne returned to the Reef, therefore, from her first voyage to the Peak, a cow was sent over in her. This change was made solely for the convenience of the milk, all the rest of the large stock being retained on the plain, where there was sufficient grass to sustain thousands of hoofs.

But the return cargo of the Anne, on this her first voyage, was composed mainly of ship-timber. Heaton had found a variety of the teak in the forests that skirted the plain, and Bigelow had got out of the trees the frame of a schooner that was intended to measure about eighty tons. A craft of that size would be of the greatest service to them, as it would enable the colonists to visit any part of the Pacific they pleased, and obtain such supplies as they might find necessary. Nor was this all; by mounting on her two of the carronades, she would effectually give them the command of their own seas, so far as the natives were concerned at least. Mark had some books on the draughting of vessels, and Bigelow had once before laid down a brig of more than a hundred tons in dimensions. Then the stores, rigging, copper, &c., of the ship, could never be turned to better account than in the construction of another vessel, and it was believed she could furnish materials enough for two or three such craft. Out of compliment to his old owner, Mark named this schooner in embryo, the 'Friend Abraham White,' though she was commonly known afterwards as the 'Abraham.'

The cutting of the frame of the intended schooner was a thing easy enough, with expert American axemen, and with that glorious implement of civilization, the American axe. But it was not quite so easy to get the timber down to the cove. The keel, in particular, gave a good deal of trouble. Heaton had brought along with him both cart and wagon wheels, and without that it is questionable if the stick could have been moved by any force then at the command of the colony. By suspending it in chains beneath the axles, however, it was found possible to draw it, though several of the women had to lend their aid in moving the mass. When at the head of the Stairs, the timber was lowered on the rock, and was slid downwards, with occasional lifts by the crowbar and handspike. When it reached the water it was found to be much too heavy to float, and it was by no means an easy matter to buoy it up in such a way that it might be towed. The Anne was three times as long making her passage with this keel in tow, as she was without it. It was done, however, and the laying of the keel was effected with some little ceremony, in the presence of nearly every soul belonging to the colony.

The getting out and raising of the frame of the 'Friend Abraham White' took six weeks. Great importance was attached to success in this matter, and everybody assisted in the work with right good will. At one time it was doubted if stuff enough could be found in the ship to plank her up with, and it was thought it might become necessary to break up the Rancocus, in order to complete the job. To Bridgets great joy, however, the good *old* Rancocus-so they called her, though she was even then only eight years old-the good old Rancocus' time had not yet come, and she was able to live in her cabin for some months longer. Enough planks were found by using those of the 'twixt decks, a part of which were not bolted down at all to accomplish all that was wanted.

Heaton was a man of singular tastes, which led him to as remarkable acquirements. Among other accomplishments, he was a very good general mechanician, having an idea of the manner in which most of the ordinary machinery ought to be, not only used, but fabricated. At the point where the rivulet descended the cliff into the sea, he discovered as noble a mill-seat as the heart of man could desire to possess. To have such a mill-seat at command, and not to use it, would, of itself, have made him unhappy, and he could not be easy until he and Peters, who had also a great taste and some skill in that sort of thing, were hard at work building a saw-mill. The saw had been brought from America, as a thing very likely to be wanted, and three months after these, two ingenious men had commenced their work, the saw was going, cutting teak, as well as a species of excellent yellow pine that was found in considerable quantities, and of very respectable size, along the cliffs in the immediate vicinity of the mill. The great difficulty to be overcome in that undertaking, was the transportation of the timber. By cutting the trees most favourably situated first, logs were got into the pond without much labour; but after they were in planks, or boards, or joists, they were quite seven miles horn the head of the Stairs, in the vicinity of which it was, on several accounts, the most desirable to dwell. Had the Abraham been kept on the stocks, until the necessary timber was brought from the mill, across the plain of Eden, she would have been well seasoned before launching; but, fortunately, that was not necessary-materials sufficient for her were got on board the ship, as mentioned, with some small additions of inch boards that were cut to finish her joiners' work.

Months passed, as a matter of course, while the schooner and the mill were in the course of construction. The work on the first was frequently intermitted, by little voyages in the other craft, and by labour necessary to be done in preparing dwellings on the Peak, to meet the rainy season, which was now again near at hand. Past experience had told Mark that the winter months in his islands, if winter a season could be termed, during which most of the trees, all the grasses, and many of the fruits continued to grow and ripen as in summer, were not very formidable. It is true it then rained nearly every day, but it was very far from raining all day. Most of the rain, in fact, fell at night, commencing a little after the turn in the day, and terminating about midnight. Still it must be very unpleasant to pass such a season beneath canvass, and, about six weeks ere the wet time commenced, everybody turned to, with a will, to erect, proper framed houses. Now that the mill was sawing, this was no great task, the pine working beautifully and easily into almost every article required.

Heaton laid out his house with some attention to taste, and more to comfort. It was of one story, but fully a hundred feet in length, and of half that in depth. Being a common American dwelling that was clap-boarded, it was soon put up and enclosed, the climate requiring very little attention to warmth. There were windows, and even glass, a small quantity of that article having been brought along by the colonists. The floors were beautiful, and extremely well laid down; nor were the doors, window-shutters, &c., neglected. The whole, moreover, was painted, the stores of the ship still furnishing the necessary materials. But there was neither chimney nor plastering, for Heaton had neither bricks nor lime. Bricks he insisted he could and would make, and did, though in no great number; but lime, for some time, baffled his ingenuity. At last, Socrates suggested the burning of oyster-shells, and by dint of fishing a good deal, among the channels of the reef, a noble oyster-bed was found, and the boats brought in enough of the shells to furnish as much lime as would put up a chimney for the kitchen; one apartment for that sort of work being made, as yet, to suffice for the wants of all who dwelt in Eden.

These various occupations and interests consumed many months, and carried the new-comers through the first wet season which they encountered as a colony. As everybody was busy, plenty reigned, and the climate being so very delicious as to produce a sense of enjoyment in the very fact of existence, everybody but Peters was happy. He, poor fellow, mourned much for his Peggy, as he called the pretty young heathen wife he had left behind him in Waally's country.

Chapter XVI

> "Forthwith a guard at every gun
> Was placed along the wall;
> The beacon blazed upon the roof
> Of Edgecombe's lofty hall;
> And many a fishing bark put out,
> To pry along the coast;
> And with loose rein, and bloody spur
> Rode inland many a post."
>
> —*The Spanish Armada.* Macauley.

The building of the houses, and of the schooner, was occupation for everybody, for a long time. The first were completed in season to escape the rains; but the last was on the stocks fully six months after her keel had been laid. The fine weather had returned, even, and she was not yet launched. So long a period had intervened since Waally's visit to Rancocus Island without bringing any results, that the council began to hope the Indians had given up their enterprises, from the consciousness of not having the means to carry them out; and almost every one ceased to apprehend danger from that quarter. In a word, so smoothly did the current of life flow, on the Reef and at Vulcan's Peak, that there was probably more danger of their inhabitants falling into the common and fatal error of men in prosperity, than of anything else; or, of their beginning to fancy that they deserved all the blessings that were conferred on them, and forgetting the hand that bestowed them. As if to recall them to a better sense of things, events now occurred which it is our business to relate, and which aroused the whole colony from the sort of pleasing trance into which they had fallen, by the united influence of security, abundance, and a most seductive climate.

As time rolled on, in the first place, the number of the colony had begun to augment by natural means. Friend Martha had presented Friend Robert with a little Robert; and Bridget made Mark the happy parent of a very charming girl. This last event occurred about the commencement of the summer, and just a twelvemonth after the happy reunion of the young couple. According to Mark's prophecy, Jones had succeeded with Joan, and they were married even before the expiration of the six months mentioned. On the subject of a marriage ceremony there was no difficulty, Robert and Martha holding a Friends' meeting especially to quiet the scruples of the bride, though she was assured the form could do no good, since the bridegroom did not belong to meeting. The governor read the church service on the occasion, too, which did no harm, if it did no good. About this time, poor Peters, envying the happiness of all around him, and still pining for his Petrina, or Peggy, as he called her himself, begged of the governor the use of the Dido, in order that he might make a voyage to Wally's group in quest of his lost companion. Mark knew how to feel for one in the poor fellow's situation, and he could not think of letting him go alone on an expedition of so much peril. After deliberating on the matter, he determined to visit Rancocus Island himself-not having been in that direction, now, for months-and to go in the Neshamony, in order to take a couple of hogs over; it having long been decided to commence breeding that valuable animal, in the wild state, on the hills of that uninhabited land.

The intelligence that a voyage was to be made to Rancocus Island seemed to infuse new life into the men of the colony, every one of whom wished to be of the party. The governor had no objection to indulging as many as it might be prudent to permit to go; but he saw the necessity of putting some restraint on the movement. After canvassing the matter in the council, it was determined that, in addition to Mark and Peters, who went of course, the party should consist of Bob, Bigelow, and Socrates. The carpenter was taken to look for trees that might serve to make the ways of the schooner, which was yet to be launched; and the latter was thought necessary in his capacity of a cook. As for Betts, he went along as the governor's counsellor and companion.

Bridget's little girl was born in the cabin of the ship; and the week preceding that set for the voyage, she and the child were taken across to the Peak, that the former might spend the period of her husband's absence with Anne, in the Garden of Eden. These absences and occasional visits gave a zest to lives that might otherwise have become too monotonous, and were rather encouraged than avoided. It was, perhaps, a little strange that Bridget rather preferred the Reef than the Peak for a permanent residence; but there was her much-beloved ship, and there she ever had her still more beloved husband for a companion.

On the appointed day, the Neshamony set sail, having on board a family of three of the swine. The plan for the excursion included a trip to the volcano, which had not yet been actually visited by any of the colonists. Mark had been within a league of it, and Bob had passed quite near to it in his voyage to the Peak; but no one had ever positively landed, or made any of those close examinations of the place, which, besides being of interest in a general way, was doubly so to those who were such near neighbours to a place of the kind. This visit Mark now decided to make on his way to leeward, taking the volcano in his course to Rancocus Island. The *détour* would lead the Neshamony some fifteen or eighteen leagues on one side; but there was abundance of time, and the volcano ought to be no longer neglected.

The wind did not blow as fresh as in common, and the Neshamony did not draw near to the volcano until late in the afternoon of the day she sailed. The party approached this place with due caution, and not without a good deal of awe. As the lead was used, it was found that the water shoaled gradually for several leagues, becoming less and less, deep as the boat drew near to the cone, which was itself a circular and very regular mountain, of some six or eight hundred feet in height, with a foundation of dry rock and lava, that might have contained a thousand acres. Everything seemed solid and permanent; and our mariners were of opinion there was very little danger of this formation ever disappearing below the surface of the sea again.

The volcano being in activity, some care was necessary in landing. Mark took the Neshamony to windward, and found a curvature in the rocks where it was possible to get ashore without having the boat knocked to pieces. He and Bob then went as near the cone as the falling stones would allow, and took as good a survey of the place as could be done under the circumstances. That there would be soil, and plenty of it, sooner or later, was plain enough; and that the island might become a scene of fertility and loveliness, in the course of ages, like so many others of volcanic origin in that quarter of the world, was probable. But that day was distant; and Mark was soon satisfied that the great use of the spot was its being a vent to what would otherwise be the pent and dangerous forces that were in the course of a constant accumulation beneath.

The party had been about an hour on the island, and was about to quit it, when a most startling discovery was made. Bob saw a canoe drawn close in among the rocks to leeward, and, on a further examination, a man was seen near it. At first, this was taken as an indication of hostilities, but, on getting a second look, our mariners were satisfied that nothing of that sort was to be seriously apprehended. It was determined to go nearer to the stranger, at once, and learn the whole truth.

A cry from Peters, followed by his immediately springing forward to meet a second person, who had left the canoe, and who was bounding like a young antelope to meet him, rendered everything clear sooner even than had been anticipated. All supposed that this eager visitor was a woman, and no one doubted that it was Peggy, the poor fellow's Indian wife. Peggy it proved to be; and after the weeping, and laughing, and caressing of the meeting were a little abated, the following explanation was made by Peters, who spoke the language of his wife with a good deal of facility, and who acted as interpreter.

According to the accounts now given by Peggy, the warfare between Ooroony and Waally had been kept up with renewed vigour, subsequently to the escape of Jones and her own husband. Fortune had proved fickle, as so often happens, and Waally got to be in the ascendant. His enemy was reduced to great straits, and had been compelled to confine himself to one of the smallest islands of the group, where he was barely able to maintain his party, by means of the most vigilant watchfulness. This left Waally at liberty to pursue his intention of following the party of whites, which was known to have gone to the southward, with so much valuable property, as well as to extend his conquests, by taking possession of the mountain visited by him the year previously. A grand expedition was accordingly planned, and a hundred canoes had actually sailed from the group, with more than a thousand warriors on board, bent on achieving a great exploit. In this expedition, Unus, the brother of Peggy, had been compelled to join, being a warrior of some note, and the sister had come along, in common with some fifty other women; the rank of Unus and Peggy not being sufficient to attract attention to their proceedings. Waally had postponed this, which he intended for the great enterprise of a very turbulent life, to the most favourable season of the year. There was a period of a few weeks every summer, when the trades blew much less violently than was usually the case, and when, indeed, it was no unusual thing to have shifts of wind, as well as light breezes. All this the Indians perfectly well understood, for they were bold navigators, when the sizes and qualities of their vessels were considered. As it appeared, the voyage from the group to Rancocus Island, a distance of fully a hundred leagues, was effected without any accident, and the while of that formidable force was safely landed at the very spot where Betts had encamped on his arrival out with the colonists. Nearly a month had been passed in exploring the mountain, the first considerable eminence most of the Indians had ever beheld; and in making their preparations for further proceedings. During that time, hundreds had seen Vulcan's Peak, as well as the smoke of the volcano, though the reef, with all its islands, lay too low to be discerned from such a distance. The Peak was now the great object to be attained, for there it was universally believed that Betto (meaning Betts) and his companions had concealed themselves and their much-coveted treasures. Rancocus Island was well enough, and Waally made all his plans for colonizing it at once, but the other, and distant mountain, no doubt was the most desirable territory to possess, or white men would not have brought their women so far in order to occupy it.

As a matter of course, Unus and Peggy learned the nature of the intended proceedings. The last might have been content to wait for the slower movements of the expedition, had she not ascertained that threats of severely punishing the two deserters, one of whom was her own husband, had been heard to fall from the lips of the dread Waally himself. No sooner, therefore, did this faithful Indian girl become mistress of the intended plan, than she gave her brother no peace until he consented to put off into the ocean with her, in a canoe she had brought from home, and which was her own property. Had not Unus been disaffected to his new chief, this might not so easily have been done, but the young Indian was deadly hostile to Waally, and was a secret friend of Ooroony: a state of feeling which disposed him to desert the former, at the first good opportunity.

The two adventurers put off from Rancocus Island just at dark, and paddled in the direction that they believed would carry them to the Peak. It will be remembered that the last could not be seen from the ocean, until about half the passage between the islands was made, though it was plainly apparent from the heights of Rancocus, as already mentioned. Next morning, when day returned, the smoke of the volcano was in sight, but no Peak. There is little question that the canoe had been set too much to the southward, and was diagonally receding from its desired point of debarkation, instead of approaching it. Towards the smoke, Unus and his sister continued to paddle, and, after thirty-six hours of nearly unremitted labour, they succeeded in landing at the volcano, ignorant of its nature, awe-struck and trembling, but compelled to seek a refuge there, as the land-bird rests its tired wing on the ship's spars, when driven from the coast by the unexpected gale. When discovered, Peggy and her brother were about to take a fresh start from their resting-place, the Peak being visible from the volcano.

Mark questioned these two friends concerning the contemplated movement of Waally, with great minuteness, Unus was intelligent for a savage, and appeared to understand himself perfectly. He was of opinion that his countrymen would endeavour to cross, the first calm day, or the first day when the breeze should be light; and that was just the time when our colonists did not desire to meet the savages out at sea. He described the party as formidable by numbers and resolution, though possessing few arms besides those of savages. There were half a dozen old muskets in the canoes, with a small supply of ammunition; but, since the desertion of Jones and Peters, no one remained who knew how to turn these weapons to much account. Nevertheless, the natives were so numerous, possessed so many weapons that were formidable in their own modes of fighting, and were so bent on success, that Unus did not hesitate to give it as his opinion, the colonists would act wisely in standing off for some other island, if they knew where another lay, even at the cost of abandoning most of their effects.

But, our governor had no idea of following any such advice. He was fully aware of the strength of his position on the Peak, and felt no disposition to abandon it. His great apprehension was for the Reef, where his territories were much more assailable. It was not easy to see how the crater, and ship, and the schooner on the stocks, and all the other property that, in the shape of hogs, poultry, &c., was scattered far and wide in that group, could be protected against a hundred canoes, by any force at his command. Even with the addition of Unus, who took service at once, with all his heart, among his new friends, Mark could muster but eight men; viz., himself, Heaton, Betts, Bigelow, Socrates, Peters, Jones and Unus. To these might possibly be added two or three of the women, who might be serviceable in carrying ammunition, and as sentinels, while the remainder would be required to look after the children, to care for the stock, &c. All these facts passed through Mark's mind, as Peters translated the communication of Unus, sentence by sentence.

It was indispensable to come to some speedy decision. Peters was now happy and contented with his nice little Peggy, and there was no longer any necessity for pursuing the voyage on his account. As for the project of placing the hogs on Rancocus, this was certainly not the time to do it, even if it were now to be done at all; we say 'now,' since the visits of the savages would make any species of property on that island, from this time henceforth, very insecure. It was therefore determined to abandon the voyage, and to shape their course back to the Peak, with as little delay as possible. As there were indications of shell-fish, sea-weed, &c., being thrown ashore at the Volcano, two of the hogs were put ashore there to seek their fortunes. According to the new plan, the Neshamony made sail on her return passage, about an hour before the sun set. As was usual in that strait, the trades blew pretty fresh, and the boat, although it had the canoe of Unus in tow, came under the frowning cliffs some time before the day reappeared. By the time the sun rose, the Neshamony was off the cove, into which she hastened with the least possible delay. It was the governor's apprehension that his sails might be seen from the canoes of Waally, long before the canoes could be seen from his boat, and he was glad to get within the cover of his little haven. Once there, the different crafts were quite concealed from the view of persons outside, and it now remained to be proved whether their cover was not so complete as effectually to baffle a hostile attempt to find it.

The quick and unexpected return of the Neshamony produced a great deal of surprise on the Plain. She had not been seen to enter the cove, and the first intimation any one in the settlement had of such an occurrence, was the appearance of Mark before the door of the dwelling. Bigelow was immediately sent to the Peak with a glass, to look out for canoes, while Heaton was called in from the woods by means of a conch. In twenty minutes the council was regularly in session, while the men began to collect and to look to their arms. Peters and Jones were ordered to go down to the magazine, procure cartridges, and then proceed to the batteries and load the carronades. In a word, orders were given to make all the arrangements necessary for the occasion.

It was not long ere a report came down from Bigelow. It was brought by his Spanish wife, who had accompanied her husband to the Peak, and who came running in, half breathless, to say that the ocean was covered with canoes and catamarans; a fleet of which was paddling directly for the island, being already within three leagues of it. Although this intelligence was expected, it certainly caused long faces and a deep gloom to pervade that little community. Mark's fears were always for the Reef, where there happened to be no one just at that moment but the black women, who were altogether insufficient to defend it, under the most favourable circumstances, but who were now without a head. There was the hope, however, of the Indians not seeing those low islands, which they certainly could not do as long as they remained in their canoes. On the other hand, there was the danger that some one might cross from the Reef in one of the boats, a thing that was done as often as once a week, in which case a chase might ensue, and the canoes be led directly towards the spot that it was so desirable to conceal. Juno could sail a boat as well as any man among them, and, as is usually the case, that which she knew she could do so well, she was fond of doing; and she had not now been across for nearly a week. The cow kept at the crater gave a large mess of milk, and the butter produced by her means was delicious when eaten fresh, but did not keep quite as well in so warm a climate as it might have done in one that was colder, and Dido was ever anxious to send it to Miss Bridget, as she still called her mistress, by every available opportunity. The boat used by the negresses on such occasions, was the Dido, a perfectly safe craft in moderate weather, but she was just the dullest sailer of all those owned by the colony. This created the additional danger of a capture, in the event of a chase. Taking all things into consideration therefore, Mark adjourned the council to the Peak, a feverish desire to look out upon the sea causing him to be too uneasy where he was, to remain there in consultation with any comfort to himself. To the Peak, then, everybody repaired, with the exception of Bigelow, Peters, and Jones, who were now regularly stationed at the carronades to watch the entrance of the cove. In saying everybody, we include not only all the women, but even their children.

So long as the colonists remained on the plain, there was not the smallest danger of anyone of them being seen from the surrounding ocean. This the woods, and their great elevation, prevented. Nor was there much danger of the party in the batteries being seen, though so much lower, and necessarily on the side of the cliff, since a strict order had been given to keep out of sight, among the trees, where they could see everything that was going on, without being seen themselves. But on the naked Peak it was different. High as it was, a man might be seen from the ocean, if moving about, and the observer was tolerably near by. Bob had seen Mark, when his attention was drawn to the spot by the report of the latter's fowling-piece; and the governor had often seen Bridget, on the look-out for him, as he left the island, though her fluttering dress probably made her a more conspicuous object than most persons would have been. From all this, then, the importance of directing the movements of the party that followed him became apparent to Mark, who took his measures accordingly.

By the time the governor reached the Peak, having ascended it on its eastern side, so as to keep his person concealed, the hostile fleet was plainly to be seen with the naked eye. It came on in a tolerably accurate line, or lines, abreast; being three deep, one distant from the other about a cable's length. It steered directly for the centre of the island, whereas the cove was much nearer to its northern than to its southern end; and the course showed that the canoes were coming on at random, having nothing in view but the island.

But Mark's eyes were turned with the greatest interest to the northward, or in the direction of the Reef. As they came up the ascent, Bridget had communicated to him the fact that she expected Juno over that day, and that it was understood she would come quite alone. Bridget was much opposed to the girl's taking this risk; but Juno had now done it so often successfully, that nothing short of a positive command to the contrary would be likely to stop her. This command, most unfortunately, as Mark now felt, had not been given; and great was his concern when Betts declared that he saw awhile speck to the northward, which looked like a sail. The glass was soon levelled in that direction, and no doubt any longer remained on the subject. It was the Dido, steering across from the Reef, distant then about ten miles; and she might be expected to arrive in about two hours! In other words, judging by the progress of the canoes, there might be a difference of merely half an hour or so between the time of the arrival of the boat and that of the canoes.

This was a very serious matter; and never before had the council a question before it which gave its members so much concern, or which so urgently called for action, as this of the course that was now to be taken to avert a danger so imminent. Not only was Juno's safety involved; but the discovery of the cove and the reef, one or both, was very likely to be involved in the issue, and the existence of the whole colony placed in extreme jeopardy. As the canoes were still more than a league from the island, Bob thought there was time to go out with the Bridget, and meet the Dido, when both boats could ply to windward until it was dark; after which, they might go into the reef, or come into the cove, as circumstances permitted. The governor was about to acquiesce in this suggestion, little as he liked it, when a new proposition was made, that at first seemed so strange that no one believed it could be put in execution, but to which all assented in the end.

Among the party on the Peak were Unus and Peggy. The latter understood a good deal of English, and that which she did not comprehend, in the course of the discussions on this interesting occasion, Bob, who had picked up something of the language of her group, explained to her, as well as he could. After a time, the girl ran down to the battery and brought up her husband, through whom the proposal was made that, at first, excited so much wonder. Peggy had told Unus what was going on, and had pointed out to him the boat of Juno, now sensibly drawing nearer to the island, and Unus volunteered to *swim* out and meet the girl, so as to give her timely warning, as well as instructions how to proceed!

Although Mark, and Heaton, and Bridget, and all present indeed, were fully aware that the natives of the South Seas could, and often did pass hours in the water, this proposal struck them all, at first, as so wild, that no one believed it could be accepted. Reflection, however did its usual office, and wrought a change in these opinions. Peters assured the governor that he had often known Unus to swim from island to island in the group, and that on the score of danger to him, there was not the least necessity of feeling any uneasiness. He did not question the Indian's power to swim the entire distance to the Reef, should it be necessary.

Another difficulty arose, however, when the first was overcome. Unus could speak no English, and how was he to communicate with Juno, even after he had entered her boat? The girl, moreover, was both resolute and strong, as her present expedition sufficiently proved, and would be very apt to knock a nearly naked savage on the head, when she saw him attempting to enter her boat. From this last opinion, however, Bridget dissented. Juno was kind-hearted, and would be more disposed, she thought, to pick up a man found in the water at sea, than to injure him. But Juno could read writing. Bridget herself had taught her slaves to read and write, and Juno in particular was a sort of 'expert,' in her way. She wrote and read half the nigger-letters of Bristol, previously to quitting America. She would now write a short note, which would put the girl on her guard, and give her confidence in Unus. Juno knew the whole history of Peters and Peggy, having taken great interest in the fate of the latter. To own the truth, the girl had manifested a very creditable degree of principle on the subject, for Jones had tried to persuade his friend to take Juno, a nice, tidy, light-coloured black, to wife, and to forget Peggy, when Juno repelled the attempt with spirit and principle. It is due to Peters, moreover, to add that he was always true to his island bride. But the occurrence had made Juno acquainted with the whole history of Peggy; and Bridget, in the few lines she now wrote to the girl, took care to tell her that the Indian was the brother of Peggy. In that capacity, he would be almost certain of a friendly reception. The rest of the note was merely an outline of their situation, with, an injunction to let Unis direct the movements.

No sooner was this important note written, than Unus hastened down to the cove. He was accompanied by Mark, Peters and Peggy; the former to give his instructions, and the two latter to act as interpreters. Nor was the sister without feeling for the brother on the occasion. She certainly did not regard his enterprise as it would have been looked upon by a civilized woman, but she manifested a proper degree of interest in its success. Her parting words to her brother, were advice to keep well to windward, in order that, as he got near the boat, he might float down upon it with the greater facility, aided by the waves.

The young Indian was soon ready. The note was secured in his hair, and moving gently in the water, he swam out of the cove with the ease, if not with the rapidity of a fish. Peggy clapped her hands and laughed, and otherwise manifested a sort of childish delight, as if pleased that one of her race should so early make himself useful to the countrymen of her husband. She and Peters repaired to the battery, which was the proper station of the man, while Mark went nimbly up the Stairs, on his way to the Peak. And here we might put in a passing word on the subject of these ascents and descents. The governor had now been accustomed to them more than a twelvemonth, and he found that the effect they produced on the muscles of his lower limbs was absolutely surprising. He could now ascend the Stairs in half the time he had taken on his first trials, and he could carry burthens up and down them, that at first he would not have dreamed of attempting even to take on his shoulders. The same was true with all the colonists, male and female, who began to run about the cliffs like so many goats —*chamois* would be more poetical-and who made as light of the Stairs as the governor himself.

When Mark reached the Peak again, he found matters drawing near to a crisis. The canoes were within a league of the island, coming on steadily in line, and paddling with measured sweeps of their paddles. As yet, the sail of Juno's boat had escaped them. This was doubtless owing to their lowness in the water, and the distance that still separated them. The Dido was about five miles from the northern end of the island, while the fleet was some five more to the southward of it. This placed the two almost ten miles apart though each seemed so near, seen from the elevation of the Peak, that one might have fancied that he could throw a shot into either.

Unus was the great point of interest for the moment. He was just coming out clear of the island, and might be seen with the naked eye, in that pure atmosphere, a dark speck floating on the undulating surface of the ocean. By the aid of the glass, there was no difficulty in watching his smallest movement. With a steady and sinewy stroke of his arms, the young savage pursued his way, keeping to windward, as instructed by his sister, and making a progress in the midst of those rolling billows that was really wonderful. The wind was not very fresh, nor were the seas high; but the restless ocean, even in its slumbers, exhibits the repose of a giant, whose gentlest heavings are formidable and to be looked to. In one particular, our colonists were favoured. Owing to some accidental circumstances of position, a current set round the northern end of the island, and diffused itself on its western side by expanding towards the south. This carried the canoes from the boat and the cove, and insomuch increased Juno's chance of escape.

The meeting between Unus and the boat took place when the latter was within a league of the land. As the sailing directions were for every craft to fall in with the island rather to windward of the Peak, on account of the very current just mentioned, it was questionable with Mark and Betts whether any in the canoes could now perceive the boat, on account of the intervening heights. It was pretty certain no one, as yet, had made this important discovery, for the impetuosity of savages would instantly have let the fact be known through their shouts and their eagerness to-chase. On the contrary, all remained tranquil in the fleet, which continued to approach the land with a steady but regulated movement, that looked as if a secret awe pervaded the savages as they drew nearer and nearer to that unknown and mysterious world. To them the approaching revelations were doubtless of vast import; and the stoutest heart among them must have entertained some such sensations as were impressed on the spirits of Columbus and his companions, when they drew near to the shores of Guanahani.

In the mean time, Juno came confidingly on, shaping her course rather more to windward than usual even, on account of the lightness of the breeze. This effectually prevented her seeing or being seen from the canoes; the parties diagonally drawing nearer, in utter ignorance of each other's existence. As for Unus, he manoeuvred quite skilfully. After getting a couple of miles off the land, he swam directly to windward; and it was well he did, the course of the boat barely permitting his getting well on her weather-bow, when it was time to think of boarding.

Unus displayed great judgment in this critical part of the affair. So accurately did he measure distances, that he got alongside of the Dido, with his hand on her weather gunwale, without Juno's having the least idea that he was anywhere near her. At one effort he was in the boat; and while the girl was still uttering her scream of alarm, he stood holding out the note, pronouncing the word "Missus" as well as he could. The girl had acquired too much knowledge of the habits of the South Sea islanders, while passing through and sojourning in the different groups she had visited, to be overwhelmed with the occurrence. What is more, she recognised the young Indian at a glance; some passages of gallantry having actually taken place between them during the two months Heaton and his party remained among Ooroony's people. To be frank with the reader, the first impression of Juno was, that the note thus tendered to her was a love-letter, though its contents instantly undeceived her. The exclamation and changed manner of the girl told Unus that all was right; and he went quietly to work to take in the sail, as the most effectual method of concealing the presence of the boat from the thousand hostile and searching eyes in the canoes. The moment Mark saw the canvas come in, he cried out 'all is well,' and descended swiftly from the Peak, to hasten to a point where he could give the necessary attentions to the movements of Waally and his fleet.

Chapter XVII

> "Ho! strike the flag-staff deep, Sir Knight, —
> Ho! scatter flowers, fair maids, —
> Ho! gunners fire a loud salute —
> Ho! gallants, draw your blades; —"
>
> —Macaulay

So much time had passed in the execution of the plan of Unus, that the canoes were close under the cliffs, when the governor and his party reached the wood that fringed their summits, directly over the northern end of their line. Even this extremity of their formation was a mile or two to leeward of the cove, and all the craft, catamarans included, were drifting still further south, under the influence of the current. So long as this state of things continued, there was nothing for the colonists to apprehend, since they knew landing at any other spot than the cove was out of the question. The strictest orders had been given for every one to keep concealed, a task that was by no means difficult, the whole plain being environed with woods, and its elevation more than a thousand feet above the sea. In short, nothing but a wanton exposure of the person, could render it possible for one on the water to get a glimpse of another on the heights above him.

The fleet of Waally presented an imposing sight. Not only were his canoes large, and well filled with men, but they were garnished with the usual embellishments of savage magnificence. Feathers and flags, and symbols of war and power, were waving and floating over the prows of most of them, while the warriors they contained were gay in their trappings. It was apparent, however, to the members of the council, who watched every movement of the fleet with the utmost vigilance, that their foes were oppressed with doubts concerning the character of the place they had ventured so far to visit. The smoke of the Volcano was visible to them, beyond a doubt, and here was a wall of rock interposed between them and the accomplishment of their desire to land. In this last respect, Rancocus Island offered a shore very different from that of Vulcan's Peak. The first; in addition to the long, low point so often mentioned, had everywhere a beach of some sort or other; while, on the last, the waves of the Pacific rose and fell as against a precipice, marking their power merely by a slight discoloration of the iron-bound coast. Those superstitious and ignorant beings naturally would connect all these unusual circumstances with some supernatural agencies; and Heaton early, gave it as his opinion that Waally, of whom he had some personal knowledge, was hesitating, and doubtful of the course he ought to pursue, on account of this feeling of superstition. When this opinion was expressed, the governor suggested the expediency of firing one of the carronades, under the supposition that the roar of the gun, and most especially the echo, of which there was one in particular that was truly terrific, might have the effect to frighten away the whole party. Heaton was in doubt about the result, for Waally and his people knew something of artillery, though of echoes they could not know anything at all. Nothing like an echo, or indeed a hill, was to be found in the low coral islands of their group, and the physical agents of producing such sounds were absolutely wanting among them. It might be that something like an echo had been heard at Rancocus Island, but it must have been of a very different calibre from that which Heaton and Mark were in the habit of making for the amusement of the females, by firing their fowling-pieces down the Stairs. As yet neither of the guns had been fired from the proper point, which was the outer battery, or that on the shelf of rock, though a very formidable roaring had been made by the report of the gun formerly fired, as an experiment to ascertain how far it would command the entrance of the cove. After a good deal of discussion, it was decided to try the experiment, and Betts, who knew all about the means necessary to produce the greatest reverberations, was despatched to the shelf-battery with instructions to scale its gun, by pointing it along the cliff and making all the uproar he could.

This plan was carried out just as Waally had assembled his chiefs around his own canoe, whither he had called them by an order, to consult on the manner in which the entire coast of the island ought to be examined, that a landing might be effected. The report of the gun came quite unexpectedly to all parties; the echo, which rolled along the cliffs for miles, being absolutely terrific! Owing to the woods and intervening rocks, the natives could see no smoke, which added to their surprise, and was doubtless one reason they did not, at first, comprehend the long, cracking, thundering sounds that, as it might be, rolled out towards them from the island. A cry arose that the strange rocks were speaking, and that the Gods of the place were angry. This was followed by a general and confused flight;—the canoes, paddling away as if their people were apprehensive of being buried beneath the tumbling rocks. For half an hour nothing was seen but frantic efforts to escape, nothing heard but the dip of the paddle and the wash of its rise.

Thus far the plan of the governor had succeeded even beyond his expectations. Could he get rid of these savages without bloodshed, it would afford him sincere delight, it being repugnant to all his feelings to sweep away rows of such ignorant men before the murderous fire of his cannon. While he and Heaton were congratulating each other on the encouraging appearances, a messenger came down from the Peak, where Bridget remained on the look-out, to report that the boat had drifted in, and was getting close under the cliffs, on the northern end of the island, which was in fact coming close under the Peak itself. A signal to push for the cove had been named to Juno, and Bridget desired to know whether it ought to be made, else the boat would shortly be too near in, to see it. The governor thought the moment favourable, for the canoes were still paddling in a body away from the spot whence the roar had proceeded, and their course carried them to the southward and westward, while Unus would approach from the northward and eastward. Word was sent, accordingly, to make the signal.

Bridget no sooner received this order than she showed the flag, which was almost immediately answered by setting the boat's sail. Unus now evidently took the direction of matters on board the Dido, It is probable he appreciated the effect of the gun and its echo, the first of which he fully comprehended, though the last was as great and as awful a mystery to him, as to any one of his countrymen. Nevertheless, he imputed the strange and fearful roar of the cliffs to some control of the whites over the power of the hills, and regarded it as a friendly roar, even while he trembled. Not so would it be with his countrymen, did he well know; they would retire before it; and the signal being given at that instant, the young Indian had no hesitation about the course he ought to take.

Unus understood sailing a boat perfectly well. On setting his sail, he stood on in the Dido until he was obliged to bear up on account of the cliffs. This brought him so close to the rocks as greatly to diminish the chances of being seen. There both wind and current aided his progress; the first drawing round the end of the island, the coast of which it followed in a sort of eddy, for some time, and the latter setting down towards the cove, which was less than two miles from the north bluff. In twenty minutes after he had made sail, Unus was entering the secret little harbour, Waally and his fleet being quite out of sight from one as low as the surface of the ocean, still paddling away to the south-west, as hard as they could.

Great was the exultation of the colonists, at this escape of Juno's. It even surpassed their happiness at the retreat of their invaders. If the boat were actually unseen, the governor believed the impression was sufficient to keep the savages aloof for a long time, if not for ever; since they would not fail to ascribe the roar, and the smoke of the volcano, and all the mysteries of the place, to supernatural agencies. If the sail *had* been seen, however, it was possible that, on reflection, their courage might revive, and more would be seen of them. Unus was extolled by everybody, and seemed perfectly happy. Peggy communicated his thoughts, which were every way in favour of his new friends. Waally he detested. He denounced him as a ruthless tyrant, and declared he would prefer death to submission to his exactions. Juno highly approved of all his sentiments, and was soon known as a sworn friend of Peggy's. This hatred of tyranny is innate in men, but it is necessary to distinguish between real oppression and those restraints which are wholesome, if not indispensable to human happiness. As for the canoes, they were soon out of sight in the south-western hoard, running off, under their sails, before the wind. Waally, himself, was too strong-minded and resolute, to be as much overcome by the echo, as his companions; but, so profound and general was the awe excited, that he did not think it advisable to persevere in his projects, at a moment so discouraging. Acquiescing in the wishes of all around him, the expedition drew off from the island, making the best of its way back to the place from which it had last sailed. All these circumstances became known to the colonists, in the end, as well as the reasoning and the more minute incidents that influenced the future movements; For the time being, however, Woolston and his friends were left to their own conjectures on the Subject; which, however, were not greatly out of the way. It was an hour after Juno and Unus were safe up on the plain, before the look-outs at the Peak finally lost sight of the fleet, which, when last seen, was steering a course that would carry it between the volcano and Rancocus Island, and might involve it in serious difficulties in the succeeding night. There was no land in sight from the highest points on Rancocus Island, nor any indications of land, in a south-westerly direction; and, did the canoes run past the latter, the imminent danger of a general catastrophe would be the consequence. Once at sea, under an uncertainty as to the course to be steered, the situation of those belonging to the expedition would be painful, indeed, nor could the results be foreseen. Waally, nevertheless, escaped the danger. Edging off to keep aloof from the mysterious smoke, which troubled his followers almost as much as the mysterious echoes, the party, most fortunately for themselves, got a distant view of the mountains for which they were running, and altered their course in sufficient time to reach their place of destination, Ly the return of light the succeeding morning.

All thoughts of the expedition to Rancocus Island were temporarily abandoned by the governor and his council. Mark was greatly disappointed, nor did his regrets cease with disappointment only. Should Waally leave a portion of his people on that island, a collision must occur, sooner or later; there being a moral impossibility of the two colonies continuing friends while so near each other. The nature of an echo would be ascertained, before many months, among the hills of Rancocus Island, and when that came to be understood, there was an end of the sacred character that the recent events had conferred on the Peak. Any straggling vagabond, or runaway from a ship, might purchase a present importance by explaining things, and induce the savages to renew their efforts. In a word, there was the moral certainty that hostilities must be renewed ere many months, did Waally remain so near them, and the question now seriously arose, whether it were better to press the advantage already obtained, and drive him back to his group, or to remain veiled behind the sort of mystery that at present enshrouded them. These points were gravely debated, and became subjects of as great interest among the colonists, as ever banks, or abolitionism, or antimasonry, or free-trade, or any other of the crotchets of the day, could possibly be in America. Many were the councils that were convened to settle this important point of policy, which, after all, like most other matters of moment, was decided more by the force of circumstances, than by any of the deductions of human reason. The weakness of the colony and the dangers to its existence, disposed of the question of an aggressive war. Waally was too strong to be assailed by a dozen enemies, and all the suggestions of prudence were in favour of remaining quiet, until the Friend Abraham White could, at least, be made available in the contest. Supported by that vessel, indeed, matters would be changed; and Mark thought it would be in his power to drive in Waally, and even to depose him and place Ooroony at the head of the natives once more. To finish and launch the schooner, therefore, was now the first great object, and, after a week of indecision and consultations, it was determined to set about that duty with vigour.

It will be easily seen, that the getting of the Abraham into the water was an affair of a good deal of delicacy, under the circumstances. The strait between the Peak and Cape South was thirty miles wide, and it was twenty more to the crater. Thus the party at work on the vessel would be fully fifty miles from the main abodes of the colony, and thrown quite out of the affair should another invasion be attempted. As for bringing the Neshamony, the Dido, the Bridget, and the fighter, into the combat, everybody was of opinion it would be risking too much. It is true, one of the swivels was mounted on the former, and might be of service, but the natives had got to be too familiar with fire-arms to render it prudent to rely on the potency of a single swivel, in a conflict against a force so numerous, and one led by a spirit as determined as that of Waally's was known to be. All idea of righting at sea, therefore, until the schooner was launched, was out of the question, and every energy was turned to effect the latter most important object. A separation of the forces of the colony was inevitable, in the meanwhile; and reliance must be placed on the protection of Providence, for keeping the enemy aloof until the vessel was ready for active service.

The labour requiring as much physical force as could be mustered, the arrangement was settled in council and approved by the governor, on the following plan, viz:—Mark was to proceed to the Reef with all the men that could be spared, and a portion of the females. It was not deemed safe, however, to leave the Peak with less than three defenders, Heaton, Peters and Unus being chosen for that important station; the former commanding, of course. Mark, Betts, Bigelow, Socrates, and Jones, formed the party *for* the Reef, to which were attached Bridget, Martha, Teresa, and the blacks. Bigelow went across, indeed, a day or two before the main party sailed, in order to look after Dido, and to get his work forward as fast as possible. When all was ready, and that was when ten days had gone by after the retreat of Waally, without bringing any further tidings from him, the governor sailed in the Neshamony, having the Bridget and the lighter in company, leaving the Dido for the convenience of Heaton and his set. Signals were agreed on, though the distance was so great as to render them of little use, unless a boat were mid-channel. A very simple and ingenious expedient, nevertheless, was suggested by Mark, in connection with this matter. A single tree grew so near the Peak as to be a conspicuous object from the ocean; it was not large, though it could be seen at a great distance, more particularly in the direction of the Reef. The governor intimated an intention to send a boat daily far enough out into the strait to ascertain whether this tree were, or were not standing; and Heaton was instructed to have it felled as soon as he had thoroughly ascertained that Waally was abroad again with hostile intentions. Other signals were also agreed on, in order to regulate the movements of the boats, in the event of their being called back to the Peak to repel an invasion.

With the foregoing arrangements completed and thoroughly understood, the governor set sail for the Reef, accompanied by his little squadron. It was an exquisitely beautiful day, one in which all the witchery of the climate developed itself, soothing the nerves and animating the spirits. Bridget had lost most of her apprehensions of the natives, and could laugh with her husband and play with her child almost as freely as before the late events. Everybody, indeed, was in high spirits, the launching of the schooner being regarded as a thing that would give them complete command of the adjacent seas.

The passage was short, a fresh breeze blowing, and four hours after quitting the cliffs, the Neshamony was under the lee of Cape South, and heading for the principal inlet. As the craft glided along, in perfectly smooth water now, Mark noted the changes that time was making on those rocks, which had so lately emerged from the depths of the ocean. The prairie, in particular, was every way worthy of his attention. A mass of sea-weed, which rested on a sort of stratum of mud immediately after the eruption, had now been the favourite pasturage of the hogs for more than a twelvemonth. These hogs at the present time exceeded fifty full-grown animals, and there were twice that number of grunters at their heels. Then the work they had done on the Prairie was incredible. Not less than hundreds of acres had they rooted over, mixing the sea-weed with the mud, and fast converting the whole into soil. The rains had washed away the salt, or converted it into manure, as well as contributing to the more rapid decay of the vegetable substances. In that climate the changes are very rapid, and Mark saw that another year or two would convert the whole of that vast range, which had been formerly computed at a surface of a thousand acres, into very respectable pastures, if not into meadows. Of meadows, however, there was very little necessity in that latitude; the eternal summer that reigned furnishing pasturage the year round. The necessary grasses might be wanting to seed down so large a surface, but those which Socrates had put in were well-rooted, and it was pretty certain they would, sooner or later, spread themselves over the whole field. In defiance of the hogs, and their increasing inroads, large patches were already green and flourishing. What is more, young trees were beginning to show themselves along the margin of the channels. Henton had brought over from Betto's group several large panniers made of green willows, and these Socrates had cut into strips, and thrust into the mud. Almost without an exception they had struck out roots, and never ceasing, day or night, to grow, they were already mostly of the height of a man. Four or five years would convert them into so many beautiful, if not very useful trees.

Nor was this all. Heaton, under the influence of his habits, had studied the natures of the different trees he had met with on the other islands. The cocoa-nut, in particular, abounded in both groups, and finding it was a tree that much affected low land and salt water, he had taken care to set out various samples of his roots and fruits, on certain detached islets near this channel, where the soil and situation induced him to believe they would flourish. Sea sand he was of opinion was the most favourable for the growth of this tree, and he had chosen the sites of his plantations with a view to those advantages. On the Peak cocoa-nuts were to be found, but they were neither very fine, nor in very large quantities. So long as Mark had that island to himself, the present, supply-would more than equal the demand, but with the increase of the colony a greater number of the trees would become very desirable. Five or six years would be needed to produce the fruit-bearing tree, and the governor was pleased to find that the growth of one of those years had been already secured, in the case of those he had himself planted, in and on the crater, near three years had contributed to their growth, and neither the Guano nor Loam Island having been forgotten, many of them were now thirty feet high. As he approached the crater, on that occasion, he looked at those promising fruits of his early and provident care for the future with great satisfaction, for seldom was the labour of man better rewarded. Mark well knew the value of this tree, which was of use in a variety of ways, in addition to the delicious and healthful fruit it bears; delicious and healthful when eaten shortly after it is separated from the tree. The wood of the kernel could be polished, and converted into bowls, that were ornamental as well as useful. The husks made a capital cordage, and a very respectable sail-cloth, being a good substitute for hemp, though hemp, itself, was a plant that might be grown on the prairies to an almost illimitable extent. The leaves were excellent for thatching, as well as for making brooms, mats, hammocks, baskets and a variety of such articles, while the trunks could be converted into canoes, gutters, and timber generally. There was also one other expensive use of this tree, which the governor had learned from Heaton. While Bridget was still confined to the ship, after the birth of her daughter. Mark had brought her a dish of greens, which she pronounced the most delicious of any thing in its way she had ever tasted. It was composed of the young and delicate leaves of the new growth, or of the summit of the cocoa-nut tree, somewhat resembling the artichoke in their formation, though still more exquisite in taste. But the tree from which this treat was obtained died,—a penalty that must ever be paid to partake of that dish. As soon as Bridget learned this, she forbade the cutting of any more for her use, at least. All the boats got into port in good season, and the Reef once more became a scene of life and activity. The schooner was soon completed, and it only remained to put her into the water. This work was already commenced by Bigelow, and the governor directed everybody to lend a hand in effecting so desirable an object. Bigelow had all his materials ready, and so perseveringly did our colonists work, that the schooner was all ready to be put into the water on the evening of the second day. The launch was deferred only to have the benefit of daylight. That afternoon Mark, accompanied by his wife, had gone in the Bridget, his favourite boat, to look for the signal tree. He went some distance into the strait, ere he was near enough to get a sight of it even with the glass; when he did procure a view, there it was precisely as he had last seen it. Putting the helm of the boat up, the instant he was assured of his fact, the governor wore short round, making the best, of his way back to the crater, again. The distances, it will be remembered, were considerable, and it required time to make the passage. The sun was setting as Mark was running along the channel to the Reef, the young man pointing out to his charming wife the growth of the trees, the tints of the evening sky, the drove of hogs, the extent of his new meadows, and such other objects as would be likely to interest both, in the midst of such a scene. The boat rounded a point where a portion of the hogs had been sleeping, and as it came sweeping up, the animals rose in a body, snuffed the air, and began scampering off in the way conformable to their habits, Mark laughing and pointing with his fingers to draw Bridget's attention to their antics.

"*There* are more of the creatures" said Bridget; "yonder, on the further side of the prairie —I dare say the two parties will join each other, and have a famous scamper, in company."

"More!" echoed Mark; "that can hardly be, as we passed some thirty of them several miles to the southward. —What is it you see, dearest, that you mistake for hogs?"

"Why, yonder-more than a mile from us; on the opposite side of the prairie and near the water, in the other channel."

"The other is not a channel at all; it is a mere bay that leads to nothing; so none of our boats or people can be there. The savages, as I am your husband, Bridget!"

Sure enough, the objects which Bridget had mistaken for mere hogs, were in truth the heads and shoulders of some twenty Indians who were observing the movements of the boat from positions taken on the other side of the plain, so as to conceal all but the upper halves of their bodies. They had two canoes; war canoes, moreover; but these were the whole party, at that point at least.

This was a most grave discovery. The governor had hoped the Reef, so accessible on every side by means of canoes, would, for years at least, continue to be a *terra incognita* to the savages. On this ignorance of the natives would much of its security depend, for the united forces of the colonists could scarcely suffice to maintain the place against the power of Waally. The matter as it was, called for all his energies, and for the most prompt measures.

The first step was to apprise the people at the Reef of the proximity of these dangerous neighbours. As the boat was doubtless seen, its sails rising above the land, there was no motive in changing its course, or for attempting to conceal it. The crater, ship and schooner on the stocks, were all in sight of the savages at that moment, though not less than two leagues distant, where they doubtless appeared indistinct and confused. The ship might produce an influence in one or two ways. It might inflame the cupidity of Waally, under the hope of possessing so much treasure, and tempt him on to hasten his assault; or it might intimidate him by its imagined force, vessels rarely visiting the islands of the Pacific without being prepared to defend themselves. The savages would not be likely to comprehend the true condition of the vessel, but would naturally suppose that she had a full crew, and possessed the usual means of annoying her enemies. All this occurred to the governor in the first five minutes after his discovery, while his boat was gliding onwards towards her haven.

Bridget behaved admirably. She trembled a little at first, and pressed her child to her bosom with more than the usual warmth, but her self-command was soon regained, and from that instant, Mark found in her a quick, ingenious, and useful assistant and counsellor. Her faculties and courage seemed to increase with the danger, and so far from proving an encumbrance, as might naturally enough have been expected, she was not only out of the way, as respects impediments, but she soon became of real use, and directed the movements of the females with almost as much skill and decision as Mark directed those of their husbands.

The boat did not reach the Reef until dusk, or for an hour after the savages had been seen. The colonists had just left their work, and the evening being cool and refreshing after a warm summer's day, they were taking their suppers under a tent or awning, at no great distance from the ship-yard, when the governor joined them. This tent, or awning, had been erected for such purposes, and had several advantages to recommend it. It stood quite near the beach of the spring, and cool fresh water was always at hand. It had a carpet of velvet-like grass, too, a rare thins for the Reef, on the outside of the crater. But, there were cavities on its surface, in which foreign substances had collected, and this was one of them. Sea-weed, loam, dead fish, and rain-water had made a thin soil on about an acre of rocks at this spot, and the rain constantly assisting vegetation, the grass-seed had taken root there, and this being its second season, Betts had found the sward already sufficient for his purposes, and caused an awning to be spread, converting the grass into a carpet. There might now have been a dozen similar places on the reef, so many oases in its desert, where soil had formed and grass was growing. No one doubted that, in time and with care, those, then living might see most of those naked rocks clothed with verdure, for the progress of vegetation in such a climate, favoured by those accidental causes which seemed to prevent that particular region from ever suffering by droughts, is almost magical, and might convert a wilderness into a garden in the course of a very few years.

Mark did not disturb the happy security in which he found his people by any unnecessary announcement of danger. On the contrary, he spoke cheerfully, complimented them on the advanced state of their work, and took an occasion to get Betts aside, when he first communicated the all-important discovery he had made. Bob was dumbfounded at first; for, like the governor himself, he had believed the Reef to be one of the secret spots of the earth, and had never anticipated an invasion in that quarter. Recovering himself, however, he was soon in a state of mind to consult intelligently and freely.

"Then we're to expect the rep*tyles* to-night?" said Betts, as soon as he had regained his voice.

"I think not," answered Mark. "The canoes I saw were in the false channel, and cannot possibly reach us without returning to the western margin of the rocks and entering one of the true passages. I rather think this cannot be done before morning. Daylight, indeed, may be absolutely necessary to them; and as the night promises to be dark, it is not easy to see how strangers can find their way to us, among the maze of passages they must meet. By land, they cannot get here from any of the islands on the western side of the group; and even if landed on the central island, there is only one route, and that a crooked one, which will bring them here without the assistance of their canoes. We are reasonably well fortified, Betts, through natural agencies, on that side; and I do not apprehend seeing anything more of the fellows until morning."

"What a misfortin 'tis that they should ever have discovered the Reef!"

"It certainly is; and it is one, I confess, I had not expected. But we must take things as they are, Betts, and do our duty. Providence-that all-seeing Power, which spared you and me when so many of our shipmates were called away with short notice-Providence may still be pleased to look on us with favour."

"That puts me in mind, Mr. Mark, of telling you something that I have lately l'arn'd from Jones, who was about a good deal among the savages, since his friend's marriage with Peggy, and before he made his escape to join us. Jones says that, as near as he can find out, about three years ago, a ship's launch came into Betto's Land, as we call it-Waally's Country, however, is meant; and that is a part of the group I never ventured into, seeing that my partic'lar friend, Ooroony, and Waally, was always at daggers drawn-but a ship's launch came in there, about three years since, with seven living men in it. Jones could never get a sight of any of the men, for Waally is said to have kept them all hard at work for himself; but he got tolerable accounts of them, as well as of the boat in which they arrived."

"Surely, Bob, you do not suppose that launch to have been ours, and those men to have been a part of our old crew!" exclaimed Mark, with a tumult of feeling he had not experienced since he had reason to think that Bridget was about to be restored to him.

"Indeed, but I do, sir. The savages told Jones that the boat had a bird painted in its starn-sheets; and that was the case with our launch, Mr. Mark, which was ornamented with a spread-eagle in that very spot. Then, one of the men was said to have a red mark on his face; and you may remember, sir, that Bill Brown had a nat'ral brand of that sort. Jones only mentioned the thing this arternoon, as we was at work together; and I detarmined to let you know all about it, at the first occasion. Depend on it, Mr. Woolston, some of our chaps is still living."

This unexpected intelligence momentarily drove the recollection of the present danger from the governor's mind. He sent for Jones, and questioned him closely touching the particulars of his information; the answers he received certainly going far towards corroborating Betts's idea of the character of the unknown men. Jones was never able even to get on the island where these men were said to be; but he had received frequent descriptions of their ages, appearances, numbers, &c. It was also reported by those who had seen them, that several of the party had died of hunger before the boat reached the group; and that only about half of those who had originally taken to the boat, which belonged to a ship that had been wrecked, lived to get ashore. The man with a mark on his face was represented as being very expert with tools, and was employed by Waally to build him a canoe that would live out in the gales of the ocean. This agreed perfectly with the trade and appearance of Brown, who had been the Rancocus's carpenter, and had the sort of mark so particularly described.

The time, the boat, the incidents of the wreck, meagre as the last were, as derived through the information of Jones, and all the other facts Mark could glean in a close examination of the man's statements, went to confirm the impression that a portion of those who had been carried to leeward in the Rancocus's launch, had escaped with their lives, and were at that moment prisoners in the power of the very savage chief who now threatened his colony with destruction.

But the emergency did not admit of any protracted inquiry into, or any consultation on the means necessary to relieve their old shipmates from a fate so miserable. Circumstances required that the governor should now give his attention to the important concerns immediately before him.

Chapter XVIII

> "To whom belongs this valley fair,
> That sleeps beneath the filmy air,
> Even like a living thing?
> Silent as infant at the breast,
> Save a still sound that speaks of rest,
> That streamlet's murmuring?"
>
> —Wilson

When the governor had communicated to his people that the savages were actually among the islands of their own group, something very like a panic came over them. A few minutes, however, sufficed to restore a proper degree of confidence, when the arrangements necessary to their immediate security were entered into. As some attention had previously been bestowed on the fortifications of the crater, that place was justly deemed the citadel of the Reef. Some thought the ship would be the most easily defended, on account of the size of the crater, and because it had a natural ditch around it, but so much property was accumulated in and around the crater that it could not be abandoned without a loss to which the governor had no idea of submitting. The gate of the crater was nothing in the way of defence, it is true; but one of the cannonades had been planted so as to command it, and this was thought sufficient for repelling all ordinary assaults. It has been said, already, that the outer wall of the crater was perpendicular at its base, most probably owing to the waves of the ocean in that remote period when the whole Reef was washed by them in every gale of wind. This perpendicular portion of the rock, moreover, was much harder than the ordinary surface of the Summit, owing in all probability to the same cause. It was even polished in appearance, and in general was some eighteen or twenty feet in height, with the exception of the two or three places, by one of which Mark and Betts had clambered up on their first visit to the Summit. These places, always small, and barely sufficient to allow of a man's finding footing on them, had long been picked away, in order to prevent the inroads of Kitty, and when the men had turned their attention to rendering the place secure against a sudden inroad, they being the only points where an enemy could get up, without resorting to ladders or artificial assistance, had, by means of additional labour, been rendered as secure as all the rest of the 'outer wall,' as the base of the crater was usually termed among them. It was true, that civilized assailants, who had the ordinary means at command, would soon have mastered this obstacle; but savages would not be likely to come prepared to meet it. The schooner, with her cradle and ways, had required all the loose timber, to the last stick, and the enemy was not likely to procure any supplies from the ship-yard. Two of the carronades were on the Summit, judiciously planted; two were on board the Abraham, as was one of the long sixes, and the remainder of the guns, (three at the rock excepted) were still on board the ship.

Mark divided his forces for the night. As Bridget habitually lived in the Rancocus' cabins, he did not derange her household at all, but merely strengthened her crew, by placing Bigelow and Socrates on board her; each with his family; while Betts assumed the command of the crater, having for his companion Jones. These were small garrisons; but the fortresses were strong, considering all the circumstances, and the enemy were uncivilized, knowing but little of fire-arms. By nine o'clock everything was arranged, and most of the women and children were on their beds, though no one there undressed that night.

Mark and Betts met, by agreement, alongside of the schooner, as soon as their respective duties elsewhere would allow. As the Reef, proper, was an island, they knew no enemy could find his way on it without coming by water, or by passing over the narrow bridge which has already been mentioned as crossing the little strait near the spring. This rendered them tolerably easy for the moment, though Mark had assured his companion it was not possible for the canoes to get to the Reef under several hours. Neither of the men could sleep, however, and they thought it as well to be on the look-out, and in company, as to be tossing about in their berths, or hammocks, by themselves. The conversation turned on their prospects, almost as a matter of course.

"We are somewhat short-handed, sir, to go to quarters ag'in them vagabonds," observed Betts, in reply to some remark of the governor's. "I counted a hundred and three of their craft when they was off the Peak the other day, and not one on 'em all had less than four hands aboard it, while the biggest must have had fifty. All told, I do think, Mr. Mark, they might muster from twelve to fifteen hundred fighting men."

"That has been about my estimate of their force, Bob; but, if they were fifteen thousand, we must bring them to action, for we fight for everything."

"Ay, ay, sir," answered Betts, ejecting the tobacco juice in the customary way, "there's reason in roasted eggs, they say, and there's reason in firing a few broadsides afore a body gives up. What a different place this here rock's got to be, sir, from what it was when you and I was floating sea-weed and rafting loam to it, to make a melon or a cucumber bed! Times is changed, sir, and we're now at war. Then it was all peace and quiet; and now it's all hubbub and disturbance."

"We have got our wives here now, and that I think you'll admit is something, Bob, when you remember the pains taken by yourself to bring so great a happiness about,"

"Why, yes, sir—I'll allow the wives is something—"

"Ship ahoy!" hailed a voice in good English, and in the most approved seaman-like tones of the voice.

The hail came from the margin of the island nearest to the Reef; or that which was connected with the latter by means of the bridge, but not from a point very near the latter.

"In the name of heavenly mercy!" exclaimed Betts, "what can that mean, governor?"

"I know that voice," said Mark, hurriedly; "and the whole matter begins to clear up to me. Who hails the Rancocus?"

"Is that ship the Rancocus, then?" answered the voice from the island.

"The Rancocus, and no other-are you not Bill Brown, her late carpenter?"

"The very same, God bless you, Mr. Woolston, for I now know *your* voice, too. I'm Bill, and right down glad am I to have things turn out so. I half suspected the truth when I saw a ship's spars this afternoon in this place, though little did I think, yesterday, of ever seeing anything more of the old 'Cocus. Can you give me a cast across this bit of a ferry, sir?"

"Are you alone, Bill-or who have you for companions?"

"There's two on us, sir, only-Jim Wattles and I—seven on us was saved in the launch; Mr. Hillson and the supercargo both dying afore we reached the land, as did the other man, we seven still living, though only two on us is here."

"Are there any black fellows with you?—Any of the natives?"

"Not one, sir. We gave 'em the slip two hours ago, or as soon as we saw the ship's masts, being bent on getting afloat in some craft or other, in preference to stopping with savages any longer. No, Mr. Woolston; no fear of them to-night, for they are miles and miles to leeward, bothered in the channels, where they'll be pretty sartain to pass the night; though you'll hear from 'em in the morning. Jim and I took to our land tacks, meeting with a good opportunity, and by running directly in the wind's eye, have come out here. We hid ourselves till the canoes was out of sight, and then we carried sail as hard as we could. So give us a cast and take us aboard the old ship again, Mr. Woolston, if you love a fellow-creatur', and an old shipmate in distress."

Such was the singular dialogue which succeeded the unexpected hail. It completely put a new face on things at the Reef. As Brown was a valuable man, and one whose word he had always relied on, Mark did not hesitate, but told him the direction to the bridge, where he and Betts met him and Wattles, after each of the parties had believed the others to be dead now fully three years!

The two recovered seamen of the Rancocus were alone, having acted in perfect good faith with their former officer, who led them to the awning, gave them some refreshment, and heard their story. The account given by Jones, for the first time that very day, turned out to be essentially true. When the launch was swept away from the ship, it drove down to leeward, passing at no great distance from the crater, of which the men in her got a glimpse, without being able to reach it. The attention of Hillson was mainly given to keeping the boat from filling or capsizing; and this furnished abundance of occupation. The launch got into one of the channels, and by observing the direction, which was nearly east and west, it succeeded in passing through all the dangers, coming out to leeward of the shoals. As everybody believed that the ship was hopelessly lost, no effort was made to get back to the spot where she had been left. No island appearing, Hillson determined to run off to the westward, trusting to fall in with land of some sort or other. The provisions and water were soon consumed, and then came the horrors usual to such scenes at sea. Hillson was one of the first that perished, his previous excesses unfitting him to endure privation. But seven survived when the launch reached an island in Waally's part of the group, so often mentioned. There they fell into the hands of that turbulent and warlike chief. Waally made the seamen his slaves, treating them reasonably well, but exacting of them the closest attention to his interests. Brown, as a ship-carpenter, soon became a favourite, and was employed in fashioning craft that it was thought might be useful in carrying out the ambitious projects of his master. The men were kept on a small island, and were watched like any other treasure, having no opportunity to communicate with any of those whites who appeared in other parts of the group. Thus, while Betts passed two months with Ooroony, and Heaton and his party nearly as much more time, these sailors, who heard of such visitors, could never get access to them. This was partly owing to the hostilities between the two chiefs-Ooroony being then in the ascendant-and partly owing to the special projects of Waally, who, by keeping his prisoners busily employed on his fleet, looked forward to the success which, in fact, crowned his efforts against his rival.

At length Waally undertook the expedition which had appeared in such force beneath the cliffs of the Peak. By this time, Brown had become so great a favourite, that he was permitted to accompany the chief; and Wattles was brought along as a companion for his shipmate. The remaining five were left behind, to complete a craft on which they had now been long employed, and which was intended to be the invincible war-canoe of those regions. Brown and Wattles had been in Waally's own canoe when the terrible echoes so much alarmed the uninstructed beings who heard it. They described them as much the most imposing echoes they had ever heard; nor did they, at first, know what to make of them, themselves. It was only on reflection, and after the retreat to Rancocus Island, that Brown, by reasoning on the subject, came to the conclusion that the whites, who were supposed to be in possession of the place, had fired a gun, which had produced the astounding uproar that had rattled so far along the cliff. As all Brown's sympathies were with the unknown people of his own colour, he kept his conjectures to himself, and managed to lead Waally in a different direction, by certain conclusions of his own touching the situation of the reef where the Rancocus had been lost.

Bill Brown was an intelligent man for his station and pursuits. He knew the courses steered by the launch, and had some tolerably accurate notions of the distances run. According to his calculations, that reef could not be very far to the northward of the Peak, and, by ascending the mountains on Rancocus Island, he either saw, or fancied he saw, the looming of land in that part of the ocean. It then occurred to Brown that portions of the wreck might still be found on the reef, and become the means of effecting his escape from the hands of his tyrants. Waally listened to his statements and conjectures with the utmost attention, and the whole fleet put to sea the very next day, in quest of this treasure. After paddling to windward again, until the Peak was fairly in sight, Brown steered to the north-east, a course that brought him out, after twenty-four hours of toil, under the lee of the group of the reef. This discovery of itself, filled Waally with exultation and pride. Here were no cliffs to scale, no mysterious mountain to appal, nor any visible obstacle to oppose his conquests. It is true, that the newly-discovered territory did not appear to be of much value, little beside naked rock, or broad fields of mud and sea-weed intermingled, rewarding their first researches. But better things were hoped for. It was something to men whose former domains were so much circumscribed and girded by the ocean, to find even a foundation for a new empire. Brown was now consulted as to every step to be taken, and his advice was implicitly followed. Columbus was scarcely a greater man, for the time being, at the court of Ferdinand and Isabella, than Bill Brown immediately became at the court of Waally. His words were received as prophecies, his opinions as oracles.

Honest Bill, who anticipated no more from his discoveries than the acquisition of certain portions of wood, iron, and copper, with, perhaps, the addition of a little rigging, certain sails and an anchor or two, acted, at first, for the best interests of his master. He led the fleet along the margin of the group until a convenient harbour was found. Into this all the canoes entered, and a sandy beach supplying fresh water in abundance having been found, an encampment was made for the night. Several hours of daylight remaining, however, when these great preliminary steps had been taken, Brown proposed to Waally an exploring expedition in a couple of the handiest of the canoes. The people thus employed were those who had given the alarm to the governor. On that occasion, not only was the boat seen, but the explorers were near enough to the reef, to discover not only the crater, but the spars of the ship. Here, then, was a discovery scarcely less important than that of the group itself! After reasoning on the facts, Waally came to the conclusion that these, after all, were the territories that Heaton and his party had come to seek; and that here he should find those cows which he had once seen, and which he coveted more than any other riches on earth. Ooroony had been weak enough to allow strangers in possession of things so valuable, to pass through *his* islands; but *he*, Waally, was not the man to imitate this folly. Brown, too, began to think that the white men sought were to be found here. That whites were in the group was plain enough by the ship, and he supposed they might be fishing for the pearl-oyster, or gathering bêche-le-mar for the Canton market. It was just possible that a colony had established itself in this unfrequented place, and that the party of which he had heard so much, had come hither with their stores and herds. Not the smallest suspicion at first crossed his mind that he there beheld the spars of the Rancocus; but, it was enough for him and Wattles that Christian men were there, and that, in all probability, they were men of the Anglo-Saxon race. No sooner was it ascertained that the explorers were in a false channel, and that it would not be in their power to penetrate farther in their canoes, than our two seamen determined to run, and attach themselves to the strangers. They naturally thought that they should find a vessel armed and manned, and ready to stand out to sea as soon as her officers were apprized of the danger that threatened them, and did not hesitate about joining their fortune with hers, in preference to remaining with Waally any longer. Freedom possesses a charm for which no other advantage can compensate, and those two old sea-dogs, who had worked like horses all their lives, in their original calling, preferred returning to the ancient drudgery rather than live with Waally, in the rude abundance of savage chiefs. The escape was easily enough made, as soon, as it was dark, Brown and Wattles being on shore most of the time, under the pretence that it was necessary, in order that they might ascertain the character of there unknown colonists by signs understood best by themselves.

Such is a brief outline of the explanations that the two recovered seamen made to their former officer. In return, the governor as briefly related to them the manner in which the ship had been saved, and the history of the colony down to that moment. When both tales had been told, a consultation on the subject of future proceedings took place, quite as a matter of course. Brown, and his companion, though delighted to meet their old shipmates, were greatly disappointed in not finding a sea-going vessel ready to receive them. They did not scruple to say that had they known the actual state of things on the Reef, they would not have left the savages, but trusted to being of more service even to their natural friends, by continuing with Waally, in their former relation, than by taking the step they had. Repentance, or regrets, however, came too late; and now they were fairly in for it, neither expressed any other determination than to stand by the service into which they had just entered, honestly, if not quite as gladly as they had anticipated.

The governor and Betts both saw that Brown and Wattles entertained a high respect for the military prowess of the Indian chief. They pronounced him to be not only a bold, but an adroit warrior; one, full of resources and ingenuity, when his means were taken into the account. The number of men with him, however, Brown assured Mark, was less than nine hundred, instead of exceeding a thousand, as had been supposed from the count made on the cliffs. As it now was explained, a great many women were in the canoes. Waally, moreover, was not altogether without fire-arms. He was master of a dozen old, imperfect muskets, and what was more, he had a four-pound gun. Ammunition, however, was very scarce, and of shot for his gun he had but three. Each of these shot had been fired several times, in his wars with Ooroony, and clays had been spent in hunting them up, after they had done their work, and of replacing them in the chief's magazine. Brown could not say that they had done much mischief, having, in every instance, being fired at long distances, and with a very uncertain aim. The business of sighting guns was not very well understood by the great mass of Christians, half a century since; and it is not at all surprising that savages should know little or nothing about it. Waally's gunners, according to Brown's account of the matter, could never be made to understand that the bore of a gun was not exactly parallel to its exterior surface, and they invariably aimed too high, by sighting along the upper side of the piece. This same fault is very common with the inexperienced in using a musket; for, anxious to get a sight of the end of their piece, they usually stick it up into the air and overshoot their object. It was the opinion of Brown, on the whole, that little was to be apprehended from Waally's fire-arms. The spear and club were the weapons to be dreaded; and with these the islanders were said to be very expert. But the disparity in numbers was the main ground of apprehension.

When Brown was told how near the schooner was to being launched, he earnestly begged the governor, to let him and Bigelow go to work and put her into the water, immediately. Everything necessary to a cruise was on board her, even to her provisions and water, the arrangements having been made to launch her with her sails bent; and, once in the water, Bill thought she would prove of the last importance to the defence. If the worst came to the worst, all hands could get on board her, and by standing through some of the channels that were clear of canoes, escape into the open water. Once there, Waally could do nothing with them, and they might be governed by circumstances.

Woolston viewed things a little differently. He loved the Reef; it had become dear to him by association and history, and he did not relish the thought of abandoning it. There was too much property at risk, to say nothing of the ship, which would doubtless be burned for its metals, should the Indians get possession, even for a day. In that ship he had sailed; in that ship he had been married; in that ship his daughter had been born; and in that ship Bridget loved still to dwell, even more than she affected all the glories of the Eden of the Peak. That ship was not to be given up to savages without a struggle Nor did Mark believe anything would be gained by depriving the men of their rest during the accustomed hours. Early in the morning, with the light itself, he did intend to have Bigelow under the schooner's bottom; but he saw no occasion for his working in the dark. Launching was a delicate business, and some accident might happen in the obscurity. After talking the matter over, therefore, all hands retired to rest, leaving one woman at the crater, and one on board the ship, on the look-out; women being preferred to men, on this occasion, in order that the latter might reserve their strength for the coming struggle.

At the appointed hour next morning, every one on the Reef was astir at the first peep of day. No disturbance had occurred in the night, and, what is perhaps a little remarkable, the female sentinels had not given any false alarm. As soon as a look from the Summit gave the governor reason to believe that Waally was not very near him, he ordered preparations to be made for the launch of the Friend Abraham White. A couple of hours' work was still required to complete this desirable task; and everybody set about his or her assigned duty with activity and zeal. Some of the women prepared the breakfast; others carried ammunition to the different guns, while Betts went round and loaded them, one and all; and others, again, picked up such articles of value as had been overlooked in the haste of the previous evening, carrying them either into the crater, or on board the ship.

On examining his fortifications by daylight, the governor resolved to set up something more secure in the way of a gate for the crater. He also called off two or three of the men to get out the boarding-netting of the ship, which was well provided in that respect; a good provision having been made, byway of keeping the Fejee people at arms' length. These two extraordinary offices delayed the work on the ways; and when the whole colony went to breakfast, which they did about an hour after sunrise, the schooner was not yet in the water, though quite ready to be put there, Mark announced that there was no occasion to be in a hurry, no canoes were in sight, and there was time to have everything done deliberately and in order.

This security came very near proving fatal to the whole party. Most of the men breakfasted under the awning, which was near their work; while the women took that meal in their respective quarters. Some of the last were in the crater, and some in the ship. It will be remembered that the awning was erected near the spring, and that the spring was but a short distance from the bridge. This bridge, it will also be recollected, connected the Reef with an island that stretched away for miles, and which had formed the original range for the swine, after the changes that succeeded the eruption. It was composed of merely two long ship's planks, the passage being only some fifty or sixty feet in width.

The governor, now, seldom ate with his people. He knew enough of human nature to understand that authority was best preserved by avoiding familiarity. Besides, there is, in truth, no association more unpleasant to those whose manners have been cultivated, than that of the table, with the rude and unrefined. Bridget, for instance, could hardly be expected to eat with the wives of the seamen; and Mark naturally wished to eat with his own family. On that occasion he had taken his meal in the cabin of the Rancocus, as usual, and had come down to the awning to see that the hands turned-to as soon as they were through with their own breakfasts. Just as he was about to issue the necessary order, the air was filled with frightful yells, and a stream of savages poured out of an opening in the rocks, on to the plain of the "hog pasture," as the adjoining field was called, rushing forward in a body towards the crater. They had crept along under the rocks by following a channel, and now broke cover within two hundred yards of the point they intended to assail.

The governor behaved admirably on this trying occasion. He issued his orders clearly, calmly, and promptly. Calling on Bigelow and Jones by name, he ordered them to withdraw the bridge, which could easily be done by hauling over the planks by means of wheels that had long been fitted for that purpose. The bridge withdrawn, the channel, or harbour, answered all the purposes of a ditch; though the South Sea islanders would think but little of swimming across it. Of course, Waally's men knew nothing of this bridge, nor did they know of the existence of the basin between them and their prey. They rushed directly towards the ship-yard, and loud were their yells of disappointment when they found a broad reach of water still separating them from the whites. Naturally they looked for the point of connection; but, by this time, the planks were wheeled in, and the communication was severed. At this instant, Waally had all his muskets discharged, and the gun fired from the catamaran, on which it was mounted. No one was injured by this volley, but a famous noise was made; and noise passed for a good deal in the warfare of that day and region.

It was now the turn of the colonists. At the first alarm everybody rushed to arms, and every post was manned, or *womaned*, in a minute. On the poop of the ship was planted one of the cannon, loaded with grape, and pointed so as to sweep the strait of the bridge. It is true, the distance was fully a mile, but Betts had elevated the gun with a view to its sending its missiles as far as was necessary. The other carronades on the Summit were pointed so as to sweep the portion of the hog pasture that was nearest, and which was now swarming with enemies, Waally, himself, was in front, and was evidently selecting a party that was to swim for the sandy beach, a sort of forlorn hope. No time was to be lost. Juno, a perfect heroine in her way, stood by the gun on the poop, while Dido was at those on the Summit, each brandishing or blowing, a lighted match. The governor made the preconcerted signal to the last, and she applied the match. Away went the grape, rattling along the surface of the opposite rocks, and damaging at least a dozen of Waally's men. Three were killed outright, and the wounds of the rest were very serious. A yell followed, and a young chief rushed towards the strait, with frantic cries, as if bent on leaping across the chasm. He was followed by a hundred warriors. Mark now made the signal to Juno. Not a moment was lost by the undaunted girl, who touched off her gun in the very nick of time. Down came the grape, hissing along the Reef; and, rebounding from its surface, away it leaped across the strait, flying through the thickest of the assailants. A dozen more suffered by that discharge. Waally now saw that a crisis was reached, and his efforts to recover the ground lost were worthy of his reputation. Calling to the swimmers, he succeeded in getting them down into the water in scores.

The governor had ordered those near him to their stations. This took Jones and Bigelow on board the Abraham, where two carronades were pointed through the stern ports, forming a battery to rake the hog pasture, which it was foreseen must be the field of battle if the enemy came by land, as it was the only island that came near enough to the Reef to be used in that way. As for Mark himself, accompanied by Brown and Wattles, all well armed, he held his party in reserve, as a corps to be moved wherever it might be most needed. At that all-important moment a happy idea occurred to the young governor. The schooner was all ready for launching. The reserve were under her bottom, intending to make a stand behind the covers of the yard, when Mark found himself at one of the spur-shores, just as Brown, armed to the teeth, came up to the other.

"Lay aside your arms," cried the governor, "and knock away your spur-shore, Bill! —Down with it, while I knock this away! —Look out on deck, for we are about to launch you!"

These words were just uttered, when the schooner began to move. All the colonists now cheered, and away the Abraham went, plunging like a battering-ram into the midst of the swimmers. While dipping deepest, Bigelow and Jones fired both their carronades, the shot of which threw the whole basin into foam. This combination of the means of assault was too much for savages to resist. Waally was instantly routed. His main body retreated into the coves of the channel, where their canoes lay, while the swimmers and stragglers got out of harm's way, in the best manner they could.

Not a moment was to be lost. The Abraham was brought up by a hawser, as is usual, and was immediately boarded by Mark, Bigelow and Wattles. This gave her a crew of five men, who were every way equal to handling her. Betts was left in command of the Reef, with the remainder of the forces. To make sail required but two minutes, and Mark was soon under way, rounding Loam Island, or what had *once* been Loam Island, for it was now connected with the hog pasture, in order to get into the reach where Waally had his forces. This reach was a quarter of a mile wide, and gave room for manoeuvring. Although the schooner bore down to the assault with a very determined air, it was by no means Mark's cue to come to close quarters. Being well to windward, with plenty of room, he kept the Abraham tacking, yawing, waring, and executing other of the devices of nautical delay, whilst his men loaded and fired her guns, as fast as they could. There were more noise and smoke, than there was bloodshed, as commonly happens on such occasions; but these sufficed to secure the victory. The savages were soon in a real panic, and no authority of Waally's could check their flight. Away they paddled to leeward, straining every nerve to get away from pursuers, whom they supposed to be murderously bent on killing them to a man. A more unequivocal flight never occurred in war.

Although the governor was much in earnest, he was riot half as bloodthirsty as his fleeing enemies imagined. Every dictate of prudence told him not to close with the canoes until he had plenty of sea-room. The course they were steering would take them all out of the group, into the open water, in the course of three or four hours, and he determined to follow at a convenient distance, just hastening the flight by occasional hints from his guns. In this manner, the people of the Abraham had much the easiest time of it, for they did little besides sail, while the savages had to use all their paddles to keep out of the schooner's way; they sailed, also, but their speed under their cocoa-nut canvas was not sufficient to keep clear of the Friend Abraham White, which proved to be a very fast vessel, as well as one easily handled.

At length, Waally found his fleet in the open ocean, where he trusted the chase would end. But he had greatly mistaken the course of events, in applying that 'flattering unction.' It was now that the governor commenced the chase in good earnest, actually running down three of the canoes, and making prisoners of one of the crews. In this canoe was a young warrior, whom Bill Brown and Wattles at once recognised as a favourite son of the chief. Here was a most important conquest, and, Mark turned it to account. He selected a proper agent from among the captives, and sent him with a palm-branch to Waally himself, with proposals for an exchange. There was no difficulty in communicating, since Brown and Wattles both spoke the language of the natives with great fluency. Three years of captivity had, at least, taught them that much.

A good deal of time was wasted before Waally could be brought to confide in the honour of his enemies. At last, love for his offspring brought him, unarmed, alongside of the schooner, and the governor met this formidable chief, face to face. He found the latter a wily and intelligent savage. Nevertheless, he had not the art to conceal his strong affection for his son, and on that passion did Mark Woolston play. Waally offered canoes, robes of feathers, whales' teeth, and every thing that was most esteemed among his own people, as a ransom for the boy. But this was not the exchange the governor desired to make. He offered to restore the son to the arms of his father as soon as the five seamen who were still prisoners on his citadel island should be brought alongside of the schooner. If these terms were rejected, the lad must take the fate of war.

Great was the struggle in the bosom of Waally, between natural affection, and the desire to retain his captives. After two hours of subterfuges, artifices, and tricks, the former prevailed, and a treaty was made. Agreeably to its conditions, the schooner was to pilot the fleet of canoes to Betto's group, which could easily be done, as Mark knew not only its bearings, but its latitude and longitude. As soon as this was effected, Waally engaged to send a messenger for the seamen, and to remain himself on board the Abraham until the exchange was completed. The chief wished to attach terms, by which the colonists were to aid him in more effectually putting down Ooroony, who was checked rather than conquered, but Mark refused to listen to any such proposition. He was more disposed to aid, than to overcome the kind hearted Ooroony, and made up his mind to have an interview with him before he returned from the intended voyage.

Some delay would have occurred, to enable Mark to let Bridget know of his intended absence, had it not been for the solicitude of Betts. Finding the sails of the schooner had gone out of sight to leeward, Bob manned the Neshamony, and followed as a support. In the event of a wreck, for instance, his presence might have been of the last importance. He got alongside of the Abraham just as the treaty was concluded, and was in time to carry back the news to the crater, where he might expect still to arrive that evening. With this arrangement, therefore, the parties separated, Batts beating back, through the channels of the Reef and the governor leading off to the northward and westward, under short canvas; all of Waally's canoes, catamarans, &c. following about a mile astern of him.

Chapter XIX

> "Nay, shrink not from the word 'farewell!'
> As if 'twere friendship's final knell;
> Such fears may prove but vain:
> So changeful is life's fleeting day,
> Whene'er we sever-hope may say,
> We part-to meet again."
>
> —Bernard Barton

The Abraham went under short canvas, and she was just three days, running dead before the wind, ere she came in sight of Waally's islands. Heaving-to to windward of the group, the canoes all passed into their respective harbours, leaving the schooner in the offing, with the hostages on board, waiting for the fulfilment of the treaty. The next day, Waally himself re-appeared, bringing with him Dickinson, Harris, Johnson, Edwards and Bright, the five seamen of the Rancocus that had so long been captives in his hands. It went hard with that savage chief to relinquish these men, but he loved his son even more than he loved power. As for the men themselves, language cannot portray their delight. They were not only rejoiced to be released, but their satisfaction was heightened on finding into whose hands they had fallen. These men had all kept themselves free from wives, and returned to their *colour*, that word being now more appropriate than *colours,* or ensign, unshackled by any embarrassing engagements. They at once made the Abraham a power in that part of the world. With twelve able seamen, all strong, athletic and healthy men, to handle his craft, and with his two carronades and a long six, the governor felt as if he might interfere with the political relations of the adjoining states with every prospect of being heard. Waally was, probably, of the same opinion, for he made a great effort to extend the treaty so far as to overturn Ooroony altogether, and thus secure to their two selves the control of all that region. Woolston inquired of Waally, in what he should be benefited by such a policy? when the wily savage told him, with the gravest face imaginable, that he, Mark, might retain, in addition to his territories at the Reef, Rancocus Island! The governor thanked his fellow potentate for this hint, and now took occasion to assure him that, in future, each and all of Waally's canoes must keep away from Rancocus Island altogether; that island belonged to him, and if any more expeditions visited it, the call should be returned at Waally's habitations. This answer brought on an angry discussion, in which Waally, once or twice, forgot himself a little; and when he took his leave, it was not in the best humour possible.

Mark now deliberated on the state of things around him. Jones knew Ooroony well, having been living in his territories until they were overrun by his powerful enemy, and the governor sent him to find that chief, using a captured canoe, of which they had kept two or three alongside of the schooner for the purpose. Jones, who was a sworn friend of the unfortunate chief, went as negotiator. Care was taken to land at the right place, under cover of the Abraham's guns, and in six hours Mark had the real gratification of taking Ooroony, good, honest, upright Ooroony, by the hand, on the quarter-deck of his own vessel. Much as the chief had suffered and lost, within the last two years, a gleam of returning happiness shone on him when he placed his foot on the deck of the schooner. His reception by the governor was honourable and even touching. Mark thanked him for his kindness to his wife, to his sister, to Heaton, and to his friend Bob. In point of fact, without this kindness, he, Woolston, might then have been a solitary hermit, without the means of getting access to any of his fellow-creatures, and doomed to remain in that condition all his days. The obligation was now frankly admitted, and Ooroony shed tears of joy when he thus found that his good deeds were remembered and appreciated.

It has long been a question with moralists, whether or not, good and evil bring their rewards and punishments in this state of being. While it might be dangerous to infer the affirmative of this mooted point, as it would be cutting off the future and its consequences from those whose real hopes and fears ought to be mainly concentrated in the life that is to come, it would seem to be presuming to suppose that principles like these ever can be nugatory in the control even of our daily concerns.

If it be true that God "visits the sins of the fathers upon the children even to the third and fourth generations of them that hate him," and that the seed of the righteous man is never seen begging his bread, there is much reason to believe that a portion of our transgressions is to meet with its punishment here on earth. We think nothing can be more apparent than the fact that, in the light of mere worldly expediency, an upright and high-principled course leads to more happiness than one that is the reverse; and if "honesty is the best policy," after all the shifts and expedients of cupidity, so does virtue lead most unerringly to happiness here, as it opens up the way to happiness hereafter.

All the men of the Abraham had heard of Ooroony, and of his benevolent qualities. It was his goodness, indeed, that had been the cause of his downfall; for had he punished Waally as he deserved to be, when the power was in his hands, that turbulent chief, who commenced life as his lawful tributary, would never have gained a point where he was so near becoming his master. Every man on board now pressed around the good old chief, who heard on all sides of him assurances of respect and attachment, with pledges of assistance. When this touching scene was over, Mark held a council on the quarter-deck, in which the whole matter of the political condition of the group was discussed, and the wants and dangers of Ooroony laid bare.

As commonly happens everywhere, civilized nations and popular governments forming no exceptions to the rule, the ascendency of evil in this cluster of remote and savage islands was owing altogether to the activity and audacity of a few wicked men, rather than to the inclination of the mass. The people greatly preferred the mild sway of their lawful chief, to the violence and exactions of the turbulent warrior who had worked his way into the ascendant; and, if a portion of the population had, unwittingly, aided the latter in his designs, under the momentary impulses of a love of change, they now fully repented of their mistake, and would gladly see the old condition of things restored. There was one island, in particular, which might be considered as the seat of power in the entire group. Ooroony had been born on it, and it had long been the residence of his family; but Waally succeeded in driving him off of it, and of intimidating its people, who, in secret, pined for the return of their ancient rulers. If this island could be again put in his possession, it would, itself, give the good chief such an accession of power, as would place him, at once, on a level with his competitor, and bring the war back to a struggle on equal terms. Could this be done with the assistance of the schooner, the moral effect of such an alliance would, in all probability, secure Ooroony's ascendency as long as such an alliance lasted.

It would not have been easy to give a clearer illustration of the truth that "knowledge is power," than the case now before us affords. Here was a small vessel, of less than a hundred tons in measurement, with a crew of twelve men, and armed with three guns, that was not only deemed to be sufficient but which was in fact amply sufficient to change a dynasty among a people who counted their hosts in thousands. The expedients of civilized life gave the governor this ascendency, and he determined to use it justly, and in moderation. It was his wish to avoid bloodshed; and after learning all the facts he could, he set about his task coolly and with prudence.

The first thing done, was to carry the schooner in, within reach of shot of Waally's principal fortress, where his ruling chiefs resided, and which in fact was the hold where about a hundred of his followers dwelt; fellows that kept the whole island in fear, and who rendered it subservient to Waally's wishes. This fortress, fort, or whatever it should be called, was then summoned, its chief being commanded to quit, not only the hold, but the island altogether. The answer was a defiance. As time was given for the reception of this reply, measures had been taken to support the summons by a suitable degree of concert and activity. Ooroony landed in person, and got among his friends on the island, who, assured of the support of the schooner, took up arms to a man, and appeared in a force that, of itself, was sufficient to drive Waally's men into the sea. Nevertheless, the last made a show of resistance until the governor fired his six-pounder at them. The shot passed through the wooden pickets, and, though it hurt no one, it made such a clatter, that the chief in command sent out a palm-branch, and submitted. This bloodless conquest caused a revolution at once, in several of the less important islands, and in eight-and-forty hours, Ooroony found himself where he had been when Betts appeared in the Neshamony. Waally was fain to make the best of matters, and even he came in, acknowledged his crimes, obtained a pardon, and paid tribute. The effect of this submission on the part of Waally, was to establish Ooroony more strongly than ever in authority, and to give him a chance of reigning peacefully for the remainder of his days. All this was done in less than a week after the war had begun in earnest, by the invasion of the Reef!

The governor was too desirous to relieve the anxiety of those he had left behind him to accept the invitations that he, and his party, now received to make merry. He traded a little with Ooroony's people, obtaining many things that were useful in exchange for old iron, and other articles of little or no value. What was more, he ascertained that sandal-wood was to be found on Rancocus Island in small quantities, and in this group in abundance. A contract was made, accordingly, for the cutting and preparing of a considerable quantity of this wood, which was to be ready for delivery in the course of three months, when it was understood that the schooner was to return and take it in. These arrangements completed, the Friend Abraham White sailed for home.

Instead of entangling himself in the channels to leeward, Mark made the land well to the northward, entering the group by a passage that led him quite down to the Reef, as the original island was now uniformly called, with a flowing sheet. Of course the schooner was seen an hour before she arrived, and everybody was out on the Reef to greet the adventurers. Fears mingled with the other manifestations of joy, when the result of this great enterprise came to be known. Mark had a delicious moment when he folded the sobbing Bridget to his heart, and Friend Martha was overcome in a way that it was not usual for her to betray feminine weakness.

Everybody exulted in the success of the colony, and it was hoped that the future would be as quiet as it was secure.

But recent events began to give the governor trouble, on other accounts. The accession to his numbers, as well as the fact that these men were seamen, and had belonged to the Rancocus, set him thinking on the subject of his duty to the owners of that vessel. So long as he supposed himself to be a cast-away, he had made use of their property without compunction, but circumstances were now changed, and he felt it to be a duty seriously to reflect on the possibility of doing something for the benefit of those who had, undesignedly it is true, contributed so much to his own comfort. In order to give this important subject a due consideration, as well as to relieve the minds of those at the Peak, the Abraham sailed for the cove the morning after her arrival at the Reef. Bridget went across to pay Anne a visit, and most of the men were of the party. The Neshamony had carried over the intelligence of Waally's repulse, and of the Abraham's having gone to that chief's island, but the result of this last expedition remained to be communicated.

The run was made in six hours, and the Abraham was taken into the cove, and anchored there, just as easily as one of the smaller craft. There was water enough for anything that floated, the principal want being that of room, though there was enough even of room to receive a dozen vessels of size. The place, indeed, was a snug, natural basin, rather than a port, but art could not have made it safer, or even much more commodious. It was all so small an island could ever require in the way of a haven, it not being probable that the trade of the place would reach an amount that the shipping it could hold would not carry.

The governor now summoned a general council of the colony. The seven seamen attended, as well as all the others, one or two at the crater excepted, and the business in hand was entered on soberly, and, in some respects, solemnly. In the first place, the constitution and intentions of the colonists were laid before the seven men, and they were asked as to their wishes for the future. Four of these men, including Brown, at once signed the constitution, and were sworn in as citizens. It was their wish to pass their days in that delicious climate, and amid the abundance of those rich and pleasing islands. The other three engaged with Mark for a time, but expressed a desire to return to America, after awhile. Wives were wanting; and this the governor saw, plainly enough, was a difficulty that must be got over, to keep the settlement contented. Not that a wife may not make a man's home very miserable, as well as very happy; but, most people prefer trying the experiment for themselves, instead of profiting by the experience of others.

As soon as the question of citizenship was decided, and all the engagements were duly made, the governor laid his question of conscience before the general council. For a long time it had been supposed that the Rancocus could not be moved. The eruption had left her in a basin, or hole, where there was just water enough to float her, while twelve feet was the most that could be found on the side on which the channel was deepest. Now, thirteen feet aft was the draught of the ship when she was launched. This Bob well knew, having been launched in her. But, Brown had suggested the possibility of lifting the vessel eighteen inches or two feet, and of thus carrying her over the rock by which she was imprisoned. Once liberated from that place, every one knew there would be no difficulty in getting the ship to sea, since in one of the channels, that which led to the northward, a vessel might actually carry out fully five fathoms, or quite thirty feet. This channel had been accurately sounded by the governor himself, and of the fact he was well assured. Indeed, he had sounded most of the true channels around the Reef. By true channels is meant those passages that led from the open water quite up to the crater, or which admitted the passage of vessels, or boats: while the false were *culs de sac*, through which there were no real passages.

The possibility, thus admitted, of taking the Rancocus to sea, a grave question of conscience arose. The property belonged to certain owners in Philadelphia, and was it not a duty to take it there? It is true, Friend Abraham White and his partners had received back their money from the insurers-this fact Bridget remembered to have heard before she left home; but those insurers, then, had their claims. Now, the vessel was still sound and seaworthy. Her upper works might require caulking, and her rigging could not be of the soundest; but, on the whole, the Rancocus was still a very valuable ship, and a voyage might be made for her yet. The governor thought that could she get her lower hold filled with sandal-wood, and that wood be converted into teas at Canton, as much would be made as would render every one contented with the result of the close of the voyage, disastrous as had been its commencement. Then Bridget would be of age shortly, when she would become entitled to an amount of property that, properly invested, would contribute largely to the wealth and power of the colony, as well as to those of its governor.

In musing on all these plans, Mark had not the least idea of abandoning the scheme for colonizing. That was dearer to him now than ever; nevertheless, he saw obstacles to their execution. No one could navigate the ship but himself; in truth, he was the only proper person to carry her home, and to deliver her to her owners, whomsoever those might now be, and he could not conceal from himself the propriety, as well as the necessity, of his going in her himself. On the other hand, what might not be the consequences to the colony, of his absence for twelve months? A less time than that would not suffice to do all that was required to be done. Could he take Bridget with him, or could he bear to leave her behind? Her presence might be necessary for the disposal of the real estate of which she was the mistress, while her quitting the colony might be the signal for breaking it up altogether, under the impression that the two persons most interested in it would never return.

Thus did the management of this whole matter become exceedingly delicate. Heaton and Betts, and in the end all the rest, were of opinion that the Rancocus ought to be sent back to America, for the benefit of those to whom she now legally belonged. Could she get a cargo, or any considerable amount of sandal-wood, and exchange it for teas by Canton, the proceeds of these teas might make a very sufficient return for all the outlays of the voyage, as well as for that portion of the property which had been used by the colonists. The use of this property was a very different thing, now, from what it was when Mark and Betts had every reason to consider themselves as merely shipwrecked seamen. Then, it was not only a matter of necessity, but, through that necessity, one of right; but, now, the most that could be said about it, was that it might be very convenient. The principles of the colonists were yet too good to allow of their deceiving themselves on this subject. They had, most of them, engaged with the owners to take care of this property, and it might be questioned, if such a wreck had ever occurred as to discharge the crew. The rule in such cases we believe to be, that, as seamen have a lien on the vessel for their wages, when that lien ceases to be of value, their obligations to the ship terminate. If the Rancocus *could* be carried to America, no one belonging to her was yet legally exonerated from his duties.

After weighing all these points, it was gravely and solemnly declared that an effort should first be made to get the ship out of her present duresse, and that the question of future proceedings should then be settled in another council. In the mean time, further and more valuable presents were to be sent to both Ooroony and Waally, from the stores of beads, knives, axes, &c., that were in the ship, with injunctions to them to get as much sandal-wood as was possible cut, and to have it brought down to the coast. Betts was to carry the presents, in the Neshamony, accompanied by Jones, who spoke the language, when he was to return and aid in the work upon the vessel.

The duty enjoined in these decisions was commenced without delay. Heaton and Unus were left at the Peak, as usual, to look after things in that quarter, and to keep the mill from being idle, while all the rest of the men returned to the Reef, and set about the work on the ship. The first step taken was to send down all the spars and rigging that remained aloft; after which everything was got up out of the hold, and rolled, or dragged ashore. Of cargo, strictly speaking, the Rancocus had very little in weight, but she had a great many water-casks, four or five times as many as would have been put into her in an ordinary voyage. These casks had all been filled with fresh water, to answer the double purpose of a supply for the people, and as ballast for the ship. When these casks were all got on deck, and the water was started, it was found that the vessel floated several inches lighter than before. The sending ashore of the spars, sails, rigging, lumber, provisions, &c., produced a still further effect, and, after carefully comparing the soundings, and the present draught of the vessel, the governor found it would be necessary to lift the last only eight inches, to get her out of her natural dock. This result greatly encouraged the labourers, who proceeded with renewed spirit. As it would be altogether useless to overhaul the rigging, caulk decks, &c., unless the ship could be got out of her berth, everybody worked with that end in view at first. In the course of a week, the water-casks were under her bottom, and it was thought that the vessel would have about an inch to spare. A gale having blown in the water, and a high tide coming at the same time, the governor determined to try the experiment of crossing the barrier. The order came upon the men suddenly, for no one thought the attempt would be made, until the ship was lifted an inch or two higher. But Mark saw what the wind had been doing for them, and he lost not a moment. The vessel was moved, brought head to her course, and the lines were hauled upon. Away went the Rancocus, which was now moved for the first time since the eruption!

Just as the governor fancied that the ship was going clear, she struck aft. On examination it was found that her heel was on a knoll of the rock, and that had she been a fathom on either side of it, she would have gone clear. The hold, however, was very slight, and by getting two of the anchors to the cat-heads, the vessel was canted sufficiently to admit, of her passing. Then came cheers for success, and the cry of "walk away with her!" That same day the Rancocus was hauled alongside of the Reef, made fast, and secured just as she would have been at her own wharf, in Philadelphia.

Now the caulkers began their part of the job. When caulked and scraped, she was painted, her rigging was overhauled and got into its places, the masts and yards were sent aloft, and all the sails were overhauled. A tier of casks, filled with fresh water, was put into her lower hold for ballast, and all the stores necessary for the voyage were sent on board her. Among other things overhauled were the provisions. Most of the beef and pork was condemned, and no small part of the bread; still, enough remained to take the ship's company to a civilized port. So reluctant was the governor to come to the decision concerning the crew, that he even bent sails before a council was again convened. But there was no longer any good excuse for delay. Betts had long been back, and brought the report that the sandal-wood was being hauled to the coast in great quantities, both factions working with right good will. In another month the ship might be loaded and sail for America.

To the astonishment of every one, Bridget appeared in the council, and announced her determination to remain behind, while her husband carried the ship to her owners. She saw and felt, the nature of his duty, and could consent to his performing it to the letter. Mark was quite taken by surprise by this heroic and conscientious act in his young wife, and he had a great struggle with himself on the subject of leaving her behind him. Heaton, however, was so very prudent, and the present relations with their neighbours-neighbours four hundred miles distant-were so amicable, the whole matter was so serious, and the duty so obvious, that he finally acquiesced, without suffering his doubts to be seen.

The next thing was to select a crew. The three men who had declined becoming citizens of the colony, Johnson, Edwards, and Bright, all able seamen, went as a matter of course. Betts would have to go in the character of mate, though Bigelow might have got along in that capacity. Betts knew nothing of navigation, while Bigelow might find his way into port on a pinch. On the other hand, Betts was a prime seaman —a perfect long-cue, in fact-whereas the most that could be said of Bigelow, in this respect, was that he was a stout, willing fellow, and was much better than a raw hand. The governor named Betts as his first, and Bigelow as his second officer. Brown remained behind, having charge of the navy in the governor's absence. He had a private interview with Mark, however, in which he earnestly requested that the governor would have the goodness "to pick out for him the sort of gal that he thought would make a fellow a good and virtuous wife, and bring her out with him, in whatever way he might return." Mark made as fair promises as the circumstances of the case would allow, and Brown was satisfied.

It was thought prudent to have eight white men on board the ship, Mark intending to borrow as many more of Ooroony's people, to help pull and haul. With such a crew, he thought he might get along very well. Wattles chose to remain with his friend Brown; but Dickinson and Harris, though ready and willing to return, wished to sail in the ship. Like Brown, they wanted wives, but chose to select them for themselves. On this subject Wattles said nothing. We may add here, that Unus and Juno were united before the ship sailed. They took up land on the Peak, where Unus erected for himself a very neat cabin. Bridget set the young couple up, giving the furniture, a pig, some fowls, and other necessaries.

At length the day for sailing arrived. Previously to departing, Mark had carried the ship through the channel, and she was anchored in a very good and safe roadstead, outside of everything. The leave-taking took place on board her. Bridget wept long in her husband's arms, but finally got so far the command of herself, as to assume an air of encouraging firmness among the other women. By this time, it was every way so obvious Mark's presence would be indispensable in America, that his absence was regarded as a necessity beyond control. Still it was hard to part for a year, nor was the last embrace entirely free from anguish. Friend Martha Betts took leave of Friend Robert with a great appearance of calmness, though she felt the separation keenly. A quiet, warm-hearted woman, she had made her husband very happy; and Bob was quite sensible of her worth. But to him the sea was a home, and he regarded a voyage round the world much as a countryman would look upon a trip to market. He saw his wife always in the vista created by his imagination, but she was at the end of the voyage.

At the appointed hour, the Rancocus sailed, Brown and Wattles going down with her in the Neshamony as far as Betto's group, in order to bring back the latest intelligence of her proceedings. The governor now got Ooroony to assemble his priests and chiefs, and to pronounce a taboo on all intercourse with the whites for one year. At the end of that time, he promised to return, and to bring with him presents that should render every one glad to welcome him back. Even Waally was included in these arrangements; and when Mark finally sailed, it was with a strong hope that in virtue of the taboo, of Ooroony's power, and of his rival's sagacity, he might rely on the colony's meeting with no molestation during his absence. The reader will see that the Peak and Reef would be in a very defenceless condition, were it not for the schooner. By means of that vessel, under the management of Brown, assisted by Wattles, Socrates and Unus, it is true, a fleet of canoes might be beaten off; but any accident to the Abraham would be very likely to prove fatal to the colony, in the event of an invasion. Instructions were given to Heaton to keep the schooner moving about, and particularly to make a trip as often as once in two months, to Ooroony's country, in order to look after the state of things there. The pretence was to be trade-beads, hatchets, and old iron being taken each time, in exchange for sandal-wood; but the principal object was to keep an eye on the movements, and to get an insight into the policy, of the savages.

After taking in a very considerable quantity of sandal-wood, and procuring eight active assistants from Ooroony the Rancocus got under way for Canton. By the Neshamony, which saw her into the offing, letters were sent back to the Reef, when the governor squared away for his port. At the end of fifty days, the ship reached Canton, where speedy and excellent sale was made of her cargo. So very lucrative did Mark make this transaction, that, finding himself with assets after filling up with teas, he thought himself justified in changing his course of proceeding. A small American brig, which was not deemed fit to double the capes, and to come-on a stormy coast, was on sale. She could run several years in a sea as mild as the Pacific, and Mark purchased her for a song. He put as many useful things on board her as he could find, including several cows, &c. Dry English cows were not difficult to find, the ships from Europe often bringing out the animals, and turning them off when useless. Mark was enabled to purchase six, which, rightly enough, he thought would prove a great acquisition to the colony. A plentiful supply of iron was also provided, as was ammunition, arms, and guns. The whole outlay, including the cost of the vessel, was less than seven thousand dollars; which sum Mark knew he should receive in Philadelphia, on account of the personal property of Bridget, and with which he had made up his mind to replace the proceeds of the sandal-wood, thus used, did those interested exact it. As for the vessel, she sailed like a witch, was coppered and copper-fastened, but was both old and weak. She had quarters, having been used once as a privateer, and mounted ten sixes. Her burthen was two hundred tons, and her name the Mermaid. The papers were all American, and in perfect rule.

The governor might not have made this purchase, had it not been for the circumstance that he met an old acquaintance in Canton, who had got married in Calcutta to a pretty and very well-mannered English girl—a step that lost him his berth, however/on board a Philadelphia ship. Saunders was two or three years Mark's senior, and of an excellent disposition and diameter. When he heard the history of the colony, he professed a desire to join it, engaging to pick up a crew of Americans, who were in his own situation, or had no work on their hands, and to take the brig to the Reef. "This arrangement was made and carried out; the Mermaid sailing for the crater" the day before the Rancocus left for Philadelphia, having Bigelow on board as pilot and first officer; while Woolston shipped an officer to supply his place. The two vessels met in the China seas, and passed a week in company, when each steered her course; the governor quite happy in thinking that he had made this provision for the good of his people. The arrival of the Mermaid would be an eventful day in the colony, on every account; and, the instructions of Saunders forbidding his quitting the islands until the end of the year, her presence would be a great additional means of security.

It is unnecessary for us to dwell on the passage of the Rancocus. In due time she entered the capes of the Delaware, surprising all interested with her appearance. Friend Abraham White was dead, and the firm dissolved. But the property had all been transferred, to the insurers by the payment of the amount underwritten, and Mark made his report at the office. The teas were sold to great advantage, and the whole matter was taken fairly into consideration. After deducting the sum paid the firm, principal and interest, the insurance company resolved to give the ship, and the balance of the proceeds of the sale, to Captain Woolston, as a reward for his integrity and prudence. Mark had concealed nothing, but stated what he had done in reference to the Mermaid, and told his whole story with great simplicity, and with perfect truth. The result was, that the young man got, in addition to the ship, which was legally conveyed to him, some eleven thousand dollars in hard money. Thus was honesty shown to be the best policy!

It is scarcely necessary to say that his success made Mark Woolston a great man, in a small way. Not only was he received with open arms by all of his own blood; but Dr. Yardley now relented, and took him by the hand. A faithful account was rendered of his stewardship; and Mark received as much ready money, on account of his wife, as placed somewhat more than twenty thousand dollars at his disposal. With this money he set to work, without losing a day, to make arrangements to return to Bridget and the crater; for he always deemed that his proper abode, in preference to the Peak. In this feeling, his charming wife coincided; both probably encouraging a secret interest in the former, in consequence of the solitary hours that had been passed there by the young husband, while his anxious partner was far away.

Chapter XX.

> "There is no gloom on earth, for God above
> Chastens in love;
> Transmuting sorrows into golden joy
> Free from alloy.
> His dearest attribute is still to bless,
> And man's most welcome hymn is grateful cheerfulness."
>
> —Moral Alchemy

The mode of proceeding now required great caution on the part of Mark Woolston. His mind was fully made up not to desert his islands, although this might easily be done, by fitting out the ship for another voyage, filling her with sandal-wood, and bringing off all who chose to abandon the place. But Woolston had become infatuated with the climate, which had all the witchery of a low latitude without any of its lassitude. The sea-breezes kept the frame invigorated, and the air reasonably cool, even at the Reef; while, on the Peak, there was scarcely ever a day, in the warmest months, when one could not labour at noon. In this respect the climate did not vary essentially from that of Pennsylvania, the difference existing in the fact that there was no winter in his new country. Nothing takes such a hold on men as a delicious climate. They may not be sensible of all its excellencies while in its enjoyment, but the want of it is immediately felt, and has an influence on all their pleasures. Even the scenery-hunter submits to this witchery of climate, which casts a charm over the secondary beauties of nature, as a sweet and placid temper renders the face of woman more lovely than the colour of a skin, or the brilliancy of fine eyes. The Alps and the Apennines furnish a standing proof of the truth of this fact. As respects grandeur, a startling magnificence, and all that at first takes the reason, as well as the tastes, by surprise, the first are vastly in advance of the last; yet, no man of feeling or sentiment, probably ever dwelt a twelve-month amid each, without becoming more attached to the last. We wonder at Switzerland, while we get to love Italy. The difference is entirely owing to climate; for, did the Alps rise in a lower latitude, they would be absolutely peerless.

But Mark Woolston had no thought of abandoning the crater and the Peak. Nor did he desire to people them at random, creating a population by any means, incorporating moral diseases in his body politic by the measures taken to bring it into existence. On the contrary, it was his wish, rather, to procure just as much force as might be necessary to security, so divided in pursuits and qualities as to conduce to comfort and civilization, and then to trust to the natural increase for the growth that might be desirable in the end. Such a policy evidently required caution and prudence. The reader will perceive that governor Woolston was not influenced by the spirit of trade that is now so active, preferring happiness to wealth, and morals to power.

Among Woolston's acquaintances, there was a young man of about his own age, of the name of Pennock, who struck him as a person admirably suited for his purposes. This Pennock had married very young, and was already the father of three children. He began to feel the pressure of society, for he was poor. He was an excellent farmer, accustomed to toil, while he was also well educated, having been intended for one of the professions. To Pennock Mark told his story, exhibited his proofs, and laid bare his whole policy, under a pledge of secresy, offering at the same time to receive his friend, his wife, children, and two unmarried sisters, into the colony. After taking time to reflect and to consult, Pennock accepted the offer as frankly as it had been made. From this time John Pennock relieved the governor, in a great measure, of the duly of selecting the remaining emigrants, taking that office on himself. This allowed Mark to attend to his purchases, and to getting the ship ready for sea. Two of his own brothers, however, expressed a wish to join the new community, and Charles and Abraham Woolston were received in the colony lists. Half-a-dozen more were admitted, by means of direct application to the governor himself, though the accessions were principally obtained through the negotiations and measures of Pennock. All was done with great secrecy, it being Mark's anxious desire, on many accounts, not to attract public attention to his colony.

The reasons were numerous and sufficient for this wish to remain unknown. In the first place, the policy of retaining the monopoly of a trade that must be enormously profitable, was too obvious to need any arguments to support it. So long as the sandal-wood lasted, so long would it be in the power of the colonists to coin money; while it was certain that competitors would rush in, the moment the existence of this mine of wealth should be known. Then, the governor apprehended the cupidity and ambition of the old-established governments, when it should be known that territory was to be acquired. It was scarcely possible for man to possess any portion of this earth by a title better than that with which Mark Woolston was invested with his domains. But, what is right compared to might! Of his native country, so abused in our own times for its rapacity, and the desire to extend its dominions by any means, Mark felt no apprehension. Of all the powerful nations of the present day, America, though not absolutely spotless, has probably the least to reproach herself with, on the score of lawless and purely ambitious acquisitions. Even her conquests in open war have been few, and are not yet determined in character. In the end, it will be found that little will be taken that Mexico could keep; and had that nation observed towards this, ordinary justice and faith, in her intercourse and treaties, that which has so suddenly and vigorously been done, would never have even been attempted.

It may suit the policy of those who live under the same system, to decry those who do not; but men are not so blind that they cannot see the sun at noon-day. One nation makes war because its consul receives the rap of a fan; and men of a different origin, religion and habits, are coerced into submission as the consequence. Another nation burns towns, and destroys their people in thousands, because their governors will not consent to admit a poisonous drug into their territories: an offence against the laws of trade that can only be expiated by the ruthless march of the conqueror. Yet the ruling men of both these communities affect a great sensibility when the long-slumbering young lion of the West rouses himself in his lair, after twenty years of forbearance, and stretches out a paw in resentment for outrages that no other nation, conscious of his strength, would have endured for as many months, because, forsooth, he *is* the young lion of the West. Never mind: by the time New Zealand and Tahiti are brought under the yoke, the Californians may be admitted to an equal participation in the rights of American citizens.

The governor was fully aware of the danger he ran of having claims, of some sort or other, set up to his islands, if he revealed their existence; and he took the greatest pains to conceal the fact. The arrival of the Rancocus was mentioned in the papers, as a matter of course; but it was in a way to induce the reader to suppose she had met with her accident in the midst of a naked reef, and principally through the loss of her men; and that, when a few of the last were regained, the voyage was successfully resumed and terminated. In that day, the great discovery had not been made that men were merely incidents of newspapers; but the world had the folly to believe that newspapers were incidents of society, and were subject to its rules and interests. Some respect was paid to private rights, and the reign of gossip had not commenced.[4]

In the last century, however, matters were not carried quite so far as they are at present. No part of this community, claiming any portion of respectability, was willing to publish its own sense of inferiority so openly, as to gossip about its fellow-citizens, for no more direct admissions of inferiority can be made than this wish to comment on the subject of any one's private concerns. Consequently Mark and his islands escaped. There was no necessity for his telling the insurers anything about the Peak, for instance, and on that part of the subject, therefore, he wisely held his tongue. Nothing, in short, was said of any colony at all. The manner in which the crew had been driven away to leeward, and recovered, was told minutely, and the whole process by which the ship was saved. The property used, Mark said had been appropriated to his wants, without going into details, and the main results being so very satisfactory, the insurers asked no further.

As soon as off the capes, the governor set about a serious investigation of the state of his affairs. In the way of cargo, a great many articles had been laid in, which experience told him would be useful. He took with him such farming tools as Friend Abraham White had not thought of furnishing to the natives of Fejee, and a few seeds that had been overlooked by that speculating philanthropist. There were half a dozen more cows on board, as well as an improved breed of hogs. Mark carried out, also, a couple of mares, for, while many horses could never be much needed in his islands, a few would always be exceedingly useful. Oxen were much wanted, but one of his new colonists had yoked his cows, and it was thought they might be made useful, in a moderate degree, until their stouter substitutes could be reared. Carts and wagons were provided in sufficient numbers. A good stock of iron in bars was laid in, in addition to that which was wrought into nails, and other useful articles. Several thousand dollars in coin were also provided, being principally in small pieces, including copper. But all the emigrants took more or less specie with them.

A good deal of useful lumber was stowed in the lower hold, though the mill by this time furnished a pretty good home supply. The magazine was crammed with ammunition, and the governor had purchased four light field-guns, two three-pounders and two twelve-pound howitzers, with their equipments. He had also brought six long, iron twelves, ship-guns, with their carriages &c. The last he intended for his batteries, the carronades being too light for steady work, and throwing their shot too wild for a long range. The last could be mounted on board the different vessels. The Rancocus, also, had an entire new armament, having left all her old guns but two behind her. Two hundred muskets were laid in, with fifty brace of pistols. In a word, as many arms were provided as it was thought could, in any emergency, become necessary.

But it was the human portion of his cargo that the governor, rightly enough, deemed to be of the greatest importance. Much care had been bestowed on the selection, which had given all concerned in it not a little trouble. Morals were the first interest attended to. No one was received but those who bore perfectly good characters. The next thing was to make a proper division among the various trades and pursuits of life. There were carpenters, masons, blacksmiths, tailors, shoemakers, &c., or, one of each, and sometimes more. Every 'man was married, the only exceptions being in the cases of younger brothers and sisters, of whom about a dozen were admitted along with their relatives. The whole of the ships' betwixt decks was fitted up for the reception of these emigrants, who were two hundred and seven in number, besides children. Of the last there were more than fifty, but they were principally of an age to allow of their being put into holes and corners.

Mark Woolston was much too sensible a man to fall into any of the modern absurdities on the subject of equality, and a community of interests. One or two individuals, even in that day, had wished to accompany him, who were for forming an association in which all property should be shared in common, and in which nothing was to be done but that which was right. Mark had not the least objection in the world to the last proposition, and would have been glad enough to see it carried out to the letter, though he differed essentially with the applicants, as to the mode of achieving so desirable an end. He was of opinion that civilization could not exist without property, or property without a direct personal interest in both its accumulation and its preservation. They, on the other hand, were carried away by the crotchet that community-labour was better than individual labour, and that a hundred men would be happier and better off with their individualities compressed into one, than by leaving them in a hundred subdivisions, as they had been placed by nature. The theorists might have been right, had it been in their power to compress a hundred individuals into one, but it was riot. After all their efforts, they would still remain a hundred individuals, merely banded together under more restraints, and with less liberty than are common.

Of all sophisms, that is the broadest which supposes personal liberty is extended by increasing the power of the community. Individuality is annihilated in a thousand things, by the community-power that already exists in this country, where persecution often follows from a man's thinking and acting differently from his neighbours, though the law professes to protect him. The reason why this power becomes so very formidable, and is often so oppressively tyrannical in its exhibition, is very obvious. In countries where the power is in the hands of the few, public sympathy often sustains the man who resists its injustice; but no public sympathy can sustain him who is oppressed by the public itself. This oppression does not often exhibit itself in the form of law, but rather in its denial. He, who has a clamour raised against him by numbers, appeals in vain to numbers for justice, though his claim may be clear as the sun at noon-day. The divided responsibility of bodies of men prevents anything like the control of conscience, and the most ruthless wrongs are committed, equally without reflection and without remorse.

Mark Woolston had thought too much on the subject, to be the dupe of any of these visionary theories. Instead of fancying that men never knew anything previously to the last ten years of the eighteenth century, he was of the opinion of the wisest man who ever lived, that 'there was nothing new under the sun.' That 'circumstances might alter cases' he was willing enough to allow, nor did he intend to govern the crater by precisely the same laws as he would govern Pennsylvania, or Japan; but he well understood, nevertheless, that certain great moral truths existed as the law of the human family, and that they were not to be set aside by visionaries; and least of all, with impunity.

Everything connected with the colony was strictly practical. The decision of certain points had unquestionably given the governor trouble, though he got along with them pretty well, on the whole. A couple of young lawyers had desired to go, but he had the prudence to reject them. Law, as a science, is a very useful study, beyond a question; but the governor, rightly enough, fancied that his people could do without so much science for a few years longer. Then another doctor volunteered his services. Mark remembered the quarrels between his father and his father-in-law, and thought it better to die under one theory than under two. As regards a clergyman, Mark had greater difficulty. The question of sect was not as seriously debated half a century ago as it is to-day; still it was debated. Bristol had a very ancient society, of the persuasion of the Anglican church, and Mark's family belonged to it. Bridget, however, was a Presbyterian, and no small portion of the new colonists were what is called Wet-Quakers; that is, Friends who are not very particular in their opinions or observances. Now, religion often caused more feuds than anything else: still it was impossible to have a priest for every persuasion, and one ought to suffice for the whole colony. The question was of what sect should that one clergyman be? So many prejudices were to be consulted, that the governor was about to abandon the project in despair, when accident determined the point. Among Heaton's relatives was a young man of the name of Hornblower, no bad appellation, by the way, for one who had to sound so many notes of warning, who had received priest's orders from the hands of the well-known Dr. White, so long the presiding Bishop of America, and whose constitution imperiously demanded a milder climate than that in which he then lived. As respects him, it became a question purely of humanity, the divine being too poor to travel on his own account, and he was received on board the Rancocus, with his wife, his sister, and two children, that he might have the benefit of living within the tropics. The matter was fully explained to the other emigrants, who could not raise objections if they would, but who really were not disposed to do so in a case of such obvious motives. A good portion of them, probably, came to the conclusion that Episcopalian ministrations were better than none, though, to own the truth, the liturgy gave a good deal of scandal to a certain portion of their number. *Reading* prayers was so profane a thing, that these individuals could scarcely consent to be present at such a vain ceremony; nor was the discontent, on this preliminary point, fully disposed of until the governor once asked the principal objector how he got along with the Lord's Prayer, which was not only written and printed, but which usually was committed to memory! Notwithstanding this difficulty, the emigrants did get along with it without many qualms, and most of them dropped quietly into the habit of worshipping agreeably to a liturgy, just as if it were not the terrible profanity that some of them had imagined. In this way, many of our most intense prejudices get lost in new communications.

It is not our intention to accompany the Rancocus, day by day, in her route. She touched at Rio, and sailed again at the end of eight and forty hours. The passage round the Horn was favourable, and having got well to the westward, away the ship went for her port. One of the cows got down, and died before it could be relieved, in a gale off the cape; but no other accident worth mentioning occurred. A child died with convulsions, in consequence of teething, a few days later; but this did not diminish the number on board, as three were born the same week. The ship had now been at sea one hundred and sixty days, counting the time passed at Rio, and a general impatience to arrive pervaded the vessel. If the truth must be said, some of the emigrants began to doubt the governor's ability to find his islands again, though none doubted of their existence. The Kannakas, however, declared that they began to smell home, and it is odd enough, that this declaration, coming as it did from ignorant men who made it merely on a fanciful suggestion, obtained more credit with most of the emigrants, than all the governor's instruments and observations.

One day, a little before noon it was, Mark appeared on deck with his quadrant, and as he cleaned the glasses of the instrument, he announced his conviction that the ship would shortly make the group of the crater. A current had set him further north than he intended to go, but having hauled up to south-west, he waited only for noon to ascertain his latitude, to be certain of his position. As the governor maintained a proper distance from his people, and was not in the habit of making-unnecessary communications to them, his present frankness told for so much the more, and it produced a very general excitement in the ship. All eyes were on the look-out for land, greatly increasing the chances of its being shortly seen. The observation came at noon, as is customary, and the governor found he was about thirty miles to the northward of the group of islands he was seeking. By his calculation, he was still to the eastward of it, and he hauled up, hoping to fall in with the land well to windward. After standing on three hours in the right direction, the look-outs from the cross-trees declared no land was visible ahead. For one moment the dreadful apprehension of the group's having sunk under another convulsion of nature crossed Mark's mind, but he entertained that notion for a minute only. Then came the cry of "sail ho!" to cheer everybody, and to give them something else to think of.

This was the first vessel the Rancocus had seen since she left Rio. It was to windward, and appeared to be standing down before the wind. In an hour's time the two vessels were near enough to each other to enable the glass to distinguish objects; and the quarter-deck, on board the Rancocus, were all engaged in looking at the stranger.

"'Tis the Mermaid," said Mark to Betts, "and it's all right. Though what that craft can be doing here to windward of the islands is more than I can imagine!"

"Perhaps, sir, they's a cruising arter us," answered Bob. "This is about the time they ought to be expectin' on us; and who knows but Madam Woolston and Friend Marthy may not have taken it into their heads to come out a bit to see arter their lawful husbands?"

The governor smiled at this conceit, but continued his observations in silence.

"She behaves very strangely, Betts," Mark, at length, said. "Just take a look at her. She yaws like a galliot in a gale, and takes the whole road like a drunken man. There can be no one at the helm."

"And how lubberly, sir, her canvas is set! Just look at that main-taw-sail, sir; one of the sheets isn't home by a fathom, while the yard is braced in, till it's almost aback!"

The governor walked the deck for five minutes in intense thought, though occasionally he stopped to look at the brig, now within a league of them. Then he suddenly called out to Bob, to "see all clear for action, and to get everything ready to go to quarters."

This order set every one in motion. The women and children were hurried below, and the men, who had been constantly exercised, now, for five months, took their stations with the regularity of old seamen. The guns were cast loose-ten eighteen-pound carronades and two nines, the new armament-cartridges were got ready, shot placed at hand, and all the usual dispositions for combat were made. While this was doing, the two vessels were fast drawing nearer to each other, and were soon within gun-shot. But, no one on board the Rancocus knew what to make of the evolutions of the Mermaid. Most of her ordinary square-sails were set, though not one of them all was sheeted home, or well hoisted. An attempt had been made to lay the yards square, but one yard-arm was braced in too far, another not far enough, and nothing like order appeared to have prevailed at the sail-trimming. But, the of the brig was the most remarkable.

Her general course would seem to be dead before the wind; but she yawed incessantly, and often so broadly, as to catch some of her light sails aback. Most vessels take a good deal of room in running down before the wind, and in a swell; but the Mermaid took a great deal more than was Common, and could scarce be said to look any way in particular. All this the governor observed, as the vessels approached nearer and nearer, as well as the movements of those of the crew who showed themselves in the rigging.

"Clear away a bow-gun," cried Mark, to Betts —"something dreadful must have happened; that brig is in possession of the savages, who do not know how to handle her!"

This announcement produced a stir on board the Rancocus, as may well be imagined. If the savages had the brig, they probably had the group also; and what had become of the colonists? The next quarter of an hour was one of the deepest expectation with all in the ship, and of intense agony with Mark. Betts was greatly disturbed also; nor would it have been safe for one of Waally's men to have been within reach of his arm, just then. Could it be possible that Ooroony had yielded to temptation and played them false? The governor could hardly believe it; and, as for Betts, he protested loudly it could not be so.

"Is that bow-gun ready?" demanded the governor.

"Ay, ay, sir; all ready."

"Fire, but elevate well-we will only frighten them, at first. We betide them, if they resist."

Betts did fire, and to the astonishment of everybody, the brig returned a broadside! But resistance ceased with this one act of energy, if it could be so termed. Although five guns were actually fired, and nearly simultaneously, no aim was even attempted. The shot all flew off at a tangent from the position of the ship; and no harm was done to any but the savages themselves, of whom three or four were injured by the recoils. From the moment the noise and smoke were produced, everything like order ceased on board the brig, which was filled with savages. The vessel broached to, and the sails caught aback. All this time, the Rancocus was steadily drawing nearer, with an intent to board; but, unwilling to expose his people, most of whom were unpractised in strife, in a hand-to-hand conflict with ferocious savages, the governor ordered a gun loaded with grape to be discharged into the brig. This decided the affair at once. Half a dozen were killed or wounded; some ran below; a few took refuge in the top; but most, without the slightest hesitation, jumped overboard. To the surprise of all who saw them, the men in the water began to swim directly to windward; a circumstance which indicated that either land or canoes were to be found in that quarter of the ocean. Seeing the state of things on board the brig, Mark luffed up under her counter, and laid her aboard. In a minute, he and twenty chosen men were on her decks; in another, the vessels were again clear of each other, and the Mermaid under command.

No sooner did the governor discharge his duties as a seaman, than he passed below. In the cabin he found Mr. Saunders, (or Captain Saunders, as he was called by the colonists,) bound hand and foot. His steward was in the same situation, and Bigelow was found, also a prisoner, in the steerage. These were all the colonists on board, and all but two who had been on board, when the vessel was taken.

Captain Saunders could tell the governor very little more than he saw with his own eyes. One fact of importance, however, he could and did communicate, which was this: Instead of being to windward of the crater, as Mark supposed, he was to leeward of it; the currents no doubt having set the ship to the westward faster than had been thought. Rancocus Island would have been made by sunset, had the ship stood on in the course she was steering when she made the Mermaid.

But the most important fact was the safety of the females. They were all at the Peak, where they had lived for the last six months, or ever since the death of the good Ooroony had again placed Waally in the ascendant. Ooroony's son was overturned immediately on the decease of the father, who died a natural death, and Waally disregarded the taboo, which he persuaded his people could have no sanctity as applied to the whites. The plunder of these last, with the possession of the treasure of iron and copper that was to be found in their vessels, had indeed been the principal bribe with which the turbulent and ambitious chief regained his power. The war did not break out, however, as soon as Waally had effected the revolution in his own group. On the contrary, that wily politician had made so many protestations of friendship after that event, which he declared to be necessary to the peace of his island; had collected so much sandal-wood, and permitted it to be transferred to the crater, where a cargo was already stored; and had otherwise made so many amicable demonstrations, as completely to deceive the colonists. No one had anticipated an invasion; but, on the contrary, preparations were making at the Peak for the reception of Mark, whose return had now been expected daily for a fortnight.

The Mermaid had brought over a light freight of wood from Betto's group, and had discharged at the crater. This done, she had sailed with the intention of going out to cruise for the Rancocus, to carry the news of the colony, all of which was favourable, with the exception of the death of Ooroony and the recent events; but was lying in the roads, outside of everything-the Western Roads, as they were called, or those nearest to the other group-waiting for the appointed hour of sailing, which was to be the very morning of the day in which she was fallen in with by the governor. Her crew consisted only of Captain Saunders, Bigelow, the cook and steward, and two of the people engaged at Canton-one of whom was a very good-for-nothing Chinaman. The two last had the look-out, got drunk, and permitted a fleet of hostile canoes to get alongside in the dark, being knocked on the head and tossed overboard, as the penalty of this neglect of duty. The others owed their lives to the circumstance of being taken in their sleep, when resistance was out of the question. In the morning, the brig's cable was cut, sail was set, after a fashion, and an attempt was made to carry the vessel over to Betto's group. It is very questionable whether she ever could have arrived; but that point was disposed of by the opportune appearance of the Rancocus.

Saunders could communicate nothing of the subsequent course of the invaders. He had been kept below the whole time, and did not even know how many canoes composed the fleet. The gang in possession of the Mermaid was understood, however, to be but a very small part of Waally's force present, that chief leading in person. By certain half-comprehended declarations of his conquerors, Captain Sauriders understood that the rest had entered the channel, with a view to penetrate to the crater, where Socrates, Unus and Wattles were residing with their wives and families, and where no greater force was left when the Mermaid sailed. The property there, however, was out of all proportion in value to the force of those whose business it was to take care of it. In consequence of the Rancocus's removal, several buildings had been constructed on the Reef, and one house of very respectable dimensions had been put up on the Summit. It is true, these houses were not very highly finished; but they were of great value to persons in the situation of the colonists. Most of the hogs, moreover, were still rooting and tearing up the thousand-acre prairie; where, indeed, they roamed very much in a state of nature. Socrates occasionally carried to them a boat-load of 'truck' from the crater, in order to keep up amicable relations with them; but they were little better than so many wild animals, in one sense, though there had not yet been time materially to change their natures. In the whole, including young and old, there must have been near two hundred of these animals altogether, their increase being very rapid. Then, a large amount of the stores sent from Canton, including most of the iron, was in store at the crater; all of which would lay at the mercy of Waally's men; for the resistance to be expected from the three in possession, could not amount to much.

The governor was prompt enough in his decision, as soon as he understood the facts of the case. The first thing was to bring the vessels close by the wind, and to pass as near as possible over the ground where the swimmers were to be found; for Mark could not bear the idea of abandoning a hundred of his fellow-creatures in the midst of the ocean, though they were enemies and savages. By making short stretches, and tacking two or three times, the colonists found themselves in the midst of the swimmers; not one in ten of whom would probably ever have reached the land, but for the humanity of their foe. Alongside of the Mermaid were three or four canoes; and these were cast adrift at the right moment, without any parleying. The Indians were quick enough at understanding the meaning of this, and swam to the canoes from all sides, though still anxious to get clear of the vessels. On board the last canoe the governor put all his prisoners, when he deemed himself happily quit of the whole gang.

There were three known channels by which the Rancocus could be carried quite up to the crater. Mark chose that which came in from the northward, both because it was the nearest, and because he could lay his course in it, without tacking, for most of the way. Acquainted now with his position, Mark had no difficulty in finding the entrance of this channel. Furnishing the Mermaid with a dozen hands, she was sent to the western roads, to intercept Waally's fleet, should it be coming out with the booty. In about an hour after the Rancocus altered her course, she made the land; and, just as the sun was setting, she got so close in as to be able to anchor in the northern roads, where there was not only a lee, but good holding-ground. Here the ship passed the night, the governor not liking to venture into the narrow passages in the dark.

Chapter XXI

> "Fancy can charm and feeling bless
> With sweeter hours than fashion knows;
> There is no calmer quietness,
> Than home around the bosom throws."
>
> —Percival

Although the governor deemed it prudent to anchor for the night, he did not neglect the precaution of reconnoitring. Betts was sent towards the Reef, in a boat well armed and manned, in order to ascertain the state of things in that quarter. His instructions directed him to push forward as far as he could, and if possible to hold some sort of communication with Socrates, who might now be considered as commander at the point assailed.

Fortunate was it that the governor bethought him of this measure. As Betts had the ship's launch, which carried two lugg-sails, his progress was both easy and rapid, and he actually got in sight of the Reef before midnight. To his astonishment, all seemed to be tranquil, and Betts at first believed that the savages had completed their work and departed. Being a bold fellow, however, a distant reconnoitring did not satisfy him; and on he went, until his boat fairly lay alongside of the natural quay of the Reef itself. Here he landed, and marched towards the entrance of the crater. The gate was negligently open, and on entering the spacious area, the men found all quiet, without any indications of recent violence. Betts knew that those who dwelt in this place, usually preferred the Summit for sleeping, and he ascended to one of the huts that had been erected there. Here he found the whole of the little garrison of the group, buried in sleep, and totally without any apprehension of the danger which menaced them. As it now appeared, Waally's men had not yet shown themselves, and Socrates knew nothing at all of what had happened to the brig.

Glad enough was the negro to shake hands with Betts, and to hear that Master Mark was so near at hand, with a powerful reinforcement. The party already arrived might indeed be termed the last, for the governor had sent with his first officer, on this occasion, no less than five-and-twenty men, each completely armed. With such a garrison, Betts deemed the crater safe, and he sent back the launch, with four seamen in it, to report the condition in which he had found matters, and to communicate all else that he had learned. This done, he turned his attention to the defences of the place.

According to Socrates' account, no great loss in property would be likely to occur, could the colonists make good the Reef against their invaders. The Abraham was over at the Peak, safe enough in the cove, as was the Neshamony and several of the boats, only two or three of the smaller of the last being with him. The hogs and cows were most exposed, though nearly half of the stock was now habitually kept on the Peak. Still, a couple of hundred hogs were on the prairie, as were no less than eight horned cattle, including calves. The loss of the last would be greatly felt, and it was much to be feared, since the creatures were very gentle, and might be easily caught. Betts, however, had fewer apprehensions touching the cattle than for the hogs, since the latter might be slain with arrows, while he was aware that Waally wished to obtain the first alive.

Agreeably to the accounts of Socrates, the progress of vegetation had been very great throughout the entire group. Grass grew wherever the seed was sown, provided anything like soil existed, and the prairie was now a vast range, most of which was green, and all of which was firm enough to bear a hoof. The trees, of all sorts, were flourishing also, and Belts was assured he would not know the group again when he came to see it by daylight, All this was pleasant intelligence, at least, to the eager listeners among the new colonists, who had now been so long on board ship, that anything in the shape of *terra firma*, and of verdure appeared to them like paradise. But Betts had too many things to think of, just then, to give much heed to the eulogium of Socrates, and he soon bestowed all his attention on the means of defence.

As there was but one way of approaching the crater, unless by water, and that was along the hog pasture and across the plank bridge, Bob felt the prudence of immediately taking possession of the pass. He ordered Socrates to look to the gate, where he stationed a guard, and went himself, with ten men, to make sure of the bridge. It was true, Waally's men could swim, and would not be very apt to pause long at the basin; but, it would be an advantage to fight them while in the water, that ought not to be thrown away. The carronades were all loaded, moreover; and these precautions taken, and sentinels posted, Betts suffered his men to sleep on their arms, if sleep they could. Their situation was so novel, that few availed themselves of the privilege, though their commanding officer, himself, was soon snoring most musically.

As might have been, expected, Waally made his assault just as the day appeared. Before that time, however, the launch had got back to the ship, and the latter was under way, coming fast towards the crater. Unknown to all, though anticipated by Mark, the Mermaid had entered the western passage, and was beating up through it, closing fast also on Waally's rear. Such was the state of things, when the yell of the assailants was heard.

Waally made his first push for the bridge, expecting to find it unguarded, and hoping to cross it unresisted. He knew that the ship was gone, and no longer dreaded *her* fire; but he was fully aware that the Summit had its guns, and he wished to seize them while his men were still impelled by the ardour of a first onset. Those formidable engines of war were held in the most profound respect by all his people, and Waally knew the importance of success in a rapid movement. He had gleaned so much information concerning the state of the Reef, that he expected no great resistance, fully believing that, now he had seized the Mermaid, his enemies would be reduced in numbers to less than half-a-dozen. In all this, he was right enough; and there can be no question that Socrates and his whole party, together with the Reef, and for that matter, the entire group, would have fallen into his hands, but for the timely arrival of the reinforcement. The yell arose when it was ascertained that the bridge was drawn in, and it was succeeded by a volley from the guard posted near it, on the Reef. This commenced the strife, which immediately raged with great fury, and with prodigious clamour. Waally had all his muskets fired, too, though as yet he saw no enemy, and did not know in what direction to aim, He could see men moving about on the Reef, it is true, but it was only at moments, as they mostly kept themselves behind the covers. After firing his muskets, the chief issued an order for a charge, and several hundreds of his warriors plunged into the basin, and began to swim towards the point to be assailed. This movement admonished Betts of the prudence of retiring towards the gate, which he did in good order, and somewhat deliberately. This time, Waally actually got his men upon the Reef without a panic and without loss. They landed in a crowd, and were soon rushing in all directions, eager for plunder, and thirsting for blood. Betts was enabled, notwithstanding to enter the gate, which he did without delay, perfectly satisfied that all efforts of his to resist the torrent without must be vain. As soon as his party had entered, the gate was closed, and Betts was at liberty to bestow all his care on the defence of the crater.

The great extent of the citadel, which contained an area of not less than a hundred acres, it will be remembered, rendered its garrison very insufficient for a siege. It is probable that no one there would have thought of defending it, but for the certainty of powerful support being at hand. This certainty encouraged the garrison, rendering their exertions more ready and cheerful. Betts divided his men into parties of two, scattering them along the Summit, with orders to be vigilant, and to support each other. It was well known that a man could not enter from without unless by the gate, or aided by ladders, or some other mechanical invention. The time necessary to provide the last would bring broad daylight, and enable the colonists to march such a force to the menaced point, as would be pretty certain to prove sufficient to resist the assailants. The gate itself was commanded by a carronade, and was watched by a guard.

Great was the disappointment of Waally when he ascertained, by personal examination, that the Summit could not be scaled, even by the most active of his party, without recourse to assistance, by means of artificial contrivances. He had the sagacity to collect all his men immediately beneath the natural walls, where they were alone safe from the fire of the guns, but where they were also useless. A large pile of iron, an article so coveted, was in plain sight, beneath a shed, but he did not dare to send a single hand to touch it, since it would have brought the adventurer under fire. A variety of other articles, almost as tempting, though not perhaps of the same intrinsic value, lay also in sight, but were tabooed by the magic of powder and balls. Eleven hundred warriors, as was afterwards ascertained, landed on the Reef that eventful morning, and assembled under the walls of the crater. A hundred more remained in the canoes, which lay about a league off, in the western passage, or to leeward, awaiting the result of the enterprise.

The first effort made by Waally was to throw a force upward, by rearing one man on another's shoulders. This scheme succeeded in part, but the fellow who first showed his head above the perpendicular part of the cliff, received a bullet in his brains. The musket was fired by the hands of Socrates. This one discharge brought down the whole fabric, several of those who fell sustaining serious injuries, in the way of broken bones. The completely isolated position of the crater, which stood, as it might be, aloof from all surrounding objects, added materially to its strength in a military sense, and Waally was puzzled how to overcome difficulties that might have embarrassed a more civilized soldier. For the first time in his life, that warrior had encountered a sort of fortress, which could be entered only by regular approaches, unless it might be carried by a *coup de main*. At the latter the savages were expert enough, and on it they had mainly relied; but, disappointed in this respect, they found themselves thrown back on resources that were far from being equal to the emergency.

Tired of inactivity, Waally finally decided on making a desperate effort. The ship-yard was still kept up as a place for the repairing of boats, &c., and it always had more or less lumber lying in, or near it. Selecting a party of a hundred resolute men, and placing them under the orders of one of his bravest chiefs, Waally sent them off, on the run, to bring as much timber, boards, planks, &c., as they could carry, within the cover of the cliffs. Now, Betts had foreseen the probability of this very sortie, and had levelled one of his carronades, loaded to the muzzle with canister, directly at the largest pile of the planks. No sooner did the adventurers appear, therefore, than he blew his match. The savages were collected around the planks in a crowd, when he fired his gun. A dozen of them fell, and the rest vanished like so much dust scattered by a whirlwind.

Just at that moment, the cry passed along the Summit that the Rancocus was in sight. The governor must have heard the report of the gun, for he discharged one in return, an encouraging signal of his approach. In a minute, a third came from the westward, and Betts saw the sails of the Mermaid over the low land. It is scarcely necessary to add, that the reports of the two guns from a distance, and the appearance of the two vessels, put an end at once to all Waally's schemes, and induced him to commence, with the least possible delay, a second retreat from the spot which, like Nelson's frigates, might almost be said to be imprinted on his heart.

Waally retired successfully, if not with much dignity. At a given signal his men rushed for the water, plunged in and swam across the basin again. It was in Betts's power to have killed many on the retreat, but he was averse to shedding blood unnecessarily. Fifty lives, more or less, could be of no great moment in the result, as soon as a retreat was decided on; and the savages were permitted to retire, and to carry off their killed and wounded without molestation. The last was done by wheeling forward the planks, and crossing at the bridge.

It was far easier, however, for Waally to gain his canoes, than to know which way to steer after he had reached them. The Mermaid cut off his retreat by the western passage, and the Rancocus was coming, fast along the northern. In order to reach either the eastern, or the southern, it would be necessary to pass within gun-shot of the Reef, and, what was more, to run the gauntlet between the crater and the Rancocus. To this danger Waally was compelled to submit, since he had no other means of withdrawing his fleet. It was true, that by paddling to windward, he greatly lessened the danger he ran from the two vessels, since it would not be in their power to overtake him in the narrow channels of the group, so long as he went in the wind's eye. It is probable that the savages understood this, and that the circumstance greatly encouraged them in the effort they immediately made to get into the eastern passage.

Betts permitted them to pass the Reef, without firing at them again, though some of the canoes were at least half an hour within the range of his guns, while doing so. It was lucky for the Indians that the Rancocus did not arrive until the last of their party were as far to windward as the spot where the ship had anchored, when she was first brought up by artificial means into those waters.

Betts went off to meet the governor, in order to make in early report of his proceedings. It was apparent that the langer was over, and Woolston was not sorry to find that success was obtained without recourse to his batteries. The ship went immediately alongside of the natural quay, and her people poured ashore, in a crowd, the instant a plank could be run out, in order to enable them to do so. In an hour the cows were landed, and were grazing in the crater, where the grass was knee-high, and everything possessing life was out of the ship, the rats and cock-roaches perhaps excepted. As for the enemy, no one now cared for them. The man aloft said they could be seen, paddling away as if for life, and already too far for pursuit. It would have been easy enough for the vessels to cut off the fugitives by going into the offing again, but this was not the desire of any there, all being too happy to be rid of them, to take any steps to prolong the intercourse.

Great was the delight of the colonists to be once more on the land. Under ordinary circumstances, the immigrants might not have seen so many charms in the Reef and crater, and hog-lot; but five months at sea have a powerful influence in rendering the most barren spot beautiful. Barrenness, however, was a reproach that could no longer be justly applied to the group, and most especially to those portions of it which had received the attention of its people. Even trees were beginning to be numerous, thousands of them having been planted, some for their fruits, some for their wood, and others merely for the shade. Of willows, alone, Socrates with his own hand had set out more than five thousand, the operation being simply that of thrusting the end of a branch into the mud. Of the rapidity of the growth, it is scarcely necessary to speak; though it quadrupled that known even to the most fertile regions of America.

Here, then, was Mark once more at home, after so long a passage. There was his ship, too, well freighted with a hundred things, all of which would contribute to the comfort and well-being of the colonists! It was a moment when the governor's heart was overflowing with gratitude, and could he then have taken Bridget and his children in his arms, the cup of happiness would have been full. Bridget was not forgotten, however, for in less than half an hour after the ship was secured Betts sailed in the Neshamony, for the Peak; he was to carry over the joyful tidings, and to bring the 'governor's lady' to the Reef. Ere the sun set, or about that time, his return might be expected, the Neshamony making the trip in much less time than one of the smaller boats. It was not necessary, however, for Betts to go so far, for when he had fairly cleared Cape South, and was in the strait, he fell in with the Abraham, bound over to the Reef. It appeared that some signs of the hostile canoes had been seen from the Peak, as Waally was crossing from Rancocus Island, and, after a council, it had been decided to send the Abraham across, to notify the people on the Reef of the impending danger, and to aid in repelling the enemy. Bridget and Martha had both come in the schooner; the first, to look after the many valuables he had left at the 'governor's house,' on the Summit, and the last, as her companion.

We leave the reader to imagine the joy that was exhibited, when those on board the Abraham ascertained the arrival of the Rancocus! Bridget was in ecstasies, and greatly did she exult in her own determination to cross on this occasion, and to bring her child with her. After the first burst of happiness, and the necessary explanations had been made, a consultation was had touching what was next to be done. Brown was in command of the Abraham, with a sufficient crew, and Betts sent him to windward, outside of everything, to look after the enemy. It was thought desirable not only to see Waally well clear of the group, but to force him to pass off to the northward, in order that he might not again approach the Reef, as well as to give him so much annoyance on his retreat, as to sicken him of these expeditions for the future. For such a service the schooner was much the handiest of all the vessels of the colonists, since she might be worked by a couple of hands, and her armament was quite sufficient for all that was required of her, on the occasion. Brown was every way competent to command, as Betts well knew, and he received the females on board the Neshamony, and put about, leaving the schooner to turn to windward.

Bridget reached the Reef before it was noon. All the proceedings of that day had commenced so early, that there had been time for this. The governor saw the Neshamony. as she approached, and great, uneasiness beset him He knew she had not been as far as the Peak, and supposed that Waally's fleet had intercepted her, Betts coming back for reinforcements. But, as the boat drew near, the fluttering of female dresses was seen, and then his unerring glass let him get a distant view of the sweet face of his young wife. From that moment the governor was incapable of giving a coherent or useful order, until Bridget had arrived. Vessels that came in from the southward were obliged to pass through the narrow entrance, between the Reef and the Hog Lot, where was the drawbridge so often mentioned. There was water enough to float a frigate, and it was possible to take a frigate through, the width being about fifty feet, though as yet nothing larger than the Friend Abraham White had made the trial. At this point, then, Woolston took his station, waiting the arrival of the Neshamony, with an impatience he was a little ashamed of exhibiting.

Betts saw the governor, in good time, and pointed him out to Bridget, who could hardly be kept on board the boat, so slow did the progress of the craft now seem. But the tender love which this young couple bore each other was soon to be rewarded; for Mark sprang on board the Neshamony as she went through the narrow pass, and immediately he had Bridget folded to his heart.

Foreigners are apt to say that we children of this western world do not submit to the tender emotions with the same self-abandonment as those who are born nearer to the rising sun; that our hearts are as cold and selfish as our manners; and that we live more for the lower and grovelling passions, than for sentiment and the affections. Most sincerely do we wish that every charge which European jealousy, and European superciliousness, have brought against the American character, was as false as this. That the people of this country are more restrained in the exhibition of all their emotions, than those across the great waters, we believe; but, that the last *feel* the most, we shall be very unwilling to allow. Most of all shall we deny that the female form contains hearts more true to all its affections, spirits more devoted to the interests of its earthly head, or identity of existence more perfect than those with which the American wife clings to her husband. She is literally "bone of his bone, and flesh of his flesh." It is seldom that her wishes cross the limits of the domestic circle, which to her is earth itself, and all that it contains which is most desirable. Her husband and children compose her little world, and beyond them and their sympathies, it is rare indeed that her truant affections ever wish to stray. A part of this concentration of the American wife's existence in these domestic interests, is doubtless owing to the simplicity of American life and the absence of temptation. Still, so devoted is the female heart, so true to its impulses, and so little apt to wander from home-feelings and home-duties, that the imputation to which there is allusion, is just that, of all others, to which the wives of the republic ought not to be subject.

It was even-tide before the governor was again seen among his people. By this time, the immigrants had taken their first survey of the Reef, and the nearest islands, which the least sanguine of their numbers admitted quite equalled the statements they had originally heard of the advantages of the place. It was, perhaps, fortunate that the fruits of the tropics were so abundant with Socrates and his companions. By this time, oranges abounded, more than a thousand trees having, from time to time, been planted in and around the crater, alone. Groves of them were also appearing in favourable spots, on the adjacent islands. It is true, these trees were yet too young to produce very bountifully; but they had begun to bear, and it was thought a very delightful thing, among the fresh arrivals from Pennsylvania, to be able to walk in an orange grove, and to pluck the fruit at pleasure!

As for figs, melons, limes, shaddocks, and even cocoa-nuts, all were now to be had, and in quantities quite sufficient for the population. In time, the colonists craved the apples of their own latitude, and the peach; those two fruits, so abundant and so delicious in their ancient homes; but the novelty was still on them, and it required time to learn the fact that we tire less of the apple, and the peach, and the potato, than of any other of the rarest gifts of nature. That which the potato has become among vegetables, is the apple among fruits; and when we rise into the mere luscious and temporary of the bountiful products of horticulture, the peach (in its perfection) occupies a place altogether apart, having no rival in its exquisite flavour, while it never produces satiety. The peach and the grape are the two most precious of the gifts of Providence, in the way of fruits.

That night, most of the immigrants slept in the ship; nearly all of them, however, for the last time. About ten in the forenoon, Brown came running down to the Reef, through the eastern passage, to report Waally well off, having quitted the group to windward, and made the best of his way towards his own islands, without turning aside to make a starting-point of Rancocus. It was a good deal questioned whether the chief would find his proper dominions, after a run of four hundred miles; for a very trifling deviation from the true course at starting, would be very apt to bring him out wide of his goal. This was a matter, however, that gave the colonists very little concern. The greater the embarrassments encountered by their enemies, the less likely would they be to repeat the visit; and should a few perish, it might be all the better for themselves. The governor greatly approved of Brown's course in not following the canoes, since the repulse was sufficient as it was, and there was very little probability that the colony would meet with any further difficulty from this quarter, now that it had got to be so strong.

That day and the next, the immigrants were busy in landing their effects, which consisted of furniture, tools and stores, of one sort and another. As the governor intended to send, at once, forty select families over to the Peak, the Abraham was brought alongside of the quay, and the property of those particular families was, as it came ashore, sent on board the schooner. Males and females were all employed in this duty, the Reef resembling a beehive just at that point. Bill Brown, who still commanded the Abraham, was of course present; and he made an occasion to get in company with the governor, with whom he held the following short dialogue:

"A famous ship's company is this, sir, you've landed among us, and some on 'em is what I calls of the right sort!"

"I understand you, Bill," answered Mark, smiling. "Your commission has been duly executed; and Phoebe is here, ready to be spliced as soon as there shall be an opportunity."

"*That* is easily enough made, when people's so inclined," said Bill, fidgeting. "If you'd be so good, sir, as just to point out the young woman to me, I might be beginning to like her, in the meanwhile."

"*Young?* Nothing was said about that in the order, Bill. You wished a wife, invoiced and consigned to yourself; and one has been shipped, accordingly. You must consider the state of the market, and remember that the article is in demand precisely as it is youthful."

"Well, well, sir, I'll not throw her on your hands, if she's old enough to be my mother; though I do rather suppose, Mr. Woolston, you stood by an old shipmate in a foreign land, and that there is a companion suitable for a fellow of only two-and-thirty sent out?"

"Of that you shall judge for yourself, Bill. Here she comes, carrying a looking-glass, as if it were to look at her own pretty face; and if she prove to be only as good as she is good-looking, you will have every reason to be satisfied. What is more, Bill, your wife does not come empty-handed, having a great many articles that will help to set you up comfortably in housekeeping."

Brown was highly pleased with the governor's choice, which had been made with a due regard to the interests and tastes of the absent shipmate. Phoebe appeared well satisfied with her allotted husband; and that very day the couple was united in the cabin of the Abraham. On the same occasion, the ceremony was performed for Unus and Juno, as well as for Peters and his Indian wife; the governor considering it proper that regard to appearances and all decent observances, should be paid, as comported with their situation.

About sunset of the third day after the arrival of the Rancocus, the Abraham sailed for the Peak, having on board somewhat less than a hundred of the immigrants, including females and children. The Neshamony preceded her several hours, taking across the governor and his family. Mark longed to see his sister Anne, and his two brothers participated in this wish, if possible, in a still more lively manner.

The meeting of these members of the same family was of the most touching character. The young men found their sister much better established than they had anticipated, and in the enjoyment of very many more comforts than they had supposed it was in the power of any one to possess in a colony still so young. Heaton had erected a habitation for himself, in a charming grove, where there were water, fruits, and other conveniences, near at hand, and where his own family was separated from the rest of the community. This distinction had been conferred on him, by common consent, in virtue of his near affinity to the governor, whose substitute he then was, and out of respect to his education and original rank in life. Seamen are accustomed to defer to station and authority, and are all the happier for the same; and the thought of any jealousy on account of this privilege, which as yet was confined to Mark and Heaton, and their respective families, had not yet crossed the mind of any one on the island.

About twelve, or at midnight, the Abraham entered the cove. Late as was the hour, each immigrant assumed a load suited to his or her strength, and ascended the Stairs, favoured by the sweet light of a full moon. That night most of the new-comers passed in the groves, under tents or in an arbour that had been prepared for them; and sweet was the repose that attended happiness and security, in a climate so agreeable.

Next morning, when the immigrants came out of their temporary dwellings, and looked upon the fair scene before them, they could scarcely believe in its reality! It is true, nothing remarkable or unexpected met their eyes in the shape of artificial accessories; but the bountiful gifts of Providence, and the natural beauties of the spot, as much exceeded their anticipations as it did their power of imagining such glories! The admixture of softness and magnificence made a whole that they had never before beheld in any other portion of the globe; and there was not one among them all that did not, for the moment, feel and speak as if he or she had been suddenly transformed to an earthly paradise.

Chapter XXII

> "You have said they are men;
> As such their hearts are something."
>
> —Byron

The colony had now reached a point when it became necessary to proceed with method and caution. Certain great principles were to be established, on which the governor had long reflected, and he was fully prepared to set them up, and to defend them, though he knew that ideas prevailed among a few of his people, which might dispose them to cavil at his notions, if not absolutely to oppose him. Men are fond of change; half the time, for a reason no better than that it is change; and, not unfrequently, they permit this wayward feeling to unsettle interests that are of the last importance to them, and which find no small part of their virtue in their permanency.

Hitherto, with such slight exceptions as existed in deference to the station, not to say rights of the governor, everything of an agricultural character had been possessed in common among the colonists. But this was a state of things which the good sense of Mark told him could not, and ought not to last. The theories which have come into fashion in our own times, concerning the virtues of association, were then little known and less credited. Society, as it exists in a legal form, is association enough for all useful purposes, and sometimes too much; and the governor saw no use in forming a wheel within a wheel. If men have occasion for each other's assistance to effect a particular object, let them unite, in welcome, for that purpose; but Mark was fully determined that there should be but one government in his land, and that this government should be of a character to encourage and not to depress exertion. So long as a man toiled for himself and those nearest and dearest to him, society had a security for his doing much, that would be wanting where the proceeds of the entire community were to be shared in common; and, on the knowledge of this simple and obvious truth did our young legislator found his theory of government. Protect all in their rights equally, but, that done, let every man pursue his road to happiness in his own way; conceding no more of his natural rights than were necessary to the great ends of peace, security, and law. Such was Mark's theory. As for the modern crotchet that men yielded *no* natural right to government, but were to receive all and return nothing, the governor, in plain language, was not fool enough to believe it. He was perfectly aware that when a man gives authority to society to compel him to attend court as a witness, for instance, he yields just so much of his natural rights to society, as might be necessary to empower him to stay away, if he saw fit; and, so on, through the whole of the very long catalogue of the claims which the most indulgent communities make upon the services of their citizens. Mark understood the great desideratum to be, not the setting up of theories to which every attendant fact gives the lie, but the ascertaining, as near as human infirmity will allow, the precise point at which concession to government ought to terminate, and that of uncontrolled individual freedom commence. He was not visionary enough to suppose that he was to be the first to make this great discovery; but he was conscious of entering on the task with the purest intentions. Our governor had no relish for power for power's sake, but only wielded it for the general good. By nature, he was more disposed to seek happiness in a very small circle, and would have been just as well satisfied to let another govern, as to rule himself, had there been another suited to such a station. But there was not. His own early habits of command, the peculiar circumstances which had first put him in possession of the territory, as if it were a special gift of Providence to himself, his past agency in bringing about the actual state of things, and his property, which amounted to more than that of all the rest of the colony put together, contributed to give him a title and authority to rule, which would have set the claims of any rival at defiance, had such a person existed. But there was no rival; not a being present desiring to see another in his place.

The first step of the governor was to appoint his brother, Abraham Woolston, the secretary of the colony. In that age America had very different notions of office, and of its dignity, of the respect due to authority, and of the men who wielded it, from what prevail at the present time.

The colonists, coming as they did from America, brought with them the notions of the times, and treated their superiors accordingly. In the last century a governor was "*the* governor," and not "*our* governor," and a secretary "*the* secretary," and not "*our* secretary," men now taking more liberties with what they fancy their own, than was their wont with what they believed had been set over them for their good. Mr. Secretary Woolston soon became a personage, accordingly, as did all the other considerable functionaries appointed by the governor.

The very first act of Abraham Woolston, on being sworn into office, was to make a registry of the entire population. We shall give a synopsis of it, in order that the reader may understand the character of the materials with which the governor had room to work, viz: —

Males,	147
Male Adults,	113
Male Children,	34
Male Married,	101
Females,	158
Female Adults,	121
Female Children,	37
Female Married,	101
Widowers,	1
Widows,	4
Seamen,	38
Mechanics,	26
Physician,	1
Student in Medicine,	1
Lawyer,	1
Clergyman,	1
Population,	305

Here, then, was a community composed already of three hundred and five souls. The governor's policy was not to increase this number by further immigration, unless in special cases, and then only after due deliberation and inquiry. Great care had been taken with the characters of the present settlers, and careless infusions of new members might undo a great deal of good that had already been done. This matter was early laid before the new council, and the opinions of the governor met with a unanimous concurrence.

On the subject of the council, it may be well to say a word. It was increased to nine, and a new election was made, the incumbents holding their offices for life. This last provision was made to prevent the worst part, and the most corrupting influence of politics, viz., the elections, from getting too much sway over the public mind. The new council was composed as follows, viz: —

Messrs. Heaton,
Pennock,
Betts,
C. Woolston, }
A. Woolston, } the governor's brothers
Charlton,
Saunders,

Wilmot, and
Warrington.

These names belonged to the most intelligent men of the colony, Betts perhaps excepted; but his claims were too obvious to be slighted. Betts had good sense moreover, and a great deal of modesty. All the rest of the council had more or less claims to be gentlemen, but Bob never pretended to that character. He knew his own qualifications, and did not render himself ridiculous by aspiring to be more than he really was; still, his practical knowledge made him a very useful member of the council, where his opinions were always heard with attention and respect. Charlton and Wilmot were merchants, and intended to embark regularly in trade; while Warrington, who possessed more fortune than any of the other colonists, unless it might be the governor, called himself a farmer, though he had a respectable amount of general science, and was well read in most of the liberal studies.

Warrington was made judge, with a small salary, all of which he gave to the clergyman, the Rev. Mr. White. This was done because he had no need of the money himself, and there was no other provision for the parson than free contributions. John Woolston, who had read law, was named Attorney-General, or colony's Attorney, as the office was more modestly styled; to which duties he added those of surveyor-general. Charles received his salary, which was two hundred and fifty dollars, being in need of it. The question of salary, as respects the governor, was also settled. Mark had no occasion for the money, owning all the vessels, with most of the cargo of the Rancocus, as well as having brought out with him no less a sum than five thousand dollars, principally in change-halves, quarters, shillings and six-pences. Then a question might well arise, whether he did not own most of the stock; a large part of it was his beyond all dispute, though some doubts might exist as to the remainder. On this subject the governor came to a most wise decision. He was fully aware that nothing was more demoralizing to a people than to suffer them to get loose notions on the subject of property. Property of all kinds, he early determined, should be most rigidly respected, and a decision that he made shortly after his return from America, while acting in his capacity of chief magistrate, and before the new court went into regular operation, was of a character to show how he regarded this matter. The case was as follows: —

Two of the colonists, Warner and Harris, had bad blood between them. Warner had placed his family in an arbour within a grove, and to "aggravate" him, Harris came and walked before his door, strutting up and down like a turkey-cock, and in a way to show that it was intended to annoy Warner. The last brought his complaint before the governor. On the part of Harris, it was contended that no *injury* had been done the property of Harris, and that, consequently, no damages could be claimed. The question of title was conceded, *ex necessitate rerum*. Governor Woolston decided, that a man's rights in his property were not to be limited by positive injuries to its market value. Although no grass or vegetables had been destroyed by Harris in his walks, he had *molested* Warner in such an enjoyment of his dwelling; as, in intendment of law, every citizen was entitled to in his possessions. The trespass was an aggravated one, and damages were given accordingly. In delivering his judgment, the governor took occasion to state, that in the administration of the law, the rights of every man would be protected in the fullest extent, not only as connected with pecuniary considerations, but as connected with all those moral uses and feelings which contribute to human happiness. This decision met with applause, and was undoubtedly right in itself. It was approved, because the well-intentioned colonists had not learned to confound liberty with licentiousness; but understood the former to be the protection of the citizen in the enjoyment of all his innocent tastes, enjoyments and personal rights, after making such concessions to government as are necessary to its maintenance. Thrice happy would it be for all lands, whether they are termed despotisms or democracies, could they thoroughly feel the justice of this definition, and carry out its intention in practice.

The council was convened the day succeeding its election. After a few preliminary matters were disposed of, the great question was laid before it, of a division of property, and the grant of real estate. Warrington and Charles Woolston laid down the theory, that the fee of all the land was, by gift of Providence, in the governor, and that his patent, or sign-manual, was necessary for passing the title into other hands. This theory had an affinity to that of the Common Law, which made the prince the suzerain, and rendered him the heir of all escheated estates. But Mark's humility, not to say his justice, met this doctrine on the threshold. He admitted the sovereignty and its right, but placed it in the body of the colony, instead of in himself. As the party most interested took this view of the case, they who were disposed to regard his rights as more sweeping, were fain to submit. The land was therefore declared to be the property of the state. Ample grants, however, were made both to the governor and Betts, as original possessors, or discoverers, and it was held in law that their claims were thus compromised. The grants to Governor Woolston included quite a thousand acres on the Peak, which was computed to contain near thirty thousand, and an island of about the same extent in the group, which was beautifully situated near its centre, and less than a league from the crater. Betts had one hundred acres granted to him, near the crater also. He refused any other grant, as a right growing out of original possession. Nor was his reasoning bad on the occasion. When he was driven off, in the Neshamony, the Reef, Loam Island, Guano Island, and twenty or thirty rocks, composed all the dry land. He had never seen the Peak until Mark was in possession of it, and had no particular claim there. When the council came to make its general grants, he was willing to come in for his proper share with the rest of the people, and he wanted no more. Heaton had a special grant of two hundred acres made to him on the Peak, and another in the group of equal extent, as a reward for his early and important services. Patents were made out, at once, of these several grants, under the great seal of the colony; for the governor had provided parchment, and wax, and a common seal, in anticipation of their being all wanted. The rest of the grants of land were made on a general principle, giving fifty acres on the Peak, and one hundred in the group, to each male citizen of the age of twenty-one years; those who had not yet attained their majority being compelled to wait. A survey was made, and the different lots were numbered, and registered by those numbers. Then a lottery, was made, each man's name being put in one box, and the necessary numbers in another. The number drawn against any particular name was the lot of the person in question. A registration of the drawing was taken, and printed patents were made out, signed, sealed, and issued to the respective parties. We say printed, a press and types having been brought over in the Rancocus, as well as a printer. In this way, then, every male of full age, was put in possession of one hundred and fifty acres of land, in fee.

As the lottery did not regard the wishes of parties, many private bargains were made, previously to the issuing of the patents, in order that friends and connections might be placed near to each other. Some sold their rights, exchanging with a difference, while others sold altogether on the Peak, or in the group, willing to confine their possessions to one or the other of these places. In this manner Mr, Warrington, or Judge Warrington, as he was now called, bought three fifty-acre lots adjoining his own share on the Peak, and sold his hundred-acre lot in the group. The price established by these original sales, would seem to give a value of ten dollars an acre to land on the Peak, and of three dollars an acre to land in the group. Some lots, however, had a higher value than others, all these things being left to be determined by the estimate which the colonists placed on their respective valuations. As everything was conducted on a general and understood principle, and the drawing was made fairly and in public, there was no discontent; though some of the lots were certainly a good deal preferable to others. The greatest difference in value existed in the lots in the group, where soil and water were often wanted; though, on the wholes much more of both was found than had been at first expected. There were vast deposits of mud, and others of sand, and Heaton early suggested the expediency of mixing the two together, by way of producing fertility. An experiment of this nature had been tried, under his orders, during the absence of the governor, and the result was of the most satisfactory nature; the acre thus manured producing abundantly.

As it was the sand that was to be conveyed to the mud, the toil was much less than might have been imagined. This sand usually lay near the water, and the numberless channels admitted of its being transported in boats along a vast reach of shore. Each lot having a water front, every man might manure a few acres, by this process, without any great expense; and no sooner were the rights determined, and the decisions of the parties made as to their final settlements, than many went to work to render the cracked and baked mud left by the retiring ocean fertile and profitable. Lighters were constructed for the purpose, and the colonists formed themselves into gangs, labouring in common, and transporting so many loads of sand to each levee, as the banks were called, though not raised as on the Mississippi, and distributing it bountifully over the surface. The spade was employed to mix the two earths together.

Most of the allotments of land, in the group, were in the immediate neighbourhood of the Reef. As there were quite a hundred of them, more than ten thousand acres of the islands were thus taken up, at the start. By a rough calculation, however, the group extended east and west sixty-three miles, and north and south about fifty,—the Reef being a very little west and a very little south of its centre. Of this surface it was thought something like three-fourths was dry land, or naked rock. This would give rather more than a million and a half of acres of land; but, of this great extent of territory, not more than two-thirds could be rendered available for the purposes of husbandry, for want of soil, or the elements of soil. There were places where the deposit of mud seemed to be of vast depth, while in others it did not exceed a few inches. The same was true of the sands, though the last was rarely of as great depth as the mud, or alluvium.

A month was consumed in making the allotments, and in putting the different proprietors in possession of their respective estates. Then, indeed, were the results of the property-system made directly apparent. No sooner was an individual put in possession of his deed, and told that the lot it represented was absolutely his own, to do what he pleased with it, than he went to work with energy and filled with hopes, to turn his new domains to account. It is true that education and intelligence, if they will only acquit themselves of their tasks with disinterested probity, may enlighten and instruct the ignorant how to turn their means to account; but, all experience proves that each individual usually takes the best care of his own interests, and that the system is wisest which grants to him the amplest opportunity so to do.

To work all went, the men forming themselves into gangs, and aiding each other. The want of horses and neat cattle was much felt, more especially as Heaton's experience set every one at the sand, as the first step in a profitable husbandry: wheelbarrows, however, were made use of instead of carts, and it was found that a dozen pair of hands could do a good deal with that utensil, in the course of a day. All sorts of contrivances were resorted to in order to transport the sand, but the governor established a regular system, by which the lighter should deliver one load at each farm, in succession. By the end of a month it was found that a good deal had been done, the distances being short and the other facilities constantly increasing by the accession of new boats.

All sorts of habitations were invented. The scarcity of wood in the group was a serious evil, and it was found indispensable to import that material. Parts of Rancocus Island were well wooded, there growing among other trees a quantity of noble yellow pines. Bigelow was sent across in the Abraham to set up a mill, and to cut lumber. There being plenty of water-power, the mill was soon got at work, and a lot of excellent plank, boards, &c., was shipped in the schooner for the crater. Shingle-makers were also employed, the cedar abounding, as well as the pine. The transportation to the coast was the point of difficulty on Rancocus Island as well as elsewhere; none of the cattle being yet old enough to be used. Socrates had three pair of yearling steers, and one of two years old breaking, but it was too soon to set either at work. With the last, a little very light labour was done, but it was more to train the animals, than with any other object.

On Rancocus Island, however, Bigelow had made a very ingenious canal, that was of vast service in floating logs to the mill. The dam made a long narrow pond that penetrated two or three miles up a gorge in the mountains, and into this dam the logs were rolled down the declivities, which were steep enough to carry anything into the water. When cut into lumber, it was found that the stream below the mill, would carry small rafts down to the sea.

While all these projects were in the course of operation, the governor did not forget the high interests connected with his foreign relations; Waally was to be looked to, and Ooroony's son to be righted. The council was unanimously of opinion that sound policy required such an exhibition of force on the part of the colony, as should make a lasting impression on their turbulent neighbours. An expedition was accordingly fitted out, in which the Mermaid, the Abraham, and a new pilot-boat built schooner of fifty tons burthen, were employed. This new schooner was nearly ready for launching when the Rancocus returned, and was put into the water for the occasion. She had been laid down in the cove, where Bigelow had found room for a sufficient yard, and where timber was nearer at hand, than on the Reef. As Rancocus Island supplied the most accessible and the best lumber, the council had determined to make a permanent establishment on it, for the double purposes of occupation and building vessels. As the resources of that island were developed, it was found important on other accounts, also. Excellent clay for bricks was found, as was lime-stone, in endless quantities. For the purposes of agriculture, the place was nearly useless, there not being one thousand acres of good arable land in the whole island; but the mountains were perfect mines of treasure in the way of necessary supplies of the sorts mentioned.

A brick-yard was immediately cleared and formed, and a lime-kiln constructed. Among the colonists, it was easy to find men accustomed to work in all these familiar branches. The American can usually turn his hand to a dozen different pursuits; and, though he may not absolutely reach perfection in either, he is commonly found useful and reasonably expert in all. Before the governor sailed on his expedition against Waally, a brick-kiln and a lime-kiln were nearly built, and a vast quantity of lumber had been carried over to the Reef. As sandal-wood had been collecting for the twelve months of her late absence, the Rancocus had also been filled up, and had taken in a new cargo for Canton. It was not the intention of the governor to command his ship this voyage; but he gave her to Saunders, who was every way competent to the trust. When all was ready, the Rancocus, the Mermaid, the Abraham, and the Anne, as the new pilot-boat schooner was called, sailed for Betto's group: it being a part of the governor's plan to use the ship, in passing, with a view to intimidate his enemies. In consequence of the revolution that had put Waally up again, every one of the Kannakas who had gone out in the Rancocus on her last voyage, refused to go home, knowing that they would at once be impressed into Waally's service; and they all now cheerfully shipped anew, for a second voyage to foreign lands. By this time, these men were very useful; and the governor had a project for bringing up a number of the lads of the islands, and of making use of them in the public service. This scheme was connected with his contemplated success, and formed no small part of the policy of the day.

The appearance of so formidable a force as was now brought against Waally, reduced that turbulent chief to terms without a battle. About twenty of his canoes had got separated from the rest of the fleet in a squall, while returning from the unsuccessful attempt on the Reef, and they were never heard of more; or, if heard of, it was in uncertain rumours, which gave an account of the arrival of three or four canoes at some islands a long way to-leeward, with a handful of half-starved warriors on board. It is supposed that all the rest perished at sea. This disaster had rendered Waally unpopular among the friends of those who were lost; and that unpopularity was heightened by the want of success in the expedition itself. Success is all in all, with the common mind; and we daily see the vulgar shouting at the heels of those whom they are ready to crucify at the first turn of fortune. In this good land of ours, popularity adds to its more worthless properties the substantial result of power; and it is not surprising that so many forget their God in the endeavour to court the people. In time, however, all of these persons of mistaken ambition come to exclaim, with Shakspeare's Wolsey —

> "Had I but served my God with half the zeal
> I served my king, he would not in mine age
> Have left me naked to mine enemies."

Waally's power, already tottering through the influence of evil fortune, crumbled entirely before the force Governor Woolston now brought against it. Although the latter had but forty whites with him, they came in ships, and provided with cannon; and not a chief dreamed of standing by the offender, in this his hour of need. Waally had the tact to comprehend his situation, and the wisdom to submit to his fortune. He sent a messenger to the governor with a palm-branch, offering to restore young Ooroony to all his father's authority, and to confine himself to his strictly inherited dominions. Such, in fact, was the basis of the treaty that was now made, though hostages were taken for its fulfilment. To each condition Waally consented; and everything was settled to the entire satisfaction of the whites and to the honour and credit of young Ooroony. The result was, in substance, as we shall now record.

In the first place, one hundred lads were selected and handed over to the governor, as so many apprentices to the sea. These young Kannakas were so many hostages for the good behaviour of their parents; while the parents, always within reach of the power of the colonists, were so many hostages for the good behaviour of the Kannakas. Touching the last, however, the governor had very few misgivings, since he believed it very possible so to treat, and so to train them, as to make them fast friends. In placing them on board the different vessels, therefore, rigid instructions were given to their officers to be kind to these youngsters; and each and all were to be taught to read, and instructed in the Christian religion. The Rev. Mr. Hornblower took great interest in this last arrangement, as did half the females of the colony. Justice and kind treatment, in fact, produced their usual results in the cases of these hundred youths; every one of whom got to be, in the end, far more attached to the Reef, and its customs, than to their own islands and their original habits. The sea, no doubt, contributed its share to this process of civilization; for it is ever found that the man who gets a thorough taste for that element, is loth to quit it again for *terra firma*.

One hundred able-bodied men were added to the recruits that the governor obtained in Betto's group. They were taken as hired labourers, and not as hostages. Beads and old iron were to be their pay, with fish-hooks, and such other trifles as had a value in their eyes; and their engagement was limited to two months. There was a disposition among a few of the colonists to make slaves of these men, and to work their lands by means of a physical force obtained in Betto's group; but to this scheme the council would not lend itself for a moment. The governor well knew that the usefulness, virtue, and moral condition of his people, depended on their being employed, and he had no wish to undermine the permanent prosperity of the colony, by resorting to an expedient that might do well enough for a short time, but which would certainly bring its own punishment in the end.

Still, an accession of physical force, properly directed, would be of great use in this early age of the colony. The labourers were accordingly engaged; but this was done by the government, which not only took the control of the men, but which also engaged to see them paid the promised remuneration. Another good was also anticipated from this arrangement. The two groups must exist as friends or as enemies. So long as young Ooroony reigned, it was thought there would be little difficulty in maintaining amicable relations; and it was hoped that the intercourse created by this arrangement, aided by the trade in sandal-wood, might have the effect to bind the natives to the whites by the tie of interest.

The vessels lay at Betto's group a fortnight, completing all the arrangements made; though the Rancocus sailed on her voyage as soon as the terms of the treaty were agreed on, and the Anne was sent back to the Reef with the news that the war had terminated. As for Waally, he was obliged to place his favourite son in the hands of young Ooroony, who held the youthful chief as a hostage for his father's good behaviour.

Chapter XXIII

> "Thou shalt seek the beach of sand
> Where the water bounds the elfin land;
> Thou shalt watch the oozy brine
> Till the sturgeon leaps in the bright moonshine,
> Then dart the glistening arch below,
> And catch a drop from his silver bow;
> The water-sprites will wield their arms,
> And dash around, with roar and rave,
> And vain are the woodland spirit's charms,
> They are the imps that rule the wave.
> Yet trust thee in thy single might;
> If thy heart be pure, and thy spirit right,
> Thou shalt win the warlike fight."
>
> —Drake

A twelvemonth passed, after the return of the expedition against Betto's group, without the occurrence of any one very marked event. Within that time, Bridget made Mark the father of a fine boy, and Anne bore her fourth, child to Heaton. The propagation of the human species, indeed, flourished marvellously, no less than seventy-eight children having been born in the course of that single year. There were a few deaths, only one among the adults, the result of an accident, the health of the colony having been excellent. An enumeration, made near the close of the year, showed a total of three hundred and seventy-nine souls, including those absent in the Rancocus, and excluding the Kannakas.

As for these Kannakas, the results of their employment quite equalled the governor's expectations. They would not labour like civilized men, it is true, nor was it easy to make them use tools; but at lifts, and drags, and heavy work, they could be, and were, made to do a vast deal. The first great object of the governor had been to get his people all comfortably housed, beneath good roofs, and out of the way of the rains. Fortunately there were no decayed vegetable substances in the group, to produce fevers; and so long as the person could be kept dry, there was little danger to the health.

Four sorts, or classes, of houses were erected, each man being left to choose for himself, with the understanding that he was to receive a certain amount, in value, from the commonwealth, by contribution in labour, or in materials. All beyond that amount was to be paid for. To equalize advantages, a tariff was established, as to the value of labour and materials. These materials consisted of lumber, including shingles, stone, lime and bricks; bricks burned, as well as those which were unburned, or adobe. Nails were also delivered from the public store, free of charge.

Of course, no one at first thought of building very largely. Small kitchens were all that were got up, at the commencement, and they varied in size, according to the means of their owners, as much as they differed in materials. Some built of wood; some of stones; some of regular bricks; and some of adobe. All did very well, but the stone was found to be much the preferable material, especially where the plastering within was furred off from the walls. These stones came from Rancocus Island, where they were found in inexhaustible quantities, partaking of the character of tufa. The largest of them were landed at the Reef, the loading and unloading being principally done by the Kannakas, while the smallest were delivered at different points along the channel, according to the wishes of the owners of the land. More than a hundred dwellings were erected in the course of the few months immediately succeeding the arrival of the immigrants. About half were on the Peak, and the remainder were in the group. It is true, no one of all these dwellings was large; but each was comfortable, and fully answered the purpose of protection against the rain. A roof of cedar shingles was tight, as a matter of course, and what was more, it was lasting. Some of the buildings were sided with these shingles; though clap-boards were commonly used for that purpose. The adobe answered very well when securely roofed, though it was thought the unburnt brick absorbed more moisture than the brick which had been burned.

The largest of all the private dwellings thus erected, was thirty feet square, and the smallest was fifteen. The last had its cooking apartment under a shed, however, detached from the house. Most of the ovens were thus placed; and in many instances the chimneys stood entirely without the buildings, even when they were attached to them. There was but one house of two stories, and that was John Pennock's, who had sufficient means to construct such a building. As for the governor, he did not commence building at all, until nearly every one else was through, when he laid the corner-stones of two habitations; one on the Peak, which was his private property, standing on his estate; and the other on the Reef, which was strictly intended to be a Government, or Colony House. The first was of brick, and the last of stone, and of great solidity, being intended as a sort of fortress. The private dwelling was only a story and a half high, but large on the ground for that region, measuring sixty feet square. The. government building was much larger, measuring two hundred feet in length, by sixty feet in depth. This spacious edifice, however, was not altogether intended for a dwelling for the governor, but was so arranged as to contain great quantities of public property in its basement, and to accommodate the courts, and all the public offices on the first floor. It had an upper story, but that was left unfinished and untenanted for years, though fitted with arrangements for defence. Fortunately, cellars were little wanted in that climate, for it was not easy to have one in the group. It is true, that Pennock caused one to be blown out with gun-powder, under his dwelling, though every one prophesied that it would soon be full of water. It proved to be dry, notwithstanding; and a very good cellar it was, being exceedingly useful against the heats, though of cold there was none to guard against.

The Colony House stood directly opposite to the drawbridge, being placed there for the purposes of defence, as well as to have access to the spring. A want of water was rather an evil on the Reef; not that the sands did not furnish an ample supply, and that of the most delicious quality, but it had to be carried to inconvenient distances. In general, water was found in sufficient quantities and in suitable places, among the group; but, at the Reef, there was certainly this difficulty to contend with. As the governor caused his brother, the surveyor-general, to lay out a town on the Reef, it was early deemed necessary to make some provision against this evil. A suitable place was selected, and a cistern was blown out of the rock, into which all the water that fell on the roof of Colony House was led. This reservoir, when full, contained many thousand gallons; and when once full, it was found that the rains were sufficient to prevent its being very easily emptied.

But the greatest improvement that was made on the Reef, after all, was in the way of soil. As for the crater, that, by this time, was a mass of verdure, among which a thousand trees were not only growing, but flourishing. This was as true of its plain, as of its mounds; and of its mounds, as of its plain. But the crater was composed of materials very different from the base of the Reef. The former was of tufa, so far as it was rock at all; while the latter was, in the main, pure lava. Nevertheless, something like a soil began to form even on the Reef, purely by the accessions caused though its use by man. Great attention was paid to collecting everything that could contribute to the formation of earth, in piles; and these piles were regularly removed to such cavities, or inequalities in the surface of the rock, as would be most likely to retain their materials when spread. In this way many green patches had been formed, and, in a good many instances, trees had been set out, in spots where it was believed they could find sufficient nourishment. But, no sooner had the governor decided to build on the Reef, and to make his capital there, than he set about embellishing the place systematically. Whenever a suitable place could be found, in what was intended for Colony House grounds, a space of some ten acres in the rear of the building, he put in the drill, and blew out rock. The fragments of stone were used about the building; and the place soon presented a ragged, broken surface, of which one might well despair of making anything. By perseverance, however, and still more by skill and judgment, the whole area was lowered more than a foot, and in many places, where nature assisted the work, it was lowered several feet. It was a disputed question, indeed, whether stone for the building could not be obtained here, by blasting, cheaper and easier, than by transporting it from Rancocus Island. Enough was procured in this way not only to construct the building, but to enclose the grounds with a sufficient wall. When all was got off that was wanted, boat-loads of mud and sand were brought by Kannakas, and deposited in the cavity. This was a great work for such a community, though it proceeded faster than, at first, one might have supposed. The materials were very accessible, and the distances short, which greatly facilitated the labour, though unloading was a task of some gravity. The walls of the house were got up in about six months after the work was commenced, and the building was roofed; but, though the gardeners were set to work as soon as the stones were out of the cavities, they had not filled more than two acres at the end of the period mentioned.

Determined to make an end of this great work at once, the Abraham was sent over to young Ooroony to ask for assistance. Glad enough was that chief to grant what was demanded of him, and he came himself, at the head of five hundred men, to aid his friend in finishing this task. Even this strong body of labourers was busy two months longer, before the governor pronounced the great end accomplished. Then he dismissed his neighbours with such gifts and pay as sent away everybody contented. Many persons thought the experiment of bringing so many savages to the Reef somewhat hazardous; but no harm ever came of it. On the contrary, the intercourse had a good effect, by making the two people better acquainted with each other. The governor had a great faculty in the management of those wild beings. He not only kept them in good-humour, but what was far more difficult, he made them work. They were converted into a sort of Irish for his colony. It is true, one civilized man could do more than three of the Kannakas, but the number of the last was so large that they accomplished a great deal during their stay.

Nor would the governor have ventured to let such dangerous neighbours into the group, had there not been still more imposing mysteries connected with the Peak, into which they were not initiated. Even young Ooroony wag kept in ignorance of what was to be found on that dreaded island. He saw vessels going and coming, knew that the governor often went there, saw strange faces appearing occasionally on the Reef, that were understood to belong to the unknown land, and probably to a people who were much more powerful than those who were in direct communication with the natives.

The governor induced his Kannakas to work by interesting them in the explosions of the blasts, merely to enjoy the pleasure of seeing a cart-load of rock torn from its bed. One of these men would work at a drill all day, and then carry off the fragments to be placed in the walls, after he had had his sport in this operation of blasting. They seemed never to tire of the fun, and it was greatly questioned if half as much labour could have been got out of them at any other work, as at this.

A good deal of attention was paid to rendering the soil of the colony garden fertile, as well as deep. In its shallowest places it exceeded a foot in depth, and in the deepest, spots where natural fissures had aided the drill, it required four or five feet of materials to form the level. These deep places were all marked, and were reserved for the support of trees. Not only was sand freely mixed with the mud, or muck, but sea-weed in large quantities was laid near the surface, and finally covered with the soil. In this manner was a foundation made that could not fail to sustain a garden luxuriant in its products, aided by the genial heat and plentiful rains of the climate. Shrubs, flowers, grass, and ornamental trees, however, were all the governor aimed at in these public grounds; the plain of the crater furnishing fruit and vegetables in an abundance, as yet far exceeding the wants of the whole colony. The great danger, indeed, that the governor most apprehended, was that the beneficent products of the region would render his people indolent; an idle, nation becoming, almost infallibly, vicious as well as ignorant. It was with a view to keep the colony on the advance, and to maintain a spirit of improvement that so much attention was so early bestowed on what might otherwise be regarded as purely intellectual pursuits which, by creating new wants, might induce their subjects to devise the means of supplying them.

The governor judged right; for tastes are commonly acquired by imitation, and when thus acquired, they take the strongest hold of those who cultivate them. The effect produced by the Colony Garden, or public grounds, was such as twenty-fold to return the cost and labour bestowed on it. The sight of such an improvement set both men and women to work throughout the group, and not a dwelling was erected in the town, that the drill did not open the rock, and mud and sand form a garden. Nor did the governor himself confine his horticultural improvements to the gardens mentioned. Before he sent away his legion of five hundred, several hundred blasts were made in isolated spots on the Reef; places where the natural formation favoured such a project; and holes were formed that would receive a boat-load of soil each. In these places trees were set out, principally cocoa-nuts, and such other plants as were natural to the situation, due care being taken to see that each had sufficient nourishment.

The result of all this industry was to produce a great change in the state of things at the Reef. In addition to the buildings erected, and to the gardens made and planted, within the town itself, the whole surface of the island was more or less altered. Verdure soon made its appearance in places where, hitherto, nothing but naked rock had been seen, and trees began to cast their shades over the young and delicious grasses. As for the town itself, it was certainly no great matter; containing about twenty dwellings, and otherwise being of very modest pretensions. Those who dwelt there were principally such mechanics as found it convenient to be at the centre of the settlement, some half a dozen persons employed about the warehouses of the merchants, a few officials of the government, and the families of those who depended mainly on the sea for their support. Each and all of these heads of families had drawn their lots, both in the group and on the Peak, though some had sold their rights the better to get a good start in their particular occupations. The merchants, however, established themselves on the Reef, as a matter of necessity, each causing a warehouse to be constructed near the water, with tackles and all the usual conveniences for taking in and delivering goods. Each also had his dwelling near at hand. As these persons had come well provided for the Indian trade in particular, having large stocks of such cheap and coarse articles as took with the natives, they were already driving a profitable business, receiving considerable quantities of sandal-wood in exchange for their goods.

It is worthy of being mentioned, that the governor and council early passed a sort of navigation act, the effect of which was to secure the carrying trade to the colony. The motive, however, was more to keep the natives within safe limits, than to monopolize the profits of the seas. By the provisions of this law, no canoe could pass from Betto's group to either of the islands of the colony, without express permission from the governor. In order to carry on the trade, the parties met on specified days at Ooroony's village, and there made their exchanges; vessels being sent from the Reef to bring away the sandal-wood. With a view to the final transportation of the last to a market, Saunders had been instructed to purchase a suitable vessel, which was to return with the Rancocus, freighted with such heavy and cheap implements as were most wanted in the colony, including cows and mares in particular. Physical force, in the shape of domestic animals, was greatly wanted; and it was perhaps the most costly of all the supplies introduced into the settlements. Of horned cattle there were already about five-and-twenty head in the colony-enough to make sure of the breed; but they were either cows, steers too young to be yet of much use, and calves. Nothing was killed, of course; but so much time must, pass before the increase would give the succour wanted, that the governor went to unusual expense and trouble to make additions to the herd from abroad.

As for the horses, but three had been brought over, two of which were mares. The last had foaled twice; and there were four colts, all doing well, but wanting age to be useful. All the stock of this character was kept on the Peak, in order to secure it from invaders; and the old animals, even to the cows, were lightly worked there, doing a vast deal that would otherwise remain undone. It was so obviously advantageous to increase the amount of this sort of force, that Saunders had strict orders to purchase the vessel mentioned, and to bring over as many beasts as he could conveniently and safely stow. With this object in view, he was directed to call in, on the western side of Cape Horn, and to make his purchases in South America. The horned cattle might not be so good, coming from such a quarter, but the dangers of doubling the Cape would be avoided.

While making these general and desultory statements touching the progress of the colony, it may be well to say a word of Rancocus Island. The establishments necessary there, to carry on the mills, lime and brick kilns, and the stone-quarry, induced the governor to erect a small work, in which the persons employed in that out-colony might take refuge, in the event of an invasion. This was done accordingly; and two pieces of artillery were regularly mounted on it. Nor was the duty of fortifying neglected elsewhere. As for the Peak, it was not deemed necessary to do more than improve a little upon nature; the colony being now too numerous to suppose that it could not defend the cove against any enemy likely to land there, should the entrance of that secret haven be detected. On the Reef, however, it was a very different matter. That place was as accessible as the other was secure. The construction of so many stout stone edifices contributed largely to the defence of the town; but the governor saw the necessity of providing the means of commanding the approaches by water. Four distinct passages, each corresponding to a cardinal point of the compass, led from the crater out to sea. As the south passage terminated at the bridge, it was sufficiently commanded by the Colony House. But all the others were wider, more easy of approach, and less under the control of the adjacent islands. But the Summit had points whence each might be raked by guns properly planted, and batteries were accordingly constructed on these points; the twelve-pounder being used for their armaments. Each battery had two guns; and when all was completed, it was the opinion of the governor that the post was sufficiently well fortified. In order, however, to give additional security, the crater was tabooed to all the Kannakas; not one of whom was permitted ever to enter it, or even to go near it.

But defence, and building, and making soil, did not altogether occupy the attention of the colonists during these important twelve months. Both the brothers of the governor got married; the oldest, or the attorney-general, to the oldest sister of John Pennock, and the youngest to a sister of the Rev. Mr. Hornblower. It was in this simple colony, as it ever has been, and ever will be in civilized society, that, in forming matrimonial connections, like looks for like. There was no person, or family at the Reef which could be said to belong to the highest social class of America, if, indeed, any one could rank as high as a class immediately next to the highest; yet, distinctions existed which were maintained usefully, and without a thought of doing them away. The notion that money alone makes those divisions into castes which are everywhere to be found, and which will probably continue to be found as long as society itself exists, is a very vulgar and fallacious notion. It comes from the difficulty of appreciating those tastes and qualities which, not possessing ourselves, are so many unknown and mysterious influences. In marrying Sarah Pennock, John Woolston was slightly conscious of making a little sacrifice in these particulars, but she was a very pretty, modest girl, of a suitable age, and the circle to choose from, it will be remembered, was very limited. In America that connection might not have taken place; but, at the crater, it was all well enough, and it turned out to be a very happy union. Had the sacrifice of habits and tastes been greater, this might not have been the fact, for it is certain that our happiness depends more on the subordinate qualities and our cherished usages, than on principles themselves. It is difficult to suppose that any refined woman, for instance, can ever thoroughly overcome her disgust for a man who habitually blows his nose with his fingers, or that one bred a gentleman can absolutely overlook, even in a wife, the want of the thousand and one little lady-like habits, which render the sex perhaps more attractive than do their personal charms.

Several other marriages took place, the scarcity of subjects making it somewhat hazardous to delay: when Hobson's choice is placed before one, deliberation is of no great use. It was generally understood that the Rancocus was to bring out very few immigrants, though permission had been granted to Capt. Saunders to take letters to certain friends of some already settled in the colony, with the understanding that those friends were to be received, should they determine to come. That point, however, was soon to be decided, for just a year and one week after the Rancocus had sailed from Betto's group, the news reached the Reef that the good ship was coming into the northern roads, and preparing to anchor. The governor immediately went on board the Anne, taking Betts with him, and made sail for the point in question, with a view to bring the vessel through the passage to the Reef. The governor and Betts were the only two who, as it was believed, could carry so large a vessel through; though later soundings showed it was only necessary to keep clear of the points and the shores, in order to bring in a craft of any draught of water.

When the Anne ran out into the roads, there she found the Rancocus at anchor, sure enough. On nearing her, Capt. Saunders appeared on her poop, and in answer to a hail, gave the welcome answer of "all well." Those comprehensive words removed a great deal of anxiety from the mind of the governor; absence being, in one sense, the parent of uncertainty, and uncertainty of uneasiness. Everything about the ship, however, looked well, and to the surprise of those in the Anne, many heads belonging to others beside the crew were to be seen above the rail. A sail was in sight, moreover, standing in, and this vessel Capt. Saunders stated was the brig Henlopen, purchased on government account, and loaded with stock, and other property for the colony.

On going on board the Rancocus it was ascertained that, in all, one hundred and eleven new immigrants had been brought out! The circle of the affections had been set at work, and one friend had induced another to enter into the adventure, until it was found that less than the number mentioned could not be gotten rid of. That which could not be cured was to be endured, and the governor's dissatisfaction was a good deal appeased when he learned that the new-comers were of excellent materials; beings without exception, young, healthful, moral, and all possessed of more or less substance, in the way of worldly goods. This accession to the colony brought its population up to rather more than five hundred souls, of which number, however, near a hundred and fifty were children, or, under the age of fourteen years.

Glad enough were the new-comers to land at a little settlement which had been made on the island which lay abreast of the roads, and where, indeed, there was a very convenient harbour, did vessels choose to use it. The roads, however, had excellent anchorage, and were perfectly protected against the prevailing winds of that region. Only once, indeed, since the place was inhabited, had the wind been known to blow *on* shore at that point; and then only during a brief squall. In general, the place was every way favourable for the arrival and departure of shipping, the trades making a leading breeze both in going and coming-as, indeed, they did all the way to and from the Reef. A long-headed emigrant, of the name of Dunks, had foreseen the probable, future, importance of this outer harbour, and had made such an arrangement with the council, as to obtain leave for himself and three or four of his connections to exchange the land they had drawn, against an equal quantity in this part of the group. The arrangement was made, and this little, out-lying colony had now been established an entire season. As the spot was a good deal exposed to an invasion, a stone dwelling had been erected, that was capable of accommodating the whole party, and pickets were placed around it in such a way as to prove an ample defence against any attempt to carry the work by assault. The governor had lent them a field-piece, and it was thought the whole disposition was favourable to the security of the colony, since no less than eleven combatants could be mustered here to repel invasion.

The immigrants, as usual, found everything charming, when their feet touched terra firma. The crops *did* look well, and the island being covered with mud, the sand had done wonders for the vegetation. It is true that trees were wanting, though the pickets, or palisades, being of willow, had all sprouted, and promised soon to enclose the dwelling in a grove. Some fifty acres had been tilled, more or less thoroughly, and timothy was already growing that was breast-high. Clover looked well, too, as did everything else; the guano having lost none of its virtue since the late arrivals.

The governor sent back the Anne, with instructions to prepare room for the immigrants in the government dwelling, which, luckily, was large enough to receive them all. He waited with the Rancocus, however, for the Henlopen to come in and anchor. He then went on board this brig, and took a look at the stock. Saunders, a discreet, sensible man, so well understood the importance of adding to the physical force of the colony, in the way of brutes, that he had even strained the point to bring as many mares and cows as he could stow. He had put on board twenty-five of the last, and twenty of the first; all purchased at Valparaiso. The weather had been so mild, that no injury had happened to the beasts, but the length of the passage had so far exhausted the supplies that not a mouthful of food had the poor animals tasted for the twenty-four hours before they got in. The water, too, was scarce, and anything but sweet. For a month everything had been on short allowance, and the suffering creatures must have been enchanted to smell the land. Smell it they certainly did; for such a lowing, and neighing, and fretting did they keep up, when the governor got alongside of the brig, that he could not endure the sight of their misery, but determined at once to relieve it.

The brig was anchored within two hundred yards of a fine sandy beach, on which there were several runs of delicious water, and which communicated directly with a meadow of grass, as high as a man's breast. A bargain was soon made with Dunks; and the two crews, that of the Rancocus, as well as that of the brig, were set to work without delay to hoist out every creature having a hoof, that was on board the Henlopen. As slings were all ready, little delay was necessary, but a mare soon rose through the hatchway, was swung over the vessel's side, and was lowered into the water. A very simple contrivance released the creature from the slings, and off it swam, making the best of its way towards the land. In three minutes the poor thing was on the beach, though actually staggering from weakness, and from long use to the motion of the vessel. The water was its first aim. Dunks was there, however, to prevent it from drinking too much, when it made its way up to the grass, which it began to eat ravenously. All the rest went through the same process, and in a couple of hours the poor things were relieved from their misery, and the brig, which smelled like a stable, was well quit of them. Brooms and water were set to work immediately, but it was a month before the Henlopen lost the peculiar odour of the cattle.

Nor were the human beings much less rejoiced to go ashore than the brutes. Dunks gave them all a hearty welcome, and though he had little fruit to offer, he had plenty of vegetables, for which they were quite as thankful. Melons, however, he could and did give them, and the human part of the cargo had an ample feast on a sort of food to which they had now so long been strangers. The horses and cows were left on Dunks's Island, where they stayed until word was sent to the governor that they had eaten down all his grass, and would soon be on allowance again, unless taken away. Means, however, were soon found to relieve him of the stock, though his meadows, or pastures rather, having been seldom cut in that climate, were much improved by the visit paid them. As for the animals, they were parcelled out among the different farms, thus giving a little milk, and a little additional force to each neighbourhood. Fowls and pigs had been distributed some time previously, so that not a man in the group was without his breeding sow, and his brood of young chickens. These were species of stock that increased so rapidly, that a little care alone was wanting to make eggs and pork plenty. Corn, or maize, grew just for the planting; though it was all the better, certainly, for a little care.

After sufficient time had been allowed to make the necessary preparations, the vessels sailed with the immigrants for the Reef. There was many a glad meeting between friends and relatives. Those who had just arrived had a great deal to tell those who had preceded then by eighteen months, and those who now considered themselves old settlers, entertained the new ones with the wonders of their novel situations.

Chapter XXIV

> "Welter upon the waters, mighty one —
> And stretch thee in the ocean's trough of brine;
> Turn thy wet scales up to the wind and sun,
> And toss the billow from thy flashing fin;
> Heave thy deep breathing to the ocean's din,
> And bound upon its ridges in thy pride,
> Or dive down to its lowest depths, and in
> The caverns where its unknown monsters hide
> Measure thy length beneath the gulf-stream's tide."
>
> —Brainard's *Sea-Serpent*.

The colony had now reached a point when its policy must have an eye to its future destinies. If it were intended to push it, like a new settlement, a very different course ought to be pursued from the one hitherto adopted. But the governor and council entertained more moderate views. They understood their real position better. It was true that the Peak, in one sense, or in that which related to soil and products, was now in a condition to receive immigrants as fast as they could come; but the Peak had its limits, and it could hold but a very circumscribed number. As to the group, land had to be formed for the reception of the husbandman, little more than the elements of soil existing over so much of its surface. Then, in the way of trade, there could not be any very great inducement for adventurers to come, since the sandal-wood was the only article possessed which would command a price in a foreign market. This sandal-wood, moreover, did not belong to the colony, but to a people who might, at any moment, become hostile, and who already began to complain that the article was getting to be very scarce. Under all the circumstances therefore, it was not deemed desirable to add to the population of the place faster than would now be done by natural means.

The cargoes of the two vessels just arrived were divided between the state and the governor, by a very just process. The governor had one-half the proceeds for his own private use, as owner of the Rancocus, without which vessel nothing could have been done; while the state received the other moiety, in virtue of the labour of its citizens as well as in that of its right to impose duties on imports and exports. Of the portion which went to the state, certain parts were equally divided between the colonists, for immediate use, while other parts of the cargo were placed in store, and held as a stock, to be drawn upon as occasion might arise.

The voyage, like most adventures in sandal-wood, teas, &c., in that day, had been exceedingly advantageous, and produced a most beneficent influence on the fortunes and comforts of the settlement. A well-selected cargo of the coarse, low-priced articles most needed in such a colony, could easily have been purchased with far less than the proceeds of the cargo of tea that had been obtained at Canton, in exchange for the sandal-wood carried out; and Saunders, accordingly, had filled the holds of both vessels with such articles, besides bringing home with him a considerable amount in specie, half of which went into the public coffers, and half into the private purse of governor Woolston. Money had been in circulation in the colony for the last twelve months; though a good deal of caution was used in suffering it to pass from hand to hand. The disposition was to hoard; but this fresh arrival of specie gave a certain degree of confidence, and the silver circulated a great deal more freely after it was known that so considerable an amount had been brought in.

It would scarcely be in our power to enumerate the articles that were received by these arrivals; they included everything in common use among civilized men, from a grind-stone to a cart. Groceries, too, had been brought in reasonable quantities, including teas, sugars, &c.; though these articles were not so much considered *necessaries* in America fifty years ago as they are to-day. The groceries of the state as well as many other articles, were put into the hands of the merchants, who either purchased them out and out, to dispose of at retail, or who took them on commission with the same object. From this time, therefore, regular shops existed, there being three on the Reef and one on the Peak, where nearly everything in use could be bought, and that, too, at prices that were far from being exorbitant. The absence of import duties had a great influence on the cost of things, the state getting its receipts in kind, directly through the labour of its citizens, instead of looking to a customhouse in quest of its share for the general prosperity.

At that time very little was written about the great fallacy of the present day, Free Trade; which is an illusion about which men now talk, and dispute, and almost fight, while no living mortal can tell what it really is. It is wise for us in America, who never had anything but free trade, according to modern doctrines, to look a little closely into the sophisms that are getting to be so much in vogue; and which, whenever they come from our illustrious ancestors in Great Britain, have some such effect on the imaginations of a portion of our people, as purling rills and wooded cascades are known to posses over those of certain young ladies of fifteen.

Free trade, in its true signification, or in the only signification which is not a fallacy, can only mean a commerce that is *totally unfettered by duties, restrictions, prohibitions, and charges of all sorts*. Except among savages, the world never yet saw such a state of things, and probably never will. Even free trade ports have exactions that, in a degree, counteract their pretended principle of liberty; and no free port exists, that is anything more, in a strict interpretation of its uses, than a sort of bonded warehouse. So long as your goods remain there, on deposit and unappropriated, they are not taxed; but the instant they are taken to the *consumer*, the customary impositions must be paid.

Freer trade-that is, a trade which is less encumbered than some admitted state of things which previously existed-is easily enough comprehended; but, instead of conveying to the mind any general theory, it merely shows that a lack of wisdom may have prevailed in the management of some particular interest; which lack of wisdom is now being tardily repaired. Prohibitions, whether direct, or in the form of impositions that the trade will not bear, may be removed without leaving trade *free*. This or that article may be thrown open to the general competition, without import duty or tax of any sort, and yet the great bulk of the commerce of a country be so fettered as to put an effectual check upon anything like liberal intercourse. Suppose, for instance, that Virginia were an independent country. Its exports would be tobacco, flour, and corn; the tobacco crop probably more than equalling in value those portions of the other crops which are sent out of the country. England is suffering for food, and she takes off everything like imposts on the eatables, while she taxes tobacco to the amount of many hundred per cent. Can that be called free trade?

There is another point of view in which we could wish to protest against the shouts and fallacies of the hour. Trade, perhaps the most corrupt and corrupting influence of life-or, if second to anything in evil, second only to politics-is proclaimed to be the great means of humanizing, enlightening, liberalizing, and improving the human race! Now, against this monstrous mistake in morals, we would fain raise our feeble voices in sober remonstrance. That the intercourse which is a consequence of commerce may, in certain ways, liberalize a man's views, we are willing to admit; though, at the same time, we shall insist that there are better modes of attaining the same ends. But it strikes us as profane to ascribe to this frail and mercenary influence a power which there is every reason to believe the Almighty has bestowed on the Christian church, and on that alone; a church which is opposed to most of the practices of trade, which rebukes them in nearly every line of its precepts, and which, carried out in its purity, can alone give the world that liberty and happiness which a grasping spirit of cupidity is so ready to impute to the desire to accumulate gold!

Fortunately, there was little occasion to dispute about the theories of commerce at the Reef. The little trade that did exist was truly unfettered; but no one supposed that any man was nearer to God on that account, except as he was farther removed from temptations to do wrong. Still, the governing principle was sound; not by canting about the beneficent and holy influences of commerce, but by leaving to each man his individuality, or restraining if only on those points which the public good demanded. Instead of monopolizing the trade of the colony, which his superior wealth and official power would have rendered very easy, governor Woolston acted in the most liberal spirit to all around him. With the exception of the Anne, which was built by the colony, the council had decided, in some measure contrary to his wishes, though in strict accordance with what was right, that all the vessels were the private property of Mark. After this decision, the governor formally conveyed the Mermaid and the Abraham to the state; the former to be retained principally as a cruiser and a packet, while the last was in daily use as a means of conveying articles and passengers, from one island to the other. The Neshamony was presented, out and out, to Betts, who turned many a penny with her, by keeping her running through the different passages, with freight, &c.; going from plantation to plantation, as these good people were in the practice of calling their farms. Indeed, Bob did little else, until the governor, seeing his propensity to stick by the water, and ascertaining that the intercourse would justify such an investment, determined to build him a sloop, in order that he might use her as a sort of packet and market-boat, united. A vessel of about forty-five tons was laid down accordingly, and put into the water at the end of six months, that was just the sort of craft suited to Bob's wishes and wants. In the mean time, the honest fellow had resigned his seat in the council, feeling that he was out of his place in such a body, among men of more or less education, and of habits so much superior and more refined than his own. Mark did not oppose this step in his friend, but rather encouraged it; being persuaded nothing was gained by forcing upon a man duties he was hardly fitted to discharge. Self-made men, he well knew, were sometimes very useful; but he also knew that they must be first *made*.

The name of this new sloop was the Martha, being thus called in compliment to her owner's sober-minded, industrious and careful wife. She (the sloop, and not Mrs. Betts) was nearly all cabin, having lockers forward and aft, and was fitted with benches in her wings, steamboat fashion. Her canvas was of light duck, there being very little heavy weather in that climate; so that assisted by a boy and a Kannaka, honest Bob could do anything he wished with his craft. He often went to the Peak and Rancocus Island in her, always doing something useful; and he even made several trips in her, within the first few months he had her running, as far as Betto's group. On these last voyages, he carried over Kannakas as passengers, as well as various small articles, such as fish-hooks, old iron, hatchets even, and now and then a little tobacco. These he exchanged for cocoa-nuts, which were yet scarce in the colony, on account of the number of mouths to consume them; baskets, Indian cloth, paddles which the islanders made very beautifully and with a great deal of care; bread-fruit, and other plants that abounded more at Betto's group than at the Reef, or even on the Peak.

But the greatest voyage Betts made that season was when he took a freight of melons. This was a fruit which now abounded in the colony; so much so as to be fed even to the hogs, while the natives knew nothing of it beyond the art of eating it. They were extraordinarily fond of melons, and Bob actually filled the cabin of the Martha with articles obtained in exchange for his cargo. Among other things obtained on this occasion, was a sufficiency of sandal-wood to purchase for the owner of the sloop as many groceries as he could consume in his family for twelve months; though groceries were high, as may well be supposed, in a place like the Reef. Betts always admitted that the first great turn in his fortune was the money made on this voyage, in which he embarked without the least apprehension of Waally, and his never-ceasing wiles and intrigues. Indeed, most of his sales were made to that subtle and active chief, who dealt very fairly by him.

All this time the Rancocus was laid up for want of something to freight her with. At one time the governor thought of sending her to pick up a cargo where she could; but a suggestion by a seaman of the name of Walker set him on a different track, and put on foot an adventure which soon attracted the attention of most of the sea-faring portion of the community.

It had been observed by the crew of the Rancocus, not only in her original run through those seas, but in her two subsequent passages from America, that the spermaceti whale abounded in all that part of the ocean which lay to windward of the group. Now Walker had once been second officer of a Nantucket craft, and was regularly brought up to the business of taking whales. Among the colonists were half a dozen others who had done more or less at the same business; and, at the suggestion of Walker, who had gone out in the Rancocus as her first officer, captain Saunders laid in a provision of such articles as were necessary to set up the business. These consisted of cordage, harpoons, spades, lances, and casks. Then no small part of the lower hold of the Henlopen was stowed with shook casks; iron for hoops, &c., being also provided.

As the sandal-wood was now obtained in only small quantities, all idea of sending the ship to Canton again, that year, was necessarily abandoned. At first this seemed to be a great loss; but when the governor came to reflect coolly on the subject, not only he, but the council generally, came to the conclusion that Providence was dealing more mercifully with them, by turning the people into this new channel of commerce, than to leave them to pursue their original track. Sandal-wood had a purely adventitious value, though it brought, particularly in that age, a most enormous profit; one so large, indeed, as to have a direct and quick tendency to demoralize those embarked in the trade. The whaling business, on the other hand, while it made large returns, demanded industry, courage, perseverance, and a fair amount of capital. Of vessels, the colonists had all they wanted; the forethought of Saunders and the suggestions of Walker furnished the particular means; and of provisions there was now a superabundance in the group.

It was exceedingly fortunate that such an occupation offered to interest and keep alive the spirit of the colonists. Man must have something to do; some main object to live for; or he is apt to degenerate in his ambition, and to fall off in his progress. No sooner was it announced that whales were to be taken, however, than even the women became alive to the results of the enterprise. This feeling was kept up by the governor's letting it be officially known that each colonist should have one share, or "lay," as it was termed, in the expected cargo; which share, or "lay," was to be paid for in provisions. Those actually engaged in the business had as many "lays" as it was thought they could earn; the colony in its collected capacity had a certain number more, in return for articles received from the public stores; and the governor, as owner of the vessels employed, received one-fifth of the whole cargo, or cargoes. This last was a very small return for the amount of capital employed; and it was so understood by those who reaped the advantages of the owner's liberality.

The Rancocus was not fitted out as a whaler, but was reserved as a ware-house to receive the oil, to store it until a cargo was collected, and then was to be used as a means to convey it to America. For this purpose she was stripped, had her rigging thoroughly overhauled, was cleaned out and smoked for rats, and otherwise was prepared for service. While in this state, she lay alongside of the natural quay, near and opposite to some extensive sheds which had been erected, as a protection against the heats of the climate.

The Henlopen, a compact clump of a brig, that was roomy on deck, and had stout masts and good rigging, was fitted out for the whaler; though the Anne was sent to cruise in company. Five whale-boats, with the necessary crews, were employed; two remaining with the Anne, and three in the brig. The Kannakas were found to be indefatigable at the oar, and a good number of them were used on this occasion. About twenty of the largest boys belonging to the colony were also sent out, in order to accustom them to the sea. These boys were between the ages of eight and sixteen, and were made useful in a variety of ways.

Great was the interest awakened in the colony when the Henlopen and the Anne sailed on this adventure. Many of the women, the wives, daughters, sisters, or sweethearts of the whalers, would gladly have gone along; and so intense did the feeling become, that the governor determined to make a festival of the occasion, and to offer to take out himself, in the Mermaid, as many of both sexes as might choose to make a trip of a few days at sea, and be witnesses of the success of their friends in this new undertaking. Betts also took a party in the Martha. The Abraham, too, was in company; while the Neshamony was sent to leeward, to keep a look-out in that quarter, lest the natives should take it into their heads to visit the group, while so many of its fighting-men, fully a hundred altogether, were absent. It is true, those who stayed at home were fully able to beat off Waally and his followers; but the governor thought it prudent to have a look-out. Such was the difference produced by habit. When the whole force of the colony consisted of less than twenty men, it was thought sufficient to protect itself, could it be brought to act together; whereas, now, when ten times twenty were left at home, unusual caution was deemed necessary, because the colony was weakened by this expedition of so many of its members. But everything is comparative with man.

When all was ready, the whaling expedition sailed; the governor leading on board the Mermaid, which had no less than forty females in her-Bridget and Anne being among them. The vessels went out by the southern channel, passing through the strait at the bridge in order to do so. This course was taken, as it would be easier to turn to windward in the open water between the south cape and the Peak, than to do it in the narrow passages between the islands of the group. The Mermaid led off handsomely, sparing the Henlopen her courses and royals. Even the Abraham could spare the last vessel her foresail, the new purchase turning out to be anything but a traveller. The women wondered how so slow a vessel could ever catch a whale!

The direction steered by the fleet carried it close under the weather side of the Peak, the summit of which was crowded by the population, to see so unusual and pleasing a sight. The Martha led, carrying rather more sail, in proportion to her size, than the Mermaid. It happened, by one of those vagaries of fortune which so often thwart the best calculations, that a spout was seen to windward of the cliffs, at a moment when the sloop was about a league nearer to it than any other vessel. Now, every vessel in the fleet had its whale-boat and whale-boat's crew: though the men of all but those who belonged to the Henlopen were altogether inexperienced. It is true, they had learned the theory of the art of taking a whale; but they were utterly wanting in the practice. Betts was not the man to have the game in view, however, and not make an effort to overcome it. His boat was manned in an instant, and away he went, with Socrates in the bows, to fasten to a huge creature that was rolling on the water in a species of sluggish enjoyment of its instincts. It often happens that very young soldiers, more especially when an *esprit de corps* has been awakened in them, achieve things from which older troops would retire, under the consciousness of their hazards. So did it prove with the Martha's boat's crew on this occasion. Betts steered, and he put them directly on the whale; Socrates, who looked fairly green under the influence of alarm and eagerness to attack, both increased by the total novelty of his situation, making his dart of the harpoon when the bows of the fragile craft were literally over the huge body of the animal. All the energy of the negro was thrown into his blow, for he felt as if it were life or death with him; and the whale spouted blood immediately. It is deemed a great exploit with whalers, though it is not of very rare occurrence, to inflict a death-wound with the harpoon; that implement being intended to make fast with to the fish, which is subsequently slain with what is termed a lance. But Socrates actually killed the first whale he ever struck, with the harpoon; and from that moment he became an important personage in the fisheries of those seas. That blow was a sort of Palo Alto affair to him, and was the forerunner of many similar successes. Indeed, it soon got to be said, that "with Bob Betts to put the boat on, and old Soc to strike, a whale commonly has a hard time on't." It is true, that a good many boats were stove, and two Kannakas were drowned, that very summer, in consequence of these tactics; but the whales were killed, and Betts and the black escaped with whole skins.

On this, the first occasion, the whale made the water foam, half-filled the boat, and would have dragged it under, but for the vigour of the negro's arm, and the home character of the blow, which caused the fish to turn up and breathe his last, before he had time to run any great distance. The governor arrived on the spot, just as Bob had got a hawser to the whale and was ready to fill away for the South Cape channel again. The vessels passed each other cheering, and the governor admonished his friend not to carry the carcass too near the dwellings, lest it should render them uninhabitable. But Betts had his anchorage already in his eye, and away he went, with the wind on his quarter, towing his prize at the rate of four or five knots. It may be said, here, that the Martha went into the passage, and that the whale was floated into shallow water, where sinking was out of the question, and Bob and his Kannakas, about twenty in number, went to work to peel off the blubber in a very efficient, though not in a very scientific, or artistical manner. They got the creature stripped of its jacket of fat that very night, and next morning the Martha appeared with a set of kettles, in which the blubber was tried out. Casks were also brought in the sloop, and, when the work was done, it was found that that single whale yielded one hundred and eleven barrels of oil, of which thirty-three barrels were head-matter! This was a capital commencement for the new trade, and Betts conveyed the whole of his prize to the Reef, where the oil was started into the ground-tier of the Rancocus, the casks of which were newly repaired, and ready stowed to receive it.

A week later, as the governor in the Mermaid, cruising in company with the Henlopen and Abraham, was looking out for whales about a hundred miles to windward of the Peak, having met with no success, he was again joined by Betts in the Martha. Everything was reported right at the Reef. The Neshamony had come in for provisions and gone out again, and the Rancocus would stand up without watching, with her hundred and eleven barrels of oil in her lower hold. The governor expressed his sense of Betts' services, and reminding him of his old faculty of seeing farther and truer than most on board, he asked him to go up into the brig's cross-trees and take a look for whales. The keen-eyed fellow had not been aloft ten minutes, before the cry of "spouts-spouts!" was ringing through the vessel. The proper signal was made to the Henlopen and Abraham, when everybody made sail in the necessary direction. By sunset a great number of whales were fallen in with, and as Capt. Walker gave it as his opinion they were feeding in that place, no attempt was made on them until morning. The next day, however, with the return of light, six boats were in the water, and palling off towards the game.

On this occasion, Walker led on, as became his rank and experience. In less than an hour he was fast to a very large whale, a brother of that taken by Betts; and the females had the exciting spectacle, of a boat towed by an enormous fish, at a rate of no less than twenty knots in an hour. It is the practice among whalers for the vessel to keep working to windward, while the game is taking, in order to be in the most favourable position to close with the boats, after the whale is killed. So long, however, as the creature has life in it, it would be folly to aim at any other object than getting to windward, for the fish may be here at one moment, and a league off in a few minutes more. Sometimes, the alarmed animal goes fairly out of sight of the vessel, running in a straight line some fifteen or twenty miles, when the alternatives are to run the chances of missing the ship altogether, or to cut from the whale. By doing the last not only is a harpoon lost, but often several hundred fathoms of line; and it not unfrequently happens that whales are killed with harpoons in them, left by former assailants, and dragging after them a hundred, or two, fathoms of line.

It may be well, here, to explain to the uninitiated reader, that the harpoon is a barbed spear, with a small, but stout cord, or whale line fastened to it. The boat approaches the fish bow foremost, but is made sharp at both ends that it may "back off," if necessary; the whale being often dangerous to approach, and ordinarily starting, when struck, in a way to render his immediate neighbourhood somewhat ticklish. The fish usually goes down when harpooned, and the line must be permitted to "run-out," or he would drag the boat after him. But a whale must breathe as well as a man, and the faster he runs the sooner he must come up for a fresh stock of air. Now, the proper use of the harpoon and the line is merely to fasten to the fish; though it does sometimes happen that the creature is killed by the former. As soon as the whale re-appears on the surface, and becomes stationary, or even moderates his speed a little, the men begin to haul in line, gradually closing with their intended victim. It often happens that the whale starts afresh, when line must be permitted to run out anew; this process of "hauling in" and "letting run" being often renewed several times at the taking of a single fish. When the boat can be hauled near enough, the officer at its head darts his lance into the whale, aiming at a vital part. If the creature "spouts blood," it is well; but if not hit in the vitals, away it goes, and the whole business of "letting run," "towing," and "hauling in" has to be gone over again.

On the present occasion, Walker's harpooner, or boat-steerer, as he is called, had made a good "heave," and was well fast to his fish. The animal made a great circuit, running completely round the Mermaid, at a distance which enabled those on board her to see all that was passing. When nearest to the brig, and the water was curling off the bow of the boat in combs two feet higher than her gunwale, under the impulse given by the frantic career of the whale, Bridget pressed closer to her husband's side, and, for the first time in her life, mentally thanked Heaven that he was the governor, since that was an office which did not require him to go forth and kill whales. At that very moment, Mark was burning with the desire to have a hand in the sport, though he certainly had some doubts whether such an occupation would suitably accord with the dignity of his office.

Walker got alongside of his whale, within half a mile of the two brigs, and to-leeward of both. In consequence of this favourable circumstance, the Henlopen soon had its prize hooked on, and her people at work stripping off the blubber. This is done by hooking the lower block of a powerful purchase in a portion of the substance, and then cutting a strip of convenient size, and heaving on the fall at the windlass. The strip is cut by implements called spades, and the blubber is torn from the carcass by the strain, after the sides of the "blanket-piece," as the strip is termed, are separated from the other portions of the animal by the cutting process. The "blanket-pieces" are often raised as high as the lower mast-heads, or as far as the purchase will admit of its being carried, when a transverse cut is made, and the whole of the fragment is lowered on deck. This "blanket-piece" is then cut into pieces and put into the try-works, a large boiler erected on deck, in order to be "tryed-out," when the oil is cooled, and "started" below into casks. In this instance, the oil was taken on board the Abraham as fast as it was "tryed-out" on board the Henlopen, the weather admitting of the transfer.

But that single whale was far from being the only fruits of Betts' discovery. The honest old Delaware seaman took two more whales himself. Socrates making fast, and he killing the creatures. The boats of the Henlopen also took two more, and that of the Abraham, one. Betts in the Martha, and the governor in the Mermaid towed four of these whales into the southern channel, and into what now got the name of the Whaling Bight. This was the spot where Betts had tried out the first fish taken, and it proved to be every way suitable for its business. The Bight formed a perfectly safe harbour, and there was not only a sandy shoal on which the whales could be floated and kept from sinking, a misfortune that sometimes occurs, but it had a natural quay quite near, where the Rancocus, herself, could lie. There was fresh water in abundance, and an island of sufficient size to hold the largest whaling establishment that ever existed. This island was incontinently named Blubber Island. The greatest disadvantage was the total absence of soil, and consequently of all sorts of herbage; but its surface was as smooth as that of an artificial quay, admitting of the rolling of casks with perfect ease. The governor no sooner ascertained the facilities of the place, which was far enough from the ordinary passage to and from the Peak to remove the nuisances, than he determined to make it his whaling haven.

The Abraham was sent across to Rancocus Island for a load of lumber, and extensive sheds were erected, in time to receive the Henlopen, when she came in with a thousand barrels of oil on board, and towing in three whales that she had actually taken in the passage between Cape South and the Peak. By that time, the Rancocus had been moved, being stiff enough to be brought from the Reef to Blubber Island, under some of her lower sails. This moving of vessels among the islands of the group was a very easy matter, so long as they were not to be carried to windward; and, a further acquaintance with the channels, had let the mariners into the secret of turning up, against the trades and within the islands, by keeping in such reaches as enabled them to go as near the wind as was necessary, while they were not compelled to go nearer than a craft could lie.

Such was the commencement of a trade that was destined to be of the last importance to our colonists. The oil that was brought in, from this first cruise, a cruise that lasted less than two months, and including that taken by all the boats, amounted to two thousand barrels, quite filling the lower hold of the Rancocus, and furnishing her with more than half of a full cargo. At the prices which then ruled in the markets of Europe and America, three thousand five hundred barrels of spermaceti, with a due proportion of head matter, was known to be worth near an hundred thousand dollars; and might be set down as large a return for labour, as men could obtain under the most advantageous circumstances.

Chapter XXV

> "The forest reels beneath the stroke
> Of sturdy woodman's axe;
> The earth receives the white man's yoke,
> And pays her willing tax
> Of fruits, and flowers, and golden harvest fields,
> And all that nature to blithe labour yields."
>
> —Paulding

Notwithstanding the great success which attended the beginning of the whaling, it was six months before the Rancocus was loaded, and ready to sail for Hamburgh with her cargo. This time the ship went east, at once, instead of sailing to the westward, as she had previously done- taking with her a crew composed partly of colonists and partly of Kannakas. Six boys, however, went in the ship, the children of reputable settlers; all of whom the governor intended should be officers, hereafter, on board of colony vessels. To prevent difficulties on the score of national character, on leaving America the last time, Saunders had cleared for the islands of the Pacific and a market; meaning to cover his vessel, let her go where she might, by the latter reservation. This question of nationality offered a good deal of embarrassment in the long run, and the council foresaw future embarrassments as connected with the subject; but, every one of the colonists being of American birth, and America being then neutral, and all the American-built vessels having American papers, it was thought most prudent to let things take their natural course, under the existing arrangement, until something occurred to render a more decided policy advisable.

As soon as the Rancocus got off, the Henlopen went out again, to cruise about two hundred leagues to windward; while the inshore fishery was carried on by Betts, in the Martha, with great spirit and most extraordinary success. So alive did the people get to be to the profit and sport of this sort of business, that boats were constructed, and crews formed all over the colony, there being often as many as a dozen different parties out, taking whales near the coasts. The *furor* existed on the Peak, as well as in the low lands, and Bridget and Anne could not but marvel that men would quit the delicious coolness, the beautiful groves, and all the fruits and bountiful products of that most delightful plain, to go out on the ocean, in narrow quarters, and under a hot sun, to risk their lives in chase of the whale! This did the colonists, nevertheless, until the governor himself began to feel the necessity of striking a whale, if he would maintain his proper place in the public opinion.

As respects the governor, and the other high functionaries of the colony, some indulgence was entertained; it being the popular notion that men who lived so much within doors, and whose hands got to be so soft, were not exactly the sort of persons who would be most useful at the oar. Heaton, and the merchants, Pennock, and the two younger Woolstons, with the clergyman, were easily excused in the popular mind; but the governor was known to be a prime seaman, and a silent expectation appeared to prevail, that some day he would be seen in the bow of a boat, lancing a whale. Before the first season was over, this expectation was fully realized; Governor Woolston heading no less than four of what were called the colony boats, or boats that belonged to the state, and fished as much for honour as profit, taking a fine whale on each occasion. These exploits of the governor's capped the climax, in the way of giving a tone to the public mind, on the subject of taking whales. No man could any longer doubt of its being honourable, as well as useful, and even the boys petitioned to be allowed to go out. The Kannakas, more or less of whom were employed in each vessel, rose greatly in the public estimation, and no *young* man could expect to escape animadversion, unless he had been present at least once at the taking of a whale. Those who had struck or lanced a fish were now held in a proportionate degree of repute. It was, in fact, in this group that the custom originally obtained, which prohibited a young man from standing at the head of the dance who had not struck his fish; and not at Nantucket, as has been erroneously supposed.

In a community where such a spirit was awakened, it is not surprising that great success attended the fisheries. The Henlopen did well, bringing in eight hundred barrels; but she found six hundred more in waiting for her, that had been taken by the in-shore fishermen; some using the Abraham, some the Martha, some the Anne, and others again nothing but the boats, in which they pursued their game. In the latter cases, however, when a fish was taken, one of the larger vessels was usually employed to take the creature into the Bight. In this way was the oil obtained, which went to make up a cargo for the Henlopen. The governor had his doubts about sending this brig on so distant a voyage, the vessel being so slow; but there was no choice, since she must go, or the cargo must remain a long time where it was. The brig was accordingly filled up, taking in seventeen hundred barrels; and she sailed for Hamburgh, under the command of a young man named Thomas. Walker remained behind, preferring to superintend the whaling affairs at home.

So high did the fever run, by this time, that it was determined to build a couple of vessels, each to measure about a hundred and eighty tons, with the sole object of using them to take the whale. Six months after laying their keels, these little brigs were launched; and lucky it was that the governor had ordered copper for a ship to be brought out, since it now came handy for using on these two craft. But, the whaling business had not been suffered to lag while the Jonas and the Dragon were on the stocks; the Anne, and the Martha, and the single boats, being out near half the time. Five hundred barrels were taken in this way; and Betts, in particular, had made so much money, or, what was the same thing, had got so much oil, that he came one morning to his friend the governor, when the following interesting dialogue took place between them, in the audience-chamber of the Colony House. It may as well be said here, that the accommodations for the chief magistrate had been materially enlarged, and that he now dwelt in a suite of apartments that would have been deemed respectable even in Philadelphia. Bridget had a taste for furniture, and the wood of Rancocus Island admitted of many articles being made that were really beautiful, and which might have adorned a palace. Fine mats had been brought from China, such as are, and long have been, in common use in America; neat and quaint chairs and settees had also been in the governor's invoices, to say nothing of large quantities of fine and massive earthenware. In a word, the governor was getting to be rich, and like all wealthy men, he had a disposition to possess, in a proportionate degree, the comforts and elegancies of civilized life. But to come to our dialogue —

"Walk in, Captain Betts-walk in, sir, and do me the favour to take a chair," said the governor, motioning to his old friend to be seated. "You are always welcome, here; for I do not forget old times, I can assure you, my friend."

"Thankee, governor; thankee, with all my heart. I *do* find everything changed, now-a-days, if the truth must be said, but yourself. To me, *you* be always, Mr. Mark, and Mr. Woolston, and we seem to sail along in company, much as we did the time you first went out a foremast-lad, and I teached you the difference between a flat-knot and a granny."

"No, no, Bob, everything is not so much changed as you pretend—I am not changed, in the first place."

"I confess it—*you* be the same, governor, blow high, or blow low."

"Then Martha is not changed, or nothing worth mentioning. A little more matronly, perhaps, and not quite as much of a girl as when you first made her acquaintance; but Martha, nevertheless. And, as for her heart, I'll answer for it, that is just the colour it was at sixteen."

"Why, yes, governor; 'tis much as you say. Marthy is now the mother of four children, and that confarms a woman's appearance, depend on't. But, Marthy is Marthy; and, for that matter, Miss Bridget is Miss Bridget, as much as one pea is like another. Madam Woolston does full credit to the climate, governor, and looks more like eighteen than ever."

"My wife enjoys excellent health, Betts; and grateful am I to God that it is so. But I think all our women have a fresh and sea-air sort of look, a cheerful freshness about them, that I ascribe to the salt and the sea-breezes. Then we have mountain air, in addition, on the Peak."

"Ay, ay, sir—I dare say you've got it right, as you do most matters. Well, governor, I don't know which counts up the fastest in the colony, children or whales?"

"Both flourish," answered Mark, smiling, "as our reports show. Mr. Secretary tells me that there were, on the first of the last month, three hundred and eighteen children in the colony under the age of ten years; of whom no less than one hundred and ninety-seven are born here-pure Craterinos, including your children and mine, Betts."

"It's a fine beginning, governor—a most capital start; and, though the young 'uns can't do much at taking a whale, or securing the ile, just now, they'll come on in their turns, and be useful when we're in dock as hulks sir."

"Talking of oil, you must be getting rich, Captain Betts. I hear you got in another hundred-barrel gentleman last week!"

"Times is altered with me, governor; and times is altered with you, too, sir, since you and I rafted loam and sea-weed, to raise a few cucumbers, and squashes, and melons. *Then*, we should have been as happy as princes to have had a good roof over our heads."

"I trust we are both thankful, where thanks are due, for all this, Betts?"

"Why, yes, sir, I endivour so to be; though men is desperate apt to believe they desarve all they get but the ill luck. I and Marthy try to think of what is all in all to us, and I believe Marthy does make out pretty well, in that partic'lar, accordin' to Friends' ways; though I am often jammed in religion, and all for want of taking to it early as I sometimes think, sir."

"There is no doubt, Betts, that men grow in Christian character, as well as in evil; and the most natural growth, in all things, is that of the young. A great deal is to be undone and unlearned, if we put off the important hour to a late period in life."

"Well, as to unl'arnin', I suppose a fellow that had as little edication as myself will have an easy time of it," answered Betts, with perfect simplicity and good faith; "for most of my schoolin' was drowned in salt water by the time I was twelve."

"I am glad of one thing," put in the governor, half in a congratulating way, and half inquiringly; "and that is, that the Rev. Mr. Hornblower takes so well with the people. Everybody appears to be satisfied with his ministrations; and I do not see that any one is the worse for them, although he is an Episcopalian."

Betts twisted about on his chair, and seemed at first unwilling to answer; but his natural frankness, and his long habits of intimacy and confidence with Mark Woolston, both as man and boy, forbade his attempting anything seriously in the way of concealment.

"Well, governor, they *do* say that 'many men, many minds,'" he replied, after a brief pause; "and I suppose it's as true about religion, as in a judgment of ships, or in a ch'ice of a wife. If all men took to the same woman, or all seamen shipped for the same craft, a troublesome household, and a crowded and onhealthy vessel, would be the upshot on't."

"We have a choice given us by Providence, both as to ships and as to wives, Captain Betts; but no choice is allowed any of us in what relates to religion. In that, we are to mind the sailor's maxim, 'to obey orders if we break owners.'"

"Little fear of 'breaking owners,' I fancy, governor. But, the difficulty is to know what orders is. Now, Friends doesn't hold, at all, to dressing and undressing in church time; and I think, myself, books is out of place in praying to God."

"And is there much said among the people, Captain Betts, about the parson's gown and surplice, and about his *reading* his prayers, instead of writing them out, and getting them by heart?"

There was a little malice in the governor's question, for he was too much behind the curtain to be the dupe of any pretending claims to sudden inspirations, and well knew that every sect had its liturgy, though only half-a-dozen have the honesty to print them. The answer of his friend was, as usual, frank, and to the point.

"I cannot say but there is, Mr. Mark. As for the clothes, women will talk about *them*, as you well know, sir; it being their natur' to be dressing themselves out, so much. Then as to praying from the book, quite half of our people think it is not any better than no praying at all. A little worse, perhaps, if truth was spoken."

"I am sorry to hear this, Betts. From the manner in which they attend the services, I was in hopes that prejudices were abating, and that everybody was satisfied."

"I don't think, governor, that there is any great danger of a mutiny; though, many men, many minds, as I said before. But, my business here is forgotten all this time; and I know it isn't with your honour now as it used to be with us both, when we had nothing to think of but the means of getting away from this place, into some other that we fancied might be better. I wish you joy, sir, in having got the two new brigs into the water."

"Thank you, Captain Betts. Does your present visit relate to either of those brigs?"

"Why, to come to the p'int, it does, sir. I've taken a fancy to the Dragon, and should like to buy her."

"Buy her! Have you any notion what such a vessel will cost, Betts?"

"Not a great way from eight thousand dollars, I should think, governor, now that the copper is on. Some things is charged high, in this part of the world, about a wessel, and other some isn't. Take away the copper, and I should think a good deal less would buy either."

"And have you eight thousand dollars at command, my friend, with which to purchase the brig?"

"If ile is money, yes; if ile isn't money, no. I've got three hundred barrels on hand, one hundred of which is head-matter."

"I rejoice to hear this, Captain Betts, and the brig you shall have. I thought to have sold both to the merchants, for I did not suppose any one else, here, could purchase them; but I would greatly prefer to see one of them in the hands of an old friend. You shall have the Dragon, Betts, since you like her."

"Done and done between gentlemen, is enough, sir; not that I set myself up for a gentleman, governor, but I've lived too long and too much in your respected society not to have l'arn'd some of the ways. The brig's mine, if ile will pay for her. And now, sir, having completed the trade, I *should* like to know if your judgment and mine be the same. I say the Dragon will beat the Jonas half a knot, the best day the Jonas ever seed."

"I do not know but you are right, Bob. In looking at the two craft, last evening, I gave the preference to the Dragon, though I kept my opinion to myself, lest I might mortify those who built the Jonas."

"Well, sir, I'm better pleased to hear this, than to be able to pay for the brig! It is something to a plain body like myself, to find his judgment upheld by them that know all about a matter."

In this friendly and perfectly confidential way did Mark Woolston still act with his old and long-tried friend, Robert Betts. The Dragon was cheap at the money mentioned, and the governor took all of the old seaman's 'ile' at the very top of the market. This purchase at once elevated Betts in the colony, to a rank but a little below that of the 'gentlemen,' if his modesty disposed him to decline being classed absolutely with them. What was more, it put him in the way of almost coining money. The brig he purchased turned out to be as fast as he expected, and what was more, the character of a lucky vessel, which she got the very first cruise, never left her, and gave her commander and owner, at all times, a choice of hands.

The governor sold the Jonas to the merchants, and took the Martha off Betts' hands, causing this latter craft to run regularly, and at stated hours, from point to point among the islands, in the character of a packet. Twice a week she passed from the Reef to the Cove at the Peak, and once a fortnight she went to Rancocus Island. In addition to her other duties, this sloop now carried the mail.

A post-office law was passed by the council, and was approved of by the governor. In that day, and in a community so simple and practical, new-fangled theories concerning human rights were not allowed to interfere with regulations that were obviously necessary to the comfort and convenience of the public.

Fortunately, there was yet no newspaper, a species of luxury, which, like the gallows, comes in only as society advances to the corrupt condition; or which, if it happen to precede it a little, is very certain soon to conduct it there. If every institution became no more than what it was designed to be, by those who originally framed it, the state of man on earth would be very different from what it is. The unchecked means of publicity, out of all question, are indispensable to the circulation of truths; and it is equally certain that the unrestrained means of publicity are equally favourable to the circulation of lies. If we cannot get along safely without the possession of one of these advantages, neither can we get along very safely while existing under the daily, hourly, increasing influence of the other-call it what you will. If truth is all-important, in one sense, falsehood is all-important too, in a contrary sense.

Had there been a newspaper at the Crater, under the control of some philosopher, who had neither native talent, nor its substitute education, but who had been struck out of a printer's devil by the rap of a composing-stick, as Minerva is reported to have been struck, full-grown, out of Jupiter's head by the hammer of Vulcan, it is probable that the wiseacre might have discovered that It was an inexcusable interference with the rights of the colonists, to enact that no one should carry letters for hire, but those connected with the regular post-office. But, no such person existing, the public mind was left to the enjoyment of its common-sense ignorance, which remained satisfied with the fact that, though it might be possible to get a letter carried from the Reef to the Cove, between which places the communications were constant and regular, for half the money charged by the office, yet it was not possible to get letters carried between some of the other points in the colony for twenty times the regulated postage. It is probable, therefore, that the people of the Crater and the Peak felt, that in supporting a general system, which embraced the good of all, they did more towards extending civilization, than if they killed the hen, at once, in order to come at the depository of the golden eggs, in the shortest way.

In the middle ages, he who wished to send a missive, was compelled, more than half the time, to be at the expense of a special messenger. The butchers, and a class of traders that corresponds, in part, to the modern English traveller, took charge of letters, on the glorious Free Trade principle; and sometimes public establishments hired messengers to go back and forth, for their own purposes. Then, the governments, perceiving the utility of such arrangements, imperfect as they were, had a sort of post-offices for their use, which have reached down to our own times, in the shape of government messengers. There can be little doubt that the man who found he could get a letter safely and promptly conveyed five hundred miles for a crown, after having been obliged previously to pay twenty for the same service, felt that he was the obliged party, and never fancied for a moment, that, in virtue of his *patronage*, he was entitled to give himself airs, and to stand upon his natural right to have a post-office of his own, at the reduced price. But, indulgence creates wantonness, and the very men who receive the highest favours from the post-offices of this country, in which a letter is carried five-and-twenty hundred miles for ten cents, penetrating, through some fourteen or fifteen thousand offices, into every cranny of a region large as half Europe, kicks and grows restive because he has not the liberty of doing a few favoured portions of the vast enterprise for himself; while he imposes on the public the office of doing that which is laborious and unprofitable! Such is man; such did he become when he fell from his first estate; and such is he likely to continue to be until some far better panacea shall be discovered for his selfishness and cupidity, than what is called 'self-government.'

But the Craterinos were thankful when they found that the Martha was set to running regularly, from place to place, carrying passengers and the mails. The two businesses were blended together for the sake of economy, and at the end of a twelvemonth it was found that the colony had nothing extra to pay. On the whole, the enterprise may be said to have succeeded; and as practice usually improves all such matters, in a few months it was ascertained that another very important step had been taken on the high-road of civilization. Certainly, the colonists could not be called a letter-writing people, considered as a whole, but the facilities offered a temptation to improve, and, in time, the character of the entire community received a beneficial impression from the introduction of the mails.

It was not long after the two brigs were sold, and just as the Martha came into government possession, that all the principal functionaries made a tour of the whole settlements, using the sloop for that purpose. One of the objects was to obtain statistical facts; though personal observation, with a view to future laws, was the principal motive. The governor, secretary, attorney-general, and most of the council were along; and pleasure and business being thus united, their wives were also of the party. There being no necessity for remaining in the Martha at night, that vessel was found amply sufficient for all other purposes, though the "progress" occupied fully a fortnight, As a brief relation of its details will give the reader a full idea of the present state of the "country," as the colonists now began to call their territories, we propose to accompany the travellers, day by day, and to give some short account of what they saw, and of what they did. The Martha sailed from the cove about eight in the morning, having on board seventeen passengers, in addition to two or three who were going over to Rancocus Island on their regular business. The sloop did not sail, however, directly for the last-named island, but made towards the volcano, which had of late ceased to be as active as formerly, and into the condition of which it was now deemed important to make some inquiries. The Martha was a very fast vessel, and was soon quietly anchored in a small bay, on the leeward side of the island, where landing was not only practicable but easy. For the first time since its existence the crater was ascended. All the gentlemen went up, and Heaton took its measurement by means of instruments. The accumulation of materials, principally ashes and scoriæ, though lava had begun to appear in one or two small streams, had been very great since the governor's first visit to the spot. The island now measured about two miles in diameter, and being nearly round, might be said to be somewhere near six in circumference. The crater itself was fully half a mile in diameter, and, at that moment, was quite a thousand feet in height above the sea. In the centre of this vast valley, were three smaller craters or chimneys, which served as outlets to the fires beneath. A plain had formed within the crater, some four hundred feet below its summit, and it already began to assume that sulphur-tinged and unearthly hue, that is so common in and about active volcanoes. Occasionally, a deep roaring would be succeeded by a hissing sound, not unlike that produced by a sudden escape of steam from a boiler, and then a report would follow, accompanied by smoke and stones; some of the latter of which were projected several hundred yards into the air, and fell on the plain of the crater. But these explosions were not one-tenth as frequent as formerly.

The result of all the observations was to create an impression that this outlet to the fires beneath was approaching a period when it would become inactive, and when, indeed, some other outlet for the pent forces might be made. After passing half-a-day on and around the volcano, even Bridget and Anne mustered courage and strength to ascend it, supported by the willing arms of their husbands. The females were rewarded for their trouble, though both declared that they should ever feel a most profound respect for the place after this near view of its terrors as well as of its beauties.

On quitting the volcano, the Martha proceeded directly to leeward, reaching Rancocus Island about sunset. Here the sloop anchored in the customary haven, and everybody but her crew landed. The fort was still kept up at this place, on account of the small number of the persons who dwelt there, though little apprehension now existed of a visit from the natives; with the exception of the Kannakas, who went back and forth constantly on board the different craft in which they were employed, not a native had been near either island of the colony since the public visit of young Ooroony, on the occasion of bringing over labourers to help to form the grounds of Colony House. The number and force of the different vessels would seem to have permanently settled the question of ascendency in those seas, and no one any longer believed it was a point to be controverted.

The population on Rancocus Island did not amount to more than fifty souls, and these included women and children. Of the latter, however, there were not yet many; though five or six were born annually, and scarcely one died. The men kept the mill going, cutting lumber of all sorts; and they made both bricks and lime, in sufficient quantities to supply the wants of the two other islands. At first, it had been found necessary to keep a greater force there, but, long before the moment of which we are writing, the people had all got into their regular dwellings, and the materials now required for building were merely such as were used in additions, or new constructions. The last, however, kept the men quite actively employed; but, as they got well paid for their work, everybody seemed contented. The Martha never arrived without bringing over quantities of fruits, as well as vegetables, the Rancocusers, lumber-men like, paying but little attention to gardening or husbandry. The island had its productions, and there was available land enough, perhaps, to support a few thousand people, but, after the group and the Peak, the place seemed so little tempting to the farmers, that no one yet thought of using it for the ordinary means of supporting life. The "visitors," as the party called themselves, had an inquiry made into the state of the animals that had been turned loose, on the pastures and mountain-sides of the island, to seek their own living. The hogs, as usual, had increased largely; it was supposed there might be near two hundred of these animals, near half of which, however, were still grunters. The labourers occasionally killed one, but the number grew so fast that it was foreseen it would be necessary to have an annual hunt, in order to keep it down. The goats did particularly well, though they remained so much on the highest peaks as to be seldom approached by any of the men. The cow had also increased her progeny, there being now no less than four younger animals, all of whom yielded milk to the people. The poultry flourished here, as it did in all that region, the great abundance of fruit, worms, insects, &c. rendering it unnecessary to feed them, though Indian-corn was almost to be had for the asking, throughout all the islands. This grain was rarely harvested, except as it was wanted, and the hogs that were fattened were usually turned in upon it in the fields.

It may be well to say, that practice and experience had taught the colonists something in the way of fattening their pork. The animals were kept in the group until they were about eighteen months old, when they were regularly transported to the cove, in large droves, and made to ascend the steps, passing the last two months of their lives amid the delightful groves of the Peak. Here they had acorns in abundance, though their principal food was Indian corn, being regularly attended by Kannakas who had been trained to the business. At killing-time, each man either came himself, or sent some one to claim his hogs; all of which were slaughtered on the Peak, and carried away in the form of pork. The effect of this change was to make much finer meat, by giving the animals a cooler atmosphere and purer food.

From Rancocus Island the Martha sailed for the group, which was visited and inspected in all its settlements by the governor and council. The policy adopted by the government of the colony was very much unlike that resorted to in America, in connection with the extension of the settlements. Here a vast extent of surface is loosely overrun, rendering the progress of civilization rapid, but very imperfect. Were the people of the United States confined to one-half the territory they now occupy, there can be little question that they would be happier, more powerful, more civilized, and less rude in manners and feelings; although it may be high treason to insinuate that they are not all, men, women and children, already at the *ne plus ultra* of each of those attainments. But there is a just medium in the density of human population, as well as in other things; and that has not yet been reached, perhaps, even in the most thickly peopled of any one of the Old Thirteen. Now, Mark Woolston had seen enough of the fruits of a concentrated physical force, in Europe, to comprehend their value; and he early set his face against the purely skimming process. He was resolved that the settlements should not extend faster than was necessary, and that as much of civilization should go with them as was attainable. In consequence of this policy, the country soon obtained a polished aspect, as far as the settlements reached. There were four or five distinct points that formed exceptions to this rule, it having been considered convenient to make establishments there, principally on account of the whalers. One, and the largest of these isolated settlements, was in the Whaling Bight, quite near to Blubber Islano, where a village had sprung up, containing the houses and shops of coopers, rope-makers, boat-builders, carpenters, blacksmiths, &c.; men employed in making casks, whaling gear, and boats. There also were the dwellings of three or four masters and mates of vessels, as well as of sundry boat-steerers. In the whole, there might have been fifty habitations at this particular point; of which about two-thirds were in a straggling village, while the remainder composed so many farm-houses. Everything at this place denoted activity and a prosperous business; the merchants taking the oil as fast as it was ready, and returning for it, hoops, iron in bars, hemp, and such other articles as were wanted for the trade.

By this time, the Rancocus had returned, and had discharged her inward-bound cargo at the Reef, bringing excellent returns for the oils sent to Hamburgh. She now lay in Whaling Bight, being about to load anew with oil that had been taken during her absence. Saunders was as busy as a bee; and Mrs. Saunders, who had come across from her own residence on the Peak, in order to remain as long as possible with her husband, was as happy as the day was long; seeming never to tire of exhibiting her presents to the other women at the Bight.

At the Reef itself, an exceedingly well-built little town was springing up. Since the removal of the whaling operations to the Bight, all nuisances were abated, and the streets, quays, and public walks were as neat as could be desired. The trees had grown wonderfully, and the gardens appeared as verdant and fresh as if they had a hundred feet of loam beneath them, instead of resting on solid lava, as was the fact. These gardens had increased in numbers and extent, so that the whole town was embedded in verdure and young trees. That spot, on which the sun had once beaten so fiercely as to render it often too hot to be supported by the naked foot, was now verdant, cool, and refreshing, equally to the eye and to the feelings. The streets were narrow, as is desirable in warm climates-thus creating shade, as well as increasing the draughts of air through them; it being in the rear that the houses obtained space for ventilation as well as for vegetation. The whole number of dwellings on the Reef now amounted to sixty-four; while the warehouses, public buildings, ships, offices, and other constructions, brought the number of the roofs up to one hundred. These buildings, Colony House and the warehouses excepted, were not very large certainly, but they were of respectable dimensions, and neat and well put together. Colony House was large, as has been mentioned; and though plain, certain ornaments had been completed, which contributed much to its appearance. Every building, without exception, had some sort of verandah to it; and as most of these additions were now embowered in shrubs or vines, they formed delightful places of retreat during the heat of the day.

By a very simple process, water was pumped up from the largest spring by means of wind-sails, and conveyed in wooden logs to every building in the place. The logs were laid through the gardens, for the double purpose of getting soil to cover them, and to put them out of the way. Without the town, a regular system had been adopted, by which to continue to increase the soil. The rock was blown out, as stone was wanted; leaving, however, a quay around the margin of the island. As soon as low enough, the cavities became the receptacles of everything that could contribute to form soil; and one day in each month was set apart for a "bee;" during which little was done but to transport earth from Loam Island, which was far from being exhausted yet, or even levelled, and scattering it on those hollow spots. In this manner, a considerable extent of surface, nearest to the town, had already been covered, and seeded, and planted, so that it was now possible to walk from the town to the crater, a distance of a quarter of a mile, and be the whole time amid flowering shrubs, young trees, and rich grasses!

As for the crater itself, it was now quite a gem in the way of vegetation. Its cocoa-nut trees bore profusely; and its figs, oranges, limes, shaddocks, &c. &c., were not only abundant, but rich and large. The Summit was in spots covered with delicious groves, and the openings were of as dark a verdure, the year round, as if the place lay twenty degrees farther from the equator than was actually the case. Here Kitty, followed by a flock of descendants, was permitted still to rove at large, the governor deeming her rights in the place equal to his own. The plain of the crater was mostly under tillage, being used as a common garden for all who dwelt in the town. Each person was taxed so many days, in work, or in money, agreeably to a village ordinance, and by such means was the spot tilled; in return, each person, according, to a scale that was regulated by the amount of the contribution, was allowed to come or send daily, and dig and carry away a stated quantity of fruits and vegetables. All this was strictly regulated by a town law, and the gardener had charge of the execution of the ordinance; but the governor had privately intimated to him that there was no necessity for his being very particular, so long as the people were so few, and the products so abundant. The entire population of the Reef proper amounted, at this visitation, to just three hundred and twenty-six persons, of whom near a hundred were under twelve years of age. This, however, was exclusively of Kannakas, but included the absent seamen, whose families dwelt there permanently.

The settlement at Dunks' Cove has been mentioned, and nothing need be said of it, beyond the fact that its agriculture had improved and been extended, its trees had grown, and its population increased. There was another similar settlement at East Cove-or Bay would be the better name-which was at the place where Mark Woolston had found his way out to sea, by passing through a narrow and half-concealed inlet. This entrance to the group was now much used by the whalers, who fell in with a great many fish in the offing, and who found it very convenient to tow them into this large basin, and cut them up. Thence the blubber was sent down in lighters to Whaling Bight, to be tryed out. This arrangement saved a tow of some five-and-twenty miles, and often prevented a loss of the fish, as sometimes occurred in the outside passage, by having it blown on an iron-bound coast. In consequence of these uses of the place, a settlement had grown up near it, and it already began to look like a spot to be civilized. As yet, however, it was the least advanced of all the settlements in the group.

At the West Bay, there was a sort of naval station and look-out port, to watch the people of the neighbouring islands. The improvements did not amount to much, however, being limited to one farm, a small battery that commanded the roads, and a fortified house, which was also a tavern.

The agricultural, or strictly rural population of the group, were seated along the different channels nearest to the Reef. Some attention had been paid, in the choice, to the condition of the soil; but, on the whole, few unoccupied spots could now be found within a league of the Reef, and on any of the principal passages that communicated with the different islands. There were foot-paths, which might be used by horses, leading from farm to farm, along the margins of the channels; but the channels themselves were the ordinary means of communicating between neighbours. Boats of all sorts abounded, and were constantly passing and repassing. Here, as elsewhere, the vegetation was luxuriant and marvellous. Trees were to be seen around the houses, that elsewhere might have required three times the number of years that these had existed, to attain the same height.

The visitation terminated at the Peak. This place, so aptly likened to the garden of Eden, and frequently so called, could receive very little addition to its picturesque beauties from the hand of man. Parts of it were cultivated, it is true; enough to supply its population (rather more than three hundred souls) with food; but much the greater portion of its surface was in pasture. The buildings were principally of stones quarried out of the cliffs, and were cool as well as solid edifices. They were low, however, and of no great size on the ground. At the governor's farm, his private property, there was a dwelling of some pretension; low, like all the rest, but of considerable extent. Here Bridget now passed much of her time; for here it was thought best to keep the children. So cool and salubrious was the air on the Peak, that two schools were formed here; and a large portion of the children of the colony, of a suitable age, were kept in them constantly. The governor encouraged this plan, not only on account of the health of the children, but because great care was taken to teach nothing but what the children ought to learn. The art of reading may be made an instrument of evil, as well as of good; and if a people imbibe false principles-if they are taught, for instance, that this or that religious sect should be tolerated, or the reverse, because it was most or least in conformity with certain political institutions, thus rendering an institution of God's subservient to the institutions of men, instead of making the last subservient to the first-why, the less they know of letters, the better. Everything false was carefully avoided, and, with no great pretensions in the way of acquisitions, the schools of the Peak were made to be useful, and at least innocent. One thing the governor strictly enjoined; and that was, to teach these young creatures that they were fallible beings, carefully avoiding the modern fallacy of supposing that an infallible whole could be formed of fallible parts.

Such is an outline of the condition of the colony at the period which we have now reached. Everything appeared to be going on well. The Henlopen arrived, discharged, loaded, and went out again, carrying with her the last barrel of oil in the Bight. The whalers had a jubilee, for their adventures made large returns; and the business was carried on with renewed spirit. In a word, the colony had reached a point where every interest was said to be prosperous—a state of things with communities, as with individuals, when they are, perhaps, in the greatest danger of meeting with reverses, by means of their own abuses.

Chapter XXVI

> "Cruel of heart, and strong of arm,
> Proud in his sport, and keen for spoil,
> He little reck'd of good or harm,
> Fierce both in mirth and toil;
> Yet like a dog could fawn, if need there were;
> Speak mildly when he would, or look in fear."
>
> —Dana —*The Buccaneer.*

After the visitation, the governor passed a week at the Peak, with Bridget and his children. It was the habit of the wife to divide her time between the two dwellings; though Mark was so necessary to her as a companion, intellectually, and she was so necessary to Mark, for the same reason, that they were never very long separated. Bridget was all heart, and she had the sweetest temper imaginable; two qualities that endeared her to her husband, far more than her beauty. Her wishes were centred in her little family, though her kindness and benevolence could extend themselves to all around her. Anne she loved as a sister and as a friend; but it would not have been impossible for Bridget to be happy, had her fortune been cast on the Reef, with no one else but Mark and her two little ones.

The Peak, proper, had got to be a sort of public promenade for all who dwelt near it. Here the governor, in particular, was much accustomed to walk, early in the day, before the sun got to be too warm, and to look out upon the ocean as he pondered on his several duties. The spot had always been pleasant, on account of the beauty and extent of the view; but a new interest was given to it since the commencement of the whaling operations in the neighbourhood. Often had Bridget and Anne gone there to see a whale taken; it being no uncommon thing for one of the boys to come shouting down from the Peak, with the cry of "a fish—a fish!" It was by no means a rare occurrence for the shore-boats to take whales immediately beneath the cliffs, and the vessels could frequently be seen to windward, working up to their game. All this movement gave life and variety to the scene, and contributed largely to the spot's becoming a favourite place of resort. The very morning of the day that he intended to cross over to the Reef, on his return from the "progress," the governor and his wife ascended to the Peak just as the sun was rising. The morning was perfectly lovely; and never had the hearts of our married couple expanded more in love to their fellows, or been more profoundly filled with gratitude to God for all his goodness to them, than at that moment. Young Mark held by his mother's hand, while the father led his little daughter. This was the way they were accustomed to divide themselves in their daily excursions, it probably appearing to each parent that the child thus led was a miniature image of the other. On that morning, the governor and Bridget were talking of the bounties that Providence had bestowed on them, and of the numberless delights of their situation. Abundance reigned on every side; in addition to the productions of the island, in themselves so ample and generous, commerce had brought its acquisitions, and, as yet, trade occupied the place a wise discrimination would give it. All such interests are excellent as *incidents* in the great scheme of human happiness; but woe betide the people among whom they get to be *principals!* As the man who lives only to accumulate, is certain to have all his nobler and better feelings blunted by the grasping of cupidity, and to lose sight of the great objects of his existence, so do whole communities degenerate into masses of corruption, venality, and cupidity, when they set up the idol of commerce to worship in lieu of the ever-living God. So far from denoting a healthful prosperity, as is too apt to be supposed, no worse signs of the condition of a people can be given, than when all other interests are made to yield to those of the mere money-getting sort. Among our colonists, as yet, commerce occupied its proper place; it was only an incident in their state of society, and it was so regarded. Men did not search for every means of increasing it, whether its fruits were wanted or not, or live in a constant fever about its results. The articles brought in were all necessary to the comfort and civilization of the settlements, and those taken away were obtained by means of a healthful industry.

As they ascended the height, following an easy path that led to the Summit, the governor and his wife conversed about the late visitation, and of what each had seen that was striking and worthy of comment. Mark had a council to consult, in matters of state, but most did he love to compare opinions with the sweet matronly young creature at his side. Bridget was so true in all her feelings, so just in her inferences, and so kindly disposed, that a better counsellor could not have been found at the elbow of one intrusted with power.

"I am more uneasy on the subject of religion than on any other," observed the governor, as he helped his little companion up a difficult part of the ascent. "While out, I took great pains to sound the people on the subject, and I found a much greater variety of opinions, or rather of feelings, among them than I could have believed possible, after the quiet time we have hitherto had."

"After all, religion is, and ought to be, more a matter of feeling, than of reason, Mark."

"That is true, in one sense, certainly; but, it should be feeling subject to prudence and discretion."

"Everything should be subject to those two qualities, though so very few are. I have all along known that the ministrations of Mr. Hornblower were only tolerated by a good number of our people. You, as an Episcopalian, have not been so much in the way of observing this; for others have been guarded before *you*; but, my family is known not to have been of that sect, and I have been treated more frankly."

"And you have not let me know this important fact, Bridget!" said the governor, a little reproachfully.

"Why should I have added to your other cares, by heaping this on your shoulder, dear Mark? The thing could not easily be prevented; though I may as well tell you, now, what cannot much longer be kept a secret-the Henlopen will bring a Methodist and a Presbyterian clergyman in her, this voyage, if any be found willing to emigrate; and I have heard, lately, that Friends expect a preacher."

"The law against the admission of an immigrant, without the consent of the governor and council, is very clear and precise," answered the husband, looking grave.

"That may be true, my love, but it would hardly do to tell the people they are not to worship God in the manner that may best satisfy their own consciences."

"It is extraordinary that, as there is but one God, and one Saviour, there should be more than one mode of worshipping them!"

"Not at all extraordinary, my dear Mark, when you come to consider the great diversity of opinion which exists among men, in other matters. But, Mr. Hornblower has a fault, which is a very great fault, in one situated as he is, without a competitor in the field. He lays too much stress on his particular mission; talking too much, and preaching too much of his apostolic authority, as a divine."

"Men should never blink the truth, Bridget; and least of all, in a matter as grave as religion."

"Quite right, Mark, when it is necessary to say anything on the subject, at all. But, after all, the apostolic succession is but a *means*, and if the end be attainable without dwelling on these means, it seems to me to be better not to conflict with the prejudices of those we wish to influence. Remember, that there are not fifty real Episcopalians in all this colony, where there is only clergyman, and he of that sect."

"Very true; but, Mr. Hornblower naturally wishes to make them all churchmen."

"It really seems to me, that he ought to be content with making them all Christians."

"Perhaps he thinks the two identical-necessary to each other," added the governor, smiling on his charming young wife, who, in her own person, had quietly consented to the priestly control of her husband's clergyman, though but half converted to the peculiar distinctions of his sect, herself.

"He should remember, more especially in his situation, that others may not be of the same way of thinking. Very few persons, I believe, inquire into the reasons of what they have been taught on the subject of religion, but take things as they find them."

"And here they find an Episcopalian, and they ought to receive him confidingly."

"That might do with children, but most of our people came here with their opinions formed. I wish Mr. Hornblower were less set in his opinions, for I am content to be an Episcopalian, with you, my dear husband; certain, if the authority be not absolutely necessary, it can, at least, do no harm."

This ended the conversation at that time, for just then the party reached the Peak. Little, however, did the governor, or his pretty wife, imagine how much the future was connected with the interest of which they had just been speaking, or dream of the form in which the serpent of old was about to visit this Eden of modern times. But occurrences of another character almost immediately attracted their attention, and absorbed all the care and energy of the colony for some time. Scarcely was the party on the Peak, when the keen, lively eyes of the younger Bridget caught sight of a strange sail; and, presently, another and another came into view. In a word, no less than three vessels were in sight, the first that had ever been seen in those seas, with the exception of the regular and well-known craft of the colony. These strangers were a ship and two brigs; evidently vessels of some size, particularly the first; and they were consorts, keeping in company, and sailing in a sort of line, which would seem to denote more of order and concert than it was usual to find among merchantmen. They were all on a wind, standing to the southward and eastward, and were now, when first seen, fairly within the strait between the Peak and the group, unquestionably in full sight of both, and distant from each some five or six leagues. With the wind as it was, nothing would have been easier for them all, than to fetch far enough to windward to pass directly beneath the western cliffs, and, consequently, directly in front of the cove.

Luckily, there were several lads on the Peak, early as was the hour, who had ascended in quest of the berries of certain plants that flourished there. The governor instantly despatched one of these lads, with a note to Heaton, written in pencil, in which he desired that functionary to send a messenger down to the cove, to prevent any of the fishermen from going out; it being the practice of many of the boys to fish in the shade of the cliffs, to leeward, ere the sun rose high enough to make the heat oppressive. Hitherto, the existence of the cove, as it was believed, remained unknown even to the Kannakas, and a stringent order existed, that no boat should ever enter it so long as craft was in sight, which might have any of those men on board it. Indeed, the whole Peak was just as much a place of mystery, to all but the colonists, as it was the day when Waally and his followers were driven away by their superstitious dread.

Having taken this precaution, and kept the other lads to send down with any farther message he might deem necessary, the governor now gave all his attention to the strangers. A couple of glasses were always kept on the Peak, and the best of these was soon in his hand, and levelled at the ship. Bridget stood at her husband's side, eager to hear his opinion, but waiting with woman's patience for the moment it might be given with safety. At length that instant came, and the half-terrified wife questioned the husband on the subject of his discoveries.

"What is it, Mark'?" said Bridget, almost afraid of the answer she was so desirous of obtaining. "Is it the Rancocus?"

"If the Rancocus, love, be certain she would not be coming hither. The ship is of some size, and appears to be armed; though I cannot make out her nation."

"It is not surprising that she should be armed, Mark. You know that the papers Captain Saunders brought us were filled with accounts of battles fought in Europe."

"It is very true that the whole world is in arms, though that does not explain the singular appearance of these three vessels, in this remote corner of the earth. It is possible they may be discovery ships, for wars do not always put a stop to such enterprises. They appear to be steering for the Peak, which is some proof that they do not know of the existence of the settlements in the group. There they might anchor; but here, they cannot without entering the cove, of which they can know nothing."

"If discovery vessels, would they not naturally come first to the Peak, as the most striking object?"

"In that you are probably right, Bridget, though I think the commodore would be apt to divide his force, having three ships, and send one, at least, towards the group, even if he came hither with the others. No nation but England, however, would be likely to have vessels of that character out, in such a war, and these do not look like English craft, at all. Besides, we should have heard something of such an expedition, by means of the papers, were there one out. It would be bad enough to be visited by explorers; yet, I fear these are worse than explorers."

Bridget very well understood her husband's apprehensions on the subject of exploring parties. As yet, the colony had got on very well, without having the question of nationality called into the account; but it had now become so far important, as, in a small way, to be a nursery for seamen; and there was much reason to fear that the ruthless policy of the strong would, in the event of a discovery, make it share the usual fortunes of the weak. It was on account of this dread of foreign interference, that so much pains had been taken to conceal the history and state of the little community, the strongest inducements being placed before all the seamen who went to Europe, to be discreet and silent. As for the Kannakas, they did not know enough to be very dangerous, and could not, at all, give any accurate idea of the position of the islands, had they been better acquainted than they were with their relation to other communities, and desirous of betraying them.

The governor now sent another note down to Heaton, with a request that orders might be forwarded along the cliffs, for every one to keep out of sight; as well as directions that care should be taken not to let any smoke even be seen to rise from the plain. This message was speedily followed by another, directing that all the men should be assembled, and the usual preparations made for defence. He also asked if it were not possible to send a whale-boat out, by keeping immediately under the cliffs, and going well to windward, in such a manner as to get a communication across to the Reef, in order to put the people on their guard in that quarter. One or two whale-boats were always in the cove, and there were several crews of capital oarsmen among the people of the Peak. If such a boat could be prepared, it was to be held in readiness, as the governor himself might deem it expedient to cross the strait.

All this time the strange vessels were not idle, but drew nearer to the Peak, at a swift rate of sailing. It was not usual for mere merchantmen to be as weatherly, or to make as much way through the water, as did all these craft. On account of the great elevation at which the governor stood, they appeared small, but he was too much accustomed to his situation not to know how to make the necessary allowances. After examining her well, when she was within a league of the cliffs, he came to the opinion that the ship was a vessel of about six hundred tons, and that she was both armed and strongly manned. So far as he could judge, by the bird's-eye view he got, he fancied she was even frigate-built, and had a regular gundeck. In that age such craft were very common, sloops of war having that construction quite as often as that of the more modern deep-waisted vessel. As for the brigs, they were much smaller than their consort, being of less than two hundred tons each, apparently, but also armed and strongly manned. The armaments were now easily to be seen, as indeed were the crews, each and all the vessels showing a great many men aloft, to shorten sail as they drew nearer to the island.

One thing gave the governor great satisfaction. The strangers headed well up, as if disposed to pass to windward of the cliffs, from which he inferred that none on board them knew anything of the existence or position of the cove. So much care had been taken, indeed, to conceal this spot from, even the Kannakas, that no great apprehension existed of its being known to any beyond the circle of the regular colonists. As the ship drew still nearer, and came more under the cliffs, the governor was enabled to get a better view of her construction, and of the nature of her armament. That she was frigate-built was now certain, and the strength of her crew became still more evident, as the men were employed in shortening and making sail almost immediately under his eye.

Great care was taken that no one should be visible on the Peak. Of the whole island, that was the only spot where there was much danger of a man's being seen from the ocean; for the fringe of wood had been religiously preserved all around the cliffs. But, with the exception of the single tree already mentioned, the Peak was entirely naked; and, in that clear atmosphere, the form of a man might readily be distinguished even at a much greater elevation. But the glasses were levelled at the strangers from covers long before prepared for that purpose, and no fear was entertained of the look-outs, who had their instructions, and well understood the importance of caution.

At length, the vessels got so near, as to allow of the glasses being pointed directly down upon the upper deck of the ship, in particular. The strangers had a little difficulty in weathering the northern extremity of the island, and they came much closer to the cliffs than they otherwise would, in order to do so. While endeavouring to ascertain the country of the ship, by examining her people, the governor fancied he saw some natives on board her. At first, he supposed there might be Kannakas, or Mowrees, among the crew; but, a better look assured him that the Indians present were not acting in the character of sailors at all. They appeared to be chiefs, and chiefs in their war-dresses. This fact induced a still closer examination, until the governor believed that he could trace the person of Waally among them. The distance itself was not such as to render it difficult to recognize a form, or a face, when assisted by the glass; but the inverted position of all on board the ship did make a view less certain than might otherwise have been the case. Still the governor grew, at each instant, more and more assured that Waally was there, as indeed he believed his son to be, also. By this time, one of the men who knew the chief had come up to the Peak, with a message from Heaton, and he was of the same opinion as the governor, after taking a good look through the best glass. Bridget, too, had seen the formidable Waally, and *she* gave it as her opinion that he was certainly on board the ship. This was considered as a most important discovery. If Waally were there, it was for no purpose that was friendly to the colonists. The grudge he owed the last, was enduring and deadly. Nothing but the strong arm of power could suppress its outbreakings, or had kept him in subjection, for the last five years. Of late, the intercourse between the two groups had not been great; and it was now several months since any craft had been across to Ooroony's islands, from the Reef. There had been sufficient time, consequently, for great events to have been planned and executed, and, yet, that the colonists should know nothing of them.

But, it was impossible to penetrate further into this singular mystery, so long as the strangers kept off the land. This they did of course, the three vessels passing to windward of the Peak, in a line ahead, going to the southward, and standing along the cliffs, on an easy bowline. The governor now sent a whale-boat out of the cove, under her sails, with orders to stand directly across to the Reef, carrying the tidings, and bearing a letter of instructions to Pennock and such members of the council as might be present. The letter was short, but it rather assumed the probability of hostilities, while it admitted that there was a doubt of the issue. A good look-out was to be kept, at all events, and the forces of the colony were to be assembled. The governor promised to cross himself, as soon as the strangers quitted the neighbourhood of the Peak.

In the mean time, Heaton mounted a horse, and kept company with the squadron as it circled the island. From time to time, he sent messages to the governor, in order to let him know the movements of the strangers. While this was going on, the men were all called in from their several occupations, and the prescribed arrangements were made for defence. As a circuit of the island required several hours, there was time for everything; and the whale-boat was fairly out of sight from even the Peak, when Heaton despatched a messenger to say that the squadron had reached the southern extremity of the island, and was standing off south-east, evidently steering towards the volcano.

Doubts now began to be felt whether the colonists would see anything more of the strangers. It was natural that navigators should examine unknown islands, cursorily at least; but it did not follow that, if trade was their object, they should delay their voyage in order to push their investigations beyond a very moderate limit. Had it not been for the undoubted presence of savages in the ship, and the strong probability that Waally was one of them, the governor would now have had hopes that he had seen the last of his visitors. Nevertheless, there was the chance that these vessels would run down to Rancocus Island, where not only might a landing be easily effected, but where the mills, the brick-yards, and indeed the principal cluster of houses, were all plainly to be seen from the offing. No sooner was it certain, therefore, that the strangers had stood away to the southward and eastward, than another boat was sent across to let the millers, brickmakers, stone-quarriers, and lumbermen know that they might receive guests who would require much discretion in their reception.

The great policy of secrecy was obviously in serious danger of being defeated. How the existence of the colony was to be concealed, should the vessels remain any time in the group, it was not easy to see; and that advantage the governor and Heaton, both of whom attached the highest importance to it, were now nearly ready to abandon in despair. Still, neither thought of yielding even this policy until the last moment, and circumstances rendered it indispensable; for so much reflection had been bestowed on that, as well as on every other interest of the colony, that it was not easy to unsettle any part of their plans-in the opinion of its rulers, at least.

A sharp look-out for the squadron was kept, not only from the Peak, but from the southern end of the cliffs, all that day. The vessels were seen until they were quite near to the volcano, when their sudden disappearance was ascribed to the circumstance of their shortening sail. Perhaps they anchored. This could only be conjecture, however, as no boat could be trusted out to watch them, near by. Although there was no anchorage near the Peak, it was possible for a vessel to anchor anywhere in the vicinity of the volcano. The island of Vulcan's Peak appears to have been projected upwards, out of the depths of the ocean, in one solid, perpendicular wall, leaving no shallow water near it; but, as respects the other islands, the coast shoaled gradually in most places; though the eastern edge of the group was an exception to the rule. Still, vessels could anchor in any or all the coves and roadsteads of the group; and *there* the holding ground was unusually good, being commonly mud and sand, and these without rocks.

The remainder of the day, and the whole of the succeeding night, were passed with much anxiety, by the governor and his friends. Time was given to receive an answer to the messages sent across to the Reef, but nothing was seen of the strangers, when day returned. The boat that came in from the Reef, reported that the coast was clear to the northward. It also brought a letter, stating that notices had been sent to all the different settlements, and that the Anne had sailed to windward, to call in all the fishermen, and to go off to the nearest whaling-ground, in order to communicate the state of things in the colony to Captain Betts and his companions, who were out. The Dragon and the Jonas, when last heard from, were cruising only about a hundred miles to windward of the group, and it was thought important, on various accounts, that they should be at once apprised of the arrival of the strangers.

The governor was perfectly satisfied with the report of what had been done, and this so much the more because it superseded the necessity of his quitting the Peak, just at the moment. The elevation of the mountain was of so much use as a look-out, that it was every way desirable to profit by it, until the time for observing was passed, and that for action had succeeded, in its stead. Of course, some trusty person was kept constantly on the Peak, looking out for the strangers, though the day passed without one of them being seen. Early next morning, however, a whale-boat arrived from Rancocus, with four stout oarsmen in it. They had left the station, after dark, and had been pulling up against the trades most of the intervening time. The news they brought was not only alarming, but it occasioned a great deal of surprise.

It seemed that the three strange vessels appeared off the point, at Rancocus Island, early on the morning of the preceding day. It was supposed that they had run across from the volcano in the darkness, after having been lost sight of from the Peak. Much prudence was observed by the colonists, as soon as light let them into the secret of their having such unknown neighbours. Bigelow happening to be there, and being now a man of a good deal of consideration with his fellow-citizens, he assumed the direction of matters. All the women and children ascended into the mountains, where secret places had long been provided for such an emergency, by clearing out and rendering two or three caves habitable, and where food and water were at hand. Thither most of the light articles of value were also transported. Luckily, Bigelow had caused all the saws at the mill, to be taken down and secreted. A saw was an article not to be replaced, short of a voyage to Europe, even; for in that day saws were not manufactured in America; nor, indeed, was scarcely anything else.

When he had given his directions, Bigelow went alone to the point, to meet the strangers, who had anchored their vessels, and had landed in considerable force. On approaching the place, he found about a hundred men ashore, all well armed, and seemingly governed by a sort of military authority. On presenting himself before this party, Bigelow was seized, and taken to its leader, who was a sea-faring man, by his appearance, of a fierce aspect and most severe disposition. This man could speak no English. Bigelow tried him in Spanish, but could get no answer out of him in that tongue either; though he suspected that what he said was understood. At length, one was brought forward who *could* speak English, and that so well as to leave little doubt in Bigelow's mind about the stranger's being either an Englishman or an American. Communications between the parties were commenced through this interpreter.

Bigelow was closely questioned touching the number of people in the different islands, the number of vessels they possessed, the present situation and employments of those vessels, the nature of their cargoes, the places where the property transported in the vessels was kept, and, in short, everything that bore directly on the wealth and movable possessions of the people. From the nature of these questions as well as from the appearance of the strangers, Bigelow had, at once, taken up the notion that they were pirates. In the eastern seas, piracies were often committed on a large scale, and there was nothing violent in this supposition. The agitated state of the world, moreover, rendered piracies much more likely to go unpunished then than would be the case to-day, and it was well known that several vessels often cruised together, when engaged in these lawless pursuits, in those distant quarters of the world. Then the men were evidently of different races, though Bigelow was of opinion that most of them came from the East Indies, the coasts, or the islands. The officers were mostly Europeans by birth, or the descendants of Europeans; but two-thirds of the people whom he saw were persons of eastern extraction; some appeared to be Lascars, and others what sailors call Chinamen.

Bigelow was very guarded in his answers; so much so, indeed, as to give great dissatisfaction to his interrogators. About the Peak he assumed an air of great mystery, and said none but birds could get on it; thunder was sometimes heard coming out of its cliffs, but man could not get up to see what the place contained. This account was received with marked interest, and to Bigelow's surprise, it did not appear to awaken the distrust he had secretly apprehended it might. On the contrary, he was asked to repeat his account, and all who heard it, though a good deal embellished this time, appeared disposed to believe what he said. Encouraged by this success, the poor fellow undertook to mystify a little concerning the Reef; but here he soon found himself met with plump denials. In order to convince him that deception would be of no use, he was now taken a short distance and confronted with Waally!

Bigelow no sooner saw the dark countenance of the chief than he knew he was in bad hands. From that moment, he abandoned all attempts at concealment, the condition of the Peak excepted, and had recourse to an opposite policy. He now exaggerated everything; the number and force of the vessels, giving a long list of names that were accurate enough, though the fact was concealed that they mostly belonged to boats; and swelling the force of the colony to something more than two thousand fighting men. The piratical commander, who went by the name of 'the admiral' among his followers, was a good deal startled by this information, appealing to Waally to know whether it might be relied on for truth. Waally could not say yes or no to this question. He had heard that the colonists were much more numerous than they were formerly; but how many fighting men they could now muster was more than he could say. He knew that they were enormously rich, and among other articles of value, possessed materials sufficient for fitting out as many ships as they pleased. It was this last information that had brought the strangers to the group; for they were greatly in want of naval stores of almost all sorts.

The admiral did not deem it necessary to push his inquiries any further at that moment; apparently, he did not expect to find much at Rancocus Island, Waally having, most probably, let him into the secret of its uses. The houses and mills were visited and plundered; a few hogs and one steer were shot; but luckily, most of the animals had been driven into a retired valley. The saw-mill was set on fire in pure wantonness, and it was burned to the ground. A new grist-mill escaped, merely because its position was not known. A great deal of injury was inflicted on the settlement merely for the love of mischief, and a brick-kiln was actually blown up in order to enjoy the fun of seeing the bricks scattered in the air. In short, the place was almost destroyed in one sense, though no attempt was made to injure Bigelow. On the contrary, he was scarcely watched, and it was no sooner dark than he collected a crew, got into his own whale-boat, and came to windward to report what was going on to the governor.

Chapter XXVII

> "All gone! 'tis ours the goodly land —
> Look round-the heritage behold;
> Go forth-upon the mountains stand;
> Then, if ye can, be cold."
>
> —Sprague

Little doubt remained in the mind of the governor, after he had heard and weighed the whole of Bigelow's story, that he had to deal with one of those piratical squadrons that formerly infested the eastern seas, a sort of successor of the old buccaneers. The men engaged in such pursuits, were usually of different nations, and they were always of the most desperate and ruthless characters. The fact that Waally was with this party, indicated pretty plainly the manner in which they had heard of the colony, and, out of all question, that truculent chief had made his own bargain to come in for a share of the profits.

It was highly probable that the original object of these freebooters had been to plunder the pearl-fishing vessels, and, hearing at their haunts, of Betto's group, they had found their way across to it, where, meeting with Waally, they had been incited to their present enterprise.

Little apprehension was felt for the Peak. A vessel might hover about it a month, and never find the cove; and should the pirates even make the discovery, such were the natural advantages of the islanders, that the chances were as twenty to one, they would drive off their assailants. Under all the circumstances, therefore, and on the most mature reflection, the governor determined to cross over to the Reef, and assume the charge of the defence of that most important position. Should the Reef fall into the hands of the enemy, it might require years to repair the loss; or, what would be still more afflicting, the freebooters might hold the place, and use it as a general rendezvous, in their nefarious pursuits. Accordingly, after taking a most tender leave of his wife and children, Governor Woolston left the cove, in the course of the forenoon, crossing in a whale-boat rigged with a sail. Bridget wished greatly to accompany her husband, but to this the latter would, on no account, consent; for he expected serious service, and thought it highly probable that most of the females would have to be sent over to the Peak, for security. Finding that her request could not be granted, and feeling fully the propriety of her husband's decision, Mrs. Woolston so far commanded her feelings as to set a good example to other wives, as became her station.

When about mid-channel, the whale-boat made a sail coming down before the wind, and apparently steering for South Cape, as well as herself. This turned out to be the Anne, which had gone to windward to give the alarm to the fishermen, and was now on her return. She had warned so many boats as to be certain they would spread the notice, and she had spoken the Dragon, which had gone in quest of the Jonas and the Abraham, both of which were a few leagues to windward. Capt. Betts, however, had come on board the Anne, and now joined his old friend, the governor, when about four leagues from the cape. Glad enough was Mark Woolston to meet with the Anne, and to find so good an assistant on board her. That schooner, which was regularly pilot-boat built, was the fastest craft about the islands, and it was a great matter to put head-quarters on board her. The Martha came next, and the whale-boat was sent in to find that sloop, which was up at the Reef, and to order her out immediately to join the governor. Pennock was the highest in authority, in the group, after the governor, and a letter was sent to him, apprising him of all that was known, and exhorting him to vigilance and activity; pointing out, somewhat in detail, the different steps he was to take, in order that no time might be lost. This done, the governor stood in towards Whaling Bight, in order to ascertain the state of things at that point.

The alarm had been given all over the group, and when the Anne reached her place of destination, it was ascertained that the men had been assembled under arms, and every precaution taken. But Whaling Bight was the great place of resort of the Kannakas, and there were no less than forty of those men there at that moment, engaged in trying out oil, or in fitting craft for the fisheries. No one could say which side these fellows would take, should it appear that their proper chiefs were engaged with the strangers; though, otherwise, the colonists counted on their assistance with a good deal of confidence. On all ordinary occasions, a reasonably fair understanding existed between the colonists and the Kannakas. It is true, that the former were a little too fond of getting as much work as possible, for rather small compensations, out of these semi-savages; but, as articles of small intrinsic value still went a great way in these bargains, no serious difficulty had yet arisen out of the different transactions. Some persons thought that the Kannakas had risen in their demands, and put less value on a scrap of old iron, than had been their original way of thinking, now that so many of their countrymen had been back and forth a few times, between the group and other parts of the world; a circumstance that was very naturally to be expected. But the governor knew mankind too well not to understand that all unequal associations lead to discontent. Men may get to be so far accustomed to inferior stations, and to their duties and feelings, as to consider their condition the result of natural laws; but the least taste of liberty begets a jealousy and distrust that commonly raises a barrier between the master and servant, that has a never-dying tendency to keep them more or less alienated in feeling. When the colonists began to cast about them, and to reflect on the chances of their being sustained by these hirelings in the coming strife, very few of them could be sufficiently assured that the very men who had now eaten of their bread and salt, in some instances, for years, were to be relied on in a crisis. Indeed, the number of these Kannakas was a cause of serious embarrassment with the governor, when he came to reflect on his strength, and on the means, of employing it.

Fully two hundred of the savages, or semi-savages, were at that moment either scattered about among the farm-houses; or working in the different places where shipping lay, or were out whaling to windward. Now, the whole force of the colony, confining it to fighting-men, and including those who were absent, was just three hundred and sixty-three. Of these, three hundred might, possibly, on an emergency, be brought to act on any given point, leaving the remainder in garrisons. But a straggling body of a hundred and fifty of these Kannakas, left in the settlements, or on the Reef, or about the crater, while the troops were gone to meet the enemy, presented no very pleasing picture to the mind of the governor. He saw the necessity of collecting these men together, and of employing them actively in the service of the colony, as the most effectual mode of preventing their getting within the control of Waally. This duty was confided to Bigelow, who was sent to the Reef without delay, taking with him all the Kannakas at Whaling Bight, with orders to put them on board the shipping at the Reef-schooners, sloops, lighters, &c., of which there were now, ordinarily, some eight or ten to be found there-and to carry them all to windward; using the inner channels of the group. Here was a twenty-four hours' job, and one that would not only keep everybody quite busy, but which might have the effect to save all the property in the event of a visit to the Reef by the pirates. Bigelow was to call every Kannaka he saw to his assistance, in the hope of thus getting most of them out of harm's way.

Notwithstanding this procedure, which denoted a wise distrust of these Indian allies, the governor manifested a certain degree of confidence towards a portion of them, that was probably just as discreet in another way. A part of the crew of every vessel, with the exception of those that went to the Peak, was composed of Kannakas; and no less than ten of them were habitually employed in the Anne, which carried two whale-boats for emergencies. None of these men were sent away, or were in any manner taken from their customary employments. So much confidence had the governor in his own authority, and in his power to influence these particular individuals, that he did not hesitate about keeping them near himself, and, in a measure, of entrusting the safety of his person to their care. It is true, that the Kannakas of both the Anne and the Martha were a sort of confidential seamen, having now been employed in the colony several years, and got a taste for the habits of the settlers.

When all his arrangements were made, the governor came out of Whaling Bight in the Anne, meeting Betts in the Martha off South Cape. Both vessels then stood down along the shores of the group, keeping a bright look-out in the direction of Rancocus Island, or towards the southward and westward. Two or three smaller crafts were in company, each under the direction of some one on whom reliance could be placed. The old Neshamony had the honour of being thus employed, among others. The south-western angle of the group formed a long, low point, or cape of rock, making a very tolerable roadstead on its north-western side, or to leeward. This cape was known among the colonists by the name of Rancocus *Needle*, from the circumstance that it pointed with mathematical precision to the island in question. Thus, it was a practice with the coasters to run for the extremity of this cape, and then to stand away on a due south-west course, certain of seeing the mountains for which they were steering in the next few hours. Among those who plied to and fro in this manner, were many who had no very accurate notions of navigation; and, to them, this simple process was found to be quite useful.

Off Rancocus Needle, the governor had appointed a rendezvous for the whole of his little fleet. In collecting these vessels, six in all, including four boats, his object had not been resistance-for the armaments of the whole amounted to but six swivels, together with a few muskets-but vigilance. He was confident that Waally would lead his new friends up towards the Western Roads, the point where he had made all his own attacks, and where he was most acquainted; and the position under the Needle was the best station for observing the approach of the strangers, coming as they must, if they came at all, from the south-west.

The Anne was the first craft to arrive off the point of the Needle, and she found the coast clear. As yet, no signs of invaders were to be seen; and the Martha being within a very convenient distance to the eastward, a signal was made to Captain Betts to stand over towards the Peak, and have a search in that quarter. Should the strangers take it into their heads to beat up under the cliffs again, and thence stretch across to the group, it would bring them in with the land to windward of the observing squadron, and give them an advantage the governor was very far from wishing them to obtain. The rest of the craft came down to the place of rendezvous, and kept standing off and on, under short sail, close in with the rocks, so as to keep in the smoothest of the water. Such was the state of things when the sun went down in the ocean.

All night the little fleet of the colonists remained in the same uncertainty as to the movements of their suspicious visitors. About twelve the Martha came round the Needle, and reported the coast clear to the southward. She had been quite to the cove, and had communicated with the shore. Nothing had been seen of the ship and her consorts since the governor left, nor had any further tidings been brought up from to leeward, since the arrival of Bigelow. On receiving this information, the governor ordered his command to run off, in diverging lines, for seven leagues each, and then to wait for day. This was accordingly done; the Anne and Martha, as a matter of course, outstripping the others. At the usual hour day re-appeared, when the look-out aloft, on board the Anne, reported the Martha about two leagues to the northward, the Neshamony about as far to the southward, though a league farther to windward. The other craft were known to be to the northward of the Martha, but could not be seen. As for the Neshamony, she was coming down with a flowing sheet, to speak the governor.

The sun had fairly risen, when the Neshamony came down on the Anne's weather-quarter, both craft then standing to the northward. The Neshamony had seen nothing. The governor now directed her commander to stand directly down towards Rancocus Island. If she saw nothing, she was to go in and land, in order to get the news from the people ashore. Unless the information obtained in this way was of a nature that demanded a different course, she was to beat up to the volcano, reconnoitre there, then stand across to the cove, and go in; whence she was to sail for the Reef, unless she could hear of the governor at some other point, when she was to make the best of her way to *him*.

The Anne now made sail towards the Martha, which sloop was standing to the northward, rather edging from the group, under short canvass. No land was in sight, though its haze could be discovered all along the eastern board, where the group was known to lie; but neither the

Peak, nor the Volcano, nor Rancocus heights could now be seen from the vessels. About ten the governor spoke Captain Betts, to ask the news. The Martha had seen nothing; and, shortly after, the three boats to the northward joined, and made the same report. Nothing had been seen of the strangers, who seemed, most unaccountably, to be suddenly lost!

This uncertainty rendered all the more reflecting portion of the colonists exceedingly uneasy. Should the pirates get into the group by either of its weather channels, they would not only find all the property and vessels that had been taken in that direction, at their mercy, but they would assail the settlements in their weakest parts, render succour more difficult, and put themselves in a position whence it would be easiest to approach or to avoid their foes. Any one understanding the place, its facilities for attacking, or its defences, would naturally endeavour to enter the group as well to windward as possible; but Waally had never attempted anything of the sort; and, as he knew little of the inner passages, it was not probable he had thought of suggesting a course different from his own to his new friends. The very circumstance that he had always approached by the same route, was against it; for, if his sagacity had not pointed out a preferable course for himself, it was not to be expected it would do it for others. Still, it was not unreasonable to suppose that practised seamen might see the advantages which the savage had overlooked, and a very serious apprehension arose in the minds of the governor and Betts, in particular, touching this point. All that could be done, however, was to despatch two of the boats, with orders to enter the group by the northern road, and proceed as far as the Reef. The third boat was left to cruise off the Needle, in order to communicate with anything that, should go to that place of rendezvous with a report, and, at the same time, to keep a look-out for the pirates. With the person in charge of this boat, was left the course to be steered by those who were to search for the governor, as they arrived off the Needle, from time to time.

The Anne and Martha bore up, in company, as soon as these arrangements were completed, it being the plan now to go and look for the strangers. Once in view, the governor determined not to lose sight of the pirates, again, but to remain so near them, as to make sure of knowing what they were about, In such cases, a close look-out should always be kept on the enemy, since an advantage in time is gained by so doing, as well as a great deal of uncertainty and indecision avoided.

For seven hours the Anne and Martha stood towards Rancocus Island, running off about two leagues from each other, thereby 'spreading a clew,' as sailors call it, that would command the view of a good bit of water. The tops of the mountains were soon seen, and by the end of the time mentioned, most of the lower land became visible. Nevertheless, the strangers did not come in sight. Greatly at a loss how to proceed, the governor now sent the Martha down for information, with orders for her to beat up to the Needle, as soon as she could, the Anne intending to rendezvous there, next morning, agreeably to previous arrangements. As the Martha went off before the wind, the Anne hauled up sharp towards the Peak, under the impression that something might have been seen of the strangers from the high land there. About four in the morning the Anne went into the cove, and the governor ascended to the plain to have an interview with Heaton. He found everything tranquil in that quarter. Nothing had been seen of the strange squadron, since it went out of sight, under the volcano; nor had even the Neshamony come in. The governor's arrival was soon known, early as it was, and he had visits from half the women on the island, to inquire after their absent husbands. Each wife was told all the governor knew, and this short intercourse relieved the minds of a great many.

At eight, the Anne sailed again, and at ten she had the Needle in sight, with three boats off it, on the look-out. Here, then, were tidings at last; but, the impatience of the governor was restrained, in order to make out the character of a sail that had been seen coming down through the straits, under a cloud of canvas. In a short time, this vessel was made out to be the Abraham, and the Anne hauled up to get her news. The two schooners spoke each other about twelve o'clock, but the Abraham had no intelligence to impart. She had been sent, or rather carried by Bigelow, out by the eastern passage, and had stood along the whole of the weather-side of the group, to give notice to the whalers where to go; and she had notified the two brigs to go in to-windward, and to remain in Weather Bay, where all the rest of the dull crafts had been taken for safety; and then had come to-leeward to look for the governor. As the Abraham was barely a respectable sailer, it was not deemed prudent to take her too near the strangers; but, she might see how matters were situated to the eastward. By keeping on the weather-coast, and so near the land as not to be cut off from it, she would be of particular service; since no enemy could approach in that quarter, without being seen; and Bigelow's familiarity with the channels would enable him, not only to save his schooner by running in, but would put it in his power to give notice throughout the whole group, of the position and apparent intentions of the strangers. The Abraham, accordingly, hauled by the wind, to beat back to her station, while the Anne kept off for the Needle.

At the rendezvous, the governor found most of his craft waiting for him. The Neshamony was still behind; but all the rest had executed their orders, and were standing off and on, near the cape, ready to report. Nothing had been seen of the strangers! It was certain they had not approached the group, for two of the boats had just come out of it, having left the colonists busy with the preparations for defence, but totally undisturbed in other respects. This information gave the governor increased uneasiness. His hope of hearing from the pirates, in time to be ready to meet them, now depended on his reports from to leeward. The Neshamony ought soon to be in; nor could it be long before the Martha would return. The great source of apprehension now came from a suspicion that some of the Kannakas might be acting as pirates, along with Waally. For Waally himself no great distrust was felt, since he had never been allowed to see much of the channels of the group; but it was very different with the sea-going Kannakas, who had been employed by the colonists. Some of these men were familiar with all the windings and turnings of the channels, knew how much water could be taken through a passage, and, though not absolutely safe pilots, perhaps, were men who might enable skilful seamen to handle their vessels with tolerable security within the islands. Should it turn out that one or two of these fellows had undertaken to carry the strangers up to windward, and to take them into one of the passages in that quarter of the group, they might be down upon the different fortified points before they were expected, and sweep all before them. It is true, this danger had been in a measure foreseen, and persons had been sent to look out for it; but it never had appeared so formidable to the governor, as now that he found himself completely at fault where to look for his enemy. At length, a prospect of fresh reports appeared. The Neshamony was seen in the southern board, standing across from the Peak; and about the same time, the Martha was made out in the south-western, beating up from Rancocus Island direct. As the first had been ordered to land, and had also been round by the volcano, the Anne hauled up for her, the governor being impatient to get her tidings first. In half an hour, the two vessels were alongside of each other. But the Neshamony had very little that was new to tell! The pirates had remained on the island but a short time after Bigelow and his companions got away, doing all the damage they could, however, in that brief space. When they left, it was night, and nothing very certain could be told of their movements. When last seen, however, they were on a wind, and heading to the southward a little westerly; which looked like beating up towards the volcano, the trades now blowing due south-east. But the Neshamony had been quite round the volcano, without obtaining a sight of the strangers. Thence she proceeded to the Peak, where she arrived only a few hours after the governor had sailed, going into the cove and finding all quiet. Of course, the Martha could have no more to say than this, if as much; and the governor was once more left to the pain of deep suspense. As was expected, when Betts joined, he had nothing at all to tell. He had been ashore at Rancocus Point, heard the complaints of the people touching their losses, but had obtained no other tidings of the wrong-doers. Unwilling to lose time, he staid but an hour, and had been beating back to the rendezvous the rest of the period of his absence. Was it possible that the strangers had gone back to Betto's group, satisfied with the trifling injuries they had inflicted? This could hardly be; yet it was not easy to say where else they had been. After a consultation, it was decided that the Martha should stand over in that direction, in the hope that she might pick up some intelligence, by meeting with fishing canoes that often came out to a large cluster of rocks, that lay several leagues to windward of the territories of Ooroony and Waally. Captain Betts had taken his leave of the governor, and had actually got on board his own vessel, in order to make sail, when, a signal was seen flying on board one of the boats that was kept cruising well out in the straits, intimating that strange vessels were seen to windward. This induced the governor to recall the Martha, and the whole of the look-out vessels stood off into the straits.

In less than an hour, all doubts were removed. There were the strangers, sure enough, and what was more, there was the Abraham ahead of them, pushing for Cape South passage, might and main; for the strangers were on her heels, going four feet to her three. It appeared, afterwards, that the pirates, on quitting Rancocus Island, had stood off to the southward, until they reached to windward of the volcano, passing however a good bit to leeward of the island, on their first stretch, when, finding the Peak just dipping, they tacked to the northward and westward, and stood off towards the ordinary whaling-ground of the colony, ever which they swept in the expectation of capturing the brigs. The pirates had no occasion for oil, which they probably would have destroyed in pure wantonness, but they were much in want of naval stores, cordage in particular, and the whaling gear of the two brigs would have been very acceptable to them. While running in for the group, after an unsuccessful search, they made the Abraham, and gave chase. That schooner steered for the straits, in the hope of finding the governor; but was so hard pressed by her pursuers, as to be glad to edge in for Cape South roads, intending to enter the group, and run for the Reef, if she could do no better.

Luckily, the discovery of the look-out boat prevented the execution of the Abraham's project, which would have led the pirates directly up to the capital. But, no sooner did the governor see how things were situated, than he boldly luffed up towards the strangers, intending to divert them from the chase of the Abraham; or, at least, to separate them, in chase of himself. In this design he was handsomely seconded by Betts, in the Martha, who hauled his wind in the wake of the Anne, and carried everything that would draw, in order to keep his station. This decision and show of spirit had its effect. The two brigs, which were most to the southward, altered their course, and edged away for the Anne and Martha, leaving the ship to follow the Abraham alone. The governor was greatly rejoiced at this, for he had a notion a vessel as large as the strange ship would hesitate about entering the narrow waters, on account of her draught; she being much larger than any craft that had ever been in before, as the Kannakas must know, and would not fail to report to the pirates. The governor supposed this ship to be a vessel of between six and seven hundred tons measurement. Her armament appeared to be twelve guns of a side, below, and some eight or ten guns on her quarter-deck and forecastle. This was a formidable craft in those days, making what was called in the English service, an eight-and-twenty gun frigate, a class of cruisers that were then found to be very useful. It is true, that the first class modern sloop-of-war would blow one of those little frigates out of water, being several hundred tons larger, with armaments, crews and spars in proportion; but an eight-and-twenty gun frigate offered a very formidable force to a community like that of the crater, and no one knew it better than the governor.

The three strangers all sailed like witches. It was well for the Abraham that she had a port so close under her lee, or the ship would have had her, beyond the smallest doubt. As it was she caught it, as she rounded the cape, as close in as she could go, the frigate letting slip at her the whole of her starboard broadside, which cut away the schooner's gaff, jib-stay, and main-topmast, besides killing, a Kannaka, who was in the main-cross-trees at the time. This last occurrence turned out to be fortunate, in the main, however, since it induced all the Kannakas to believe that the strangers were their enemies, in particular; else why kill one of their number, when there were just as many colonists as Kannakas to shoot at!

As the governor expected, the ship did not venture to follow the Abraham in. That particular passage, in fact, was utterly unknown to Waally, and those with him, and he could not give such an account of it as would encourage the admiral to stand on. Determined not to lose time unnecessarily, the latter hauled short off shore, and made sail in chase of the Anne and Martha, which, by this time, were about mid-channel, heading across to the Peak. It was not the wish of the governor, however, to lead the strangers any nearer to the cove than was necessary, and, no sooner did he see the Abraham well within the islands, her sails concealed by the trees, of which there was now a little forest on this part of the coast, and the ship drawing well off the land in hot pursuit of himself, than he kept away in the direction of Rancocus Island, bringing the wind on his larboard quarter. The strangers followed, and in half an hour they were all so far to leeward of Cape South, as to remove any apprehension of their going in there very soon.

Thus far, the plan of the governor had succeeded to admiration. He had his enemies in plain sight, within a league of him, and in chase of his two fastest craft. The best sailing of the Anne and Martha was on a wind, and, as a matter of course, they could do better, comparatively, in smooth water, than larger craft. No sooner, therefore, had he got his pursuers far enough off the land, and far enough to leeward, than the governor wore, or jibed would be the better word, running off northwest, with the wind on his starboard quarter. This gave the strangers a little the advantage, in one sense, though they lost it in another. It brought them on his weather-beam; pretty well forward of it, too; but the Needle was directly ahead of the schooner and sloop, and the governor foresaw that his pursuers would have to keep off to double that, which he was reasonably certain of reaching first.

Everything turned out as the governor anticipated. The pirates had near a league of water more to pass over, before they could double the Needle, than the Anne and the Martha had; and, though those two crafts were obliged to haul up close to the rocks, under a distant fire from all three of their pursuers, no harm was done, and they were soon covered by the land, and were close-hauled in smooth water, to leeward of the group. Twenty minutes later, the strangers came round the cape, also, bearing up sharp, and following their chase. This was placing the enemy just where the colonists could have wished. They were now to-leeward of every point in the settlements, looking up towards the roads, which opened on the western passage, or that best known to Waally, and which he would be most likely to enter, should he attempt to pilot the strangers in. This was getting the invaders precisely where the governor wished them to be, if they were to attack him at all. They could not reach the Reef in less than twenty-four hours, with their knowledge of the channel; would have to approach it in face of the heaviest and strongest batteries, those provided for Waally; and, if successful in reaching the inner harbour, would enter it under the fire of the long twelves mounted on the crater, which was, rightly enough, deemed to be the citadel of the entire colony-unless, indeed, the Peak might better deserve that name.

Chapter XXVIII

> "It scares the sea-birds from their nests;
> They dart and wheel with deafening screams;
> Now dark-and now their wings and breasts
> Flash back amid disastrous gleams.
> O, sin! what hast thou done on this fair earth?
> The world, O man! is wailing o'er thy birth."
>
> —Dana

It was the policy of the colonists to lead their pursuers directly up to the Western Roads. On the small island, under which vessels were accustomed to anchor, was a dwelling or two, and a battery of two guns-nine-pounders. These guns were to command the anchorage. The island lay directly in front of the mouth of the passage, making a very beautiful harbour within it; though the water was so smooth in the roads, and the last were so much the most convenient for getting under-way in, that this more sheltered haven was very little used. On the present occasion, however, all the colony craft beat up past the island, and anchored inside of it. The crews were then landed, and they repaired to the battery, which they found ready for service in consequence of orders previously sent.

Here, then, was the point where hostilities would be likely to commence, should hostilities commence at all. One of the boats was sent across to the nearest island inland, where a messenger was landed, with directions to carry a letter to Pennock, at the Reef. This messenger was compelled to walk about six miles, the whole distance in a grove of young palms and bread-fruit trees; great pains having been taken to cultivate both of these plants throughout the group, in spots favourable to their growth. After getting through the grove, the path came out on a plantation, where a horse was kept for this especial object; and here the man mounted and galloped off to the Reef, soon finding himself amid a line of some of the most flourishing plantations in the colony. Fortunately, however, as things then threatened, these plantations were not on the main channel, but stood along the margin of a passage which was deep enough to receive any craft that floated, but which was a *cul-de-sac*, that could be entered only from the eastward. Along the margin of the ship-channel, there was not yet soil of the right quality for cultivation, though it was slowly forming, as the sands that lay thick on the adjacent rocks received other substances by exposure to the atmosphere.

The Anne and her consorts had been anchored about an hour, when the strangers hove-to in the roads, distant about half a mile from the battery. Here they all hoisted white flags, as if desirous of having a parley. The governor did not well know how to act. He could not tell whether or not it would do to trust such men; and he as little liked to place Betts, or any other confidential friend, in their power, as he did to place himself there. Nevertheless, prudence required that some notice should be taken of the flag of truce; and he determined to go off a short distance from the shore in one of his own boats, and hoist a white flag, which would be as much as to say that he was waiting there to receive any communication that the strangers might chose to send him.

It was not long after the governor's boat had reached her station, which was fairly within the short range of the two guns in the battery, ere a boat shoved off from the ship, showing the white flag, too. In a few minutes, the two boats were within the lengths of each other's oars, riding peacefully side by side.

On board the stranger's boat, in addition to the six men who were at the oars, were three persons in the stern-sheets. One of these men, as was afterwards ascertained, was the admiral himself; a second was an interpreter, who spoke English with a foreign accent, but otherwise perfectly well; and the third was no other than Waally! The governor thought a fierce satisfaction was gleaming in the countenance of the savage when they met, though the latter said nothing. The interpreter opened the communications.

"Is any one in that boat," demanded this person, "who is empowered to speak for the authorities ashore?"

"There is," answered the governor, who did not deem it wise, nevertheless, exactly to proclaim his rank. "I have full powers, being directly authorized by the chief-magistrate of this colony."

"To what nation does your colony belong?"

This was an awkward question, and one that had not been at all anticipated, and which the governor was not fully prepared to answer.

"Before interrogatories are thus put, it might be as well for me to know by what authority I am questioned at all," returned Mr. Woolston. "What are the vessels which have anchored in our waters, and under what flag do they sail?"

"A man-of-war never answers a hail, unless it comes from another man-of-war," answered the interpreter, smiling.

"Do you, then, claim to be vessels of war?"

"If compelled to use our *force*, you will find us so. We have not come here to answer questions, however, but to ask them. Does your colony claim to belong to any particular nation, or not?"

"We are all natives of the United States of America, and our vessels sail under her flag."

"The United States of America!" repeated the interpreter, with an ill-concealed expression of contempt. "There is good picking among the vessels of that nation, as the great European belligerents well know; and while so many are profiting by it, *we* may as well come in for our share."

It may be necessary to remind a portion of our readers, that this dialogue occurred more than forty years ago, and long before the republic sent out its fleets and armies to conquer adjacent states; when, indeed, it had scarce a fleet and army to protect its own coasts and frontiers from insults and depredations. It is said that when the late Emperor of Austria, the good and kind-hearted Francis II., was shown the ruins of the little castle of Habsburg, which is still to be seen crowning a low height, in the canton of Aarraw, Switzerland, he observed, "I now see that we have not *always* been a great family." The governor cared very little for the fling at his native land, but he did not relish the sneer, as it indicated the treatment likely to be bestowed on his adopted country. Still, the case was not to be remedied except by the use of the means already provided, should his visitors see fit to resort to force.

A desultory conversation now ensued, in which the strangers pretty plainly let their designs be seen. In the first place they demanded a surrender of all the craft belonging to the colony, big and little, together with all the naval stores. This condition complied with, the strangers intimated that it was possible their conquests would not be pushed much further. Of provisions, they stood in need of pork, and they understood that the colony had hogs without number. If they would bring down to the island a hundred fat hogs, with barrels and salt, within twenty-four hours, it was probable, however, no further demand for provisions would be made. They had obtained fifty barrels of very excellent flour at Rancocus Island, and could not conveniently stow more than that number, in addition to the demanded hundred barrels of pork. The admiral also required that hostages should be sent on board his ship, and that he should be provided with proper pilots, in order that he, and a party of suitable size, might take the Anne and the Martha, and go up to the town, which he understood lay some twenty or thirty miles within the group. Failing of an acquiescence in these terms, war, and war of the most ruthless character, was to be immediately proclaimed. All attempts to obtain an announcement of any national character, on the part of the strangers was evaded; though, from the appearance of everything he saw, the governor could not now have the smallest doubt that he had to do with pirates.

After getting all out of the strangers that he could, and it was but little at the best, the governor quietly, but steadily refused to accede to any one of the demands, and put the issue on the appeal to force. The strangers were obviously disappointed at this answer, for the thoughtful, simple manner of Mark Woolston had misled them, and they had actually flattered themselves with obtaining all they wanted without a struggle. At first, the anger of the admiral threatened some treacherous violence on the spot, but the crews of the two boats were so nearly equal, that prudence, if not good faith, admonished him of the necessity of respecting the truce. The parties separated, however, with denunciations, nay maledictions, on the part of the strangers, the colonists remaining quiet in demeanor, but firm.

The time taken for the two boats to return to their respective points of departure was but short; and scarcely was that of the stranger arrived alongside of its vessel, ere the ship fired a gun. This was the signal of war, the shot of that first gun falling directly in the battery, where it took off the hand of a Kannaka, besides doing some other damage. This was not a very favourable omen, but the governor encouraged his people, and to work both sides went, trying who could do the other the most harm. The cannonading was lively and well sustained, though it was not like one of the present time, when shot are hollow, and a gun is chambered and, not unfrequently, has a muzzle almost as large as the open end of a flour-barrel, and a breech as big as a hogshead. At the commencement-of this century a long twelve-pounder was considered a smart piece, and was thought very capable of doing a good deal of mischief. The main battery of the ship was composed of guns of that description, while one of the brigs carried eight nines, and the other fourteen sixes. As the ship mounted altogether thirty, if not thirty-two, guns, this left the governor to contend with batteries that had in them at least twenty-six pieces, as opposed to his own two. A couple of lively guns, nevertheless, well-served and properly mounted, behind good earthen banks, are quite equal to several times their number on board ship. Notwithstanding the success of the first shot of the pirates, this truth soon became sufficiently apparent, and the vessels found themselves getting the worst of it. The governor, himself, or Captain Betts pointed every gun that was fired in the battery, and they seldom failed to make their marks on the hulls of the enemy. On the other hand, the shot of the shipping was either buried in the mounds of the battery, or passed over its low parapets. Not a man was hurt ashore, at the end of an hour's struggle, with the exception of the Kannaka first wounded, while seven of the pirates were actually killed, and near twenty wounded.

Had the combat continued in the manner in which it was commenced, the result would have been a speedy and signal triumph in favour of the colony. But, by this time, the pirate admiral became convinced that he had gone the wrong way to work, and that he must have recourse to some management, in order to prevail against such stubborn foes. Neither of the vessels was anchored, but all kept under way, manoeuvring about in front of the battery, but one brig hauled out of the line to the northward, and making a stretch or two clear of the line of fire, she came down on the north end of the battery, in a position to rake it. Now, this battery had been constructed for plain, straightforward cannonading in front, with no embrasures to command the roads on either flank. Curtains of earth had been thrown up on the flanks, to protect the men, it is true, but this passive sort of resistance could do very little good in a protracted contest. While this particular brig was gaining that favourable position, the ship and the other brig fell off to leeward, and were soon at so long a shot, as to be out of harm's way. This was throwing the battery entirely out of the combat, as to anything aggressive, and compelled a prompt decision on the part of the colonists. No sooner did the nearest brig open her fire, and that within short canister range, than the ship and her consort hauled in again on the southern flank of the battery, the smallest vessel leading, and feeling her way with the lead. Perceiving the utter uselessness of remaining, and the great danger he ran of being cut off, the governor now commenced a retreat to his boats. This movement was not without danger, one colonist being killed in effecting it, and two more of the Kannakas wounded. It succeeded, notwithstanding, and the whole party got off to the Anne and Martha.

This retreat, of course, left the island and the battery at the mercy of the pirates. The latter landed, set fire to the buildings, blew up the magazine, dismounted the guns, and did all the other damage to the place that could be accomplished in the course of a short visit. They then went on board their vessels, again, and began to beat up into the Western Passage, following the colonists who preceded them, keeping just out of gun-shot.

The Western Passage was somewhat crooked, and different reaches were of very frequent occurrence. This sometimes aided a vessel in ascending, or going to windward, and sometimes offered obstacles. As there were many other passages, so many false channels, some of which were *culs-de-sacs,* it was quite possible for one ignorant of the true direction to miss his way; and this circumstance suggested to the governor an expedient which was highly approved of by His friend and counsellor, captain Betts, when it was laid before that plain, but experienced, seaman. There was one false passage, about a league within the group, which led off to the northward, and far from all the settlements, that offered several inducements to enter it. In the first place, it had more of the appearance of a main channel, at its point of junction, than the main channel itself, and might easily be mistaken for it; then, it turned right into the wind's eye, after beating up it for a league; and at the end of a long reach that ran due-south-east, it narrowed so much as to render it questionable whether the Anne and Martha could pass between the rocks, into a wide bay beyond. This bay was the true *cul-de-sac,* having no other outlet or inlet than the narrow pass just mentioned; though it was very large, was dotted with islands, and reached quite to the vicinity of Loam Island, or within a mile, or two, of the Reef.

The main question was whether the schooner and the sloop could pass through the opening which communicated between the reach and the bay. If not, they must inevitably fall into the hands of the pirates, should they enter the false channel, and be followed in. Then, even admitting that the Anne and Martha got through the narrow passage, should the pirates follow them in their boats, there would be very little probability of their escaping; though they might elude their pursuers for a time among the islands. Captain Betts was of opinion that the two vessels *could* get through, and was strongly in favour of endeavouring to lead the enemy off the true course to the Reef, by entangling them in this *cul-de-sac.* If nothing but delay was gained, delay would be something. It was always an advantage to the assailed to have time to recover from their first alarm, and to complete their arrangements. The governor listened to his friend's arguments with favour, but he sent the Neshamony on direct to the Reef, with a letter to Pennock, acquainting that functionary with the state of things, the intended plan, and a request that a twelve-pounder, that was mounted on a travelling carriage, might be put on board the boat, and sent to a landing, whence it might easily be dragged by hand to the narrow passage so often mentioned. This done, he took the way into the false channel himself.

The governor, as a matter of course, kept at a safe distance ahead of the pirates in the Anne and the Martha. This he was enabled to do quite easily, since fore-and-aft vessels make much quicker tacks than those that are square-rigged. As respects water, there was enough of that almost everywhere; it being rather a peculiarity of the group, that nearly every one of its passages had good channels and bold shores. There was one shoal, however, and that of some extent, in the long reach of the false channel named; and when the governor resolved to venture in there, it was not without the hope of leading the pirate ship on it. The water on this shoal was about sixteen feet deep, and there was scarce a hope of either of the brigs fetching up on it; but, could the ship be enticed there, and did she only strike with good way on her, and on a falling tide, her berth might be made very uncomfortable. Although this hope appeared faintly in the background of the governor's project, his principal expectation was that of being able to decoy the strangers into a *cul-de-sac,* and to embarrass them with delays and losses. As soon as the Neshamony was out of sight, the Anne and Martha, therefore, accompanied by the other boats, stood into the false channel, and went off to the northward merrily, with a leading wind. When the enemy reached the point, they did not hesitate to follow, actually setting studding sails in their eagerness not to be left too far behind. It is probable, that Waally was of but little service to his allies just then, for, after all, the knowledge of that chief was limited to a very imperfect acquaintance with such channels as would admit of the passage of even canoes. The distances were by no means trifling in these crooked passages. By the true channel, it was rather more than seven and twenty miles from the western roads to the Reef; but, it was fully ten more by this false channel, even deducting the half league where there was no passage at all, or the bottom of the *bag.* Now, it required time to beat up such a distance, and the sun was setting when the governor reached the shoal already mentioned, about which he kept working for some time, in the hope of enticing the ship on it in the dark. But the pirates were too wary to be misled, in this fashion. The light no sooner left them than they took in all their canvas and anchored. It is probable, that they believed themselves on their certain way to the Reef, and felt indisposed to risk anything by adventuring in the obscurity. Both parties, consequently, prepared to pass the night at their anchors. The Anne and Martha were now within less than a mile of the all-important passage, through which they were to make their escape, if they escaped at all. The opportunity of ascertaining the fact was not to be neglected, and it was no sooner so dark as to veil his movements than the governor went on board the Martha, which was a vessel of more beam than the Anne, and beat her up to the rocks, in order to make a trial of its capacity. It was just possible to take the sloop through in several places; but, in one spot, the rocks came too near together to admit of her being hauled between them. The circumstances would not allow of delay, and to work everybody went, with such implements as offered, to pick away the rock and to open a passage. By midnight, this was done; and the Martha was carried through into the bay beyond. Here she stood off a short distance and anchored. The governor went back to his own craft and moved her about a mile, being apprehensive of a boat attack in the darkness, should he remain where he was. This precaution was timely, for, in the morning, after day had dawned, no less than seven boats were seen pulling down to the pirates, which had, no doubt, been looking for the schooner and the sloop in vain. The governor got great credit for this piece of management; more even than might have been expected, the vulgar usually bestowing their applause on acts of a glittering character, rather than on those which denote calculation and forethought.

As the day advanced the pirates re-commenced their operations. The delay, however, had given the colonists a great advantage. There had been time to communicate with the Reef, and to receive the gun sent for. It had greatly encouraged the people up at the town, to hear that their enemies were in the false channel; and they redoubled their efforts, as one multiplies his blows on a retreating enemy. Pennock sent the governor most encouraging reports, and gave him to understand that he had ordered nearly all the men in from the out-posts, leaving just enough to have a look-out, and to keep the Kannakas in order. As it was now understood that the attack must be on the capital, there was every reason for taking this course.

All the vessels were soon under way again. The pirates missed the Martha, which they rightly enough supposed had gone ahead. They were evidently a good deal puzzled about the channel, but supposed it must be somewhere to windward. In the mean time, the governor kept the Anne manoeuvring around the shoal, in the hope of luring the ship on it. Nor was he without rational hopes of success, for the brigs separated, one going close to each side of the sound, to look for the outlet, while the ship kept beating up directly in its centre, making a sinuous course towards the schooner, which was always near the shallow water. At length the governor was fully rewarded for his temerity; the admiral had made a stretch that carried him laterally past the lee side of the shoal, and when he went about, he looked directly for the Anne, which was standing back and forth near its weather margin. Here the governor held on, until he had the satisfaction of seeing the ship just verging on the weather side of the shoal, when he up helm, and stood off to leeward, as if intending to pass out of the *cul-de-sac* by the way he had entered, giving his pursuers the slip. This bold manoeuvre took the pirate admiral by surprise, and being in the vessel that was much the nearest to the Anne, he up helm, and was plumped on the shoal with strong way on him, in less than five minutes! The instant the governor saw this, he hauled his wind and beat back again, passing the broadside of the ship with perfect impunity, her people being too much occupied with their own situation, to think of their guns, or of molesting him.

The strange ship had run aground within half a mile of the spot where the twelve-pounder was planted, and that gun now opened on her with great effect. She lay quartering to this new enemy, and the range was no sooner obtained, than every shot hulled her. The governor now landed, and went to work seriously, first ordering the Anne carried through the pass, to place her beyond the reach of the brigs. A forge happened to be in the Anne, to make some repairs to her iron work, and this forge, a small one it was true, was taken ashore, and an attempt was made to heat some shot in it. The shot had been put into the forge an hour or two before, but a fair trial was not made until the whole apparatus was landed. For the next hour the efforts of both sides were unremitted. One of the brigs went to the assistance of the admiral, while the other endeavoured to silence the gun, which was too securely placed, however, to mind her broadsides. One shot hulling her, soon drove her to leeward; after which, all the attention of the pirates was bestowed on their ship.

The admiral, beyond all doubt, was very awkwardly placed. He had the whole width of the shoal to leeward of him, could only get off by working directly in the face of the fire, and had gone on with seven knots way on his ship. The bottom was a soft mud; and the colonists knew that nothing but anchors laid to windward, with a heavy strain and a good deal of lightening, would ever take that vessel out of her soft berth. Of this fact the pirates themselves soon began to be convinced, for they were seen pumping out their water. As for the brigs, they were by no means well handled. Instead of closing with the battery, and silencing the gun, as they might have done, they kept aloof, and even rendered less assistance to the ship than was in their power. In point of fact, they were in confusion, and manifested that want of order and submission to authority, as well as self-devotion, that would have been shown among men in an honest service: guilt paralysed their efforts, rendering them timid and distrustful.

After near two hours of cannonading, during which the colonists had done the pirates a good deal of damage, and the pirates literally had not injured the colonists at all, the governor was ready with his hot shot, which he had brought to something more than a red heat. The gun was loaded with great care, and fired, after having been deliberately pointed by the governor himself. The ship was hulled, and a trifling explosion followed on board. That shot materially added to the confusion among the pirates, and it was immediately followed by another, which struck, also. It was now so apparent that confusion prevailed among the pirates, that the governor would not take the time necessary to put in the other hot shot, but he loaded and fired as fast as he could, in the ordinary way.

In less than a quarter of an hour after the first hot shot was fired, smoke poured out of the admiral's main-deck ports; and, two minutes later, it was succeeded by flames.

From that moment the result of the conflict was no longer doubtful. The pirates, among whom great confusion prevailed, even previously to this disaster, now lost all subordination, and it was soon seen that each man worked for himself, striving to save as much as he could of his ill-gotten plunder. The governor understood the state of the enemy, and, though prudence could scarcely justify his course, he determined to press him to the utmost. The Anne and Martha were both brought back through the pass, and the twelve-pounder was taken on board the former, there being room to fight it between her masts. As soon as this was done, the two craft bore down on the brigs, which were, by this time, a league to leeward of the burning ship, their commanders having carried them there to avoid the effects of the expected explosion. The admiral and his crew saved themselves in the boats, abandoning nearly all their property, and losing a good many men. Indeed, when the last boat left the ship, there were several of her people below, so far overcome by liquor, as to be totally helpless. These men were abandoned too, as were all the wounded, including Waally, who had lost an arm by the fire of the battery.

Neither did the governor like the idea of passing very near the ship, which had now been burning fully an hour. In going to leeward, he gave her a berth, and it was well he did, for she blew up while the Anne and Martha, as it was, were considerably within a quarter of a mile of her. The colonists ever afterwards considered an incident connected with this explosion, as a sort of Providential manifestation of the favour of Heaven. The Martha was nearest to the ship, at the instant of her final disaster, and very many fragments were thrown around her; a few even on her decks. Among the last was a human body, which was cast a great distance in the air, and fell, like a heavy clod, across the gunwale of the sloop. This proved to be the body of Waally, one of the arms having been cut away by a shot, three hours before! Thus perished a constant and most wily enemy of the colony, and who had, more than once, brought it to the verge of destruction, by his cupidity and artifices.

From this moment, the pirates thought little of anything but of effecting their retreat, and of getting out into open water again. The governor saw this, and pressed them hard. The twelve-pounder opened on the nearest brig, as soon as her shot would tell; and even the Martha's swivel was heard, like the bark of a cur that joins in the clamour when a strange dog is set upon by the pack of a village. The colonists on shore flew into the settlements, to let it be known that the enemy was retreating, when every dwelling poured out its inmates in pursuit. Even the females now appeared in arms; there being no such incentive to patriotism, on occasions of the kind, as the cry that the battle has been won. Those whom it might have been hard to get within the sound of a gun, a few hours before, now became valiant, and pressed into the van, which bore a very different aspect, before a retreating foe, from that which it presented on their advance.

In losing Waally, the strangers lost the only person among them who had any pretension to be thought a pilot. He knew very little of the channels to the Reef, at the best, though he had been there thrice; but, now he was gone, no one left among them knew anything about them at all. Under all the circumstances, therefore, it is not surprising that the admiral should think more of extricating his two brigs from the narrow waters, than of pursuing his original plan of conquest. It was not difficult to find his way back by the road he had come; and that road he travelled as fast as a leading breeze would carry him along it. But retreat, as it now appeared, was not the only difficulty with which this freebooter had to contend. It happened that no kind feeling existed between the admiral and the officers of the largest of the brigs. So far had their animosity extended, that the admiral had deemed it expedient to take a large sum of money, which had fallen to the share of the vessel in question, out of that brig, and keep it on board the ship, as a guaranty that they would not run away with their craft. This proceeding had not strengthened the bond between the parties; and nothing had kept down the strife but the expectation of the large amount of plunder that was to be obtained from the colony. That hope was now disappointed; and, the whole time the two vessels were retiring before the Anne and the Martha, preparations were making on board one of the brigs to reclaim this ill-gotten treasure, and on board the other to retain it. By a species of freemasonry peculiar to their pursuits, the respective crews were aware of each other's designs; and when they issued nearly abreast out of the passage, into the inner bay of the Western Roads, one passed to the southward of the island, and the other to the northward; the Anne and Martha keeping close in their wakes.

As the two vessels cleared the island and got into open water, the struggle commenced in earnest; the disaffected brig firing into the admiral. The broadside was returned, and the two vessels gradually neared each other, until the canopies of smoke which accompanied their respective movements became one. The combat now raged, and with a savage warmth, for hours; both brigs running off the land under short canvas. At length the firing ceased, and the smoke so far cleared away as to enable the governor to take a look at the damages done. In this respect, there was little to choose; each vessel having suffered, and seemingly each about as much as the other. After consuming an hour or two in repairing damages, the combat was renewed; when the two colony craft, seeing no prospects of its soon terminating, and being now several leagues to leeward of the group, hauled up for the roads again. The brigs continued their fight, always running off before the wind, and went out of sight, canopied by smoke, long after the reports of their guns had become inaudible. This was the last the governor ever saw or heard of these dangerous enemies.

Chapter XXIX

VOX POPULI, VOX DEI.

—Venerable Axiom

After this unlooked-for termination of what the colonists called the 'Pirate-War,' the colony enjoyed a long period of peace and prosperity. The whaling business was carried on with great success, and many connected with it actually got rich. Among these was the governor, who, in addition to his other means, soon found himself in possession of more money than he could profitably dispose of in that young colony. By his orders, no less than one hundred thousand dollars were invested in his name, in the United States six per cents, his friends in America being empowered to draw the dividends, and, after using a due proportion in the way of commissions, to re-invest the remainder to his credit.

Nature did quite as much as art, in bringing on the colony; the bounty of God, as the industry of man. It is our duty, however, to allow that the colonists did not so regard the matter. A great change came over their feelings, after the success of the 'Pirate-War,' inducing them to take a more exalted view of themselves and their condition than had been their wont. The ancient humility seemed suddenly to disappear; and in its place a vainglorious estimate of themselves and of their prowess arose among the people. The word "people," too, was in everybody's mouth, as if the colonists themselves had made those lovely islands, endowed them with fertility, and rendered them what they were now fast becoming-scenes of the most exquisite rural beauty, as well as granaries of abundance. By this time, the palm-tree covered more or less of every island; and the orange, lime, shaddock and other similar plants, filled the air with the fragrance of their flowers, or rendered it bright with the golden hues of their fruits. In short, everything adapted to the climate was flourishing in the plantations, and plenty reigned even in the humblest dwelling.

This was a perilous condition for the healthful humility of human beings. Two dangers beset them; both coloured and magnified by a common tendency. One was that of dropping into luxurious idleness-the certain precursor, in such a climate, of sensual indulgences; and the other was that of "waxing fat, and kicking." The tendency common to both, was to place self before God, and not only to believe that they merited all they received, but that they actually created a good share of it.

Of luxurious idleness, it was perhaps too soon to dread its worst fruits. The men and women retained too many of their early habits and impressions to drop easily into such a chasm; on the contrary, they rather looked forward to producing results greater than any which had yet attended their exertions. An exaggerated view of self, however, and an almost total forgetfulness of God, took the place of the colonial humility with which they had commenced their career in this new region. These feelings were greatly heightened by three agents, that men ordinarily suppose might have a very different effect-religion, law, and the press.

When the Rancocus returned, a few months after the repulse of the pirates, she had on board of her some fifty emigrants; the council still finding itself obliged to admit the friends of families already settled in the colony, on due application. Unhappily, among these emigrants were a printer, a lawyer, and no less than four persons who might be named divines. Of the last, one was a presbyterian, one a methodist, —the third was a baptist, and the fourth a quaker. Not long after the arrival of this importation, its consequences became visible. The sectaries commenced with a thousand professions of brotherly love, and a great parade of Christian charity; indeed they pretended that they had emigrated in order to enjoy a higher degree of religious liberty than was now to be found in America, where men were divided into sects, thinking more of their distinguishing tenets than of the Being whom they professed to serve. Forgetting the reasons which brought them from home, or quite possibly carrying out the impulses which led them to resist their former neighbours, these men set to work, immediately, to collect followers, and believers after their own peculiar notions. Parson Hornblower, who had hitherto occupied the ground by himself, but who was always a good deal inclined to what are termed "distinctive opinions," buckled on his armour, and took the field in earnest. In order that the sheep of one flock should not be mistaken for the sheep of another, great care was taken to mark each and all with the brand of sect. One clipped an ear, another smeared the wool (or drew it over the eyes) and a third, as was the case with Friend Stephen Dighton, the quaker, put on an entire covering, so that his sheep might be known by their outward symbols, far as they could be seen. In a word, on those remote and sweet islands, which, basking in the sun and cooled by the trades, seemed designed by providence to sing hymns daily and hourly to their maker's praise, the subtleties of sectarian faith smothered that humble submission to the divine law by trusting solely to the mediation, substituting in its place immaterial observances and theories which were much more strenuously urged than clearly understood. The devil, in the form of a "professor," once again entered Eden; and the Peak, with so much to raise the soul above the grosser strife of men, was soon ringing with discussions on "free grace," "immersion," "spiritual baptism," and the "apostolical succession." The birds sang as sweetly as ever, and their morning and evening songs hymned the praises of their creator as of old; but, not so was it with the morning and evening devotions of men. These last began to pray *at* each other, and if Mr. Hornblower was an exception, it was because his admirable liturgy did not furnish him with the means of making these forays into the enemy's camp.

Nor did the accession of law and intelligence help the matter much. Shortly after the lawyer made his appearance, men began to discover that they were wronged by their neighbours, in a hundred ways which they had never before discovered. Law, which had hitherto been used for the purpose of justice, and of justice only, now began to be used for those of speculation and revenge. A virtue was found in it that had never before been suspected of existing in the colony; it being discovered that men could make not only very comfortable livings, but, in some cases, get rich, by the law; not by its practice, but by its practices. Now came into existence an entire new class of philanthropists; men who were ever ready to lend their money to such of the needy as possessed property, taking judgment bonds, mortgages, and other innocent securities, which were received because the lender always *acted on a principle* of not lending without them, or had taken a vow, or made their wives promises; the end of all being a transfer of title, by which the friendly assistant commonly relieved his dupe of the future care of all his property. The governor soon observed that one of these philanthropists rarely extended his saving hand, that the borrower did not come out as naked as the ear of the corn that has been through the sheller, or nothing but cob; and that, too, in a sort of patent-right time. Then there were the labourers of the press to add to the influence of those of religion and the law. The press took up the cause of human rights, endeavouring, to transfer the power of the state from the public departments to its own printing-office; and aiming at establishing all the equality that can flourish when one man has a monopoly of the means of making his facts to suit himself, leaving his neighbours to get along under such circumstances as they can. But the private advantage secured to himself by this advocate of the rights of all, was the smallest part of the injury he did, though his own interests were never lost sight of, and coloured all he did; the people were soon convinced that they had hitherto been living under an unheard-of tyranny, and were invoked weekly to arouse in their might, and be true to themselves and their posterity. In the first place, not a tenth of them had ever been consulted on the subject of the institutions at all, but had been compelled to take them as they found them. Nor had the present incumbents of office been placed in power by a vote of a majority, the original colonists having saved those who came later to the island all trouble in the premises. In these facts was an unceasing theme of declamation and complaint to be found. It was surprising how little the people really knew of the oppression under which they laboured, until this stranger came amongst them to enlighten their understandings. Nor was it less wonderful how many sources of wrong he exposed, that no one had ever dreamed of having an existence. Although there was not a tax of any sort laid in the colony, not a shilling ever collected in the way of import duties, he boldly pronounced the citizens of the islands to be the most overburthened people in Christendom! The taxation of England was nothing to it, and he did not hesitate to proclaim a general bankruptcy as the consequence, unless some of his own expedients were resorted to, in order to arrest the evil. Our limits will not admit of a description of the process by which this person demonstrated that a people who literally contributed nothing at all, were overtaxed; but any one who has paid attention to the opposing sides of a discussion on such a subject, can readily imagine how easily such an apparent contradiction can be reconciled, and the proposition demonstrated.

In the age of which we are writing, a majority of man kind fancied that a statement made in print was far more likely to be true than one made orally. Then he who stood up in his proper person and uttered his facts on the responsibility of his personal character, was far less likely to gain credit than the anonymous scribbler, who recorded his lie on paper, though he made his record behind a screen, and half the time as much without personal identity as he would be found to be without personal character, were he actually seen and recognised. In our time, the press has pretty effectually cured all observant persons at least of giving faith to a statement merely because it is in print, and has become so far alive to its own great inferiority as publicly to talk of conventions to purify itself, and otherwise to do something to regain its credit; but such was not the fact, even in America, forty years since. The theory of an unrestrained press has fully developed itself within the last quarter of a century, so that even the elderly ladies, who once said with marvellous unction, "It must be true, for it's in print," are now very apt to say, "Oh! it's only a newspaper *account!*" The foulest pool has been furnished by a beneficent Providence with the means of cleansing its own waters.

But the "Crater Truth-Teller" could utter its lies, as a privileged publication, at the period of this narrative. Types still had a sanctity; and it is surprising how much they deceived, and how many were their dupes. The journal did not even take the ordinary pains to mystify its readers, and to conceal its own cupidity, as are practised in communities more advanced in civilization. We dare say that journals *are* to be found in London and Paris, that take just as great liberties with the fact as the Crater Truth-Teller; but they treat their readers with a little more outward respect, however much they may mislead them with falsehoods. Your London and Paris publics are not to be dealt with as if composed of credulous old women, but require something like a plausible mystification to throw dust in their eyes. They have a remarkable proneness to believe that which they wish, it is true; but, beyond that weakness, some limits are placed to their faith and appearances must be a good deal consulted.

But at the crater no such precaution seemed to be necessary. It is true that the editor did use the pronoun "we," in speaking of himself; but he took all other occasions to assert his individuality, and to use his journal diligently in its behalf. Thus, whenever he got into the law, his columns were devoted to publicly maintaining his own side of the question, although such a course was not only opposed to every man's sense of propriety, but was directly flying into the teeth of the laws of the land; but little did he care for that. He was a public servant, and of course all he did was right. To be sure, other public servants were in the same category, all they did being wrong; but he had the means of telling his own story, and a large number of gaping dunces were ever ready to believe him. His manner of filling his larder is particularly worthy of being mentioned. Quite as often as once a week, his journal had some such elegant article as this, viz: —"Our esteemed friend, Peter Snooks" —perhaps it was Peter Snooks, *Esquire* —"has just brought us a fair specimen of his cocoa-nuts, which we do not hesitate in recommending to the housekeepers of the crater, as among the choicest of the group." Of course, Squire Snooks was grateful for this puff, and often brought *more* cocoa-nuts. The same great supervision was extended to the bananas, the bread-fruit, the cucumbers, the melons, and even the squashes, and always with the same results to the editorial larder. Once, however, this worthy did get himself in a quandary with his use of the imperial pronoun. A mate of one of the vessels inflicted personal chastisement on him, for some impertinent comments he saw fit to make on the honest tar's vessel; and, this being matter of intense interest to the public mind, he went into a detail of all the evolutions of the combat. Other men may pull each other's noses, and inflict kicks and blows, without the world's caring a straw about it; but the editorial interest is too intense to be overlooked in this manner. A bulletin of the battle was published; the editor speaking of himself always in the plural, out of excess of modesty, and to avoid egotism(!) in three columns which were all about himself, using such expressions as these: —"*We* now struck *our* antagonist a blow with *our* fist, and followed this up with a kick of *our* foot, and otherwise *we* made an assault on him that he will have reason to remember to his dying day." Now, these expressions, for a time, set all the old women in the colony against the editor, until he went into an elaborate explanation, showing that his modesty was so painfully sensitive that he could not say *I* on any account, though he occupied three more columns of his paper in explaining the state of *our* feelings. But, at first, the cry went forth that the battle had been of *two* against *one*; and *that* even the simple-minded colonists set down as somewhat cowardly. So much for talking about *we* in the bulletin of a single combat!

The political, effects produced by this paper, however, were much the most material part of its results. Whenever it offended and disgusted its readers by its dishonesty, selfishness, vulgarity, and lies-and it did this every week, being a hebdomadal-it recovered the ground it had lost by beginning to talk of 'the people' and their rights. This the colonists could not withstand. All their sympathies were enlisted in behalf of him who thought so much of their rights; and, at the very moment he was trampling on these rights, to advance his own personal views, and even treating them with contempt by uttering the trash he did, they imagined that he and his paper in particular, and its doctrines in general, were a sort of gift from Heaven to form the palladium of their precious liberties!

The great theory advanced by this editorial tyro, was, that a majority of any community had a right to do as it pleased. The governor early saw, not only the fallacies, but the danger of this doctrine; and he wrote several communications himself, in order to prove that it was false. If true, he contended it was true altogether; and that it must be taken, if taken as an axiom at all, with its largest consequences. Now, if a majority has a right to rule, in this arbitrary manner, it has a right to set its dogmas above the commandments, and to legalize theft, murder, adultery, and all the other sins denounced in the twentieth chapter of Exodus. This was a poser to the demagogue, but he made an effort to get rid of it, by excepting the laws of God, which he allowed that even majorities were bound to respect. Thereupon, the governor replied that the laws of God were nothing but the great principles which ought to govern human conduct, and that his concession was an avowal that there was a power to which majorities should defer. Now, this was just as true of minorities as it was of majorities, and the amount of it all was that men, in establishing governments, merely set up a standard of principles which they pledged themselves to respect; and that, even in the most democratical communities, all that majorities could legally effect was to decide certain minor questions which, being necessarily referred to some tribunal for decision, was of preference referred to them. If there was a power superior to the will of the majority, in the management of human affairs, then majorities were not supreme; and it behooved the citizen to regard the last as only what they really are, and what they were probably designed to be-tribunals subject to the control of certain just principles.

Constitutions, or the fundamental law, the governor went on to say, were meant to be the expression of those just and general principles which should control human society, and as such should prevail over majorities. Constitutions were expressly intended to defend the rights of minorities; since without them, each question, or interest, might be settled by the majority, as it arose. It was but a truism to say that the oppression of the majority was the worst sort of oppression; since the parties injured not only endured the burthen imposed by many, but were cut off from the sympathy of their kind, which can alleviate much suffering, by the inherent character of the tyranny.

There was a great deal of good sense, and much truth in what the governor wrote, on this occasion; but of what avail could it prove with the ignorant and short-sighted, who put more trust in one honeyed phrase of the journal, that flourished about the 'people' and their 'rights,' than in all the arguments that reason, sustained even by revelation, could offer to show the fallacies and dangers of this new doctrine, As a matter of course, the wiles of the demagogue were not without fruits. Although every man in the colony, either in his own person, or in that of his parent or guardian, had directly entered into the covenants of the fundamental law, as that law then existed, they now began to quarrel with its provisions, and to advance doctrines that would subvert everything as established, in order to put something new and untried in its place. *Progress* was the great desideratum; and *change* was the hand-maiden of progress. A sort of 'puss in the corner' game was started, which was to enable those who had no places to run into the seats of those who had. This is a favourite pursuit of man, all over the world, in monarchies as well as in democracies; for, after all that institutions can effect, there is little change in men by putting on, or in taking off ermine and robes, or in wearing 'republican simplicity,' in office or out of office; but the demagogue is nothing but the courtier, pouring out his homage in the gutters, instead of in an ante-chamber.

Nor did the governor run into extremes in his attempts to restrain the false reasoning and exaggerations of the demagogue and his deluded, or selfish followers. Nothing would be easier than to demonstrate that their notions of the rights of numbers was wrong, to demonstrate that were their theories carried out in practice, there could be, and would be nothing permanent or settled in human affairs; yet not only did each lustrum, but each year, each month, each week, each hour, each minute demand its reform. Society must be periodically reduced to its elements, in order to redress grievances. The governor did not deny that men had their natural rights, at the very moment he insisted that these rights were just as much a portion of the minority as of the majority. He was perfectly willing that equal laws should prevail, as equal laws did prevail in the colony, though he was not disposed to throw everything into confusion merely to satisfy a theory. For a long time, therefore, he opposed the designs of the new-school, and insisted on his vested rights, as established in the fundamental law, which had made him ruler for life. But "it is hard to kick against the pricks." Although the claim of the governor was in every sense connected with justice, perfectly sacred, it could not resist the throes of cupidity, selfishness, and envy. By this time, the newspaper, that palladium of liberty, had worked the minds of the masses to a state in which the naked pretension of possessing rights that were not common to everybody else was, to the last degree, "tolerable and not to be endured." To such a height did the fever of liberty rise, that men assumed a right to quarrel with the private habits of the governor and his family, some pronouncing him proud because he did not neglect his teeth, as the majority did, eat when they ate, and otherwise presumed to be of different habits from those around him. Some even objected to him because he spat in his pocket-handkerchief, and did not blow his nose with his fingers.

All this time, religion was running riot, as well as politics. The next-door neighbours hated each other most sincerely, because they took different views of regeneration, justification, predestination and all the other subtleties of doctrine. What was remarkable, they who had the most clouded notions of such subjects were the loudest in their denunciations. Unhappily, the Rev. Mr. Hornblower, who had possession of the ground, took a course which had a tendency to aggravate instead of lessening this strife among the sects. Had he been prudent, he would have proclaimed louder than ever "Christ, and him crucified;" but, he made the capital mistake of going up and down, crying with the mob, "the church, the church!" This kept constantly before the eyes and ears of the dissenting part of the population-dissenting from his opinions if not from an establishment-the very features that were the most offensive to them. By "the church" they did not understand the same divine institution as that recognised by Mr. Hornblower himself, but surplices, and standing up and sitting down, and gowns, and reading prayers out of a book, and a great many other similar observances, which were deemed by most of the people relics of the "scarlet woman." It is wonderful, about what insignificant matters men can quarrel, when they wish to fall out. Perhaps religion, under these influences, had quite as much to do with the downfall of the governor, which shortly after occurred, as politics, and the newspaper, and the new lawyer, all of which and whom did everything that was in their power to destroy him.

At length, the demagogues thought they had made sufficient progress to spring their mine. The journal came out with a proposal to call a convention, to alter and improve the fundamental law. That law contained a clause already pointing out the mode by which amendments were to be made in the constitution; but this mode required the consent of the governor, of the council, and finally, of the people. It was a slow, deliberative process, too, one by which men had time to reflect on what they were doing, and so far protected vested rights as to render it certain that no very great revolution could be effected under its shadow. Now, the disaffected aimed at revolution-at carrying out, completely the game of "puss in the corner," and it became necessary to set up some new principle by which they could circumvent the old fundamental law.

This was very easily accomplished in the actual state of the public mind; it was only to carry out the doctrine of the sway of the majority to a practical result; and this was so cleverly done as actually to put the balance of power in the hands of the minority. There is nothing new in this, however, as any cool-headed man may see in this enlightened republic of our own, daily examples in which the majority-principle works purely for the aggrandizement of a minority clique. It makes very little difference how men are ruled; they will be cheated; for, failing of rogues at head-quarters to perform that office for them, they are quite certain to set to work to devise some means of cheating themselves. At the crater this last trouble was spared them, the opposition performing that office in the following ingenious manner.

The whole colony was divided into parishes, which exercised in themselves a few of the minor functions of government. They had a limited legislative power, like the American town meetings. In these parishes, laws were passed, to require the people to vote 'yes' or 'no,' in order to ascertain whether there should, or should not be, a convention to amend the constitution. About one-fourth of the electors attended these primary meetings, and of the ten meetings which were held, in six "yes" prevailed by average majorities of about two votes in each parish. This was held to be demonstration of the wishes of the majority of the people to have a convention, though most of those who staid away did so because they believed the whole procedure not only illegal, but dangerous. Your hungry demagogue, however, is not to be defeated by any scruples so delicate. To work these *élites* of the colony went, to organise an election for members of the convention. At this election about a third of the electors appeared, the candidates succeeding by handsome majorities, the rest staying away because they believed the whole proceedings illegal. Thus fortified by the sacred principle of the sway of majorities, these representatives of a minority, met in convention, and formed an entirely new fundamental law; one, indeed, that completely subverted the old one, not only in fact, but in theory. In order to get rid of the governor to a perfect certainty, for it was known that he could still command more votes for the office than any other man in the colony, one article provided that no person should hold the office of governor, either prospectively, or perspectively, more than five years, consecutively. This placed Mr. Mark Woolston on the shelf at the next election. Two legislative bodies were formed, the old council was annihilated, and everything was done that cunning could devise, to cause power and influence to pass into new hands. This was the one great object of the whole procedure, and, of course, it was not neglected.

When the new constitution was completed, it was referred back to the people for approval. At this third appeal to the popular voice, rather less than half of all the electors voted, the constitution being adopted by a majority of one-third of those who did. By this simple, and exquisite republican process, was the principle of the sway of majorities vindicated, a new fundamental law for the colony provided, and all the old incumbents turned out of office. 'Silence gives consent,' cried the demagogues, who forgot they had no right to put their questions!

Religion had a word to say in these changes. The circumstance that the governor was an Episcopalian reconciled many devout Christians to the palpable wrong that was done him; and it was loudly argued that a church government of bishops, was opposed to republicanism, and consequently ought not to be entertained by republicans. This charming argument, which renders religious faith secondary to human institutions, instead of human institutions secondary to religious faith, thus completely putting the cart before the horse, has survived that distant revolution, and is already flourishing in more eastern climes. It is as near an approach to an idolatrous worship of self, as human conceit has recently tolerated.

As a matter of course, elections followed the adoption of the new constitution. Pennock was chosen governor for two years; the new lawyer was made judge, the editor, secretary of state and treasurer; and other similar changes were effected. All the Woolston connection were completely laid on the shelf. This was not done so much by the electors, with whom they were still popular, as by means of the nominating committees. These nominating committees were expedients devised to place the power in the hands of a few, in a government of the many. The rule of the majority is so very sacred a thing that it is found necessary to regulate it by legerdemain. No good republican ever disputes the principle, while no sagacious one ever submits to it. There are various modes, however, of defeating all 'sacred principles,' and this particular 'sacred principle' among the rest. The simplest is that of caucus nominations. The process is a singular illustration of the theory of a majority-government. Primary meetings are called, at which no one is ever present, but the wire-pullers and their puppets. Here very fierce conflicts occur between the wire-pullers themselves, and these are frequently decided by votes as close as majorities of one, or two. Making the whole calculation, it follows that nominations are usually made by about a tenth, or even a twentieth of the body of the electors; and this, too, on the supposition that they who vote actually have opinions of their own, as usually they have not, merely wagging their tongues as the wires are pulled. Now, these nominations are conclusive, when made by the ruling party, since there are no concerted means of opposing them. A man must have a flagrantly bad character not to succeed under a regular nomination, or he must be too honest for the body of the electors; one fault being quite as likely to defeat him as the other.

In this way was a great revolution effected in the colony of the crater. At one time, the governor thought of knocking the whole thing in the head, by the strong arm; as he might have done, and would have been perfectly justified in doing. The Kannakas were now at his command, and, in truth, a majority of the electors were with him; but political jugglery held them in duress. A majority of the electors of the state of New York are, at this moment, opposed to universal suffrage, especially as it is exercised in the town and village governments, but moral cowardice holds them in subjection. Afraid of their own shadows, each politician hesitates to 'bell the cat.' What is more, the select aristocrats and monarchists are the least bold in acting frankly, and in saying openly what they think; leaving that office to be discharged, as it ever will be, by the men who —*true* democrats, and not canting democrats-willing to give the people just as much control as they know how to use, or which circumstances will allow them to use beneficially to themselves, do not hesitate to speak with the candour and manliness of their principles. These men call things by their right names, equally eschewing the absurdity of believing that nature intended rulers to descend from male to male, according to the order of primogeniture, or the still greater nonsense of supposing it necessary to obtain the most thrifty plants from the hotbeds of the people, that they may be transplanted into the beds of state, reeking with the manure of the gutters.

The governor submitted to the changes, through a love of peace, and ceased to be anything more than a private citizen, when he had so many claims to be first, and when, in fact, he had so long been first. No sovereign on his throne, could write *Gratia Dei* before his titles with stricter conformity to truth, than Mark Woolston; but his right did not preserve him from the ruthless plunder of the demagogue. To his surprise, as well as to his grief, Pennock was seduced by ambition, and he assumed the functions of the executive with quite as little visible hesitation, as the heir apparent succeeds to his father's crown.

It would be untrue to say that Mark did not feel the change; but it is just to add that he felt more concern for the future fate of the colony, than he did for himself or his children. Nor, when he came to reflect on the matter, was he so much surprised that he could be supplanted in this way, under a system in which the sway of the majority was so much lauded, when he did not entertain a doubt that considerably more than half of the colony preferred the old system to the new, and that the same proportion of the people would rather see him in the Colony House, than to see John Pennock in his stead. But Mark-we must call him the governor no longer-had watched the progress of events closely, and began to comprehend them. He had learned the great and all-important political truth, that the more a people attempt to extend their power DIRECTLY over state affairs, the less they, in fact, control them, after having once passed the point of naming lawgivers as their representatives; merely bestowing on a few artful managers the influence they vainly imagine to have secured to themselves. This truth should be written in letters of gold, at every corner of the streets and highways in a republic; for truth it is, and truth, those who press the foremost on another path will the soonest discover it to be. The mass *may* select their representatives, *may* know them, and *may* in a good measure so far sway them, as to keep them to their duties; but when a constituency assumes to enact the part of executive and judiciary, they not only get beyond their depth, but into the mire. What *can*, what *does* the best-informed layman, for instance, know of the qualifications of this or that candidate to fill a seat on the bench! He has to take another's judgment for his guide; and a popular appointment of this nature, is merely transferring the nomination from an enlightened, and, what is everything, a responsible authority, to one that is unavoidably at the mercy of second persons for its means of judging, and is as irresponsible as air.

At one time, Mark Woolston regretted that he had not established an opposition paper, in order to supply an antidote for the bane; but reflection satisfied him it would have been useless. Everything human follows its law, until checked by abuses that create resistance. This is true of the monarch, who misuses power until it becomes tyranny; of the nobles, who combine to restrain the monarch, until the throes of an aristocracy-ridden country proclaim that it has merely changed places with the prince; of the people, who wax fat and kick! Everything human is abused; and it would seem that the only period of tolerable condition is the transition state, when the new force is gathering to a head, and before the storm has time to break. In the mean time, the earth revolves, men are born, live their time, and die; communities are formed and are dissolved; dynasties appear and disappear; good contends with evil, and evil still has its day; the whole, however, advancing slowly but unerringly towards that great consummation, which was designed from the beginning, and which is as certain to arrive in the end, as that the sun sets at night and rises in the morning. The supreme folly of the hour is to imagine that perfection will come before its stated time.

Chapter XXX

> "This is thy lesson, mighty sea!
> Man calls the dimpled earth his own,
> The flowery vale, the golden lea;
> And on the wild gray mountain-stone
> Claims nature's temple for his throne!
> But where thy many voices sing
> Their endless song, the deep, deep tone
> Calls back his spirit's airy wing,
> He shrinks into himself, when God is king!"
>
> —Lunt

For some months after the change of government, Mark Woolston was occupied in attending to the arrangement of his affairs, preparatory to an absence of some length. Bridget had expressed a strong wish to visit America once more, and her two eldest children were now of an age when their education had got to be a matter of some solicitude. It was the intention of their father to send them to Pennsylvania for that purpose, when the proper time arrived, and to place them under the care of his friends there, who would gladly take the charge. Recent events probably quickened this intention, both as to feeling and time, for Mark was naturally much mortified at the turn things had taken.

There was an obvious falling-off in the affairs of the colony from the time it became transcendantly free. In religion, the sects ever had fair-play, or ever since the arrival of the parsons, and that had been running down, from the moment it began to run into excesses and exaggerations. As soon as a man begins to *shout* in religion, he may be pretty sure that he is "hallooing before he is out of the woods." It is true that all our feelings exhibit themselves, more or less, in conformity to habits and manners, but there is something profane in the idea that the spirit of God manifests it presence in yells and clamour, even when in possession of those who have not been trained to the more subdued deportment of reason and propriety. The shouting and declamatory parts of religion may be the evil spirits growling and yelling before they are expelled, but these must not be mistaken for the voice of the Ancient of Days.

The morals decayed as religion obtained its false directions. Self-righteousness, the inseparable companion of the quarrels of sects, took the place of humility, and thus became prevalent that most dangerous condition of the soul of man, when he imagines that *he* sanctifies what he does; a frame of mind, by the way, that is by no means strange to very many who ought to be conscious of their unworthiness. With the morals of the colony, its prosperity, even in worldly interests, began to lose ground. The merchants, as usual, had behaved badly in the political struggle. The intense selfishness of the caste kept them occupied with the pursuit of gain, at the most critical moments of the struggle, or when their influence might have been of use; and when the mischief was done, and they began to feel its consequences, or, what to them was the same thing, to fancy that the low price of oil in Europe was owing to the change of constitution at the Crater, they started up in convulsed and mercenary efforts to counteract the evil, referring all to money, and not manifesting any particular notions of principles concerning the manner in which it was used. As the cooler heads of the minority-perhaps we ought to say of the majority, for, oddly enough, the minority now actually ruled in Craterdom, by carrying out fully the principle of the sway of the majority-but, as the cooler heads of the colony well understood that nothing material was to follow from such spasmodic and ill-directed efforts, the merchants were not backed in their rising, and, as commonly happens with the slave, the shaking of their chains only bound them so much the tighter.

At length the Rancocus returned from the voyage on which she had sailed just previously to the change in the constitution, and her owner announced his intention to go in her to America, the next trip, himself. His brothers, Heaton, Anne, their children, and, finally, Captain Betts,

Friend Martha, and their issue, all, sooner or later, joined the party; a desire to visit the low shores of the Delaware once more, uniting with the mortification of the recent changes, to induce them all to wish to see the land of their fathers before they died. All the oil in the colony was purchased by Woolston, at rather favourable prices, the last quotations from abroad being low: the ex-governor disposed of most of his movables, in order to effect so large an operation. He also procured a glorious collection of shells, and some other light articles of the sort, filling the ship as full as she could be stowed. It was then that the necessity of having a second vessel became apparent, and Betts determined to withdraw his brig from the fishery, and to go to America in her. The whales had been driven off the original fishing-ground, and the pursuit was no longer as profitable as it had been, three fish having been taken formerly to one now; a circumstance the hierarchy of the Crater did not fail to ascribe to the changes in the constitution, while the journal attributed it to certain aristocratical tendencies which, as that paper averred, had crept into the management of the business.

The vessels were loaded, the passengers disposing of as many of their movables as they could, and to good advantage, intending to lay in fresh supplies in Philadelphia, and using the funds thus obtained to procure a freight for the brig. At the end of a month, both vessels were ready; the different dwellings were transferred to new occupants, some by lease and others by sales, and all those who contemplated a voyage to America were assembled at the crater. Previously to taking leave of a place that had become endeared to him by so many associations and interests, Mr. Woolston determined to take the Anne, hiring her of the government for that purpose- Governor Pennock condescendingly deciding that the public interests would not suffer by the arrangement-and going in her once more through the colony, on a tour of private, if not of official inspection. Bridget, Heaton, Anne, and Captain Betts, were of the party; the children being left at the crater, in proper custody.

The first visit was paid to Rancocus Island. Here the damage done by the pirates had long been repaired; and the mills, kilns and other works, were in a state of prosperous industry. The wild hogs and goats were now so numerous as to be a little troublesome, particularly the former; but, a good many being shot, the inhabitants did not despair of successfully contending with them for the possession of the place. There were cattle, also, on this island; but they were still tame, the cows giving milk, and the oxen being used in the yoke. These were the descendants of the single pair Woolston had sent across, less than twelve years before, which had increased in an arithmetical proportion, care having been taken not to destroy any. They now exceeded a hundred, of whom quite half were cows; and the islanders occasionally treated themselves to fresh beef. As cows had been brought into the colony in every vessel that arrived, they were now in tolerably good numbers, Mark Woolston himself disposing of no less than six when he broke up his farming establishment for a visit to America. There were horses, too, though not in as great numbers as there were cows and oxen. Boats were so much used, that roadsters were very little needed; and this so much the less, on account of the great steadiness of the trades. By this time, everybody understood the last; and the different channels of the group were worked through with almost the same facility as would have been the case with so many highways. Nevertheless, horses were to be found in the colony, and some of the husbandmen preferred them to the horned cattle in working their lands.

A week was passed in visiting the group. Something like a consciousness of having ill-treated Mark was to be traced among the people; and this feeling was manifested under a well-known law of our nature, which rendered those the most vindictive and morose, who had acted the worst. Those who had little more to accuse themselves of than a compliant submission to the wrong-doing of others, in political matters everywhere the most numerous class of all, received their visiters well enough, and in many instances they treated their guests with delicacy and distinction. On the whole, however, the late governor derived but little pleasure from the intercourse, so much mouthing imbecility being blended with the expressions of regret and sympathy, as to cause him to mourn over the compliance of his fellow-creatures, more than to rejoice at their testimony in his own favour.

But, notwithstanding all these errors of man, nature and time had done their work magnificently since the last "progress" of Woolston among the islands. The channels were in nearly every instance lined with trees, and the husbandry had assumed the aspect of an advanced civilization. Hedges, beautiful in their luxuriance and flowers, divided the fields; and the buildings which contribute to the comforts of a population were to be found on every side. The broad plains of soft mud, by the aid of the sun, the rains, the guano, and the plough, had now been some years converted into meadows and arable lands; and those which still lay remote from the peopled parts of the group, still nine-tenths of its surface, were fast getting the character of rich pastures, where cattle, and horses, and hogs were allowed to roam at pleasure. As the cock crowed from the midst of his attendant party of hens and chickens, the ex-governor in passing would smile sadly, his thoughts reverting to the time when its predecessor raised its shrill notes on the naked rocks of the Reef!

That Reef itself had undergone more changes than any other spot in the colony, as the Peak had undergone fewer. The town by this time contained more than two hundred buildings, of one sort and another, and the population exceeded five hundred souls. This was a small population for so many tenements; but the children, as yet, did not bear a just proportion to the adults. The crater was the subject of what to Mark Woolston was a most painful law-suit. From the first, he had claimed that spot as his private property; though he had conceded its use to the public, under a lease, since it was so well adapted, by natural formation, to be a place of refuge when invasions were apprehended. But the crater he had found barren, and had rendered fertile; the crater had even seemed to him to be an especial gift of Providence bestowed on him in his misery; and the crater was his by possession, as well as by other rights, when he received strangers into his association. None of the older inhabitants denied this claim. It is the last comers who are ever the most anxious to dispute ancient rights. As they can possess none of these established privileges themselves, they dislike that others should enjoy them; and association places no restraints on their cupidity. Pennock, once in the hands of "the people," was obliged to maintain their rights, or what some among them chose to call their rights; and he authorized the attorney-general to bring an action of ejectment against the party in possession. Some pretty hard-faced trickery was attempted in the way of legislation, in order to help along the claim of the public; for, if the truth must be said, the public is just as wont to resort to such unworthy means to effect its purposes as private individuals, when it is deemed necessary. But there was little fear of the "people's" failing; they made the law, and they administered it, through their agents; the power being now so completely in their hands that it required twice the usual stock of human virtue to be able to say them nay, as had formerly been the case. God help the man whose rights are to be maintained against the masses, when the immediate and dependent nominees of those masses are to sit in judgment! If the public, by any inadvertency, have had the weakness to select servants that are superior to human infirmities, and who prefer to do right rather than to do as their masters would have them, it is a weakness that experience will be sure to correct, and which will not be often repeated.

The trial of this cause kept the Woolstons at the crater a week longer than they would have remained. When the cause was submitted to the jury, Mr. Attorney-General had a great deal to say about aristocracy and privileged orders, as well as about the sacred rights of the people. To hear him, one might have imagined that the Woolstons were princes in the full possession of their hereditary states, and who were dangerous to the liberties or the mass, instead of being what they really were, citizens without one right more than the meanest man in the colony, and with even fewer chances of maintaining their share of these common rights, in consequence of the prejudice, and jealousy, and most of all, the *envy*, of the majority. Woolston argued his own cause, making a clear, forcible and manly appeal to the justice and good sense of the jury, in vindication of his claims; which, on every legal as well as equitable principle, was out of all question such as every civilized community should have maintained. But the great and most powerful foe of justice, in cases of this sort, is SLANG; and SLANG in this instance came very near being too much for law. The jury were divided, ten going for the 'people,' and two for the right; one of the last being Bigelow, who was a fearless, independent fellow, and cared no more for the bug-bear called the 'people,' by the slang-whangers of politics, than he did for the Emperor of Japan.

The day after this fruitless trial, which left Mark's claim in abeyance until the next court, a period of six months, the intended travellers repaired on board ship, and the brig, with her party, went to sea, under her owner, captain Betts, who had provided himself with a good navigator in the person of his mate. The Rancocus, however, crossed over to the Peak, and the passengers all ascended to the plain, to take leave of that earthly paradise. Nature had done so much for this place, that it had been the settled policy of Mark Woolston to suffer its native charms to be marred as little as possible. But the Peak had ever been deemed a sort of West-End of the Colony; and, though the distribution of it had been made very fairly, those who parted with their shares receiving very ample compensations for them, a certain distinction became attached to the residence on the Peak. Some fancied it was on account of its climate; some, because it was a mountain, and was more raised up in the world than the low islands near it; some, because it had most edible birds, and the best figs; but none of those who now coveted residences there for their families, or the name of residences there, would allow even to themselves, what was the simple fact, that the place received it highest distinction on account of the more distinguished individuals who dwelt on it. At first, the *name* was given to several settlements in the group, just as the Manhattanese have their East and West Broadway; and, just for the very same reasons that have made them so rich in Broadways, they will have ere long, first-fifth, second-fifth, and third-fifth avenue, unless common sense begins to resume its almost forgotten sway among the aldermen. But this demonstration in the way of names, did not satisfy the minor-majority, after they got into the ascendant; and a law was passed authorizing a new survey, and a new subdivision of the public lands on the Peak, among the citizens of the colony. On some pretence of justice, that is not very easily to be understood, those who had property there already were not to have shares in the new lottery; a lottery, by the way, in which the prizes were about twice as large as those which had originally been distributed among the colonists.

But, Mark and Bridget endeavoured to forget everything unpleasant in this visit to their much-loved home. They regarded the place as a boon from Providence, that demanded all their gratitude, in spite of the abuses of which it was the subject; and never did it seem to them more exquisitely beautiful, perhaps it never had been more perfectly lovely, than it appeared the hour they left it. Mark remembered it as he found it, a paradise in the midst of the waters, wanting only in man to erect the last great altar in his heart, in honour of its divine creator. As yet, its beauties had not been much marred; though the new irruption menaced them, with serious injuries.

Mr. and Mrs. Woolston took leave of their friends, and tore themselves away from the charming scenery of the Peak, with heavy hearts. The Rancocus was waiting for them, under the lee of the island, and everybody was soon on board her. The sails were filled, and the ship passed out from among the islands, by steering south, and hauling up between the Peak and the volcano. The latter now seemed to be totally extinct. No more smoke arose from it, or had indeed risen from it, for a twelvemonth. It was an island, and in time it might become habitable, like the others near it.

Off Cape Horn the Rancocus spoke the Dragon; Captain Betts and his passengers being all well. The two vessels saw no more of each other until the ship was coming out of the Bay of Rio, as the brig was going in. Notwithstanding this advantage, and the general superiority of the sailing of the Rancocus, such was the nature of the winds that the last encountered, that when she passed Cape May lights the brig was actually in the bay, and ahead of her; This circumstance, however, afforded pleasure rather than anything else, and the two vessels landed their passengers on the wharves of Philadelphia within an hour of each other.

Great was the commotion in the little town of Bristol at the return of all the Woolstons, who had gone off, no one knew exactly whither; some saying to New Holland; others to China; and a few even to Japan. The excitement extended across the river to the little city of Burlington, and there was danger of the whole history of the colony's getting into the newspapers. The colonists, however, were still discreet, and in a week something else occurred to draw the attention of the multitude, and the unexpected visit was soon regarded like any other visit.

Glad enough, notwithstanding, were the near relatives of Bridget and Anne, in particular, to see those two fine young women again. Neither appeared much more than a twelvemonth older than when she went away. This was owing to the delicious, yet not enervating climate, in which both had lived. They were mothers, and a little more matronly in appearance, but none the less lovely; their children, like themselves, were objects of great interest, in their respective families, and happy indeed were the households which received them. It in no degree lessened the satisfaction of any of the parties, that the travellers had all returned much better off in their circumstances than when they went away. Even the two younger Woolstons were now comfortable, and early announced an intention not to return to the islands. As for the ex-governor, he might be said to be rich; but his heart was still in the colony, over the weaknesses of which his spirit yearned, as the indulgent parent feels for the failings of a backsliding child. Nevertheless, Bridget was persuaded to remain with her father a twelvemonth longer than her husband, for the health of the old gentleman had become infirm, and he could not bear to part with his only child so soon again, after she had once been restored to his arms. It was, therefore, decided, that Mr. Mark Woolston should fill the Rancocus with such articles as were deemed the most useful to the colony, and go back in that vessel, leaving his wife and children at Bristol, with the understanding he would return and seek them the succeeding summer. A similar arrangement was made for the wife and children of Captain Betts, Friend Martha Betts being much in the practice of regulating her conduct by that of Friend Bridget Woolston. Betts sold his brig, and consented to go in the Rancocus as a passenger, having no scruples, now he had become comparatively wealthy, about eating with his old shipmate, and otherwise associating with him, though it was always as a sort of humble companion.

The Heatons determined to remain in America, for a time at least. Mr. Heaton felt the ingratitude of the colonists even more keenly than his brother-in-law; for he knew how much had been done for them, and how completely they had forgotten it all. Anne regretted the Peak, and its delicious climate; but her heart was mainly concentred in her family, and she could not be otherwise than happy, while permitted to dwell with her husband and children.

When the Rancocus sailed, therefore, she had no one on board her but Mark Woolston and Betts, with the exception of her proper crew. Her cargo was of no great intrinsic value, though it consisted in articles much used, and consequently in great demand, in the colony. As the vessel had lain some months at Philadelphia, where she had been thoroughly repaired and new-coppered, she sailed well, and made an excellent run to Rio, nor was her passage bad as far as the straits of La Maire. Here she encountered westerly gales, and the Cape may be said to have been doubled in a tempest. After beating about for six weeks in that stormy ocean, the ship finally got into the Pacific, and went into Valparaiso, Here Mark Woolston received very favourable offers for most of his cargo, but, still feeling desirous to serve his colony, he refused them all, setting sail for the islands as soon as he had made a few repairs, and had a little refreshed his crew.

The passages between Valparaiso and the Crater had usually consumed about five weeks, though somewhat dependent on the state of the trades. On this occasion the run was rather long, it having been attempted to find a new course. Formerly, the vessels had fallen in with the Crater, between Betto's group and the Reef, which was bringing them somewhat to leeward, and Mr. Woolston now thought he would try a more southern route, and see if he could not make the Peak, which would not only bring him to windward, but which place was certainly giving him a more striking object to fall in with than the lower islands of the group.

It was on the morning of one of the most brilliant days of those seas, that Captain Saunders met the ex-governor on the quarter-deck, as the latter appeared there for the first time since quitting his berth, and announced that he had just sent look-outs aloft to have a search for the land. By his reckoning they must be within twelve leagues of the Peak, and he was rather surprised that it was not yet visible from the deck. Make it they must very shortly; for he was quite certain of his latitude, and did not believe that he could be much out of the way, as respected his longitude. The cross-trees were next hailed, and the inquiry was made if the Peak could not be seen ahead. The answer was, that no land was in sight, in any part of the ocean!

For several hours the ship ran down before the wind, and the same extraordinary vacancy existed on the waters! At length an island was seen, and the news was sent down on deck. Towards that island the ship steered, and about two in the afternoon, she came up close under its lee, and backed her topsail. This island was a stranger to all on board! The navigators were confident they must be within a few leagues of the Peak, as well as of the volcano; yet nothing could be seen of either, while here was an unknown island in their places! This strange land was of very small dimensions, rising out of the sea about three hundred feet. Its extent was no great matter, half a mile in diameter perhaps, and its form nearly circular. A boat was lowered, and a party pulled towards it.

As Mr. Woolston approached this as yet strange spot, something in its outlines recurred to his memory. The boat moved a little further north, and he beheld a solitary tree. Then a cry escaped him, and the whole of the terrible truth flashed on his mind. He beheld the summit of the Peak, and the solitary tree was that which he had himself preserved as a signal. The remainder of his paradise had sunk beneath the ocean!

On landing, and examining more minutely, this awful catastrophe was fully confirmed. No part of Vulcan's Peak remained above water but its rocky summit, and its venerable deposit of guano. All the rest was submerged; and when soundings were made, the plain, that spot which had almost as much of Heaven as of earth about it, according to the unenlightened minds of its inhabitants, was found to be nearly a hundred fathoms deep in the ocean!

It is scarcely possible to describe the sickening awe which came over the party, when they had assured themselves of the fatal facts by further observation. Everything, however, went to confirm the existence of the dire catastrophe. These internal fires had wrought a new convulsion, and the labours and hopes of years had vanished in a moment. The crust of the earth had again been broken; and this time it was to destroy, instead of to create. The lead gave fearful confirmation of the nature of the disaster, the soundings answering accurately to the known formation of the land in the neighbourhood of the Peak. But, in the Peak itself, it was not possible to be mistaken: there it was in its familiar outline, just as it had stood in its more elevated position, when it crowned its charming mountain, and overlooked the whole of that enchanting plain which had so lately stretched beneath. It might be said to resemble, in this respect, that sublime rock, which is recognised as a part of the "everlasting hills," in Cole's series of noble landscapes that is called "the March of Empire;" ever the same amid the changes of time, and civilization, and decay, there it was the apex of the Peak; naked, storm-beaten, and familiar to the eye, though surrounded no longer by the many delightful objects which had once been seen in its neighbourhood.

Saddened, and chastened in spirit, by these proofs of what had befallen the colony, the party returned to the ship. That night, they remained near the little islet; next day they edged away in the direction of the place where the volcano had formerly risen up out of the waves. After running the proper distance, the ship was hove to, and her people sounded; two hundred fathoms of line were out, but no bottom was found. Then the Rancocus bore up for the island which had borne her own name. The spot was ascertained, but the mountain had also sunk into the ocean. In one place, soundings were had in ten fathoms water, and here the vessel was anchored. Next day, when the ship was again got under way, the anchor brought up with it, a portion of the skeleton of a goat. It had doubtless fallen upon the remains of such an animal, and hooking it with its flukes thus unexpectedly brought once more to the light of day, the remains of a creature that may have been on the very summit of the island, when the earthquake in which it was swallowed, occurred.

The Rancocus next shaped her course in the direction of the group. Soundings were struck near the western roads, and it was easy enough to carry the vessel towards what had formerly been the centre of those pleasant isles. The lead was kept going, and a good look-out was had for shoals; for, by this time, Mr. Woolston was satisfied that the greatest changes had occurred at the southward, as in the former convulsion, the group having sunk but a trifle compared with the Peak; nevertheless, every person, as well as thing, would seem to have been engulfed. Towards evening, however, as the ship was feeling her way to windward with great caution, and when the ex-governor believed himself to be at no great distance from the centre of the group, the look-outs proclaimed shoal-water, and even small breakers, about half a mile on their larboard beam. The vessel was hove-to, and a boat went to examine the place, Woolston and his friend Betts going in her.

The shoal was made by the summit of the crater; breakers appearing in one or two places where the hill had been highest. The boat met with no difficulty, however, in passing over the spot, merely avoiding the white water. When the lead was dropped into the centre of the crater, it took out just twenty fathoms of line. That distance, then, below the surface of the sea, had the crater, and its town, and its people sunk! If any object had floated, as many must have done, it had long before drifted off in the currents of the ocean, leaving no traces behind to mark a place that had so lately been tenanted by human beings. The Rancocus anchored in twenty-three fathoms, it being thought she lay nearly over the Colony House, and for eight-and-forty hours the exploration was continued. The sites of many a familiar spot were ascertained, but nothing could be found on which even a spar might be anchored, to buoy out a lost community.

At the end of the time mentioned, the ship bore up for Betto's group. There young Ooroony was found, peacefully ruling as of old. Nothing was known of the fate of the colonists, though surprise had been felt at not receiving any visits from their vessels. The intercourse had not been great of late, and most of the Kannakas had come away. Soon after the Woolstons had left, the especial friends of humanity, and the almost exclusive lovers of the "people" having begun to oppress them by exacting more work than was usual, and forgetting to pay for it. These men could say but little about the condition of the colony beyond this fact. Not only they, but all in the group, however, could render some account of the awful earthquake of the last season, which, by their descriptions, greatly exceeded n violence anything formerly known in those regions. It was in that earthquake, doubtless, that the colony of the crater perished to a man.

Leaving handsome and useful presents with his friend, young Ooroony, and putting ashore two or three Kannakas who were in the vessel, Woolston now sailed for Valparaiso. Here he disposed of his cargo to great advantage, and purchased copper in pigs at almost as great. With this new cargo he reached Philadelphia, after an absence of rather more than nine months.

Of the colony of the crater and its fortunes, little was ever said among its survivors. It came into existence in a manner that was most extraordinary, and went out of it in one that was awful. Mark and Bridget, however, pondered deeply on these things; the influence of which coloured and chastened their future lives. The husband often went over, in his mind, all the events connected with his knowledge of the Reef. He would thus recall his shipwreck and desolate condition when suffered first to reach the rocks; the manner in which he was the instrument in causing vegetation to spring up in the barren places; the earthquake, and the upheaving of the islands from out of the waters: the arrival of his wife and other friends: the commencement and progress of the colony; its blessings, so long as it pursued the right, and its curses, when it began to pursue the wrong; his departure, leaving it still a settlement surrounded with a sort of earthly paradise, and his return, to find all buried beneath the ocean. Of such is the world and its much-coveted advantages. For a time our efforts seem to create, and to adorn, and to perfect, until we forget our origin and destination, substituting self for that divine hand which alone can unite the elements of worlds as they float in gasses, equally from His mysterious laboratory, and scatter them again into thin air when the works of His hand cease to find favour in His view.

Let those who would substitute the voice of the created for that of the Creator, who shout "the people, the people," instead of hymning the praises of their God, who vainly imagine that the masses are sufficient for all things, remember their insignificance and tremble. They are but mites amid millions of other mites, that the goodness of providence has produced for its own wise ends; their boasted countries, with their vaunted climates and productions, have temporary possessions of but small portions of a globe that floats, a point, in space, following the course pointed out by an invisible finger, and which will one day be suddenly struck out of its orbit, as it was originally put there, by the hand that made it. Let that dread Being, then, be never made to act a second part in human affairs, or the rebellious vanity of our race imagine that either numbers, or capacity, or success, or power in arms, is aught more than a short-lived gift of His beneficence, to be resumed when His purposes are accomplished.

Footnotes

1. Some few of our readers may require to be told that, in Spanish, y, pronounced as e, is the simple conjunction "and;" thus this name is de Castro *and* Muños.

2. Absurd and forced as these strange appellations may appear, they are all genuine. The writer has collected a long list of such names from real life, which he may one day publish-Orchistra, Philena, and Almina are among them. To all the names ending in a, it must be remembered that the sound of a final y is given.

3. This last phrase has often caused the writer to smile, when he has heard a countryman say, with a satisfied air, as is so often the case in this good republic, that "such or such a thing here is good enough for *me*;" meaning that he questions if there be anything of the sort that is better anywhere else. It was uttered many years since, by a shrewd Quaker, in West-Chester, who was contending with a neighbour on a subject that the other endeavoured to defend by alluding to the extent of his own observation. "Oh, yes, Josy," answered the Friend, "thee's been to meeting and thee's been to mill, and thee knows all about it!" America is full of travellers who have been to meeting and who have been to mill. This it is which makes it unnecessarily provincial.

4. We hold in our possession a curious document, the publication of which might rebuke this spirit of gossip, and give a salutary warning to certain managers of the press, who no sooner hear a rumour than they think themselves justified in embalming it among the other truths of their daily sheets. The occurrences of life brought us in collision, legally, with an editor; and we obtained a verdict against him. Dissatisfied with defeat, as is apt to be the case, he applied for a new trial. Such an application was to be sustained by affidavits, and he made his own, as usual. Now, in this affidavit, our competitor swore distinctly and unequivocally, to certain alleged facts (we think to the number of six), every one of which was untrue. Fortunately for the party implicated, the matter sworn to was purely *ad captandum* stuff, and, in a legal sense, not pertinent to the issue. This prevented it from being perjury in law. Still, it was all untrue, and nothing was easier than to show it. Now, we do not doubt that the person thus swearing *believed* all that he swore to, or he would not have had the extreme folly to expose himself as he did; but he was so much in the habit of publishing gossip in his journal, that, when an occasion arrived, he did not hesitate about swearing to what he had read in other journals, without taking the trouble to inquire if it were true! One of these days we may lay all this, along with much other similar proof of the virtue there is in gossip, so plainly before the world, that he who runs may read.

www.ingramcontent.com/pod-product-compliance
Lightning Source LLC
LaVergne TN
LVHW011933070526
838202LV00054B/4614